Remaking a Lost Harmony

Stories from the Hispanic Caribbean

❖

Edited by
Margarite Fernández Olmos
&
Lizabeth Paravisini-Gebert

❖

WHITE PINE PRESS • FREDONIA, NY

These are works of fiction. Names, characters, places, and incidents either are the product of the author's imagination or are used fictitiously, and any resemblances to actual persons, living or dead, events, or locales is purely coincidental.

ACKNOWLEDGEMENTS
"Colonel Bum Vivant" ©1994 by Rosario Ferré. Translation ©1994 by Rosario Ferré. Used by permission of Rosario Ferré and Susan Bergholz Literary Services, New York.

"Truffle Hunters" by Humberto Arenal translated by Paula Sharp. Translation copyright 1985.

"After the Hurricane" by Edgardo Sanabria Santaliz previously appeared in the *New England Review and Bread Load Quarterly*.

An exhaustive effort has been made to locate all rights holders and to clear reprint permissions. If any required acknowledgements have been overlooked, it is unintentional and forgiveness is requested. If notified, the publishers will be pleased to rectify any omission in future editions.

Publication of this book was made possible, in part, by grants from the New York State Council on the Arts and the National Endowment for the Arts.

Book design by Elaine LaMattina

Cover painting: *Cemeterio pequeño de Culebra* by María de Mater O'Neill.©1990 María de Mater O'Neill. Oil crayons, oils on linen. 64" x 94". Collection of Iliana Font.

ISBN 1-877727-36-9

Manufactured in the United States of America

First printing 1995

Published by
WHITE PINE PRESS
10 Village Square • Fredonia, NY 14063

Remaking a Lost Harmony

❖ CONTENTS ❖

INTRODUCTION

We are storytellers because words are one of our last refuges.
We tell jokes because reality is almost unbearable, we tell sto-
ries to console, entertain and to tell the truth.
— Alan West, *Being América*

S hort-story writers from Cuba, the Dominican Republic, and Puerto
Rico, in their efforts to "console, entertain and to tell the truth,"
have created some of the most innovative work in Spanish in recent
decades. Writing with humor, compassion, imagination, and daring,
writers from the Hispanic Antilles have breathed new life into a genre
that has always been quintessentially Caribbean.

Yet, for a variety of reasons, English-, and, in many cases, Spanish-
speaking readers have lacked opportunities to acquaint themselves
with the writings of Hispanic Caribbean authors. Not usually afforded
adequate representation in anthologies that span the entire Latin
American region, the Cuban, Puerto Rican, and Dominican writers
featured in this collection have, until very recently, also been exclud-
ed from pan-Caribbean anthologies as well: editors and anthologists
have seemed to work under the assumption that the Spanish-speak-
ing islands are separated, not only linguistically, but also culturally,
from their Antillean neighbors. A review of their shared histories,
however – of the legacy of European colonialism, African slavery,
plantation economies, and massive migrations – reveals the error of
that belief.

The dissemination of these authors' works has also faced difficulties of a political nature: Cuba's uneasy relationship with the United
States following the 1959 revolution kept Cuban literature from
reaching the United States public. While a handful of scholars have,
often under great hardship, brought Cuban writers to the attention of
a largely academic audience, the vast majority of North Americans
have been virtually cut off from Cuban culture for the past thirty-four
years.

In the case of Puerto Rican and Dominican literatures, linguistic barriers have been a major obstacle: only a few authors available in English translation, like Luis Rafael Sánchez and Rosario Ferré, or those who write in English, like Julia Álvarez, have reached wide audiences in the United States. This anthology hopes to remedy this lack.

Some years ago, noted Cuban-American literary critic Roberto González Echevarría observed that while it is not possible to speak of a specific Hispanic-Caribbean literature, it is possible to pinpoint certain features that allow one to speak of a literature of the Hispanic Caribbean. One of these features, he argues, is the " . . . conception of a syncretic social myth giving a sense of national and regional identity, a myth whose outward manifestation is popular music . . . an atavistic desire to remake a lost harmony . . . ."[1] Despite the development in each of the islands of a specific literary history corresponding to their diverse political, social, and economic evolutions, this myth resounds in the works presented here, echoing across the gaps separating the islands to give them their grace and strength.

❖

The largest of the Greater Antilles, Cuba experienced a deep social transformation in recent decades as a result of the 1959 Revolution, an event that has had a profound impact on the region, both culturally and politically. The stories in this collection, all written after 1959, share in the impetus for a search into the genuine roots of Caribbean and Latin American culture spawned by the Cuban Revolution.

The dramatic social changes taking place in Cuba in the 1960s resulted in works of literature that condemned past societal abuses, and served as testimony to revolutionary gains and the Cuban people's hope for a better future. Many new writers emerged from the now famous literacy campaign of the 1960s, an effort that broadened the country's readership to a degree never before seen in Latin America. By the end of the decade, however, the revolution had begun to harden its position regarding free literary expression, and a trying period referred to as the "grey quinquennium" followed. The imprisonment of Heberto Padilla in 1971 for the publication of poems considered counter-revolutionary, known internationally as "the Padilla affair," coincided with an official preference for social-realist works and the discouragement of more imaginative writing. In the mid-1970s, however, the National Council of Culture was replaced by the Ministry of Culture which brought about a more open attitude towards artistic creativity.

Cuban narrative from the late 1970s to the present reflects a renewed vision of the role of the artist, particularly among the generation of writers who have lived the greater part of their lives in a post-revolutionary Cuba. Cuban author and critic Leonardo Padura Fuentes sees recent Cuban writing as undergoing a vigorous revitalization: "Far from reflecting, admiring, praising, or reaffirming—historical or present—reality, it questions it from an essentially ethical perspective, one engaged solely with the aesthetic responsibility of the artist and reflective of his or her engagement with reality."[2]

Among the more interesting of the younger generation of Cuban authors is the award-winning writer Senel Paz. In an interview with Emilio Bejel, Paz offers his own perspective on the comparison between his generation and earlier post-revolutionary Cuban narrators:

> Perhaps the new angle we have found is that of the imagination, of fantasy, and we opted for a literature weighed more heavily towards the imagination and a narrative more responsive to poetry . . . We have softened the tone of our literature: it is now more tranquil, lighter, more self-searching and intimate, less marked by the impact of the plot and sub- ject matter, but having gained in reflection. There is more concern with the trivial pursuit of everydayness and also, and in this we all agree, with the ethical preoccupations that stem from the construction of socialism.[3]

Important changes were also taking place in the Dominican Republic during the 1960s. Dominican dictator Rafael Leonidas Trujillo was assassinated in 1961, ending thirty-two years of political, economic, and cultural repression. Dominican literary production had naturally suffered the consequences of the Trujillo era, and many have observed that the majority of internationally-recognized works by Dominican authors were produced by writers in exile, as in the case of Juan Bosch and Pedro Mir.

The generation of young writers that emerged in the post-Trujillo period was in many ways still reeling from the effects of the regime and the consequent lack of a solid, on-going literary tradition. And, despite the growing urbanization of Dominican society, they had to confront a literary discourse still deeply entrenched in the neo-realism of the 1930s and 1940s, with its focus on the Dominican peasant. Authors such as Miguel Alfonseca and René del Risco Bermúdez were more concerned, however, with the ever-growing capital city of Santo Domingo; there they could observe a society growing increasingly more politicized as the impact of the Cuban revolution spread throughout the Caribbean, and as the political possibilities opened by Trujillo's demise were debated. Many of the emerging generation of writers were members of an urban middle class anxious for change and innovation. Committed to a politically-conscious writing, they were also aware of the latest trends in Latin American literature, very much in tune with the literary developments that would become known as the Latin American literary "Boom."

In the mid-1960s, historical events on the island caused politically-conscious writing to give way, in many cases, to a more direct political activism. The United States' invasion of the country for the second time in the twentieth century frustrated the attempts of progressive segments of the armed forces to combat more reactionary elements of the Dominican military establishment. The death of Trujillo had not meant the death of *trujillismo,* and the country continued to struggle against social inequities deeply rooted in the past.

Like their Cuban counterparts, post-1960s Dominican authors have grown more introspective, more dedicated to the task of examining their personal and historical past and searching for answers for the future. Many of the writers of the 1960s retreated from their earlier militant literary positions and either found newer avenues for their writings or abandoned writing altogether. The short stories written in the Dominican Republic from the 1970s to the present are marked by their attempts to come to grips with the complexities of Dominican reality with renewed creativity and freedom. No longer bound to any one trend or tradition, Dominican narrators are re-examining their culture and themselves, engaging, as author and critic José Alcántara Almánzar has argued, " . . . in a ceaseless search to recreate the everyday through language . . . ."

❖

The social upheavals of the 1960s and 1970s, as well as worldwide movements for change that included racial and sexual liberations, would also have a profound impact on Puerto Rico. The 1950s had witnessed the rapid industrialization of the island under Operation Bootstrap, a program designed to attract light manufacturing industries, heralding the transformation of an economy based on the plantation system into one dominated by industrial-technological production. This process naturally affected traditional values and institutions associated with the patriarchal, agrarian society of the past. Combined with an expansion in the educational system, it also opened new employment possibilities for both men and women and led to the growing urbanization of Puerto Rican society.

These rapid processes and their consequences have inspired Puerto Rican short story writers. From the groundbreaking 1966 collection by Luis Rafael Sánchez, *En cuerpo de camisa* (In Shirtsleeves) to the present, Puerto Rican short fiction has voiced the writers' ongoing concerns with the political status of the island (a commonwealth of the United States since 1898), and the defense of Puerto Rican language and culture in the face of the cultural influence of the United States (a concern shared by Cuba and the Dominican Republic).

The new generation of Puerto Rican writers, influenced by the enormous growth and evolution of Latin American fiction in the last several decades, is changing the traditional image of many segments of Puerto Rican society through profound changes in the discourse of Puerto Rican literature. Efraín Barradas, Puerto Rican critic and anthologist, finds in recent Puerto Rican writing the attempt to create new forms of expression out of the language of the streets, a fascination with the historical in aesthetic terms, a new identification with the Puerto Rican working class, with the Antillean world and the rest of Latin America, increased literary experimentation and a feminist and anti-machista trend that may be explained, in part, by the marked increase in the number of important women authors in the past two decades. The ample representation of female writing in this anthology attests to the fact that women writers have been at the forefront of literary innovation, not only in Puerto Rico, but in the region as a whole, having produced some of the most daring and controversial works in recent years.

❖

Finally, some mention should be made of the selections and their translation. As editors, we wished to offer the reader the full range and variety of contemporary Hispanic-Caribbean stories, attempting a balance of styles and subject matter, selecting among countless works that merit translation into English. We have combined well-known, often-translated authors with their less-known counterparts, and chosen works that allow for convincing and authentic translations.

As translators, we were painfully aware of the linguistic difficulties we would encounter, particularly in the case of authors writing in *puertorriqueño* or using *cubanismos* or *dominicanismos* in the expression of a renewed sense of identity and cultural uniqueness. We hope that as you read the stories you will delight in their remaking of a lost harmony and agree with us that the result was well worth the effort.

— Margarite Fernández Olmos
Lizabeth Paravisini-Gebert
New York 1994

[1]Roberto González Echevarría, "Literature of the Hispanic Caribbean," *Latin American Literary Review* 16 (Spring-Summer 1980), p. 17.

[2]Leonardo Padura Fuentes, "El derecho de nacer: la cuentística cubana de los 80, imagen y posibilidad," *La Gaceta de Cuba* 2 (marzo-abril 1992), p. 39.

[3]Emilio Bejel, ed. *Escribir en Cuba: entrevistas con escritores cubanos, 1979-1989* (Puerto Rico: Editorial de la Universidad de Puerto Rico, 1991), pp. 304-305.

❖ ACKNOWLEDGEMENTS ❖

We would like to express our deepest appreciation to the authors of the stories included in this collection for their interest in our project and their generosity; and to the translators – Beth Baugh, Carmen C. Esteves, Paula Sharp, and Beth Wellington – for the excellence of their work. Special thanks are due to Leonardo Padura Fuentes and Héctor Delgado, for their help in the identification and selection of Cuban manuscripts; to the Professional Staff Congress of the City University of New York for a timely grant that allowed Margarite Fernández Olmos to travel to Cuba to conduct research for the project; to Iraida López of the CUNY Caribbean Exchange Program for her help in facilitating communications with authors in Cuba; to Ángela Hernández in the Dominican Republic and Daisy Cocco de Filippis of York College (CUNY) for their assistance in identifying Dominican authors and securing the necessary permissions for publication; to Joy De Jesús, a student at Harvard University, and Juliet Lynd, a Vassar College student, who, as Lizabeth Paravisini-Gebert's research assistants did most of the text entry. Ruth Churchill and Luis Bothwell Travieso gave generously of their time and talents to help us with tricky translation problems. Gordon A. Gebert dealt with the countless difficulties posed by our use of incompatible computers with his usual patience and good humor.

Remaking a Lost Harmony

Truffle Hunters

❖

Humberto Arenal

I say: Pucho called me to tell me that he caught a swordfish this big. How big? says Emelina. I say, Well about fifty pounds or more, I think. Fifty pounds? Are you sure? says Emelina. Well, more or less, I say, that's what Pucho says. Then how much is he asking for it? says Emelina. I say, Pucho says, you can be sure he won't give it away for less than seventy pesos. That's steep, says Emelina. It's steep and that's the truth. Steep? I say, you're crazy, girl, look what you're saying . . . Then Emelina says, Mama, that's steep, the truth is he's taking advantage of you, that's the truth, Pucho's a cutthroat, he's always been a cutthroat. I say, Look girl, the way things are, that's not expensive at all, you know? Prices are sky high for everything nowadays. I've known Pucho I don't know how long, since your father was working for Shell or before, and he's aways sold me fish and he's never cheated me, and he's always sold to me at a good price. The way things are, I really don't see how you can talk like that. Emelina says: Remember, remember that rotten yellowtail snapper he sold us, remember that time when from the moment it arrived I said or someone said, I don't remember who, that it was rotten, remember that. I say: It was all due to María Pepa, María Pepa's carelessness, I say. Emelina says: The truth, Mama, is that it was rotten. Don't bother to discuss it any further. From the minute Papa brought it home it smelled bad. It wasn't rotten I say. Oh yes it was, says Emelina. No it wasn't, I say. Yes it was, says Emelina. Not it wasn't. Yes it was. Until I tell her: You've made your point. We've talked about this plenty now. Fine, says Emelina, let's leave it right there. But the truth is, the price is steep. Damnation! I say. Look girl, do we buy it or don't we? The deal's still good, I have to let Pucho know this very afternoon, because he's waiting for me.

He can sell it off to anyone, you know? As you're sure to know he won't find any shortage of buyers. Nowadays people spend their whole lives asking if Pucho can get me a porgy, if Pucho can get me a saw-fish, if he can get me this and that. He came and told me: Señora, you're the first on my list. After all, I know you and like to be at your service. I have to ask Ismael, says Emelina. OK, I say. Your brother Jorge agrees that we should buy the fish. Says Emelina: We can call María Luisa to ask her to go in on it. And I say: No, no, no. You don't have to call anyone. This is just between us. You guys, Arturo, and me. Arturo? says Emelina. Arturo too? Yes, I say. Then Emelina tells me that she'll let me know at lunch time. Arturo, and Arturo's money? I answer: I'm putting down Arturo's money.

Pucho brought the swordfish and Julia measured it with a meter stick. From head to tail it measured one meter and 60 centimeters exactly. As Pucho had told her, it weighed more than fifty pounds. Exactly 53 pounds. She was satisfied. She hung up the fish in the kitchen and called her cousin Arturo. He said he wasn't feeling well. Arturo had suffered two heart attacks and hardly ever left his house. For the exceptional occasions on which he went out he had a Rolls Royce and a chauffeur. She asked him to come over. It was something important. Arturo said he would. She sat down in front of the sword-fish to look at it and smile. It had been a long time since she last smiled. Now she felt happy. She felt the way she had in the old days when her husband Pepe was alive and used to bring home fish on Saturday noons or Sunday mornings. Huge porgies or yellowtails or sea bass or halibuts or swordfish, like this one. Since her husband's death three years before she had not bought any more fish. Pucho had come other times and she hadn't made up her mind to buy anything from him. Now she felt as if her husband were there. She thought that perhaps this was a nice way of remembering him, at least of not forgetting him. She was always afraid that she would forget him over time. Perhaps this was why she had now bought the fish, and she wanted to take great pains in preparing it. She thought that her husband would have liked her to do that.

He would come and tell her, "Bilina, what a beautiful fish," and he would put his arm around her shoulders.

She would look at him and smile. "Do you like it, do you really like it?"

"I sure do."

She would feel his hot hand on her shoulder and then say, "I bought it for you. If you hadn't been here I wouldn't have bought it. I bought it especially for you."

When Arturo arrived she led him to the kitchen to show him the fish, without giving away her secret.

"Here it is," she gestured toward the fish and tilted back her head. She smiled.

Arturo also smiled.

"A swordfish. An honest to God swordfish."

He approached it, arms akimbo, and scrutinized the fish, smelled it, touched it several times with his right index finger. He stepped back. He looked at her.

"It's so pretty," he said. "It's flawless, a treasure. Congratulations."

"It looks good, doesn't it?" she smiled modestly. She bowed her head a little.

"Exquisite. You've made a great buy, a great buy." Arturo had long legs, and he began to pace in lengthy strides, cutting a triangular path twice in front of her. He was old, she knew it, but when he got excited he seemed like a young man. Now he looked young again to her. Like he had when they used to summer in Varadero, the most famous beach in Cuba, and she had watched him swim, row and play tennis. Or like the times he visited her in Havana, in the house here on Sixth Street in the high class Vedado neighborhood, or in the other house on Seventeenth Street where her three children were born. Arturo had always played tennis and habitually visited her in the afternoons dressed in a white shirt, cream colored flannel pants and white tennis shoes. He carried his racquet in his right hand and the cylindrical three-ball container in his left.

Arturo stopped walking. He drew near her, breathing a little heavily now as he spoke.

"It must be treated like the thing it is: an *emperador* — a swordfish and an emperor. You have made me come out of my cave for something that's really worth it."

They laughed. They laughed loud and afterwards they sat down in front of the fish, which seemed to be watching them with foreboding from its gelatinous and silvery eye. Arturo said that the swordfish had to be cooked in a special manner. They would buy the ingredients together. He would tell Julia how to do it. She had to leave it just as it was. She shouldn't cut it or section it in any way, so that it could be cooked whole in the oven. She was worried about where she would keep it. She didn't know anyone who could refrigerate such a large fish.

"You keep it here in your refrigerator," said Arturo. "Gut it and stick it inside."

"Inside, inside the refrigerator, whole like this? It won't fit."

"Remove all the shelves and take everything out and there you have it."

"I don't know . . . You really think so? So much trouble."

"It's worth it. It's a very beautiful fish. A real live swordfish." Arturo smiled again, standing up.

He was excited, loquacious, happy, enthusiastic. It had been a long time since Julia had seen him like that. She was reminded again of the times he had visited her after playing tennis.

"And what will María Pepa say?"

"What will she say, girl?"

"You know how she is. She doesn't like anyone to poke around in her kitchen. Pepe was the only one she'd let get away with it."

"Forget María Pepa, you've let that woman become too important. "

"She's very loyal. Even though she has a nasty disposition."

"She's nothing more than a servant, you've trained her very badly."

Julia repeated that María Pepa was very loyal.

"Pepe cared a lot for her and she for him. That's true." Arturo smiled.

"She used to call Pepe the Big Gentleman."

"The Big Gentleman."

"Yes."

"That's ridiculous! She's crazy."

"She's very strange, it's true, but she's a very good woman. She loves animals a lot. I wish you could see her with Pretty Boy."

"Cucu's dog?"

"Yes. Ever since her girl went up north María Pepa's taken care of him. She loves that dog like a son. She's given him a last name and everything. Pretty Boy Oliver. She wanted to write it in the ration book and everything. I had to put up with it. She's capable of making trouble for me with the committee."

"How ridiculous."

They fell silent. Arturo had seated himself a moment before, while Julia was speaking. Now he looked grave and was breathing hard. Julia bent forward with her hands folded in her lap and looked at the floor. Arturo raised his right hand to his chest. Julia looked at him.

"Do you feel bad?"

"A little. I can't overexert myself."

"Get going then, leave here this instant. Don't let yourself start feeling worse. I'm sorry I made you come all the way over here."

They both stood up.

"You have to take great pains with that swordfish. It's precious. How are you going to cook it?"

"I don't know. How do you think I should?"

He walked toward the front door.

"I think the best way is *a la Jardinera, a la Gran Jardinera.* Nowadays it's difficult to make but that fishy deserves it. I'll help you look for the ingredients."

Fish a la Gran Jardinera
Scale, clean and wash well one fish of ten, twenty or more pounds. Put in a sauce pan a generous amount of cooking oil or lard, one pound of veal cut into small pieces, a quarter pound of fresh pork rinds, one cup of sherry and a pinch of white flour. Cook over low heat until the veal is well cooked, stirring constantly. Strain the veal and pork rinds through a cheesecloth, squeezing well so that all their juices go into the sauce.

I say as I'm standing around to catch a bus you just have to wait and wait for the number twenty-two and the miserable bus doesn't come I'm sick and tired of these damn buses I say a full one comes by and doesn't stop have to wait for the next one I say patience the next one comes by not too full and it doesn't stop either what's this Mother of God I say I'm still full of patience and I keep waiting after a while someone says they changed the corner where the bus stops now it's on Tenth I walk toward Tenth and wait I catch the twenty-two it also comes filled to the gills jam packed I get in one way or another I tell you almost crawl my way in on all fours however I can the thing is to get to Marianao I say I run into Cuca in the bus she there at the back and me up here next to the bus driver she's deafer than ever, I don't understand anything she says, she asks me screaming whether Jorge is living in Miami now, if he's very well, if he has a new car or something like that, I don't know to tell you the truth because I'm stupefied and I don't hear anything she's saying and she's way off in outer space and doesn't notice anything and I say I can't hear her very well can she get closer can she get closer and she says nothing but eh? eh? and puts her right hand to her ear I motion to her to come closer and in the end accomplish nothing and I move toward her and I say in a very quiet voice that I'm going to Marianao to look on the black market for some cooking ingredients then she yells to me which aunts, is someone sick? she asks and I say not my aunts, no one's sick, I said ingredients, in-gred-i-ents for cooking a swordfish and she asks at the top of her lungs, ingredients for a swordfish? putting on a very surprised expression and I nod yes and she asks me again INGREDIENTS? even louder still and I say let the earth swallow me up because everyone is watching and listening to us especially a military man in a green beret to everything going on between us and he won't take his eyes off me, you see I'm going to go stop at the Cabaña I say and Cuca just stands there like an idiot waiting for me to answer her and then I in order to say something ask about Florentino and she tells me he's improved a little a whole lot although afterwards she tells me that there's something wrong with his vision cataracts or something else that's making him half blind and his heart's very bad and there's something wrong with his prostate gland, a tumor or something and they can't operate on him because he has high blood sugar or something I'm not exactly sure and I say to myself, so what's any better about him then? then I realize I'm at Crucero de la Playa and then I say good-bye and she screams at me when am I coming over to visit her soon soon I tell her and push to get to the door and the bus is already pulling out and I'm yelling: Wait wait I'm getting off here and I wanted to stop in this part of Marianao to look for a little Sensat Spanish olive oil and a bottle of sherry and thinking that I had to get the pork rind because the swordfish wouldn't turn out right without it and the sun sticking to

my back like a cat because now it was around twelve o'clock noon
and it turned out there was a black vendor an old vendor that I knew
from Cerro although he didn't have olive oil or sherry or anything
except a few lemons from a tree he had growing on the patio back at
his house.

> *Into a separate bowl, pass through a colander the juice
> of thirty stewed tomatoes, a cup of olive oil, two onions
> diced in a mixer, finely chopped parsley, one crushed
> garlic clove, ground pepper, a pinch of nutmeg, slivered
> asparagus, mushrooms, petit-pois, sliced truffles, salt
> and the juice of one or two lemons. Add this preparation
> to the first. Pour the sauce into the baking dish, being
> careful not to spill any of the truffles, mushrooms,
> asparagus, petit-pois, etc.*

"Señora Julia, you have to cook that fish. It's got my whole kitchen
tied up."

María Pepa was complaining because the fish took up all the space
in the refrigerator. That woman took out all the dividing shelves and
put the fish in diagonally, so that it's hogging all the space. The potatoes were spoiling, along with the tomatoes. The chilies, the garlic, the
onions, the lemons were spread out all over the kitchen. Some of the
potatoes had to be thrown out, and the tomatoes too.

"That fish smell is driving me crazy, Señora. It's horrible, I can't
stand it, I think the swordfish smells like it's gone a little bad, it
seems to be beginning to rot. Pretty Boy comes up, smells it and runs
off with an awful look on his face. He knows, animals know."

"Be quiet, María Pepa, be quiet this instant. It's not in the least rotten. It's a beautiful swordfish. Just like Pepe used to love."

"I don't know Señora, I don't know. It doesn't smell good to me.
The Big Gentleman . . ."

> *Put the fish in the baking dish and cover it with the
> remainder of the sauce and cook over a low flame.*

Then the taxi driver says he used to be a teacher and that now I
can see him for myself and I say life life you know nobody knows
who he's working for my husband used to criticize me because I

always wanted to save and now I think he was right life is a crock of shit says the driver and pardon my language in front of a lady but it's just that and then I say that he liked to enjoy what he had and share it with others he was a good man a very good man I say too good and the driver says people aren't like that excuse me says the driver but people are full of shit and please excuse my language in front of a lady the truth is he wasn't the type of man who only cared about his own house he did everything for his family and even his friends he spent his life working for others for his mother for his brothers for his aunts he was always giving this thing with the fish stings my conscience but I am doing it in part for him since he loved a big fish broiled in the oven my cousin Arturo recommended that I make it a la Gran Jardinera that's why I'm looking for Sensat olive oil and sherry the driver says that if we don't find it in Arroyo Apolo we can go to Mantilla to see a woman he knows who has Spanish oil and wine and asparagus, asparagus too? I say at the least says the man I know I'll find it don't waste your time in Cerro in Miramar wherever it might be, you need help in these things all right I say because the man has an honest face and seems like someone you can trust . . .

and upon serving, smother with slices of hard boiled egg, cucumbers and small pickled onions, with the truffles, mushrooms, etc, and the rest of the sauce. Before pouring the sauce, thicken it with breadcrumbs.

"Mama isn't well, I tell you," the woman says.

"It's the business with father," the man says.

"I've told her, you know, I'm very gruff with her in order to see if she reacts, I've told her: If you feel like that, then kill yourself, girl, kill yourself and get it over with. Why don't you do it? The truth is she's more woman than mother, you know? Now I'm finally realizing this."

"You shouldn't talk to her like that."

"It's just to get a reaction."

"Acting that way won't get you a reaction. You're mistreating her. "

The woman looks at her brother. "Now this thing with the taxi driver. When he called me today I said, oh, this is the last straw, I'm calling Jorge. The driver took her all over Havana and charged her twenty-five pesos, twenty-five pesos that I had to pay because she had spent her money on olive oil and wine and I don't know what else.

She spent her last cent because she wants to make that fish, as you already know. You have to help me."

"I don't have any money to spare. You know I don't have anything, I'm out of work. I'm putting up with the little I have until I can leave."

"And until you leave for Miami . . . ?"

"For New York."

"For New York or wherever, leaving me to take care of everything. That won't do, you know? You and Marta are going and I'm supposed to take care of everything. That won't do."

"I didn't invent this business with the fish, that's you guys' problem."

"It's Mama's idea."

"To hell with all of you.

"Why don't you tell that to Mama? You're always the good and noble son and I'm the bad daughter. But I'm staying with Mama and you and Marta are going away."

"You and your husband are revolutionaries. I leave that to you, swordfish and all."

Calmly, no, at first, to be more precise, slowly, perhaps lazily, but not calmly, or tranquilly, or pacifically; and later, a little later, he began to move faster, less sleepily, less peacefully, less placidly. In truth, he knew it better than anyone, he was always restless, or perhaps not restless, but yes vexed and annoyed from the moment the woman told him that she had spent twenty-five pesos on a taxi ride looking through all of Havana for Sensat olive oil and sherry and mushrooms and asparagus and she had only gotten a tiny bottle of sherry in Mantilla which had cost her ten pesos and the olive oil she had bought was Spanish but not Sensat, and the little can of mushrooms was in bad shape. The woman had been crying and he had said a moment before that he would help her. He had called Jaime the chauffeur and had told him to come look for the Rolls Royce and grease it up and fill it with gas and pump up the tires and put oil in the motor and then come looking for him. Arturo was walking from the telephone to the table in front of it, exactly three steps from one to the other, thinking of his friends or acquaintances he was going to visit. Ramón in Miramar and Cristina in Old Havana and Sigifredo in Víbora and Juan on Animas Street. Maybe they would have the truffles or the asparagus or the Sensat oil or would know someone who had them. These were difficult times and he had to help Julia, who had always been like a sister to Arturo. He climbed the stairs. Faster than usual and when he came to the last step he was gasping for breath more than usual. His wife was in the bedroom when he entered and she noticed. He told her he was going out. His wife heard him trying to catch his breath and told him he shouldn't get himself too excited. He had to help Julia find the ingredients he said. He was feeling fine. He had to do it, for her and for the others. His wife really didn't know who the others were that he was referring to, but she repeated he shouldn't get himself too excited. He sent her to get his blue cashmere suit, his black patent leather shoes, his white shirt of Irish linen, his silk socks, and his fine red cotton tie. He took a bath and he shaved. As he was just finishing shaving he felt the first pain in his chest. He closed his eyes and lifted his right hand to the middle of his chest. He breathed slowly and deeply and the pain almost disappeared. He went to the medicine cabinet and took out a small flask and emptied out a tiny pill and swallowed it. He went to the bedroom and dressed. As he was climbing down the stairs he felt the pain again but he did not lift his hand to his chest because his wife was coming up the stairs. He told her he would spend the whole day out and asked her if Jaime had arrived. Jaime had not arrived. Arturo went to the garden and occupied himself looking at the flowers. He no longer personally tended the garden and it wasn't as well kept as it had been in the old days. He stepped forward and picked a rose and put it in the button-hole of his jacket. He went up to the iron gate and looked toward the corner and paced back to the rosebush. He returned to the gate. He opened it and went out onto the sidewalk. He walked to the corner. He returned to the gate and began to walk toward the corner. In the middle of his path he felt the pain in his chest. Perhaps this was the last thing he remembered. Then Jaime came around the corner. Arturo's wife, at the exact same moment, neither before nor after, also appeared on the sidewalk and saw him all stretched out.

María Pepa was in the center of the kitchen looking at the refrigerator. From where she stood, which was not close by, she could smell the stench, but she wanted to open the refrigerator door to show Señora Julia the state the fish was in. A moment before María Pepa had told her and the woman had yelled to leave her alone. The fish was not rotten. There wasn't any smell in the house. It was an excuse on María Pepa's part not to help her. She would cook it alone. The

Señora was sitting now in the living room, or on the terrace — María Pepa wasn't sure which — with her eyes closed and covered with a handkerchief soaked in alcohol because she had a potent migraine. Someone rang the doorbell and María Pepa went to open it. She approached the Señora, touched her on the shoulder, and told her that someone, the next-door-neighbor, had to speak with her. The Señora didn't answer. The other woman touched her again on the shoulder. Señora Julia opened her eyes.

"What is it now, María?"

When she called her María, María Pepa knew the Señora was in a bad mood.

"It's the young man from next door, Señora, who wants to see you."

She closed her eyes again. "What does he want?"

"I don't know."

"Tell him I'm not here."

"It has to do with the fish, Señora."

Señora Julia opened her eyes. "What's wrong with the fish?"

The other woman bit her lower lip and crossed her arms.

"The guy's saying, hey come on! Look, Señora." She had braced herself, legs spread apart, and now she began to rock back and forth. "Talk with him. I'm already tired of this."

"I don't have to talk with anyone."

The other woman began walking away.

"I don't care about either of you, but the truth is that no one can stand the smell. That's the truth. Pretty Boy has been missing from the house since yesterday." When she finished speaking, María Pepa was three or four yards away from the kitchen.

The woman sitting down stood up. Now she walked quickly. From the kitchen the other woman heard the man's grave and monotonous voice and the now sharp and nervous voice of the Señora, but could not make out the details of the conversation. She only heard when the Señora began to shout:

"There's no smell! There's no smell! There's no smell!"

María Pepa stayed in the kitchen heating the leftover breakfast coffee in a can.

She heard the Señora's steps and saw her when she reached the door, but María Pepa didn't turn her head.

"I don't know why you had to call me, María. That stupid idiot made my headache worse. Bring me an aspirin."

When María Pepa turned around, she said: "Señora." She looked at the Señora, the can of coffee in her right hand and her other hand on her hip.

"The truth is that no one can stand it. The smell is unbearable." Then she walked to the refrigerator and opened the door. "Look at this, look how the fish is all bunched up in the corner."

The fish was now crumbling into pieces and had slumped over.

Señora Julia couldn't see it from where she stood and she began shouting, "It doesn't smell, it doesn't smell!"

"It's rotten, Señora, it's rotten, you can't see it, it's rotten!" María Pepa cried.

"It's not rotten, there's no smell, it's not rotten, there's no smell, there's no smell . . ." Julia walked toward María Pepa and began to push her and closed the door of the refrigerator. "Get out, get out of here, you're all against me because I'm alone, you're abusing me, there's no smell, Pepe is the only one who's with me, he'll never abandon me, he never abandoned me. Get out of here, get out of here!"

María Pepa was going to leave and then she looked at Señora Julia. The woman was crying, she was pale and her hair was all disheveled.

"Señora," María Pepa said and held out her hand

"Get out of here, María, I'm telling you to get out of here!"

María Pepa walked to the patio. Then she stopped and looked at Señora Julia through the window. She was standing in the same place. Then María Pepa continued walking without turning around.

When Señora Julia heard the iron gate close, she began to pace and say: "It's not rotten, it's not rotten. There's no smell. There's no smell. It's not rotten, it's not rotten."

She walked through the dining room, the hallways, the living room, the three bedrooms, the bathroom, all the time repeating: "It's not rotten, it's not rotten. There's no smell. There's no smell. It's not rotten. It's not rotten." She paced back through the dining room, the hallways, the living room, the three bedrooms and the bathroom.

Then she went to her bedroom and lay down. A while, a long while. She couldn't say how long. She lay on her right side and cried. Her tears soaked the pillow. She gradually stopped feeling the pillow's dampness.

María Pepa and Arturo approached the head of her bed to tell her to come with them to the kitchen. She was very tired, Julia said, very tired, she repeated, and she wanted to rest. She asked them to leave her alone. María Pepa insisted that she come, pulling on her foot. She protested. She was very tired. The other woman pulled on her foot, forcing her to get up. Arturo took her by the hand and steered her. María Pepa opened the refrigerator door. Pretty Boy was at her side, at María Pepa's side. The swordfish was not in the refrigerator, she said. Julia didn't want to look. María Pepa insisted. Julia came closer because Arturo pushed her from behind and said something in her ear that she didn't understand but which vexed her because she heard Bilina, the name her husband had called her by. Arturo was coming closer to her, pressing his hand against her back. María Pepa opened the door wider and Julia put her hands over her face. María and Arturo began yelling at her to look, look. She looked backward, toward where Arturo was standing, and he pointed to the refrigerator. Now she looked. She looked again at Arturo and saw that he wasn't there any longer. Then María Pepa shouted at her: "Look, Señora, look." Now she looked well. Inside the refrigerator was her husband's naked body. She hurried to take it out and the body began to fall away in pieces. She took the right hand, the right forearm. The head came free from the body and fell at her feet. María Pepa stepped forward, gathered up the head carefully and put it on the table as she kept repeating the Big Gentleman, the Big Gentleman, the Big Gentleman. The dog pranced at her side, barking and jumping up and down. Julia hurried to the inside of the refrigerator to take out the rest of the body. Now she was breaking the body up into smaller pieces that she tried to take out with the help of María Pepa who stood at her side: a shoulder, a thigh, a buttock, a foot, the other shoulder, part of the chest, the intestines, the heart. She was kneeling and she stood up. She walked clutching the heart, which was still beating, it was the only part of the body that felt alive and hot. María Pepa approached and Julia drew the heart to her chest and covered it with her hands and arms. Pretty Boy ran at her side. The other woman asked for the heart. Julia said no, it was hers, it was her husband's heart, the only thing she had left of him. Then María Pepa rushed toward the table and took the head. The dog followed her leaping. Julia ran behind yelling at her to give it back; the other woman yelled no. They kept running and yelling. While this was happening, she didn't know when, the heart fell to the ground and the dog carried it off between his teeth. And she didn't see it again. She let out a cry, a howl, a shriek. Then she didn't know if she had been dreaming before or was dreaming now. The accelerated rhythm and the sound of her own breathing were tugging her back to reality. She lay stretched out for a while. She began to smell the fish. The stench that she hadn't noticed until then. Immediately, almost immediately, or maybe she lingered a while, she went to the kitchen. She stretched out some papers on the floor in front of the refrigerator, and opened it. She began to pull out the rotten pieces of fish that had fallen about. She made a large package and took it out to the patio where the garbage can was. She threw the fish inside and walked away, without looking back. The flies immediately began to swarm over the swordfish and settle on it. The silvery and white fish began to turn black.

She walked toward her bedroom. She would await the arrival of María Pepa and tell her: "It was rotten, María Pepa, it was rotten. You were right."

"I knew it, Señora, I've known it for a long time," María Pepa would say.

Julia stretched out on the bed, facing upward, with her legs extended, her eyes closed and her hands laced together on her chest. Feeling her own breathing. Less and less. Less, less. Until she didn't feel anything.

Translated by Paula Sharp

Black Alleluia

Luis Rafael Sánchez

The mulatta is slicked-up with bright-colored rags, smiling from head to toes, seasoned in crimson and rouge, white teeth seated on the front row.

"Listen up, Granma."

The *tum* crawls through the sand, caressing the ears of the rabble.

"Damn black niggers got the devil inside 'em."

The Grandmother shifts her wad and stains the floor with the rank spittle.

"Damn Carmelo. Dey made dat one on top a bongo drum. And dey must've really toss for him!"

The *tum* inches up the round bellies, furrowing into the heart.

Ay Bacumbé
of the three halos
Bacumbé!
Ay Bacumbé
I am so jealous
Bacumbé!

"Granma, lemme go."

"You too uppity. Dose are black niggers with the devil in 'em. You stayin' put."

"Please, Granma, please."

"I tol' you no. You too conceited!"

The kettle drums let out a reverberant cry, and the females hurry to suck macho nails. Gentlemen tucking in their buttocks, faggots sucking their own dicks, carnival devils licking their fingers, brazen hussies displaying their tits!

"Granma, just a bit."

"You crazy. You a yard nigger. Dose are shore niggers who don' brush deir behinds."

"Please, Granma, is only to watch."

Granma Rufa puckers her lips, scratches her hip and grumbles.

"Can't believe I'm givin' in to dis brat. All right. Go an come back an don' tarry. But don' get too close. Dose niggers got the devil in 'em."

The girl runs out, shedding sweatdrops that sprinkle the drums, slipping through the seagrapes, her arms akimbo, a fleeting, smokey gazelle.

"She looks good enough to gnaw to the bone."

"To nibble bit by bit."

"Good enough to toss round."

Her nigger-wool is covered-up, cropped close to the skull, hard, red, she's kinky to the eyebrows. Checking over the other girls, whipping up molasses and sighs, swaying her rump, she's lying on the ground, trying to shake off the quivers that the ebony has put in her soul. And so fiery is she that coconuts don't dare fall off the trees! Startled, Caridad watches the toothy mascarade sparkling joy in a rumba-line.

Ay Bacumbé
of the three halos
Bacumbé!
Ay Bacumbé
I am so jealous
Bacumbé!

Legs contort in leaps, pirouettes and somersaults. The night orchestrates rhythms while drummers pound away with bleeding fingers.

Ay Bacumbé
what has she got
Bacumbé!

Caridad skips over dry fronds and moves through the starlight, framed by two tall palms. And Ace-of-Spades Carmelo, the most evil-tempered nigger of the palm grove, sees her. He feels a stiff longing in his groin, a stirring of hard yearning, raunchy, horny. He watches her swishing her buttocks on the sand and dreams of them throbbing chest against chest, of digging his drumming fingers into the pulp he can almost taste between her thighs.

"Hey, black mamma, let me fill you with syrup."

Caridad crosses herself and prays, "Saint Ives, open his eyes. Saint John, make him be gone."

Caridad flees and the palm grove drowns in cries and ay's.

"She's built like a brick shithouse."

"Manatee, I'd even suck her pee."

"I'd like to show her my stuff."

"I'd like to munch her clam."

It's the vile alleluia of the buck niggers, the stinking voice of the shore that knows nothing of the good manners of dolled-up little negresses, scrubbed-up little negresses who don't toss in bed with just anyone, slippery little negresses who hide their navels from their confessors!

"The shore is where it's at!"

The *tum* breaks out in beats and slithers. *Tum* on the coconuts. *Tum* on the fronds. *Tum* on the palm trees. *Tum* on the sand. *Tum* on the lips. *Tum* on the souls. Caridad stops, aroused.

The bucks wipe off their urges by plunging into the Río Grande in search of their new god: Bacumbé, god of mischief, trickster god who can just as quickly cure a bellyache as turn a prayer into gibberish, a jesting god who distills moonshine, beautifully black god, blessedly black, marvelously black. The thick lips stretch towards the water to soothe their weariness.

Ay Bacumbé
of the three halos
Bacumbé!

Caridad's eyes bulge and the round little snout begins to quiver.

"Damn niggers flirtin' me up, 'cause I'm pretty and cute. Stinkin' niggers that don't even put cream in deir armpit. Damn niggers with the devil inside 'em."

The *tum* is a savage howl. She tries to open her mouth but she feels five fingers over her lips. The scream is drowned by the broad and knotty hand. Now she feels the *tum* drifting away until it becomes a piercing throb.

"Lemme go. Lemme go."

"You gonna get what's yours."

"Let me go, bully, you got the devil in you."

They're on the ground, the lips burst in blood, the bellies rub against each other, the hands open in skin and hide.

"You gonna see."

Caridad feels the flower bursting through and sobs to the beat of a sad *tum*. She hears the voice of her Granma. "Dose niggers got the devil in 'em." She feels Ace-of-Spades Carmelo's breath trampling her neck.

"Dat was good."

The long tongue wipes up the drool.

"Dat was good."

"Shut up."

And she rises horror-stricken at what her Grandmother will think when she learns that now she too belongs to the shore, she too has the devil under her skin.

"Let's go."

The shadows dart until they reach the Bacumbé of the three halos.

The other niggers lick their lips.

"Brazen nigger.

"He ate her up."

"Lucky nigger."

Caridad skips past the dance circle and heads straight to Colasa's hut.

"Open up, Colasa, and cook me up some brew, or take it out with hook, broom, or knife, but leave my innards clean."

Colasa's eyes dart out of her sockets and she makes the sign of the cross upon Caridad.

"What is it."

"Ace-of-Spades Carmelo put the devil inside me."

Colasa retreats into her room of roots. Caridad continues to hear Granma's voice.

"Drink this."

Like fire to the flesh it lacerates. An excruciating pain that turns her entrails into a searing sore. Each one of her organs feels the bile dragging with it water and blood. She has to open her legs, as if she were playing hopscotch. And she feels the devil descend.

When she left the hut she noticed that the moon was full. She walked across two or three yards. The *tum* hissed its sorcery in the distance. Granma was at the door.

"Damn niggers. Not true dey got the devil in 'em?"

Caridad went straight to the cot and buried herself in the sheets. Granma asked again:

"Not true dey got the devil in 'em?"

The throbbing beat resounded on the palm trees. Caridad turned over on her back. A star slipped in through a crack on the roof. The Bacumbé whirled till dawn. Granma asked for the third time.

"Not true dey got the devil in 'em?"

But the mulatta was already dreaming.

Translated by Lizabeth Paravisini-Gebert
and Margarite Fernández Olmos

Now That I'm Back, Ton

❖

René del Risco Bermúdez

You really were a character, Ton; with that cap from the Licey tigers that wasn't blue anymore but streaked and faded and the khaki pants that you used to wear ironed to a tee for our Saturday afternoon get togethers at the bandstand in Salvador park, seeing the Boy Scouts parade along the avenue and running and horsing around until suddenly night fell and the park was in darkness and our shouts died away in the streets of the barrio. I remember you, because today I have learned to love guys like you and so I try to remember that tired, shy voice of yours and that persistent limp that would make the hop at every step but didn't keep you from running from home to first base, when Juan would come up to you and whisper in your ear "we're gonna surprise 'em, Ton; hit one to third and run like crazy." And because you used to play with the guys of the "Aurora," many times you joined us in the fun of forming that circle in the stands "Rosi, Rosi, shish boom bah – Aurora-Aurora-ra-ra-ra!" and that thing about how you couldn't play every inning in a game, because you had to wait for us to get ahead of the teams from "Miramar" or "La Barca" in order to "give Ton a chance 'cuz he got here early" and "don't worry Ton, you're about to go in as a pinch hitter."

How did you end up in the barrio? When? Who got you into the gang? What story did Tonín tell about Pedro the Boogey man that night, Ton? Do you remember the radio program at Candelario's house every night at nine "Mejoral," the best sedative of them all, presenting "Jailhouse of Women," and then someone clapping their hands from the doorway and it was already time to go to bed, and the spell was broken?

I don't know if you'd recognize me now, looking up at me with that squint of yours with the sun in your eyes. Probably the pipe clenched in my teeth makes me look like a stranger to you, or the extra pounds that are rounding out my face and my receding hairline have wiped out what could have been recalled about that boy who parted his hair on the side, and who sometimes went with you in the afternoon to see Kid Barquerito and Kid 22-22 at boxing practice in the outdoor ring in the days of "Barquero fights Acevedo in Havana" and Efraín, the trainer with his Joaquín Pardave moustache, "Come on, come on, you got it, the left, now the jab, that's it!" and later you poised on one leg, "pow-pow-pow-pow-pow" hitting the air with your fists, going down Sánchez street, "pow-pow-pow" you would shadow box against the wall, always hopping because of your permanent limp and I would say "cut it out, Ton" but you would keep it up and then, right in the middle of the barrio, I would take off your cap, exposing the huge oval of your zeppelin-like head, the head of "Ton Melíton, Melonhead, cripple bone!" which got skinny Pérez to join in with a drum roll from the Boy Scout drums to make you so mad that you would yell at him "you stinking sonofabitch," and so we would run one after the other until we got to my doorway where as you put your cap back on, you would always say the same thing: "I'm through with you!"

In those days the barrio wasn't so sad Ton, that faded dusty light didn't fall on the houses and there wasn't this depressing clammy smell of old boards that permeates the skin like a resigned and tender vapor of poverty, through the streets where minutes before I came uselessly longing for the bushy eyebrows and close-set gaze of "Owl" Pujols, the charcoal tins by the door of the yellow house, the Pascual family's black and white dog, the babble at Pin Baez's birthday parties where his father used to drink beer with his friends sitting against a brick wall in a shady corner of the patio, all of us, me with my starched white suit; now I remember the punctual and melancholy strumming of Negro Alcántara's guitar, while we ran and shouted around the well and all the while the noise of the churning ice cream maker and Asia's shouting, her buck teeth flashing whenever she opened her mouth.

It was enough to make you die laughing, Ton, to get your shoes muddy, to stand on tiptoe at the edge of the well, to see yourself in its dark mirror, face of concentric circles, hair of ferns, spit in the eye, and later "look what you've done to yourself, it's enough to drive any-one crazy, you lost two buttons, wise guy, that's what you are, a good for nothing, Arturo, someone is going to have to beat some sense into this kid"; but then we were so alike, so "two peas in a pod whatever happens happens," Ton, that life was all the same, "a blast: a gas," for all of us.

Obviously it isn't the same now. Years have passed. They started passing the day I looked into the putrid green waters in the street gut-ter, when Papa turned the key in the black lock and Mama kept look-ing at the house out of the back window of the car and I waved at you all, you, Fremio, Juan, Tonín, on the street corner and I kept remembering the way you all looked, a little sad, a little angry, when we left the barrio and the town for good that morning (eight-fifteen by the car radio).

You would all remain forever leaning against the gray wall of Ulises' corner store. The spindle of the toy top boring a hole in the soft pavement, its string hurled into the air with wild abandon, play-ing a game of skill for coins, black from rolling in the street; from then on you could always be found alongside this wall which would grow darker with the years, vulgar graffiti written in charcoal there and the days passing by with a deaf listlessness that would end in memory, in a remote and blurry image of a time inexplicably lost for-ever.

One morning I happened to tell my friends from San Carlos what you all were like; I told them about Fremio, who discovered that traces of brown sugar were always left behind on the floors of the box cars on the wharf whenever the boats were being loaded, and that we could take fistfuls of it, even fill up a bag and sit down and eat it on the steps leading to the old customs house; I also told them about the times we used to plunge into the river, swimming out to the schooner, beached in the mud on one of its sides, and once we got there, with our feet dangling in the water, looking at the town, the smoke from the chimney, the carts that came back up from the port carrying goods, we passed the time away, pissing off the boat, talking, chasing each other from bow to stern, until it was late by the church clock and once again, thrashing our way through the water we made it to shore in an uproar of splashing that I can hear even now, believe it or not, Ton.

The guys were fascinated by our world of mangrove thickets, locomotives, greenheart trees, crab holes, and from then on they made me tell stories that as the days went by I altered little by little until I ended up attributing to you and to myself veritable epic poems that I myself believed and repeated to myself for who knows how long, perhaps until the day I understood that it was completely useless, this passion for reviving the outlines of an image which like old photographs inevitably yellow and fade.

Life was changing, Ton; then I was a little inclined towards books and I got caught up in a strange world, a mixture of the Natural Science of Fesquet, the poetry of Bécquer and the illustrations in *Billiken;* I liked the walk to school each morning under the trees of Avenida Independencia, and the face of Rita Hayworth on the small yellow screen of the "Capitolio" movie house made me forget about Flash Gordon and the Three Stooges. By that time Papa was earning good money in his job at the Ministry of Education and we moved to a house which gave me a view of the sea and of Ivette, with her striped shorts and golden braids that punctuated the lively rhythm of her eyes and head; she introduced me to Nat King Cole, Fernando Fernández, the old records by the Modernaires, and I learned to keep up with the beat of her shots at the ping pong table; I never talked about you with her, that's the truth, maybe because there was never any opportunity to do so or perhaps because my days with Ivette went by so fast, so full of "come-look-this-is-Gretchen-Dad's-Pontiac-Albertico-says-I'm-going-to-Canada" that I never had the time or the need to remember.

Do you know what became of the Andrea Doria, Ton? You probably don't know; I remember it from some photographs in the *Miami Herald* and because the latino crowd at the university, we used to go to a cafe in Coral Gables to sing together with pitchers of beer, "Arrivederci Roma," tipping back in our chairs as if we were on a life boat; I was studying English and I got a kick out of pronouncing the "Good-bye" in the song, dropping my jaw in the strange way peculiar to the kids of that country. And you know what, Ton? Once I thought about you guys. It was the morning we went walking along the pier looking at yachts and I saw a group of dirty unkempt boys that were taking sardines out of a rusty can, sticking them onto the tips of their fish hooks. I watched that gang of kids for awhile and I saw the portrait of ourselves on the wharf in Macorís come to life, only we weren't blond and we didn't wear sneakers and didn't have fishing poles, then and there the spell of my reverie was broken and I went on looking at yachts with my Nicaraguan friend, a real sailing buff.

And the years fall with all their weight on memories, on life that has been lived, and the burial of the past begins in some unknown place, in a region of the heart and in dreams where it will maybe remain intact but covered with the grime of day to day living, buried beneath the books read, impressions of other countries, handshakes, afternoons of soccer, drinking bouts, misunderstandings, love, indigestion, work. That's why, Ton, when I graduated in medicine years later, the party wasn't with you all in San Pedro, but in various places, racing crazily in that Triumph without a muffler that blasted over the pavement, dancing to exhaustion in the Country Club, popping corks on the terrace while Mama brought in plates of sandwiches and Papa called me "Doctor" to the hilarity of my friends; you all weren't there and I wasn't in the mood to reconstruct old and melancholy images of crumbling walls, dusty streets, the whistle of locomotives, and bare feet wading in the muddy water of the river; now the names were Héctor, Fred, Américo and we would talk about Parkinson's disease, allergies and tests by Jung and Adler as well as certain works by Thoman Mann and Francois Mauriac.

All this must seem so strange to you, Ton; it probably seems so "once upon a time and two and two are four beggars can't be choosers" that I can see you straddling the dirty wall of the Avenida, your wandering eyes lost in the red branches of the almond trees, listening to Juan tell fabulous tales about his uncle the sailor who was shipwrecked on the Mona Canal and who during the war was taken prisoner on a German submarine near Curaçao. Your eyes always had a sad and naive vagueness about them whenever something made you see that the world had other dimensions that you, sleeping among the sacks of charcoal and rotten oranges, would never know save for Juan's stories, or Bayer Aspirin film clips, or the sports illustrations in "Carteles."

I don't know what you dreamt of then, Ton, or if you had dreams; I don't know if people like you have dreams or if the crude awareness of the realities you face don't allow for them, but in any case I wouldn't let you dream, I would keep you up telling you all this so that I can somehow become one of you again if only for this afternoon. Now I would tell you how years later, while studying Psychiatry in Spain, I met Rossina, a recent arrival from Italy with a group of travelers which included two brothers, Piero and Francesco, who wore striped tee shirts and had hair that fell into their eyes. We met by accident, Ton, just as people met in certain novels by Françoise Sagan; we were drinking "Valdepeñas" in a tavern after a bullfight, and Rossina, accustomed to making sweeping gestures while speaking, raised her arms showing a belly button about an inch above her white pants. After that I only remember that someone spilled a bottle of wine on my jacket and Piero exchanged discreet smiles with the pianist in a dark place that I never found again. Months later, Rossina came back to Madrid and we set ourselves up in a tiny flat at the end of Avenida Generalissimo; we went to the soccer games, the museums, the cine-club, the fairs and to the theatre; we read, spent summers together, played the guitar, wrote poetry and once my specialization was finished, we put the books, the records, the camera, the guitar and our clothes in huge suitcases and went to sea. "What is Santo Domingo like?" Rossina had asked me a week before when we'd decided to get married, and I limited myself to answering, "something more than the palm trees and drums that you've seen in the posters at the Consulate."

That happened sometime ago, Ton; Papa was still living when we returned. Did you know that Papa died? You must know that. We buried him here because he always said that in this town he would rest among comrades. If you had seen how the old man changed, you who made fun of his hurried way of walking and his jumpy, marionette-like manner, would never have recognized him; the sparse gray hair, the contorted face, his hoarse voice and breathing, he painfully wasted away until he died one afternoon among the shadows and the strong odor of medicines in his bedroom. Mama was to die in the same place, hardly a year later; she died sound of mind with her eyes hard and bright, with the same expression that always used to frighten us so much, Ton.

As for me, things with Rossina didn't go as well as I'd hoped; we got a nice apartment on Avenida Bolívar and began to work with relative success in my own private practice. Months went by at a normal pace for those of us who come from a foreign country and begin to establish a social network: invitations to the beach on Sundays, dinners, dancing on the weekends, hikes in the mountains, get togethers with artists and colleagues, invitations to the art galleries, phone calls from friends, in a nutshell, the relaxed pace that one falls into when one arrives married and with a degree from abroad. Rossina adjusted to the environment with natural ease and, save for a few small protests, showed herself to be happy and interested in everything that was beginning to form the center of our lives. But soon things began to change, I began to give lectures at the University while my number of clients increased, which meant that my worries and responsibilities grew greater and greater, by this time Francesco José was born, and all of this taken together, turned our relationship upside down. Rossina began to complain about being overweight and between the can of Metrecal and the bathroom scales, she would launch into a litany of bitter and nasty remarks, life was so expensive in this country, in Italy the taxis aren't like this, here it's raining all the time and when it's not, the dust swallows everyone up, the baby's hair is going to be too coarse, the household help is despicable, young marrieds shouldn't turn into a couple of bores, one needed so much to be in Europe, no one should spend their time sewing on buttons every two minutes. The goddamn bottle of "Sucaryl" broke this morning, and so everything went sour, Ton my friend, until one day all my reserves of restraint and common sense ran out and Rossina flew to Rome on "Alitalia" and all I know of my son Francesco arrives in two letters a month and a few color photos which I keep here in my wallet, to feel him growing up next to me. That's the story.

The rest won't be strange, Ton. Tomorrow is the Day of the Dead and I have come in order to stand for a moment by my parents' grave; I wanted to come today because for a long time now, the thought of this homecoming has been rattling around in my mind. I thought about coming back to walk the streets of the barrio, to go down its alleyways, breathing in the fragrances of the cherry and kinup trees, the grass in the house plots, going over to that window which looks out onto the river and its boats; finding all of you hanging around the gray wall of Ulises' corner store, pulling "Owl" Pujos' hair, wrestling with Fremio, joking around with Tonín and Pericles, going to the bandstand in Salvador park to search in the breeze for the uniform sound of the Boy Scouts' drumroll. But perhaps I should admit that it's already a little late, that I won't be able to go back over my tracks in search of a part of life that was perhaps more genuine.

That's why a moment ago I left the barrio, Ton, and I've come here to this table and found myself ordering, almost without hesitating to, the bottles of beer that I'm drinking down without realizing it, because when I saw you a while ago, I saw you come in with that same limp that could never escape me and that look of guarded candor and that unmistakable head of "Ton Melíton, Melonhead, cripple bone" looking at me as if I were a stranger, without recognizing me. I've only had time to understand that you haven't changed a bit, Ton; your honest heart is still the same, just as it was in those days, because only guys like you can really remain uncorrupted, even after all the years of neglect and poverty and that bitterness that always made you look at the red branches of the almond trees when you thought about certain things. I'm the one who has changed, Ton; that's why I think that I'll be going tonight and that's also why I don't know if I should tell you who I am right now and talk about all of this with you or simply let you finish polishing my shoes and leave this town forever.

Translated by Beth Wellington

The Fire

❖

Hilma Contreras

It started near the summit, a scarlet burst of laughter at sunset. Later, the youngest pines hurled their red wail at the sky. With every flare-up, the smoke—the dense bluish pain of the boiling resin—intensified.

At the beginning it was a distraction for the five or six people resting from the city bustle at the Bella Vista hotel, located at an altitude of 1,400 meters. People of modest means yielding to the illusion of a change in fortune because the half-rates just before the tourist season made a luxury hotel accessible to them.

Jorge Núñez was among them, although he had not come to loaf, but to escape the annoying interruptions that made it difficult for him to concentrate on the creation of his novel. He had had two fruitful, extremely fruitful, days before the constant flow of curious valley inhabitants began. Barely an hour after word spread of the fire in the pine groves it was no longer possible to remain on the terrace, facing the imposing panorama of the mountains. All the bustle and confusion would eventually force him to seek refuge in his room if he wanted to continue writing. But before going up he went to the bar for a Coke. They too were there, their eyes fixed on the uncommon spectacle they could observe at their leisure through the window, without rising from the table where they sat, leaning on their elbows. His voice distracted the woman from her contemplation.

Even though he had his back to her, Jorge felt the gaze of her profoundly black eyes. *What an absurd couple,* he thought. *What is it about that man that I dislike?* He had never spoken to him, had barely exchanged a greeting at mealtimes, but the man's presence nonetheless exasperated him, even when he had his back to him, like now.

"It's useless, it won't light!" the woman said impatiently, the cigarette still on her lips. "This lighter is a disaster, just like you."

"Emilia!" her companion reproached her, reddening, "they can hear you!"

"Allow me . . . "

The woman smiled imperceptibly and concentrated on the act of lighting her cigarette from the flame Jorge was offering in the hollow of his palm. She thanked him with a puff of smoke on his face. The other squirmed restlessly on his chair. Jorge looked straight at him. *So it was just that, after all. A simple delay in fetal development, something unfinished, something insufficiently formed in his being, a latent deformity. I would swear that . . .*

He didn't want to accept the couple's invitation to join them for dinner and he withdrew, ruminating on his discovery. *I would swear that he had been a sickly child, rickety and snooty-nosed . . . What an absurd couple. What is this woman doing with that guy?*

In the silence of the night the insects had grown quiet, making the roar of the fire more audible. The flames were racing down the slope.

"Do you think there's any danger to the hotel?" Emilia asked.

"We are at the mercy of the breeze (Jorge took pleasure in frightening her). A change in direction will bring it upon us."

"You see, Emilia? This gentleman confirms my opinion. We should have left this afternoon (the little man was fidgeting nervously, pointing here and there). If it runs to the south it can block our retreat."

"I have made it clear that I won't miss this spectacle for all the gold in the world." As he was grumbling, torn between his desire to vanquish her stubbornness and his fear of her cutting replies in the presence of strangers, Emilia grew sarcastic: "Why don't you go to bed? You've had a day plum-full of emotions, and may find yourself having to rise early to save your life."

"We can all go to bed without worry," Jorge intervened, appeasingly. "The river will protect our sleep."

Not only Jorge but all of the men trusted in the river, which in effect kept the fire at bay, at a prudent distance from the hotel. But unwilling to admit defeat, it wasn't long in slipping south along the riverbanks, burning pines and apple trees. Then the crackle of the flames joined the sharp blows of the fire's aggressiveness.

"Rodolfo insists that we are in danger . . . "

Jorge glanced at the time on his watch. One o'clock . . . and the woman was pestering him once again. Despite the acrid smell of the air full of black feathery ash he had remained on the terrace, savoring the feeling of finding himself alone on the threshold of a beautiful inferno. Alone until now . . . He noticed that the fire's red radiance filled Emilia's insistent pupils.

"You don't love your husband."

"What is it to you?" she asked, seating herself on an armchair next to him.

"It was just an idle comment . . . "

The truth is he felt simultaneously attracted and mistrustful.

"You may have noticed he drives me to distraction. Rodolfo is a wimp, and I'm eager for adventure."

He seemed not to be listening.

"Am I bothering you?"

Jorge smiled . . . The conflagration enveloped the woman in a demonic halo. *Goddess of the inferno.*

On the fourth day the fire got the best of the men, crossed the river, jumped over the waters and clung to the trees on the opposite bank. The alarm spread:

"Up and at it, everyone, if it climbs up here it will burn the hotel!"

Rodolfo jumped to his feet.

"Who was right?" He sobbed, frantic. "If you had followed my advice we wouldn't be in this mess now."

"And you wouldn't have the opportunity to participate in a heroic action," his wife replied, impassively caressing her tumbler of whisky on the rocks.

It was eleven in the morning. They were alone in the bar, Emilia's favorite place at that hour.

"What do you mean?"

The husband asked the question in a suspicious tone.

"Mr. Núñez," Emilia called out. Jorge had just come in, still clutching his machete, asking for a Coke. "Are you going with the crew?"

"Naturally, of course"

"Take my husband with you."

"Emilia!"

Jorge's attention rested momentarily on the couple. He was chok-ing with indignation. She was arching her brows, a strange gleam in her eyes.

"There's no need for him to come now," he assured them. "There'll be other brigades."

And he left, swigging his bottle of Coke.

From the river valley rose ever-renewing mushrooms of smoke—slow, thick and continuous, suffocating the mountain. Everything in the hotel was being coated with ashes. In an uninterrupted relay the men battled the conflagration with machete blows.

Jorge joined another brigade at sundown. Emilia caught up with him as he was crossing the terrace.

"Mr. Núñez . . . you need rested men, let my husband go with you."

Her insistence aroused his uneasiness.

"Please, let him be good for something."

Her manicured hand had rested on his well-muscled arm.

"Do you understand?"

"I'll go get him," he said reluctantly, but his heart was beating wild-ly when he crossed the threshold of the bar.

They worked until very late, zealously, with singleminded energy and the determined will to win the battle against the voracious ele-ment. In the darkness, where the fire had passed, the incandescent pine cones opened their hungry pupils. They sprung from the night, cautiously, steadying themselves into scarlet dots. After hour upon hour of uncertainty, it became evident that the machetes had the upper hand . . . The men returned in small groups to the hotel, where they were served coffee and rum amidst exclamations and commen-taries.

Emilia opened the door to her bedroom when she heard the man's steps approaching on the hallway. Jorge stopped, his hair singed, cov-ered in soot, smelling of burnt resin, of half-burned logs, of stale sweat. Despite his fatigue he again felt powerfully attracted to the woman devouring him with eyes dilated by anxiety.

Outside, the long-awaited rain began falling. It was raining heavily. Under the first lash of the rainstorm, the flames that had persisted at the mountain top hurled a gigantic crimson rose against the black sky.

"Well? . . . " Emilia could hardly contain the desire to clasp the man's vigorous body.

"Everything went according to plan," he informed her in a low voice, his gaze fixed on her.

"An accident?"

"An . . . ?"

His gasp of surprise dissolved into an irrepressible burst of laughter.

"Your husband is waiting for you at the bar," he said when he recovered his breath.

Translated by Lizabeth Paravisini-Gebert

Mambrú Did Not Go to War

❖

Aída Cartagena Portalatín

"No, there isn't, and never was, a more
deplorable caste . . ."

Mambrú went off to war
What pain, what pain, what sorrow.
Mambrú went off to war
Don't know when he'll be back.
Oh, do, re mi; oh do, re fa.
Don't know when he'll be back.
　　　　　　　　　　　 — Nursery Rhyme[1]

I'm among the broken-up. You are broken up. He is broken up. We are broken up. We are all broken up. But your fissure is not like ours. You lost your balance before you got to the top, and powerless to counteract the force of gravity, you rolled downhill. Your falls multiplied themselves dizzily like in the Physics theory of the inclined plane, which you understood well enough to get excellent grades in school but appalling results in real life. In your place, I would have remained silent about it all. Not even with a noose around my neck, on the verge of being hanged, would I have uttered a single word, but you believe in a conscience, and though not quite repenting of the things you've done, you love to vomit out your affairs to one and all. You speak about yourself. It doesn't offend you to spill things out. You want to be listened to. We're finally listening.

You go on and on and on. Talking. Talking. Talking. Talking until its very neverendingness tires me out, and without stopping I let out a scream, a halt, leaving those still alive to consume themselves in rectifying their intimacies until time immemorial, amen, and to think this is the Boulevard St. Michel, from numbers 27 to 31. I let my eyes fall on the newspaper vending machine and read the *France Soir* headlines: *Black Crusade. African Liberation.* These are not front-page headlines; Black Africa has been wishing and struggling for its freedom for decades. I gaze at another headline: *The Secret Life of Cats.* That business about cats on roofs meowing erotic nonsense is such a hackneyed theme it can't rouse my curiosity. I laugh a mocking, negative laugh that infuriates a guy walking along the same sidewalk, close to me. This is the Boulevard St. Michel in the Latin Quarter of Paris, in the year nineteen hundred and . . . something. I'm sorry about that guy, I would like to offer him an explanation, and while I try to locate him, glancing up an down the street, I sense upon me a band of male and female teenagers going by, squeezing each other. Male or female. Female or male. I can't identify them by gender, it's impossible to tell them apart, because they wear the same outfits. As they walk they push me against a restaurant window. Behind the glass I read: today's special 10.50 francs. I can't believe they want so much money, very soon I'll go hungry again, I won't have anything to eat, I'll roam the bad neighborhoods, I'll sleep on park or boulevard benches, or on the angles formed by the walls and buttresses of St. Severino. I think of so many things at once, even of those coffins at the Louvre Metro exit across from Ponte Neuf which made such an impression on me. To die, what a dammed thing it is to die. People have no right to die in Paris. I think of my life and that of Lilá. She repeated it to me three days ago: you have to find yourself another room before the whole thing blows up, I don't want to compromise you. But now I am waiting for the bus, I'm looking out for the number 21, the one that climbed from the University City up Glaciere-Berthóllet-Claude Bernard and at the end of Guy Lussad entered St. Michel, going on across the Seine to Chatelet, to the Opera and ending its run at St. Lazaire. It was my route when I arrived in Paris as a student. A few buses have gone by. And I kept waiting for one that took a long while to appear, finally showing up with its luminous green eye on which you could read the number 21. It is an indescribable thing, as if two clandestine lovers had suddenly found each other again in an inexplicable place. All this notwithstanding, I let the bus go by.

I am Claudio, trying to find lost time and nail it to a panelled wall. Today it occurs to me that my brain is not working well, that something is failing, that I have fallen from I don't know where to this corner. Claudio, Claudio, I tell myself, calling myself over and over again and several times more. Hurry up, you must go further on. My brain cannot fix on ideas very well. I would say that it is somewhat foggy. At eight o'clock in the morning Paris is all fog. It is June. All is fog just like my brain, and guided by that very brain I march on until, tired of walking up and down, I decide to sit down on one of the empty chairs on the improvised sidewalk terrace of the Select Latin, with its scandalous prices. On the opposite sidewalk, under Marcuset, is the brasserie Glaciére, which further excites my hunger. I have ten francs in my wallet. I have a little bit more money in the room I occupy in the hotel. I need to put it all together and I remind myself several times that I must go and get it. I also remember the guy that works as a receptionist behind the counter. I will have to greet him and observe his oh-so-carefully coiffed mane, done at a woman's beauty shop. He is exaggeratedly unpleasant, but I must go back, and the necessity of doing so means that I must humiliate myself, I must beg him: *la clé, s'il vous plait, monsieur.* I must go—I will go. I am before him. I speak to him like an automaton, without looking at him. He hands me the key, I walk to the elevator, push the button, and climb up. The door opens and I'm on the third floor. The staircase is at the end of the hallway. I must still climb eighteen steps to the landing right across the door to Room number 46, which is on the fourth floor. I go in, take the money, and go back out. Once on the street again I stop and re-read: University of Paris—School of Sciences. It's on the Place de la Sorbonne with its statue of Auguste Comte in the center. The world advances, crowds up with people, with ideas, with vehicles, with car accidents and deaths. Auguste Comte is not now a positivist who ignites intellectual fires. He did that once, but he has been assimilated. The monument serves to guide the parking of vehicles, those who enter, those who exit, those who remain. It also serves as a support for peeing dogs. I remember: I forgot to return the key to the receptionist guy but I will not go back to drop it off. Guided by my right index finger the disc with the 46 gyrates with the key. Six months with all their details clench my memory, swallowing almost all of my time on this humid and misty morning.

Last night when we walked past Notre Dame, Lilá held on to me tightly, squeezing my arm. I thought we would both collapse; we joined efforts in an attempt to avoid a tragedy. A few steps ahead, at the entrance to rue de l'Arcade, in front of the Quasimodo Bar, a stream of blood came down her legs. She said, anguished: let's hurry, let's hurry, it's getting worse. She began to lose her strength, I don't know how we advanced several more meters, which seemed like an endless distance. I don't know how we made it, I don't know. Right at the entrance to the Hotel Dieu she collapsed. She yelled at me: run, run, you must avoid the police. I left her. No, I didn't leave her. I abandoned her at the entrance to the Hotel Dieu, the public maternity clinic in Paris. She aborted right then and there. I was the only witness to that misfortune. I didn't agree with her, I didn't want her to get rid of the creature. On various occasions she had said to me: this has to be gotten rid of, it would be such a humiliation for my family, it's not worth our being forced to get married, you are not the type of man who accepts responsibility, besides, they would stop sending the dollars that we both live on.

Lilá aborted last night. Now it is morning, I reach the corner, sit down, and glance up and down the Boulevard. The great human river circulates up and down, running to cars, buses, entering or exiting the Metro. I get up and retreat to the narrow rue Champollion, the one with the moviehouses for students but with rich-people prices. Yesterday Lilá and I attended the 4 o'clock showing. I'm ashamed to admit it, but we had quite an argument over Z, the film by Vasilis Vassiloff. She was very supportive of the actions of the revolutionaries and applauded deliriously when they sentenced the military officers. The disruption of the entire web of spying and torture excited her so much that I had to force her to control herself. She wanted to get up and yell like the other revolutionary students who were applauding and stomping their feet like madmen. The press has said that they are FLN members from the colonies. I shouldn't have felt uncomfortable, but my nature rebels against these types who clamor for the liberation of this or that region or country. I was upset and kept riling her because it bothered me that she could think like her fellow university students. And besides, she shouldn't forget that I fled the war of 1965 in Santo Domingo. However, we left Z holding hands and walked to a small restaurant across form the Seine where we frequently had dinner. While they got our order ready I took a pencil out and calculated how many francs the ZZZ had cost—tickets, tip to the usherette, a pack of hot chestnuts, etc. Lilá interrupted me: Claudio, it doesn't matter, I love feeling well-to-do, it's so pleasant. Whatever it cost has been paid, why are you always counting pennies, don't be melodramatic, you knew that the prices weren't for cheapskates. She was humiliating me, making me turn pale, forcing me to admit to myself that I was also a cheapskate living at her expense. She had the upper hand in our situation, but emotionally and sexually she was lost without me, she needed me. I am conscious that she has a problem with sex but that she is incapable of taking a different man every day. She is not sleeping around. Her links to her family prevent her from going from one man to the next. Poor girl, so generous with me. She appreciates my wisdom so.

I finally get to the corner of St. Michel and the St. Germain des Prés-Cluny Metro. I enter the Metro. On a second class coach I go up to Menilmontant. I make several line changes on the Metro. Above, on the surface, is Lilá. I'm still thinking of her. She has aborted. Last night she was picked up at the door of the Hotel Dieu, the public maternity hospital in Paris. The clock strikes ten o'clock in the morning. I take it as a fact that by this time she has been questioned over and over again. Her identity card has been withheld. She has refused to give the name of her uncle, the ambassador. I, rolling underneath the city in the Metro, sweating from the disagreeable, metallic heat let off by the machines, choking in this dirty heat that remains suspended in the closed-off vacuum of the tunnels, or sticking to the tunnel walls. It isn't coal, it's electrical, I don't know, but it's dirty, and I'm letting myself be dragged through the Parisian underground like a rat. When the engine stops I read: Gare de Austerlitz, my heart contracts again, I think of the police who must have taken all of Lilá's things, even her School of Letters identity card. No, she is not a professional prostitute. The doctor must have noticed that it was her first loss. The engine follows its established route. I am an idiot, I reproach myself, but I'm comforted by the fact that in three days they will leave her in peace and will drop her off at a doorway she will say is hers. No, she will not go to the embassy. I roll on. This is a heaven beneath the ground. I feel the engine take off again, slow down again. I transfer to the number 5 line, to Eglise de Pantin. I am sleepy and move like an automaton. My eyes close and I keep them closed. I count with my eyes closed as the engine slams its brakes down seven times before reaching República.

I immediately transfer to the number 3 line, Pte. des Lilas, and one, two, three more stops: Pére Lachaise. I leave the car and run to the number 2 line, Nation Etoile. One station more and I'm at Menilmontant. When I exit the Metro the clarity of the daylight and the overwhelming crowd jolt me so that I feel revealed in the nakedness of my own weak nature and I must accept that I'm a failure. It's true I fled my country in 65, when it was again occupied by the Yankees. It wasn't just that I was not going to fight against a superior foe, but that I was also not interested in defending my own people. Lilá knows all my shortcomings, and I have the suspicion that she won't return with me to the Rosetta apartment.

She will not go back to that dilapidated dwelling where we installed ourselves six months ago to enjoy our love or to make love. One single dingy room we had, but we lacked nothing. She took pains to make me feel secure, and I accepted without argument everything she offered me in that Rue de Solferino with its aura of a hideaway. We possessed the enchantment of the Rive Gauche; we walked the narrow winding alleys. We hopped around in zigzag. We zigzagged in an embrace until we reached Cluny, and four blocks to the west, the School of Letters where I left Lilá every morning.

I don't know, but one day someone will finish this story and call it Mambrú, Mambrú didn't go to war. I can't continue it now.

Translated by Lizabeth Paravisini-Gebert

[1]Translator's addition.

The Path to the Ministry

❖

Marcio Veloz Maggiolo

Are you sure this is the address?"

"Of course, absolutely."

The General rang the bell and chimes playing the notes of Mozart's Fourth Symphony fell like "a soft breeze of unhurried spinnings" on the ears of Mr. and Mrs. Ternejo.

"Felipe, someone's at the door."

"And . . . ?" responded Mr. Ternejo peevishly.

"Open it, open it . . ."

Felipe Ternejo, a well-experienced ex-Minister, never could refute or reject, as happens with almost all of those of his former rank, the orders of his wife.

"Bah!," he exclaimed, "I'd better check the peephole."

With his eye in the viewer he manifested surprised at his unexpected visitors. The General and Tola, his wife, appeared through the perspective of the "magic eye" like two greasy little balls in the night.

"Mary, Mary, it's none other than General Castrillo and his wife Tola . . . Can you believe it? Just like that, without warning."

Before ringing the bell again Tola asked her husband:

"But are you certain that the invitation said eight-thirty?"

"Of course I'm accurate, Tola, . . . Are you forgetting my training?"

Mary went to the fish-eye to confirm the news her husband had "cabled" to her, barely moving his lips. Having done so she ran up the stairs, hastily put on the dress from the preceding night — still smelling of perfume and cigarettes — and descended hurriedly so that Felipe could do the same while she opened the door.

"But how wonderful; the two of you here," she said, allowing the General to enter, examine his surroundings and say:

"We're sorry to be so early."

Mary immediately grasped the mistake contained in that voice that had issued so many commands, eliminated so many guerrillas, installed and expelled so many so-called constitutional presidents and filled Central America with communiques supporting interventions, non-interventions, the right, the left of center, the right wing of center, etcetera and more etceteras. A man of great power, General Castrillo was one of those few names that held influence "at every level."

"Come in, come in," Mary indicated, while she thought of the argument she would use to avoid displeasing Castrillo and his wife. "Felipe is upstairs getting dressed."

The guests made their way into the great dining room, which appeared untidy and disorganized.

"Be seated, be seated," Mary insisted, pointing her visitors towards an elegant striped sofa for eight.

The General and Tola did not hesitate. Felipe, who had been listening to the conversation from the second floor, descended wearing his favorite dinner jacket and with reverent gestures presented himself:

"My dear friends and guests. My dear General, my dear and always well-cherished Tola, you don't know how pleased we are."

"Well, well, we were more than honored by your invitation. It's always nice to see that there are friends that remember their friends," said Tola, who was more tactful than her husband.

The General glanced towards the patio and saw half-empty glasses, crumpled napkins abandoned in flower pots, and a grass-colored parrot saying between his teeth — or rather between his beak— greetings, greetings, at your service, at your service.

Mary, who did not wish to lose her guests despite the fact that the party had been yesterday — a complicated matter given the presence today of these two erratic tardy pests —began to figure out an excuse and find a way to retain, with some sort of sociable logic, such important national figures.

"Felipe, attend to Tola and General Castrillo; a whiskey, gin, a glass of beer, make them comfortable as the party will be ready soon."

General Castrillo preferred — he himself — to mix his own rum and soda, and placed a Tom Collins in Tola's hands. He pointed out that he had been a barman during his years at the academy, when each cadette had to learn to make his own drinks.

Given the lack of new arrivals, Tola inquired:

"Have we mistaken the hour?"

"Oh, no, not at all, Mary will explain later. It's something rather unique. And by the way, General Sir, I received your letter of recommendation for my niece Sandra in the Washington consulate, and also the Bank is studying the loan application with your guarantee from a week ago. We don't know, really, how to thank you, as well as for the magnificent time we spent a year and a half ago when you last invited us to the officer's club, and moreover" — Felipe laughed nervously — "we are so pleased that your son Julitín visits our daughter Gertrudis frequently, he seems to have hit it off with her so well . . ."

With cunning and an embarrassed effortlessness, Felipe handed the General and Tola a photo album in which Gertrudis was featured wearing her first diapers and her first five-year-old dress, and later her formal gown at Club Paradise, where she had her coming-out party, displaying the pearl necklace given to her by General Cámpora, whom General Castrillo later overthrew to place in power the present ruler-of-the-moment, Dr. Alzaga, with whom, naturally, the Ternejos kept a good, nay, an excellent, relationship.

"A lovely necklace," said the General as if sensing this.

"We bought it in Capri, General Sir. On a trip," Felipe pointed out peremptorily . . ."Another drink, General Sir?"

"Sure, sure," said the General, beginning to grow lively. "Yes, Felipe my friend," he continued, "yes, every time I see a pearl necklace like that I remember all the ones that son of a bitch Cámpora gave away; Central America is full of those necklaces."

"But not this one, General Sir, this one, this one you see here we purchased in Capri."

Mary had taken advantage of this conversation to contact her neighbor Emilia, whose gardener doubled in the evenings as a waiter for certain families and who, moreover, had a uniform and everything.

Lautaro, the waiter-chauffeur-gardener, leapt over the flowering adobe wall of the patio and immediately found a tray, pink cloth, cocktail napkins, soda, glasses and drinks, arriving through the blue glass door that ex-Minister Ternejo had installed more to block outside onlookers than the violent tropical sun.

"At your orders, Sirs," said Lautaro, whose smudgy beard denoted his former domestic duties, and whose smell of sour perspiration reverberated in the tepid atmosphere, declaring his having preceded his new transformation with harsh work that clashed with the black and white uniform he now bore so gallantly.

Tola asked for another drink, this time a Martini. Lautaro served it rapidly while Mary tried to locate some of their friends to create a genial atmosphere for General Castrillo, who assuredly had his "wires crossed" when he confused today with yesterday.

"My dear General, — although you should be a Generalissimo by now, since your work for the benefit of the country and the region is unequaled —... shall we have another? ... The guests may arrive at any moment, and then we won't have you to ourselves, we would have to share your gracious presence ... That is why we have organized a small get-together, very small ..."

"We organized it in your honor, and wished to give you a friendly surprise, General Sir," Mary informed from the distant hollows of the telephone where she had been unsuccessful in locating anyone disposed to joining in so that the General might have the pleasure of finding himself in a traditional cocktail party.

General Castrillo felt almost moved, at least that is how he appeared. He was a man who could be moved. When he ordered the execution of eleven students in 1980 he was profoundly moved, no one would have believed it, but it was so. To categorize him as indifferent would have been, according to him, unjust; that is what he replied when Felipe said to him:

" . . . and we then discovered that in that situation you became sentimental."

"Well, duty is duty. Today I would execute them again and I would still get sentimental. One thing is having a sensitive nature, and another is the Fatherland."

The chimes with Mozart's music rang and Mary ran to the door, peered through the fish-eye and discerned the watchman who had come to collect his wages. She opened the door somewhat violently and peering out told him:

"We have guests today. Bring the bill back another day."

She closed it again and sat down next to Tola, with whom she commented on politics, the possible new cabinet ministers and the important research concerning the life of General Castrillo carried out by her husband Felipe Ternejo who, besides being an ex-minister, was also a history enthusiast, even though he had never revealed it. Tola became very interested when Mary added:

"And you know? . . . Felipe thinks that it is about time the General decided to take over the reigns of this little country. Men like the General should not be supporting insignificant civilians."

"Yes, I'm always telling Purito," said Tola, referring to her husband, "either do things yourself or don't do them . . . Purito, come over here and listen to Mary, she too, like many of our friends, believes that it is time that you did things for yourself."

General Puro Castrillo took out a Honduran cigar, lit it circumspectly and asked:

"Well, are the guests arriving or not?"

Felipe Ternejo, balancing himself on his grey moccasins, outdone by the bluntness of the question, replied:

"General Sir, there are no guests. You are the guests."

Castrillo opened his eyes wide, sleeked down his grey moustache, looked around and remarked:

"I don't believe it."

"Well yes, believe it, believe it," said Felipe. "If you wish you can blame us for this little farce. We wanted you all to ourselves and invented an non-existent reception in which only we would be present. Imagine, General Sir, if we had invited you individually you wouldn't have felt like you do now, surprised and surrounded by our exclusive affection. An ambush, that's it, an ambush; our strategy didn't fail, General Sir."

Castrillo's face was neither somber nor smiling. Felipe and Mary searched for some sign that would indicate the effect produced by the situation. General Castrillo thought that he could very well find himself being mocked, but he caught a glimpse of Ternejo's admiration for him. As was always the case when similar things happened, he allowed his heart to reply.

"Look, Felipe, look, Mary, I am grateful. It is the second time that something like this has happened to me. Last night we visited

Joaquín Tades, the industrialist, and something very similar took place. We arrived at the door, rang the bell, classical music chimed and we quickly discovered that having been invited to a reception what was really taking place was a family gathering, just for us. It was simply like that. Curious. The same. We conversed for a long time. Joaquín spoke to me about his debts. I promised to promote his two sons, and tomorrow the honorable President Alzaga will appoint them colonel and major. They're young. But it was all the same. A repetition."

Mary, who was aware that Joaquín Tades' party had been the day before yesterday and not yesterday, was struck by a silence as red as porphyry. So Joaquín Tades and Mirna had played the same game with the General. They concocted a little rendezvous among friends; they summoned up a waiter and they made the General believe that it was an original party arranged in an intimate fashion to show their esteem for him and his wife.

Felipe glanced out of the corner of his eye at his wife, but she could not resist the impulse:

"How many people were in the Tades home, General Sir?"

"Oh, very few, him, his wife, his sisters and one of the younger sons; not even the two military men. A party, not as intimate as this one, of course."

"But very touching," Felipe noted, trying to make amends for his own actions.

Mary excused herself to go the bathroom. The coincidence was amazing. While General Castrillo and Felipe Ternejo spoke of the difficulties caused by the resurgence of the guerrillas, Mary telephoned the home of Joaquín Tades. The person who answered was, in fact, Mirna, the industrialist's wife:

"How are you, Mirna dearest? . . . I want you to hear this. I'm sorry, dear, General Castrillo and Tola are visiting us and we know that they were in your house yesterday . . ."

"The strangest thing, dearest. We invited him to a get-together on Friday and he shows up a day later."

"The same happened with us, we invited him for our thing yesterday at home, and he shows up today. Isn't that odd?"

"He's past it, honey, but he offered Joaquín the post of Minister of Industry."

"Nothing for Felipe yet. We're making him believe that this is an intimate party."

"That's what we did. He is always mixing up the dates."

"We'll talk later, dear. I'm going because I told them I had to take a leak; now I feel better."

Mary reappeared and the General had begun to rise from his seat when Felipe detained him to ask:

"General Sir, do you think . . . there will be a change of government in the near future? This Alzaga is a bit soft . . . I mean . . ."

Tola was about to answer when the General sat down again. He put his hand to his chin and half-closed his eyes as if listening to a philosophical dictum or to one of Toña la Negra's finest boleros. At that moment the grass-colored parrot began to scream some new gibberish which to the General sounded like: "better to piss, better to piss."

Almost no one heard it, but the General turned around and said to himself: "an intelligent parrot, that it is."

He excused himself to go to the bathroom, or rather the half-bath that found itself strategically located under the stairway leading to the upper floors.

While the General urinated, Tola, already quite inebriated, went on about behind-the-scenes political intrigues. The General was willing to toss Alzaga out on his ear, to change posts in the administration and even to find a ministry for Felipe. Tola had not discussed it with her husband, but she knew him well. Undoubtedly the General would offer Felipe the post of Minister of Industry. Mary considered saying "but he has offered that post to Tades," but she realized she would be committing an indiscretion.

The General returned with his cap in hand and his trouser fly all wet.

"We must retire. Tomorrow is a workday."

"It has been a splendid party and a surprise," Tola said.

"If there are changes, and there will be, you could well be on the list," the General affirmed.

The General bid goodbye to the waiter. Before a surprised Mary and Felipe the waiter said to him:

"You know, Castrillo, you're ok." And General Castrillo bent over with laughter.

"The thing is that his father" — he said pointing to the young man — "was a cadet with me. He died of despair on the northern frontier when he was still a sergeant. I had seen this fellow working as a gardener in the Alpaca district and he approached me one day to ask for something. I've just told him that undoubtedly now, with the coming changes, I'll name him Minister of Industry."

The phrase whirled around the room and crammed itself into the ears of Felipe Ternejo and Mary, who felt the urge to call Mirna and repeat it to her.

They said their farewells soberly. The General and Tola entered their Mercedes 480 and they watched as, after discharging a turbo-diesel belch, it took off with a cackling sound.

When they returned inside they noticed that Lautaro had left his waiter's uniform on the sofa without explanations.

In silence, Mary and Felipe Ternejo gazed upon one another like two beings that have just awakened from a dream and still do not recognize each other. At that moment the phone rang. Mary ran to it and caught Mirna's voice, as if from a faraway fog:

"Oh, dearest, I forgot to tell you, the General, when he's had a few too many, offers minister's posts even to the gardeners."

Translated by Margarite Fernández Olmos

The Marked One

❖

Norberto Fuentes

He had bathed, and the smell no longer clung to him. That smell of bandit, that mixture of humid cloth, live-skin sweat, trampled grass, and the rust of weapons. But he retained the imperceptible marks within the pores of his wrists, deep, insistent, red, like particles of earth and salt from the mountain encrusted in the cuff of his shirt and then into his skin with all the fury of the thorns, the rocks, and the sun.

I wanted to be kind: would you like a cigarette? and I placed the pack on the desk. I have my own, he told me, and showed me a pack with half a dozen cigars thick as fingers. These are stronger, chest-busters, and I like them better.

We lit his chestbuster and my ultra-mild with a single match. So, give me your full name.

"You want it again? I already gave it in previous questionings."

"It doesn't matter. Tell me your full name."

"Claudio Garate Guzmán."

I wrote on my pad: Claudio Garate Guzmán. And Claudio followed the traces of my fountain pen.

"Sir, why did you call me in?"

"Tell me how long you spent with the rebels."

"Sixteen months, yes, about sixteen months."
"You took part in the Tomás San Gil offensive."
"No, sir, I had nothing to do with that offensive, I was in the north then."
"Where?"
"In Llanadita de Perea, sir."
I turned to my pad and spelled out what I was writing:
Assigned to Llanadita de Perea during the March offensive.
"Please, sir, I did not participate in that offensive."
"Why are you behaving so badly? The chief keeps telling me: Claudio is not behaving well."
"I do want to help."
"The chief is right. You're not cooperating" — I stated. With the fountain pen I wrote in big strokes: IS NOT COOPERATING.
"Sir, am I not being helpful?"
I placed the pen on the pad and leaned my chair against the wall.
"The chief has gotten it into his head and insists that you're no good. I do my best to convince him otherwise, but as you can see . . . the chief continues to say you're no good."
"Sir, tell him it isn't true, tell him I am good. Why don't you tell him?"
"I have told him, I have told him many times, but he won't budge."
"The chief wants to send me to the firing squad."
I didn't reply.
"Sir, I don't want to be shot. You have confirmed that I've killed no one. Do something for me. Tell the chief the truth."
I shrugged my shoulders and crushed my ultra-mild in the clay ashtray. Claudio still had half of his chestbuster left. I explained:
"The chief is stubborn."
"Sir."
"Well, then, you took part in the offensive."
"Look here, sir, I tell you I didn't."
"You're nervous today, Claudio. If you'd like I could have them bring your pills, or maybe you want some coffee? I'm going to send for some coffee" — and I cranked the field telephone installed on the desk. Center replied:
"Pass me through to Service!" — I yelled. Center always delays, and I covered the receiver to tell Claudio:
"Center always delays." — Claudio smiled, turning his eyes to the

fast-burning chestbuster. A voice from Service finally came through.

"Listen! Who's this? Listen, send me two mugs of coffee. Here to the interrogation room. Two mugs of coffee. What? Two mugs of coffee! Yes. The interrogation room. But, listen here, I mean fast. Good."

I hung up.

"What kind of weapons did you have in the mountains, Claudio?"

"I had a Springfield, sir. A rifle that is about this long."

"Yes, I know, I know what a Springfield looks like" — and I asked him — "have you seen my pistol?" — I took it out of the holster, placing it on the center of the desk, with the barrel pointing towards me and the handle within Claudio's reach.

"Is it Russian?"

"No, it's a Colt 45."

"It's nice."

"Yes, look at the handle. It's made of a very light metal. Pick it up so you can see."

Claudio moved his right hand near it and his nails grazed the grooves where the magazine clicks, but he did not move his hand closer.

"Pick it up, man."

"Sir."

"Pick it up, man, so you can see."

Claudio pulled his hand back and placed it between his thighs.

"You're very nervous today. Look how you're shaking."

"I don't want to pick it up, sir."

"Why?"

"No, I don't want to."

I pressed the clip of the magazine: half of it stuck out, then I pulled it out completely and showed Claudio the bullets it was loaded with.

"Do you know what blanks are?"

"No, sir."

"These are blanks" — I told him.

There was a knock at the door. I yelled: Come in! A cook from Service entered the room. He was carrying a metal tray and two tin cups. The tray was pretty banged up, the water from the kitchen dripped through some of the cracks and the cups were steaming.

"The coffee," the cook announced.

"Serve him first," I ordered.

"Good coffee, eh?"

"Yes," Claudio replied. I picked up the cup. Then we lit new cigarettes and the cook left.

"How do you feel now?"

"I feel very bad, sir."

"I only want to know one thing."

"I feel very bad, my head hurts."

"That doesn't matter."

"I don't want to talk today. Let me go back to my cell."

"Stay where you are."

"Let me go back, please."

"Take your clothes off."

"My clothes?"

"Yes, your clothes."

Claudio unbuttoned his yellow shirt and began to show a hairless
chest — the few hairs he had circled his nipples and opened a triangle
moving down below his navel. Claudio bundled his shirt and put it
on his thighs. He had two purple bruises bordering his shoulders as if
they were bands. The belts of his backpack had left their imprint.

"I feel like a woman. Why are you ordering me to do this?"

"You have to speak to a person. A person you know," and I picked
up the field phone. "I want you to speak to Nono Madruga."

"I can't speak to that man."

"Yes.

"Listen, sir, aren't you listening to me?" Claudio said, leaning forward on his seat and resting both elbows on the desk. "I can't speak
to that man."

I turned the telephone crank several times.

"That man is dead," Claudio assured me.

"Dead?" I feigned surprised. "No, man, Nono Madruga is alive and
I'm going to call him now." I turned the crank. Center replied.

"Listen, Center, have Nono Madruga brought to me."

"Don't you understand me?" he said, and he nailed his open hand
on the cradle of the phone and cut it off. "Don't you understand?
That man is dead." I grabbed his wrist and moved his arm off the cradle. "Sit down," I ordered him.

I returned to the telephone.

"Listen, Center, have them bring me Nono Madruga."

I said nothing else. Neither did Claudio and he returned to his
seat, wiping his sweat occasionally with his yellow shirt — which now

and then showed the black P on its back — as a towel. I pretended to read from the pages on the pad: Claudio Garate Guzmán. He was assigned to Llanadita de Perea during the March offensive. IS NOT COOPERATING. The steps approached from the yard behind us, turning onto on the hallway, leather creaking over cement.

"I don't want to talk to the dead."

"Why did you do it, Claudio?"

"I won't speak to a dead man."

The steps reached the door and stopped there.

"I don't want to speak to the dead!" he screamed, pounding the desk with his fists.

"Why did you do it, Claudio?" I rose to open the door. Claudio dropped onto his seat, his arms lifeless, and his shirt on the floor.

"Tomás San Gil told me I was not a man," he mumbled.

"And you will take me to the place?"

Claudio nodded. I returned to the desk and requested a jeep and two guards on the telephone. "Put your shirt on," I told Claudio and picked up the pistol from the desk.

"Let's go, Claudio." I opened the door. The hallway was deserted. We left between the two guards. The jeep arrived immediately. I sat next to the driver and Claudio sat behind between the guards.

"Where to?" the driver asked me.

"Where is it?" I asked Claudio.

"At Limones Cantero," Claudio said.

"To Limones Cantero," I told the driver.

We arrived three hours later because one has to skirt all of Escambray and come in from the north. Claudio indicated a rocky road, narrow and steep, which the jeep could not climb. We tied Claudio up and climbed on foot. Then we dug at the place Claudio indicated and made a bundle with the driver's t-shirt in which we gathered what we found of Nono Madruga: some bones, a pair of boots, and a belt. Then we headed back. On the way back, Claudio said to me:

"Sir, now the chief is going to be very displeased with me."

"I'm afraid so, Claudio."

"Will you help me?"

"Listen, Claudio, your case has taken a turn for the worse."

"Sir, then there's no hope?"

"I think not, Claudio."

The t-shirt bundle laid on the floor. It was jolted open by the bumpy road. Some frightened cockroaches jumped out of it.

"Sir, does it hurt?"

I turned towards Claudio. I felt sorry for him and said:

"No, Claudio, what happens at the wall is over very quickly."

Translated by Lizabeth Paravisini-Gebert

Delicatessen

Miguel Alfonseca

DELICATESSEN. I've really liked that sign ever since I first saw it. I remember that I was still a girl with braids down to my waist and I would pass by the place on my way to school, nimbly skipping around the park benches, happy with the sun over the trees and the old church, grey and small, feeling the wind blow past me, indecently, getting itself between my legs and searching for my breasts under the white blouse. What an unfamiliar sensation when the freshness of the wind blew between my legs! I felt like running, jumping happily to exhaustion, or a sweet dreaminess, and without resisting I'd remain on the bench, receiving the sun fully, allowing the wind to squeeze me. That's why I was late so often and had to wait for the next class. I'd go underneath the large, shady elms of the square and watch the couples walk by, sit down with open books and note pads, and start to neck. There was nothing better to do at that hour than watching the boys. I couldn't avoid looking at their groins and experienced the same intoxicating sensation as that of the wind trapping me in the park.

The brown skirt had just been pressed and I walked contentedly with my new socks, white with a blue border, tight against my legs. When I got to the park I noticed the movements of several men, some climbing ladders and others pushing a huge box. In an instant they lifted the sign and fixed it onto the facade of a house with large new windows. I suddenly realized that there were some twenty people in the place, all smiling. A blond, fleshy man moved from one side to the next disappearing through one door and appearing again with plates and other things in his hands. He would hand them to a washed-out woman with sagging breasts who smiled and ran two or three fingers through her hair while she went among those present handing out the goods in her hands. The red letters shone over the grey, blinking, pretty, tilting to the side. DELICATESSEN. The fleshy, blond man went out to the sidewalk and noisily called everyone. The avalanche took place at once; the first to arrive, pushing and laughing, were the boys from the park. I approached the windows carefully. Behind them lured several kinds of cheeses and delicate meats as well as sweets unfamiliar to us. I entered. DELICATESSEN.

Now the red letters are a bit faded and the old man, fatter and more tired, moves as if he had to drag along the whole park. I've been a client since the beginning. I should say, I was a client; I don't go there anymore. Things have changed: there are more stores with names in English, I've seen other place like this one (Delicatessen means "delicacies" in German, according to the French "Mme.," back in high school), and I . . . I've grown a lot, changed a lot, plenty, so much that I can hardly recognize myself. According to some old hags with black mantillas and sour faces, the kind that, fortunately, you don't see around much anymore, I am what I was meant to be. "That girl will come to no good." And then they'd go off to the church in the park to breakfast with Christ. I don't know if they're right, but I don't accept it. It would be a disaster to accept the triumph of these deadly people. The truth is, it took a lot of work to finish High School. Not because of the studies, no, but because of the teachers who hated me; the boys would come over to me and I'd laugh, move my hips, turn my head looking back over my shoulder while I eyed their bodies up and down. Life was great in school! The best years. Why did I have to become what I am? Papa went to Korea during the war and we never heard from him again. The memory I have of Papa is his morning bath, and me peeking in to see his naked body under the spray of the shower, my mother jerking at my hair and making me cry. Ever since the accident during Holy Week in '55 I haven't been the same and never will be. My brother buried Mama while I writhed in a hospital bed. When I got out everything had changed, the city, the days and the people; the people had changed terribly. Around that time I was beginning to develop gloriously. My figure got noticed in the tight pants, I let my hair fall to one side of my face. I understood that I was at a disadvantage, I didn't have the luxury to choose like other girls. Naturally, in the neighborhood the men pretended, greeting me in the street indifferently. But I know that when I undressed before an open window many would observe me hidden in the neighboring houses. Little by little the barriers came down and they began to come secretly, at night, and consume themselves with me, even though the next morning they would ignore me. I don't blame them. The girls hated me, were repulsed by me, and the men kept up appearances, because sooner or later they would marry them. I was just their entertainment.

Even my brother couldn't take it. He did his best, but I understood the tremendous effort it took to accept the awful reality of his sister. Finally he left. "I'm going to New York. There life is a breeze, kid. Don't worry, Violeta, I'll send you an allowance." I felt better living alone. I'd stroll in my shorts and sandals, moving as I pleased, laughing and scandalizing. When I finished High School I looked for work in vain. So now I'm in my element: I get up when I feel like it, go to the street and walk around the park, enter the shops as I please, go to the movies frequently and some weekends go off to the beaches. The evenings are my reward, then it's my turn. The ones that turn up go crazy with my body. They don't want to see my face so they won't feel obligated, ashamed to be with someone like myself. That's why they turn off the light the moment they arrive and close the window, trying to darken the room as much as possible. After those nights I would get up, and after washing myself, powdering myself, and putting on my scanty but comfortable clothing, I'd go to the DELICATESSEN. The young men would crowd the place along the bars and the tables; I'd enter as if it were a saloon from a Western movie. But DELICATESSEN ceased to be what I had loved so much, that important part of my world. The woman with the sagging breasts was miserly, and since one day they took her out in a black box attended by Mister Feldstein's greasy tears, things have changed. Mister Feldstein had big aspirations, he redecorated the place, raised the prices, made it "chic," converted it into a genuine "delicacy." I didn't fit there anymore. So I stayed in the park.

One day a boy got off a bus and asked for an address on a certain street in the neighborhood. With shiny hair over clear eyes, slender lips half-opened in a smile, his adolescent body sharply dressed, he came near and I heard his soft, slow voice. He moved into a crummy room; it was a shame to see something so beautiful trapped in a narrow and smelly pigsty. He was studying the first year of college and in his free time worked in a store. I approached him from the outset; I was the first to reach the solitary one in his new and unfamiliar surroundings, so large and monstrous compared to the life he had led. He seemed not to notice, or he didn't notice, what I was. He has been the best of them all, the only one really worth something. We would go to the movies with our bags of popcorn and laugh; he would grab my hands, dig between my legs. Some nights on the weekends we would thrill to exhaustion in Coney Island, enjoying ourselves in front of everyone, in front of the girls surprised at this good-looking boy who slapped them in the face by appearing in public with me. I did whatever I could for him: I washed and ironed his clothes to spare him the expense, and kept his room decent, taking whatever I could to dress it up a bit. When he needed some books I would buy them and kept it a surprise, and also shirts which he accepted reluctantly. I would wait for him after his classes and we would go to some bar for lunch, and in the afternoons I'd await for him to appear, frowning and beautiful, under the neon-lit night. I didn't do more because he forbid me to receive men, he wanted me for himself. Even though I only had the allowance my brother sent me I was happy, blissful with this opportunity that appeared in the form of a man, alive and so near. Frank didn't even turn off the light. He allowed the bulb to expose my nakedness, with no way to conceal me, and he would run over me lovingly, burying his head in my neck. My fingers would search for the lamp and the darkness would unite us even more. He kissed me. He kissed me! I never expected to find this extraordinary privilege that life was giving me. Maybe Frank . . . with time . . . What a surprise to find myself thinking such thoughts!

For Christmas I gave him a watch with my name on the back and we made love like never before despite the fact that in certain moments he would remain pensive and sad, always looking up towards a sky so hot and blue, tranquil with the season's coolness. We'd walk a long time examining the store windows with their fantasy mountains of snow and sleds, and the children's music that emerged, and behind or on the sides, wrapped in brilliantly-colored papers, the gifts that called to passers-by. I enjoyed myself a lot; but Frank wasn't very happy, he seemed tired. He was living a busy life. It was impossible for him to continue with the two things for very long: study and work. His gaze would get lost sometimes through the window of my bedroom where the breeze entered to dry our sweat, calming us, those Sunday afternoons when the city would flee to the beaches and restaurants and we could feel undisturbed, masters of ourselves; and I would imagine his family in his large, dark eyes. Those people hardly sent him money for his college registration and lately not even that; they left Frank on his own. Poor Frank, so anxious to have a career. Those afternoons, with my head resting on his chest glancing at his strong face, slowly caressing the soft hairs at my side while feeling the curly nearness of his legs that cradled mine, I would take his wrist and lift it; there was the watch heralding the night; on the shiny metal winked the letters: Violeta.

Little by little Frank began to disappear. I understood that I wasn't Frank's future. From the looks of it, I'm not anyone's future. I don't want to judge him, I don't even want to think that . . . No, I owe Frank a lot! He gave me what no one else did; he treated me like a woman. He even made me take back the watch and I felt that something crumpled within me; I sold the watch, promising myself not to give anyone anything again. Sometimes I see him from afar. I prefer it that way; I prefer to keep him intact in my memory, now that I've gone back to those who foully arrive with their shame, almost with repugnance, to relieve themselves between my legs.

I don't change my habits and every afternoon I pass in front of the church before the stares and dirty comments of the bums in the park. Above all I like to look at the sign and repeat its syllables to myself: DEL-I-CA-TES-SEN. The letters are no longer red. Blue, a deep blue and new, without the dust of the former. How strange! I met Frank when I stopped going to the DELICATESSEN, when it was no longer a place for people like me. The park doesn't change. People still go up or down towards the center, the trees shade without charging a cent, the shoeshine boys, the drunks, the girls that go to school with brown skirts and white blouses, the people that sit facing north waiting for the buses that take them to nearby towns, and the wind, soft and alive. And I'm still here. Still here, with my shorts, my swaying, my hair over my face and this strange feeling that I never felt before: this feeling of doing things without realizing it.

A few days ago someone told me that Frank is going around with a rich girl. He's doing very well; it looks like he has no money problems and he's wearing expensive suits. On Tuesday I saw him by accident, he's healthy and calm. How I love to lie to myself! I know everything. She's the daughter of the owner of the store, the girl that goes out with him in the Chevelle. He thinks he's made a good match. Sure! He'd be marrying the father and the store. I feel sorry for him. I'm used to getting the short end. But he's putting himself down, selling out his manhood. Pig! That's why he avoids me, turns his back, crosses the street when he sees me coming. As if I didn't know about his trips to the DELICATESSEN with that girl! Margot told me about it and I wanted to see it with my own eyes. It's true; there's the grey Chevelle. And me strolling about like a jerk in front of those bums around the church! There he is. With polite gestures and smiles one after the other. He takes in the parents with his chatter while he squeezes the hand of the colorless virgin at his side, and she puts on her cow eyes.

I've pounded the hateful tires of the Chevelle and arrived at the windows of the DELICATESSEN. Frank has gone livid, concealing it by turning his face. He pretends he hasn't seen me, but he knows I'm here. I gather up my hair and tie it back. Let them really see what I am. When I push the glass door my image is reflected momentarily on the immaculate surface: the bronzed thighs, the hips, the hard breasts under the sleeveless blouse, my face: the violet-colored gash that starts at one eye plunging down one side of my face until it reaches a corner of my lips, exposing several teeth. This air conditioning is so cool! I'm going to sit on Frank's lap.

Translated by Margarite Fernández Olmos

Sad Though Brief the Rituals

❖

Tomás López Ramírez

Forgive me for not telling this with sorrow, in a redeeming tone of contrition, but I can't. I can't because I have never known how to face minor or major tragedies, and what has happened is neither one nor the other, no matter how many times we twist it around. Nothing can be changed now. The hotel was closed one fine day, when it wasn't profitable anymore, and everyone went their own way. Everything returned to its usual harmony, which was partly shattered a month later when I read the obituary that announced the manager's death. Because I am not going to talk about myself, a poor reception-ist at a cheap hotel, but about him. It is in honor of his memory, then, that I decided to recount this. Because the manager – the poor guy – who used to look at me with his penetrating tiny eyes, searching in mine for a reprieve, a benevolent forgiveness, was never able to recover, and he went to his grave carrying his own sins as well as ours. I say "ours" because a few of us shared the thankless task of keeping the run-down hotel going – a decaying hotel, once grand among the grand, where the most distinguished couples from the interior came to spend their honeymoons, where so many foreign guests praised the view of the bay, and which now was no more than a vulgar refuge to hide who knows what sad though brief rituals – and in a certain way we all contributed to its lamentable end. Because we did nothing to save it and everything to destroy it. And with it went the manager, who had been a prosperous businessman, who had to take over, after an interminable parade of inept and irresponsible candidates had come and gone.

Everything began in room 405, where I, very kindly and no less astutely, placed the sweet-smelling, smooth-skinned, young North American lady who begged to have her room changed, because the one I have smells bad, the furniture is very old. And to win her over — I am not going to deny it — I gave her the best room, with the best view of the bay. One afternoon when I arrived for my shift, the manager came to me and questioned me without any ceremony: who is making the little peepholes in the doors? You must know, you stay here at night. I looked at him — I had to — with my most incredulous expression: little holes in the doors? When, how? Who would think of such a thing! He had questioned the chambermaids, the porter, the day receptionists, no one knows anything, do you? The sweet-smelling, smooth-skinned, young North American lady had denounced the small peephole under the doorhandle, and had left in an outrage. Afterwards, many other sweet-smelling and white-skinned North American young ladies arrived, young tourist couples, and I do not know how many more guests, and the peepholes in the doors multiplied. The manager, clenching his teeth in a gesture of restrained anger, gathered the employees in his office and warned that the guilty one would be fired immediately. In the meantime the guests continued discovering peepholes and complaining to the manager, who would come down from his office worn out, perturbed in the face of the exodus of guests, who accused him of running a center for impotent and smiling satyrs hiding behind their good-afternoon-what-can-I-do-for you's. That same day he ordered us to cover the peepholes with plaster, but not without first regaling me with a harangue about the morality and good habits that had always been the guiding principle of his life — what an atrocity! I, like everyone else, shrugged my shoulders and swore I didn't know anything.

His final disaster coincided with the arrival of the young Haitian woman. And here is where I have to confess my greatest complicity and guilt. Because the manager fell for the Haitian woman, and she — Françoise — fell for me. Françoise would spend long periods conversing with me in the hotel lobby, while the manager watched us, not understanding, eager to let her know how much he liked her, how much he wanted to invite her to his office to have a drink. The manager — the poor distressed man — threw off the weapons of old morality that he had defended all his life, that he struggled to uphold before us, and surrendered. And the peepholes in the doors appeared again. And this time in all the best-kept rooms, where there were guests all the time, some young and soft-skinned young woman who was surely spied upon during her bath, or upon her return from the beach when her tanned skin could tolerate no clothing. And surely Françoise was spied upon too when she put on her strong aromatic perfumes, or her wigs and blush, at dusk. Françoise, who also turned down my advances because *on ne fait pas ça chez nous,* she said cuttingly, was not as compassionate as I was with the manager. She made fun of him in her language and one afternoon confessed to me that he had invited her, with gestures, to go up to his office, and she laughed as she told me about the old man's libidinous face and about his sad expression when she turned him down.

The peepholes in the doors were not covered again. Although the guests complained and left suddenly, although letters arrived canceling reservations for the winter season, the peepholes ruled the roost. In the meantime Françoise and I continued to have lively chats. The manager did not mention the peepholes again. Truly he did not dare. He would look at Françoise shyly and ask me what she had said. That you are very nice and very amusing, I would reply, since Françoise had once said: Could we get something out of this old man? He did not mention again the peepholes in the doors which were spreading like a plague, and only I knew why he didn't. Little by little I took control of the situation; an embittered complicity was woven between the manager and me, in which I — I am not ashamed to say — had the upper hand. Because Françoise would lavish her attentions on me and became increasingly diffident towards him. I found out that he insisted on inviting her, that he had begged her to come to his office for only just a moment. Until he dared ask me to intercede for him. That was his most pitiable mistake. I told Françoise and we both laughed heartily.

We both laughed heartily, Françoise, and then it occurred to me what would be the greatest joke, the crowning mockery that would also grant me a power I never dared imagine. That was his most pitiable mistake. I didn't tell you then what I was plotting, you agreed because you thought it was funny and because deep inside you wanted to humiliate the old man. Each time I look at you I remember it. Each day the hotel had fewer clients, the house was falling in on us and the manager would scratch his head and count the small amount of money made each day. I devoted myself to walking through the hotel's halls at night to inform the manager that I had not see any furtive voyeur. It was on one of those nights that I managed to catch a glimpse of a gray jacket moving away, the color of the jacket he always wore.

After a short time it was I who counted the day's earnings, and if any money was missing I did not assume responsibility for it. The manager would leave at dusk saying goodbye to me with a laconic hand signal. It was I who accepted or rejected guests, the one who dealt with details and small mishaps. He would remain in his office and he would come down at six smelling of whiskey and lamenting the hotel's lack of business. He never again blamed the peepholes for the deplorable situation.

Each time I look at you, Françoise, I remember the mean trick we played on him. You invited him to your room and he ran to his office to get the whiskey before you could change your mind. He returned jubilant, trembling with lust. The poor guy got drunk too quickly, but in just enough time for me to make my planned appearance. You left the door ajar and precisely at the moment when he was struggling to embrace you, I opened it arrogantly, stopping on the threshold with ironed sheets in my arms, your clean sheets, miss, oh, excuse me for interrupting, I managed to say, and he stood there, bent, livid, finally accepting his defeat. I closed the door and withdrew after showing him my best triumphant smile, poor old man, finally surrendering what was left of his old and well-defended honor. You should not have laughed so hard, Françoise, in spite of everything, such an outburst of laughter had not been necessary.

Unfortunately, no happiness is complete. The enjoyment of my power ended soon, too soon. To be more precise, at Christmas of that year. While Françoise was there I reigned over the others, and I even deigned answer the manager's questions with supreme arrogance. The manager — I decided to narrate this to honor his memory, not because of any remorse — became my faithful and unswerving vassal. I never mentioned the incident in Françoise's room but he understood that it was not necessary, that if I were to do so he would not be able to remain there, humiliated before the eyes of all the employees. I said that no happiness is complete, and everything ended when Françoise decided to return to her country. She had not done as well as she had expected here, and in her country she did well enough. I truly feared that the end was near. On Christmas Eve the manager arranged to gather all the employees for a small party, with the few guests we had, in the empty floor the hotel had for receptions. We arrived as our shifts allowed us and there he had been, with his gray and somewhat disheveled hair, a grieving expression on his face, and I knew that I would no longer have anything to do there. We drank a few whiskeys and enjoyed a very sparse cold dinner. After a while the manager raised his voice and in a very solemn tone announced the definite closing of the hotel, since it was impossible to absorb further losses and the unsustainable situation forced us to do so. We all looked at each other, somewhat saddened, and I looked at Françoise, who gave me a broad smile while I poured the manager a whiskey. We went down in the narrow and slow elevator three at a time, chatting about what we would do in the future. He came down last, and I saw him come out with drooping shoulders and without looking at me whispered his greetings with a voice too weak to be sincere. The next day I left with Françoise.

Yes, Françoise, I don't know why you laughed so hard. The thing is that we are here now, I let myself be carried away by enthusiasm, and you were the true instigator of everything, the true mistress of destinies, and I watch you parade up and down the corridors and the halls greeting the customers avid with passion, who wait impatiently for me to assign them the rooms they will occupy for a while, or for the night, in this hotel in Port-au-Prince where I am at your service, perhaps until my hair turns gray or until the day you bring a jovial and distinguished substitute for me.

Translated by Carmen C. Esteves

After the Hurricane

❖

Edgardo Sanabria Santaliz

I.

After the hurricane, the house and the whole immense and hours before green and raised area of the coconut grove would appear completely desolate, covered with fish. One would see octopus, squid and cuttlefish tentacles hanging from the cornices, opalescent, moist with a gentle teary lustre that would form slow phosphorescent puddles on the floor, a large curtain in tremulous tatters of stalactites in the round – as if the roof – or what remained of the roof – were melting beneath the hot grey mist that would still fall. Through the enormous hole between the tiles, through the unprotected shattered glass windows, torrents of spray would have burst, devastating everything, pulverizing the little fragile objects, pulling the heavy mahogany furniture from the floor in whirlpools and making it sail with the lightness of rafts from room to room, dragging some things forever, driving out others – pictures, carpets, an old pendulum clock – that would then be found kilometers away on the boundaries of the coconut grove, ornamenting the countryside. It would prove to be almost impossible to walk through the salons and to climb the stairs with all the sargasso tangling the feet, with all the moving water making it slippery: it would be easy to discover sea horses and starfish, purple or cinnamon-colored crabs of elusive and exquisite forms, conches, snails, minuscule fishes sparkling like gems in the drawers, within armoires and trunks, adhering to the backs of chairs, tables and mattresses. One would find everything that could contain any volume of water — bathtubs, kettles, sinks, vases — in ebullient precipitation, overflowing with groupers, snappers, sturgeon by the dozens, sifting and showing an inanimate and perfectly circular eye for one, two seconds on the surface of that sea that would dazzle with its scanty proportions and absence of sand. Outside, looking from the detritus-filled terrace in the direction of the beach, not even a trace would be seen of the stone barrier that used to separate the sand from the smooth terrain of emerald grass in which the house was set. Only stretches of a filth of weeds mixed with sand and palm fronds, gravel, split coconuts: the avenue that would open the tottering rows of coconut palms would signal the passing of the Great Wave that came from the ocean in the most extreme moment of the cyclone.

When Acisclo Aroca returned from his hurried flight his eyes filled with tears of grief and consternation, and he had to cover his nose with a handkerchief against the stench of rotting shellfish that was beginning to spread all over, as was the black cloud of flies. It had been a sudden unavoidable flight, principally determined by the fact that Acisclo lived alone, almost never seeing anyone in a house that could have comfortably held an entire army: at the last minute, the horizon now filling with monstrous clouds, some fishermen from around there remembered him and gave warning. He hadn't time to take anything with him, even less to secure the windows or to gather up what loose things remained here and there. He escaped because he saw in the fisherman's terrified look — sweaty below the growing, pressing shadow — that what he was saying was true: "Leave, or you won't wake here tomorrow!" Now, facing all this, he understood that the fisherman had been right. But he wasn't thanking him, he would have preferred a thousand times more to disappear with his possessions than to face what he was seeing. Nevertheless, at the crucial moment he didn't believe so much destruction was possible. He thought of his life, and that it was better to run the risk of some adequately reparable destruction than to lose the only thing that couldn't be replaced. Never had the idea of a similar devastation passed through his mind, that in one night what had taken him so many years to construct had been demolished.

Acisclo Aroca will walk alone through the ruins of his house. With his rubber boots he will move dead fish, fragments of tile, remains of objects. He will recognize them if he pays careful attention to retain some trace or appearance of yesterday. Painstakingly, he will travel from one room to another, from the first to the second floor, stopping now and then to bend over and pick something from the floor, and to contemplate it in his fingers, stupefied, as if he were dealing with a prehistoric tool or with something he might have seen in his childhood and that he just now came to remember. It's not possible, he will murmur, lost as if he carried a useless compass in the middle of an infinite forest. In the last room he will turn in circles, already tired of the chaos, and he will begin the path again. Suddenly though, he will turn aside towards the terrace with the speed of someone heeding a summons. Going out into the afternoon air, Acisclo will look as though he has aged ten years. To the left, out of the corner of his eye, before finally orienting his vision in that direction, he will be able to make out the silver-blue luminosity of the swimming pool.

It looks to have suffered the least destruction of his property. Branches, leaves and every kind of debris had accumulated around the spotless surface of the turquoise oval, creating the impression that the wind had refrained from flinging anything in or that someone had taken charge of cleaning any residue from the water. The pool reflects the platinum light of the huge clouds the hurricane has left behind; the mist (now tenuous, invisible) dots the smooth water, filling it with microscopic waves that break in concentric circles, as though created by the almost weightless alighting of an insect. Acisclo can't take his eyes off it. Time passes by him unnoticed. When he comes to (moving has broken the enchantment) he discovers that there is a burning elliptical sun floating between a tight string of clouds and the coconut palms that have remained standing: the ellipse of fire threatens to singe what remains of their lopped-off crowns. Again he turns his attention to the pool. When he focuses his gaze he notices, astonished, that his strange hours-long intoxication was in no way one of sight, but rather one of sound, a suspension such that he seemed to be seeing within sound. What he has been hearing is a sort of song, he doesn't know for certain if he can call it that, but he can't think of any other word to describe it. It is a song. The most inconceivably beautiful voice that he has ever heard in his life. Singing. The most extraordinary and supernatural music that human ears have heard.

Then he would see her for the first time. A barely perceptible agitation (not of breeze or lagging raindrops) at the center of the oval. A rising, fountainlike tremor. And suddenly the head crowned with orange coral would emerge, and then the thick, greenish, mossy hair, braided with pearls and covering her shoulders, her back, her breasts, each one in turn veiled by a clinging star stone. She would be looking directly at the terrace, inexplicably immobile in the deepest part of the pool, half submerged in the water that would now have taken on a pewter tone, gilded from the waist up by the slanting glare of late afternoon. She would no longer be singing (yes, it was she who was singing!) but the face turned towards him would be as wondrous as the voice. Never in his life would Acisclo Aroca forget that vision. A little while would pass before he asked himself what the woman was doing there, and seconds later the thought of having been conscious of the song long before she emerged would make him tremble.

Even though he climbed downstairs as quickly as the debris permitted, upon drawing near to the pool he didn't see the woman anywhere, neither in nor out of the water. Night had already almost fallen, the oval was a limitless eye with a half-closed eyelid, falling, hiding the diaphanous, sapphire-colored iris. Acisclo went around the pool several times, stopping when he called out — as if movement would have impeded the use of his voice — and then did the same thing around the structure of the house, finally arriving at the boundary where the entanglement of the bent, split, unearthed trunks of the coconut grove began. She couldn't have gone so soon, without leaving so much as a trace of her damp footprints. Unless . . . it had all been his imagination. But that was impossible, he had heard her, he had distinguished her so clearly! Where was she? How was she able to disappear like that? He approached the pool again. He then remained very quiet, his five senses concentrated on the dark and serene water. He was unconsciously moving his lips, as if counting the minutes a person is capable of withstanding a deep dive. Nothing happened. Now the oval looked like an eye that had hypnotized him. For an instant he believed he had fallen and was sinking — the moon had just risen and its reflection colored the air blue with the weightlessness of the ocean bottom. Suddenly the pool was a mirror through which clouds passed and stars swam. Drained, Acisclo moved back and sat in the grass, supporting his back against the trunk of some tree that had lost its branches in the night. His head nodded sleepily. The distinct, resurgent song, spreading as if exhaled from the heart of an opened and deadly flower (the song that he would have heard, had he been more awake) finished by lulling him to sleep.

Then he will see her again. He will find himself still reclining against the tree, dozing off; an unexpected splash will make him raise his head. She will be there. Appearing beyond the marble border of the pool, observing him with eyes like drops of the bluest ocean on earth. Acisclo will not dare to move, for fear that she will submerge and never rise again. The coral will shimmer under the moon, over her hair braided with pearls that will radiate an arcane inner light. Perhaps he will say (whisper) something like who are you, but he won't hear himself pronounce a single word. Later, when he makes a deliberate attempt to speak, she will draw back suddenly, as if driven by his voice. She will swim in wide expert circles, with the undulating skill of a fish, her arms at her sides, her raised head leaving the green-white wake of her skin mingled with foam. A second before she disappears in the water, he will make out the sweeping iridescent tail. Without knowing how he got there, Acisclo will find himself on his knees at the pool's edge, leaning over the subtle reflection of his searching face. It will seem to him that centuries have passed before an almost imaginary fluctuation on the surface finally reveals itself, followed by the more fleeting representation of a figure hurriedly sliding by. Swift as lightning he will shoot out his arm, catch and remove something. When he takes the string of pearls from the water, their lustre will illuminate his face.

Acisclo Aroca wakes up. In his hands he discovers the string of pearls gleaming in the sun.

II.

The truck reappeared as soon as the sun set, bursting into the plaza from some street through which the nocturnal wave of murkiness and stars advanced. At once it proceeded to circle the tree-lined rectangle a number of times — secret, stealthy — like an animal searching for somewhere to rest. The old men sitting in a row on the long half-moon-shaped concrete bench turned their heads in time to see it make its slow entrance. It passed in front of them (its dark blue brimming with shoals of luminescent decal art) and, turning off the headlights in the very center, stopped to one side of an arbor blown over a short while before by the hurricane. It was the same enormous, outlandish truck that had gone through the pueblo that afternoon, deafening everyone with its loudspeaker (as the crow flies, or from the top of the belfry, it would have been easy to follow it by ear through the maze of streets). It was a navy blue truck, covered with decals of fish, that ended by circling around and around the plaza, from where the echo reverberated, moving away through the series of side-streets that fed into it. Then the truck had gone into one of them and disappeared, creating an unusual momentary silence everywhere, as if it had robbed the entire village of sound. Now it was here again, and a man got out, who seemed with his glance to take in the atmosphere of the public park and the white and gravid heights of the temple, dotted with already sleeping doves. He moved towards the back part of the vehicle and struggled with the doors for a while: from inside he brought out several bolts of a grayish material that he unrolled on the ground. In about half an hour the bolts proved to be canvas, forming a small tent attached to the truck. The entrance to this sort of country house was covered with an arch of multi-colored lightbulbs that, once turned on, outlined three shining words: THE BEAUTIFUL MELUSINE in the black air of the night. At once the man went inside like a mollusk into the shell, and he didn't show himself again until the town clock struck eight. By then the line of spectators already extended several times around the square of the plaza.

Upon entering they are received all of a sudden by a man who holds a kind of large money-box in his hands (like the ones held in churches by those wooden surplice-clad altarboys with lifelike gaze and the size of an eleven-year-old child) in which the cost of admission is deposited. Crammed into the space behind the man a dolphin-print curtain reveals, when moved to one side, another space, six times larger and filled with chairs — some twenty in all — which face an opening with no canvas: there the back of the truck shows its closed doors. A single lightbulb hangs from the tent like an enormous drop of honey ready to fall on the audience. Once the seats are all occupied, the man appears and stops further entry into the tent by zipping the curtain shut. Then he turns and passes through the curving border of light outlined on the dirt floor. He walks to the front, faces the public, and begins to speak with an impassive expression in which it is impossible to detect any sentiment or thought, as if he spoke in a dream, or like someone who was releasing words from the ungraspable interior of a memory or a vision. He reaffirms what the loudspeaker had proclaimed earlier (that they are present for a fantastic, incomprehensible, unforgettable spectacle), but on his lips, the assertion had lost that quality of coarse clamorous propaganda, turning instead into a smooth dreamlike recitation. He says they are going to come face to face with a being of fable, a glorious sea creature of which the world has heard tell since the beginning of time, although no one has ever, ever seen her. Only now, thanks to the formidable power of the whirlwind that whipped the island weeks before, had she been torn from the icy shadowy abyss in which she reigned and dragged towards the coast where he himself had the fortune to recover her. They, those who listened to him that night, were the first human beings to set eyes on Melusine. "Here she is," he concludes quickly . . . . He turns his back to the wall of the auditorium and heads towards the truck and opens the doors wide. One, two, three lights go on in rapid sequence, aiming towards the interior where something glazed, sparkling, green-in-blue flashes, framed by strips of gleaming nickel. No sooner does the blindness dissipate than, one by one, they begin to glimpse, peering in, amazed at the proportions of the giant fish tank.

III.

From time to time he would ask himself amazedly if what was happening was real. Had he torn away those pearls that illuminated his fingers with a lustre that stayed in his nails? Contemplating the pearls, had he perceived the control he could attain and thanked his luck which, along with desolation, had sent him relief? Had it actually occurred to him to sell them (although he saved three or four so as not to lose influence over her), acquire the truck and have the colossal fishtank lodged in the cargo area? Afterwards had he really cast the net into that caricature of an ocean (to which she surely must have acclimated herself by now, resigned, reduced to going around in circles like an ornamental fish in its aquarium), to catch the fish that he never imagined in his dreams, a fish of queer unattainable beauty that existed nevertheless because he carried it (carried it?) there in the back, in dark murky water, stirred by the countless jolts and bumps of streets and roads, plowing through the swell of the mountains, from village to village behind the demolition spread by the hurricane? Did he now habitually park the truck at night on the outskirts of the villages, withdrawing into jungles of yagrumos and bamboo, and shut himself up in the back, seated between the bolts of canvas, opposite the gleaming fishtank? Did he then awaken quite numb and open up to the breeze, to the first light of the morning, disoriented, surveying the sky full of birds, the vegetation, astonished that the world was not submerged, that it didn't partake of the water except for a short while, when it rained; that it was inhabited by people (of which he, unfortunately, was one) who fled, opening parasols and umbrellas, or who feared drowning in rivers or in the sea. Was it true that he avoided stopping twice in the same village, because he had realized that those who entered to see her left with their gaze turned in upon themselves, flickering in short bursts, and that with enraptured faces they asked to see her again as if inside they had surrendered the power, the will that they had exercised over themselves minutes before? And was he filled with fear because he knew (knew?) from his own experience the irreconcilable consequences that a second examination of the roseate, phosphorescent breasts (as if made of the most downy sand of the ocean depths); of the scaly hip, embellishing the silvered water in a dancing boil of swishing tail; of the voice, whose echo could take over and settle forever in the hearer's soul could bring? But he would know that he wasn't dreaming when what would happen happened.

That night, for the first time, he recognized the three men. He has already visited almost all the towns on the island, he has spent weeks going through cities neighborhood by neighborhood. Thousands of people have filed through the tent, casting short, perplexed looks at the crystal coffer of his treasure; it is frankly impossible to remember so many faces of women, children and men. But he identifies these three as the three that he has seen the day before yesterday and yesterday (yes, it's them, that's all there is to it!) entering and leaving during the stops he has made in the last two towns. The great numbers of people, the severe exhaustion that he has already begun to feel — months of travel which have raced by like so many hours, all of it indistinct: alone, driving, making stops, setting up the tent, taking it down and driving, solitary apostle of something that doesn't know (does it?) for certain what it is, impelled by the unshakable incandescence he harbors — perhaps these are the reasons he hasn't taken notice of them. Three big brown guys with black moustaches, mustard colored teeshirts with stains of sweat at the armpits and greasy mechanic's overalls. He trembles from head to toe. He decides to take drastic action: when he comes to the end of that group, he announces to the large line of customers still remaining that the show has been canceled. The customers protest but they finally disperse, seeing that the man has begun to dismantle the tent. That night, instead of following the planned route, he travels in the opposite direction towards a tiny village in the mountains, far away and not easily accessible. But on the following night, when he opens for spectators, the same three men appear, and this time their swollen lips break into sarcastic little smiles as they avidly pay their entry fee. Now the persecution is a certainty. As best he can, he cancels the show once again and leaves the village after driving about the deserted streets a dozen times to assure himself that no one is following him. That night he hides the vehicle on a road funneled into the brush and shuts himself up in the back to contemplate the fishtank with sponge-like eyes that want to drink in all the water. When he notices the morning light penetrating the crack between the doors, he stands up and opens them. At the very instant he jumps to the ground he hears a motor starting and turning, discovers through the dustcloud it is making the truck moving off. After a second of paralysis he gives chase, but he is unable to catch up. The mermaid thrashes her tail in the silvery water, frightened by the giddy vision of the countryside and that man, ever smaller waving his arms like an octopus. The man hears bursts of laughter mixed with the dust and monoxide which he breathes while crying out and gasping.

He will know he wasn't dreaming when he finds himself alone on that back road. He will know definitely that it wasn't a hoax, that the creature enclosed in the fishtank was superhuman, when he no longer feels the influence of her presence. It will be as if he himself were a being who spent hundreds of years submerged under the sea, and who someone suddenly took from the water. During the unbearable minute of suffocation another type of world will enter through his terrified and incredulous eyes, a world which, no sooner than he discovers it, annihilates him. He will take a few steps as if trying out the impossible sense of balance coming from this pair of extremities that have replaced his tail. He will open his mouth but rather than bubbles a shout will come out: Melusine. He will begin to run again. Melusine. At some moment on the road he will trip and fall on his face in the dust: four pearls will come rolling out of his shirt pocket. They will roll towards the grass like luxurious insects that he will start trapping. With the four of them in the palm of his hand, a lunatic giggle will escape him. The polished luminescence will make him happy, their possession will show him the way, finding her is inevitable, nothing else can happen while he has them. He won't know the time that has passed walking, sleeping beneath the trees, eating fruit and roots, asking all if they have seen a truck of such and such appearance. Slowly he will go, descending the mountains towards the sea. The sea. His hopelessness will be so great when he faces it that he will hurl the pearls over the precipice. He will regret this immediately. Looking over the rocky edge he will see the truck, smashed at the foot of the precipice, at the very edge of the water where the waves are soaping with foam the already rusting body.

The back doors were open, one hanging by the top hinge, the heavy panes of glass of the fishtank crushed, and nothing inside, not a trace of her ever having been there. The same thing in the front seats of the truck. The men had disappeared, perhaps the undercurrents had dragged the bodies (how were they going to survive a fall from such a height?) and they would now be three skeletons at the bottom of the ocean, their flesh food for the fish, sea-moss and coral beginning to colonize the bones, schools of fish swimming through the ribcage of each one. The truck was pushed nose-first into the waves, up to the shattered windshield. Acisclo sat in the sand, distressed and worn out. His eyes wandered from the shore to the horizon, from the horizon to the shore, while he called to her with his mind, not wanting to think about the overturning and the violent impact of the fall. The whole rig, months and months of effort lost as if the hurricane had struck again. But nothing was as important to him as the fact that she had disappeared. What was he going to do now? How was he going to be able to live without her company? He would have preferred to find her dead to not knowing where she was. Suddenly he began to crawl around the beach: the pearls, the pearls, if he found them it could be that . . . But he didn't see them anywhere. He had thrown them in an attack of frustration, never imagining he would find what he was seeking at the very edge of the sea. No, he couldn't see them, couldn't find them. He was an enormous and absurd baby clambering from one side to the other and wailing. After a while he went back to sitting and remained immobile for a long time. The waves wet his heels, there were shadows of seagulls sliding in circles over the sand. When his hope was at the point of evaporating he thought he saw something shiny carried in and out by the surf. He jumped and rolled until enclosing it in his fist. He felt something take hold of his wrist below the water. When he pulled, the milk white, delicate hand emerged, grasping him with the virulence of a giant clam. At first he tried to free himself, but gave up when in front of his head — which now floated in the sea up to his chin — appeared that magnificent head that looked at him, laughing. It didn't even cross his mind to shout when a second hand gripped his other wrist with equal force. He felt the viscous tail striking against his legs while she maneuvered into the sea. Then, with his ears already plugged with water, he heard the song, bidding him welcome.

Translated by Beth Baugh

Lulú or the Metamorphosis

❖

José Alcántara Almánzar

When night falls everything grows confusing, there are no precise contours or defined faces, nothing but blurry edges, formless masses, shadows gliding from place to place. Lulú is aware of this as she prepares for this big carnival night, on this impatiently-awaited February, long anticipated in minute rites, minuscule savings, restrained impulses, the zealous selling of sweets, and the singsong with which she hawks her merchandise. There's the basket, on the table covered by a flowered tablecloth, still bearing traces of pine-nut candy, guava crystals in cellophane half melted from the sun, and other leftovers from her daily work trekking from office building to office building, starting early in the morning, delivering her candied oranges in syrup to the chubby secretary at the Municipal Hall, the ever-yearned-for bread pudding to the Corporation archivist, the plum mini-tarts to the peroxide blonde at Internal Revenue, the nuts-and-honey nougat to the cutie-pie of a chauffeur at Bagrícola, the one who always croons at her with a voice ripe with inspiration: "Lulú, honey, no one makes these sweets better than you." And she glances at him, melting, incredulous, an impish hand on her smiling lips, and sighs, warbles, flutters her curly eyelashes. She leaves swinging a tiny ass imprisoned in tight blue jeans, and saying, no longer looking at him: "Oh, what a lying rascal this Guelo is!," heedless of the bursts of laughter behind her.

As she went out she felt the hot breeze laden with humidity, dragging along heavy clouds, hoisting dust and papers off the street, tickling her legs, and making her wonder once again if it was worth going to the park and risk ruining under a rain shower what she had put such an effort into creating. She locked her door and started walking with awkward steps. As she walked she displayed the fruits of her labors for all to see, making herself deaf to stupid comments, smiling at those who appreciated the rosiness of her cheeks, the exuberance of her dress, the sparkle of her glittery tinsel jewelry. The streets, swarming with carousers, had become an extension of a grand fiesta, a frolicking revelry spilling drunk and dusky men and women, with their flamboyant masks and costumes and their contagious shrills of happiness, onto the sidewalk. She went on, falsely majestic, betrayed by trips and burps, by the convulsive swishing of her hips, the agitated flailing of her excessively bejeweled arms, the nervous contortions of her head, the troubled and searching eyes.

Now the ceremony must begin. It doesn't matter how long this transformation into the carnival's most fabulous rumba dancer takes. Her ironed dress, ready, pleased as punch in its court of festoons and ruffles, hangs on the clothes rack, almost dancing with the sling-back high-heeled shoes, the scintillating bracelets, the necklaces of iridescent bijouterie, the long earrings of deceptive sparkle, and everything that adorned the famous dancers that Lulú never grows tired of going to see at the Julia Cinema, the very same ones that she used as models in making her dress, the flame-colored turban that will cover her head, the plastic roses she has sewn to her shoes, the tones of that exuberant make-up she has reserved for today.

The park was packed with people, with hawkers of every sort of tidbit to satisfy the carnival revelers' every possible whim as they swaggered in the park's inner paths, watching the performance of the municipal band. From the gazebo wafted the strains of a danzón that invaded the reveries of the old, making them yearn for an era decidedly dead. She made her entrance with an undisguisable awkwardness which seemed to increase as the effects of the three beers she had drunk intensified. She walked down the center of the main path, shaking

the festoons of her slithering multicolor train. From the bench-
es flanking the path, now occupied by strange characters, she
began to hear insidious taunts and catcalls that prompted her
to raise her head too high, exposing her to tripping on the
mosaics dislodged by the tree roots.

Lulú is lying on the bed like a wet and porous leaf. She is soothing herself before initiating the beautification ritual. Although seemingly at peace, her body quivers on the bed, her skin vibrates as it makes contact with the clean white cotton of the bedclothes. She picks up the hand-held mirror and looks at herself. Her face betrays the apprehension that perturbs her. She drops the mirror, turns on the radio, and instantly the honey-and-molasses voice of an announcer explodes into the room, counseling brief rests between household chores, touting the importance of relaxation for remaining young and beautiful, my dear home maker, the benefits of that cleansing cream you bought to keep your face smooth like that of a porcelain doll, even though it may not lighten your dark skin. That's why she won't be dressing up as a sassy Spaniard or a little Dutch girl. Who has ever heard – Lulú says it herself – of black Europeans, thick-lipped, with straightened hair and meatball noses? What Dutch and Spanish women lack is her slender wasp waist, the long strong legs she exercises every day, walking from office to office, up and down stairs and hallways, asking leave to drop off orders, bending to put her basket down somewhere to sell a macaroon to a busy passerby, placing it again on the *babonuco* of rolled-up rags crowning her head before going on her way with an old Lola Flores song on her lips.

Despite the laughter from the crowd, she advanced to the
gazebo, trying with discombobulated steps to climb up to the
platform for a chat with the band leader. The catcalls
increased with each stride on the worn-out steps. The initial
uproar gave way to cruel and provoking taunts. A young boy
almost made her fall down by stepping on her train. She
turned around and, goaded by anger, spat a phrase at him
that was drowned out by the cymbals and drumbeats of the
song's final crescendo. She raised a menacing fist against the
mob, grabbed her train, wrapped it around her arm and con-
tinued her climb to the gazebo.

She picks up the razor, lathers up her arms and legs and starts to shave off the growth of the last few days. There can't be a trace of hair left on the skin. The razor glides down the arm to the beat of a piercing *salsa* coming from the radio. The hairs slide down the drain and the arm glistens, silky, still streaked with mentholated foam. The legs are a more difficult terrain. They resist the blade's depilatory action, proffering obstacles that bog the razor down, causing tiny sharp cuts that sting like scratches from a cat's claws. She replaces the blade on the razor and the new edge removes the stubborn hairs, vanquishing their stiff resistance. Now they are two sleek and pliant legs, speckled with white foam, legs that can slide easily into the net of a pair of nylon stockings.

The band leader glanced at her from head to toe and couldn't repress a smile in which mingled derision and compassion. He nodded his agreement, promising her that after the pasodoble *his boys would play the rumba she was requesting. She thanked him by extending a limp hand and making a long and ceremonious bow. Then the band leader turned to his musicians, raised his hands, and launched into the next selection of the concert program. She climbed down the steps to the martial strains of an operatic march.*

She goes to the refrigerator, takes out a beer, opens it, introduces the opening of the bottle into her mouth, sips the golden liquid, drinks it in until the cold stuns her and makes it impossible for her to continue swallowing. The melody of a romantic *bolero* pierces through her body, making her forget momentarily the razor and what remained of the procedure. Lulú closes her eyes and thinks of Ciro. He will be at the park selling peanuts when she appears in her rumba-dancer costume, joining the phoney ladies and the gentlemen decked out in suits rented for the occasion. She will provide the sorely-needed spice. She will go to the gazebo and ask the director of the band to play something hot and then she will dance — and she will steal the show. If Ciro approaches her she will offer to buy him a drink, and she knows he will accept, as she knows he will go home with her because he needs both the money and the affection, and who but she could give them to him, as she always has.

During the pasodoble *she saw her man in the throng. He was carrying on his daily work, oblivious to the bustle of the crowd and the roar of the cars climbing the hill on the broad avenue, stopping at the park entrance or blowing their horns at the distracted pedestrians. The alcohol rushed to her head, she felt her legs giving way and shuddered at the thought of an encounter with him. She hesitated for an instant. It would be better if he tried to make his way towards her first. She took a powder case from between her breasts and looked in the tiny mirror at her own face covered with wee beads of sweat that were beginning to make her makeup run. She dusted fresh powder on her face with the small puff.*

The indecisive razor moves down her underarm, detaching a clump of hard bristles. More lather, more water, another blade, the third. The hairs give way, the body is becoming as hairless as that of a fifteen-year-old girl, only the belly remains before everything looks like the surface of polished mahogany, without scratchy or rough patches that could lead to rejection, that could discourage caresses from robust hands or betray the scandalous contradictions of her body.

The rumba burst as she was putting the powder case away. She immediately ran to the gazebo and started to dance, surrounded by the crowd that had gathered to watch the spectacle. Her body was moving without restraint; the feet drew sparks from the mosaics; the legs, lengthened by the high heels, dashed to and fro furiously, as if deranged; the hips contorted; the bracelet-laden arms whirled, tracing circles in the air; the head gaily followed the rhythm of the music. In the midst of the frenzied uproar, she danced with eyes closed, seemingly enthralled in a brutal trance. She advanced and retreated, shook the bare shoulders, got down on her knees and up again, now completely barefoot. Her two massive feet, finally liberated from the high heels, took hold of the pavement, zigzagging, filling her with pleasure.

The eyebrows are more used to the punishment of the tweezers. The coarse hairs wrench themselves from their root systems following the jittery progress of the small metallic jaws. Each plucked hair wrings a tear out of Lulú. Her watery eyes watch how the recently-bared flesh swells, and the line of black dots that used to be her eyebrows disappears, leaving a clear smooth surface for a perfect stroke of an eyebrow pencil.

She continued to move, totally possessed by the madness of the dance. Then the pirates burst in, vociferating, pushing their way through the crowd. The group was captained by a

*Francis Drake too dwarfish and pot-bellied to be convincing.
They hurled fierce curses at the crowd, threatening it with
wooden swords, tin knives, cudgels, and toothless mouths with
sewer breath. The dancer, furious at their stealing her audience's attention, pounced on the intruders with a savage cry.
The rumba was coming to an end, precipitated by the band
leader, who sensed the chaos of the approaching brawl.*

Lulú spreads the lotion over her body, and the dusky, chocolate-
colored skin glistens, thirstily absorbing the oil from the cleansing
substance. Her flexible body quivers under the warmth of the mas-
sage, the epidermis throbs as it is stroked by the caresses from her
own hand, now descending to her groin and stopping, hesitatingly,
anxiously, at the edge of an immense appendage which the hand
squeezes and abandons in sudden bursts, intermittently, going as if
from fury to repentance. Lulú lies on the bed, gulps down the rest of
the beer, closes her eyes, and buries her head in the pillow. Her temples pulsate, she gropes for air, the rebellious hand continues its task,
Ciro's face emerges from the bottom of a river, his body covered with
drops of water, but he's not dead, just playing with the liquid, and he
waves goodbye with a victorious hand. He dives in again for an
instant, the hand goes up and down, slides on the slippery phallus.
Ciro returns to the surface and this time signals to Lulú to dive in
after him, he wants her to accompany him. Lulú dips her foot in the
warm water, then drops her body in, and the river swallows her. It
seems to her as if she were going to die, but Ciro rescues her, he lifts
her up in the air as if he could not hold her for long or find a
foothold under water. Then he takes her to a safe place. Up and
down, charging forcefully, the member bulges to its utmost, nearing
the climax. Lulú feels Ciro's warm body next to her, looks at his face
in the sunlight, their breaths mingle, she holds on to the man's
equine neck and then she feels his hand on the penis which her hand
now grabs convulsively, and Lulú explodes in obscene cries which
the pillow silences so that only she can witness the volcano's erup-
tion.

*From every corner of the park emerged frenzied characters
joining the fray. In jumped little devils with rubber pitch-forks,
followed by Death chasing an almost naked Lothario, a
Carioca band which materialized from another corner, several
gladiators carrying shields and spears, Don Quixote mounted*

on a donkey, and a multitude of magicians, soldiers, and peas-
ants. The witches appeared at the most unexpected moment,
brandishing brooms that they wielded as clubs. The dancer
clung to Drake's tangled locks, digging her teeth into the cor-
sair's flabby neck. They had fallen to the ground, circled by a
crowd egging them on. From time to time others also fell,
spurred by the example of the dancer and the corsair. Not very
far from them, a goblin strangled two ape-men and a harle-
quin, decked in jingling bells, ribbons, and bit and pieces of
mirror, attempted to finish off a manly nun growling in a
thicket.

She is immediately overtaken by an inescapable slackness, her ten-
dons go limp, the muscles yield to an compulsory lethargy which
yearns to be infinite. Suddenly the flesh slackens, the extremities
slump, the skin oozes the effluvium of fulfilled desire, the fires that
fed her fantasy die out. The image of Ciro in the river also fades,
replaced by an immediate and more humdrum reality. Lulú's head
emerges from the depths of the pillow: there's the table with its flowered tablecloth, the basket encircled by a line of gluttonous ants, the
refrigerator with its voiceless hum, the alarm clock, the sink still leak-
ing, the battery-operated radio still tuned on, the landscapes cut out
of old calendars, and an armoire with its doors open where the regal
carnival dress still hangs, imperturbable. Lulú drops her head back
on the pillow while she wipes away the jelly-like remains of the erup-
tion and bit by bit reinitiates the inventory of what has already been
done and calculates what's still left to do. She jumps to her feet and
opens a drawer in the lower half of the armoire. She rummages
through the contents and takes out a pair of panties into which she
introduces her long legs. The sex is reduced to a mound that she
compresses further with a pair of pantyhose. Her vital problem
resolved, her androgynous figure moves from one end of the room to
another. She takes out her makeup implements and finally settles
down on a stool before the armoire's mirror.

Her dress torn, her turban gone, her eyelashes unglued, the
dancer still hangs onto the corsair. The band has dispersed.
The musicians fled the gazebo, their instruments above their
heads, protecting them from irreparable harm. The band
leader had tried to calm tempers down and break up the fight,
but two mischievous harlequins prevented him, holding him by

the arms and leading him on a dance through the park.

She's dazzled by the resplendent layer of cream that her fingers spread on her cheeks, jaws, and forehead. The mutations of her face bring forth memories that are like electrical charges, remote and undesirable. As in a dream, Lulú recalls the sweet singsong of Guelo's voice when he says to her "Honey, nobody makes these sweets better than you," before he takes the nuts-and-honey nougat and smiles at her with his gold-capped teeth. A few brush strokes of rouge on her cheekbones. Or the day she tripped and the basket rolled down the staircase to the landing and the sweets spilled all over the steps. Two fine lines on the tired eyelids, a trace of blue shadow right along the lash line, higher up a broad though brief silvery stroke arching up to the brows. Or that afternoon when she was on her way home, dead tired, and ran into Ciro, and, although he saw her, he wouldn't return her greeting, wouldn't or was ashamed to, since he looked the other way and went on selling his peanuts, ignoring the cashew-nut paste she had made just for him. The firm movements of the lipstick over the thick lips, furious movements like the ones she used when she threw the cashew paste in the garbage for the flies and the rats to eat, movements that leave her lips red and creamy. Or the day she was chased by some thugs yelling "faggot," "queer freak," throwing orange rinds and food scraps at her and all because she had not agreed to let them have some sweets on credit, yelling at them that "no son of a bitch is going to live at my expense." A thick layer of mascara coats her lashes, turning them into two long dark brushes. And she locked herself in her room, a knife at hand in case one of them dared force the door. The mirror reflects the gaily-colored face the occasion requires. "I'll gut the son of a bitch who dares come in here." The face of a tropical rumba dancer. "I swear by my blessed mother." A very coquettish face. And then the crowd dispersed amidst guffaws and threats. The face of an ecstatic Latin dancer. Now she gets up, opens another beer, gulps down the bubbling foam that makes her forget the bad times.

The folding chairs flew from the gazebo to the crowd, cata-
pulted by some buccaneers and several men wearing goat
masks. The confusion grew when the patrons of the Atenas cin-
ema started coming out of the movie house. The blows and the
punches turned into a rocks-and-bottles battle waged by three
or four ferocious gangs. The dancer tried to disentangle herself

*from Drake's hands which were closed tightly around her slen-
der seagull neck. She dug her fingernails into the diminutive
corsair's eyes and was finally able to extricate herself from the
large hands trying to choke her.*

She adjusts the false breasts on the thoracic expanse, trying to
place them right where they belong. She shifts the mounds of foam
from left to right, fixing them at the precise point that she judges
equidistant from the center of the chest. The third beer leaves her
shuddering, tottering awkwardly up and down the room, searching
for shoes and bracelets for the culmination of the ritual. She unhangs
the dress, coils it up her body like a boa, from her feet to her waist
and from there to her shoulders. She is enraptured by the corolla of
flounces that engirdles her body as the teeth of the zipper are welded
together in a seemingly eternal embrace.

*The crowd roared. The gangs carried on their volleys of
rocks and bottles. The black helmets emerged from the police
station, and in a matter of seconds crossed José Martí Avenue
and entered the park. She tried to find her man in the midst of
the melee but the commotion was such that she saw only the
hysterical masked fugitives fleeing from the pacifying billy-
clubs. A few thick drops of rain began falling, turning quickly
into a downpour. She felt a blow on her back and tried to
escape, but the policeman grabbed her by the arm as he continued hurling blows at the dancer's soaked body, thrusting
her into the line of prisoners heading for the station in a forced
march.*

"That's it," Lulú says in front of the mirror, raising her voice so she
could be heard, "there's no resisting this flair and this style. I'd just
like them to show me a queen that could be compared to me, let
them bring her to me." And she hides a powder case between her
falsies, perfumes herself, and exits the room with a joyous expression
on her face that makes her look radiant, as if she were floating in
space.

Translated by Lizabeth Paravisini-Gebert

Colonel Bum Vivant

Rosario Ferré

> *Gradually I perceived its capitals and*
> *astragals, its triangular pediments*
> *and its domes, its bubbles of*
> *granite and of marble. Thus I was*
> *chosen to ascend to the blind*
> *region of black labyrinths*
> *which wove their way into the*
> *resplendent city.*
>
> "The Immortal"
> Jorge Luis Borges

I am pleased you are taking a tour of the White House with us today, my friend. I see you love this city, capital of our great nation and one of the most beautiful places in the world. Otherwise you wouldn't have come to visit us, you wouldn't have been willing to travel for miles just to get to Washington D.C.

Major Pierre Charles L'Enfant, the brilliant French corps engineer of General Washington, laid out the plans for our capital two centuries ago in what was almost a wilderness. A year after he was commissioned to draw the plans Major L'Enfant was dismissed for insubordination. He tore down the houses of rich and poor alike when they got in the way of his architectural plans without so much as a "May I please," and this was too much for the landed gentry of the time. But although he never saw it, his plans were put to good use by our founding father.

Major L'Enfant planned the city in circles in order to thwart the advance of enemy troops in case of war and to facilitate the deployment of our own armies in an invasion. He designed its great avenues, Wisconsin, Connecticut, Massachusetts, Rhode Island, in diagonals across the foggy swamps of our meandering Potomac River. This was a carefully planned strategy. Thanks to L'Enfant, Washington D.C. today is a city of dreams, a marvelous garden of forked paths.

I doubt whether anybody knows this city better than I do — its domes and courtyards, its rolling parks and tranquil fountains, its columned galleries where snow flurries dance silently in winter. In broad daylight its marble monuments look cold and unapproachable, as if they had been carved in ice, but as evening approaches they slowly acquire a delicate rose tint. As I walk down its avenues suddenly a simple detail — a finely chiseled face carved over an archway, the curl of an acanthus leaf high up on a Corinthian capital — makes me stop in my tracks and stare in wonder.

In Washington D.C. every monument is home to an immortal. President Lincoln, President Jefferson, President Roosevelt reside in their own marble halls, built thanks to the generosity of our people. When I walk down the city's streets I feel as if they were still alive because their monuments keep me company. Before he lived in an obelisk, General Washington lived at Mount Vernon. The White House was designed by James Hoban, an Irish carpenter turned architect who lived in Charleston. For a long time the General's shirts were hung out to dry from the colonnade of the East wing and flapped humbly in the wind next to his wife's petticoats.

The obelisk where the General lives today is a fascinating structure; at night it looks like a sword and my friends, the other homeless of Washington, like to call it "Excalibur." The obelisk was once buried in the mire of the Civil War. For years it was abandoned; construction on it was resumed only when that terrible conflict came to an end. The hill on which it stands is a beautiful spot, although it tends to be cold in winter because of the wind that gusts up from Lincoln's Reflecting Pool and the Vietnam Memorial nearby. But the hill where the obelisk stands is usually a sunny, happy spot – something Grandma Moses should have painted. At noon it looks like a birthday cake, with dozens of small flags fluttering around it like candles and a long line of tourists curling sleepily at its feet.

President Jefferson's monument is without doubt the most beautiful one of all. At night its delicate marble cupola floats over the Potomac Basin like a halo. The air smells faintly of cherry blossoms all year round, as if Spring were reluctant to leave, but when the frosts begin a cold vapor rises from the pond and swirls about the cupola, making a prolonged stay dangerous.

President Lincoln's monument is my favorite to spend the night in. Its coffered ceiling, carved in gold with the words of the Gettysburg Address cut deep into its beams, protects one from unfriendly weather. Lincoln's statue always reminds me a little of Rodin's "The Thinker," only Lincoln is dressed in tails. The way he looks straight at you, his large hands resting heavily on the arms of his chair, makes one feel secure and at the same time recalls Lincoln's goodness and wisdom. The words of the Gettysburg Address glow comfortingly over one's head: *To that cause for which they gave their last full measure of devotion; that we are highly resolved that these dead shall not have died in vain; that this nation, under God, shall have a new birth of freedom; that the government of the people, by the people, for the people, shall not perish from the earth . . .*

When I'm lying on the floor bundled up in my Salvation Army blanket, I love to read them over and over again until I finally fall asleep. Spending the night under Lincoln's armchair always makes me feel safe because I can listen to his breathing in the dark. He was a fearless man; the darkness outside, the darkness inside, it was all the same to him and he was never afraid of it. If he were still alive we would have comfortable places to sleep in, a mattress and a bed with a real pillow on which to lay our heads.

You may well ask yourself who is this man who dares whisper to us about the founding fathers of our nation? Where is he from? What is his name and occupation? Why has he been allowed to tour the White House with us?

My name is Sam Roger and I am a retired Army Colonel who served honorably in the Vietnam War. My comrades in arms, the men who walk the streets with me, sometimes call me "Colonel Bum Vivant" because they resent my West Point education. But I never let it upset me; this type of thing often happens during missions and they are still my men.

We know we are not looked upon with approval by the Capital's establishment. They call us "the lost troop," but I prefer to think of us as wanderers. The wanderer, as Mahler and the Romantics well knew, is always voyaging in search of a better world, and that is precisely our purpose. Our duty is to stoically relinquish our homes to assure that freedom is still possible as a way of life in our country.

The younger and more resilient of us like to sleep outdoors. Like the Algonquin Indians who once roamed this valley, they let the heavens turn freely above their heads. At night some of us sleep on park benches, others on train station platforms, or in bus stops decorated with posters from Benetton and The Gap. On winter Sundays we warm ourselves on the grates of the Capital's major museums. During weekends almost all public buildings are closed, and that's why museums are so popular. The grate in front of the Corcoran Museum, for example, can accommodate up to six of us at a time when temperatures plummet.

One day I was standing there with five of my men and wondered why people coming in and out of the Corcoran stared at us before walking to their cars. A visitor dropped a catalog on the sidewalk and I saw the Museum was holding an exhibition of George Segal. Segal's work is very popular in D. C.; for some reason he appeals to the taste of Washingtonians. You can see his sculptures in all the parks and plazas and sometimes it's very difficult to tell if they're dead or alive.

The highlight of the exhibit was a sculpture of six beggars standing on a grate, shivering and trying to warm themselves. Their faces were black with soot and they had a hungry look on their faces, like birds sitting on a branch in winter. The sculpture wasn't about us, of course; Segal's models weren't wearing Salvation Army clothes, but there *was* a faint resemblance. My men were so ashamed from that day on they never stood on the Corcoran grate again. They found a more secluded one behind the Air and Space Museum, where they can warm themselves on Sundays. At least there one has some measure of privacy; people don't come up to poke and sniff you, to see if you're a George Segal sculpture.

Some days we have our casualties. Every once in a while one of our young troopers freezes to death inside a telephone booth. We open the door and there he stands, a sentry at attention, proud of a hero's death. He died guarding the city at night; it doesn't make us sad. The oldest ones among us rarely take these chances, however. During winter we prefer to take refuge in the Metro, where we spend the night changing trains from station to station, not coming up to the surface for hours. It's a nice way to keep warm. You buy a ticket for fifty cents; sit on a contoured plastic chair, your feet on an orange carpet – the D.C. Metro must be the only carpeted subway in the world – and let yourself be rocked to sleep as you enter the Green line and exit on the Red line. This strategy is only necessary in winter, however. During the summer we can sleep peacefully on the wrought iron benches of the Smithsonian's Victorian Garden, or on the marble steps of Congress, the ones facing East, which is where mornings are sunniest.

As I said before, I'm a retired Army Colonel. I live on the streets of Washington D.C. because I want to, not because I have to. My mission is to defend our capital from enemy invasion, and that's why I always wear army fatigues and carry a knapsack. My helmet is furnished with half a dozen toothbrushes which serve as radio antennae. I picked up this trick in the jungles of Vietnam, where toothbrushes were very useful in detecting enemy activity in the underbrush.

I believe in the importance of what I do. A wanderer's life is a hero's life; one has to survive on nothing, by the skin of one's teeth. Every day I wake up at five a.m. and jog to Lafayette Park. This is another of my favorite spots, especially in Spring, when it's full of white and red tulips mingled with blue pansies, the colors of our flag. Then I run up to the Federal Research Building on Pennsylvania Avenue, which has two large black marble basins in front, and do a few jumping jacks and pushups. When I finish my routine I take off my clothes under a copse of cedar pines. At five thirty on summer mornings there's no one around and I can bathe in style, floating on my belly like a walrus or swooping and swilling to my heart's content. When I finally step out of my Roman bath I shave carefully and sit on the Federal Reserve's Art Deco portico, thinking all the while of the poor bank officers who will be trudging in just two hours later. They work so hard, and what with the national debt widening the way it is, they never have time to look out the windows at those beautiful cedar pines.

When I'm spic and span again I walk down Pennsylvania Avenue, past the Archives and the Natural History Museum, to the East Wing of the National Gallery. This is another of my favorite spots, because Mario Pei's pyramid is always good hunting ground. I love to peek into its diamond-shaped windows and look down at the underground cafeteria, where the Museum's lunch queue is already moving ahead. I could stand there for hours watching them, hiding behind the pyramid so the guards can't see me and picking up all the wishing coins I need from the fountain.

When you see a city full of fountains you immediately think it's a lucky city, but I tell you we're the fortunate ones to live in it. People come here from all over the country: from Little Rock, Phoenix, New Orleans, Seattle, to throw money in our fountains and to make a wish. It's a wonderful experience to stand in front of Pei's pyramid with your eyes closed and say to yourself: "I wish Patrick falls madly in love with me tonight"; or "I wish David would give me a nice down-filled parka for Christmas." It's cheerful, happy money; it's not culled from the exploitation of others. It feels good to pay for one's breakfast with it; and sometimes even lunch and dinner, too.

I've told my men many times not to beg, not to stoop to panhandling. I hate to see them stick out their hand like a black claw or bang an empty tin plate against the wall. Especially when they say "God bless you" when a passerby doesn't give them anything. That "God bless you" really gets me, it's so steeped in bitterness you can almost taste it. Every day I repeat the same thing to them: "Better to go hungry than to beg. Patrol the streets with your heads held high. Survive with the money our people have wished you well."

In Saint John's gospel, Christ said: "Be not afraid of those who kill the body, but of those who might stifle the soul. Not a single sparrow falls to the ground but that He knows about it, and even the hairs on your head have been accounted for." I think of these words every day when I stand in front of Pei's glass and silver fountain. That's why, when I walk up to the hot dog stand on the corner and ask the Vietnamese boy for one with everything, I do it with a light heart and a quiet conscience, because I know we're at peace and that I'm standing up for my rights.

As you can see, one can live with very little in our Capital; with almost nothing, truth be known. It always surprises me when our Senators and Congressmen claim they need such high salaries to come and live here, tens of thousands of dollars, because the cost of living is so high. They've lost the *frontiersman's* spirit; David

Crockett's marvelous ingenuity, Daniel Boone's craftiness in learning to survive. I tell you, the homeless of the city are heroes, they are the last true *frontiersmen* of our nation. I have the greatest admiration for them.

Because I'm a colonel I have to set an example for my men all the time. I keep my uniform spotless and at night I never abandon my observation post at the Q Street Metro entrance. Washington, D.C. has a military tradition; you probably noticed it the minute you arrived. There are statues of military heroes all over the place, so people hardly look at them as they rush by on their way to the office or to the shopping arcades. There's a statue of General Lafayette, one of General Grant, one of General Jackson, even of one Simón Bolívar, that great Latin American statesman and man-at-arms whose nick name was "iron butt," because his campaigns carried him across the continent on horseback several times. But there are very few statues of poets — Henry Wadsworth Longfellow and Kahil Gibran are about the only two exceptions — and not a single statue of a woman. Thank God I wasn't born a woman because if I had, there could never have been a statue of me in Washington D.C. I'm my own statue, you know, the statue of Colonel Bum Vivant, the Colonel who fought in Vietnam.

There are many types of living statues among us, and I have had the good fortune of befriending several of them. I remember a young orange-clad Buddhist priest who used to sing on the Mall. He looked just like John Glenn. He made you feel like he had just stepped out of the Air Space Museum, with his finely chiseled nose, his half-inch crew-cut, and the serene gaze of a pilot lost in space. He had painted his nose with gold dust and wrapped himself in a flame-colored cape. He sat on the Mall as if on a green carpet, legs crossed lotus-style in front of a xylophone, and sang to the sky as he played. I would have liked to be like him, but he never noticed as I sat behind him and mimed all his gestures.

I remember poor Meredith who was a photo-buff, and loved to have his photograph taken with the Presidents. He would walk up to the Iranian photographer in front of the White House and stare for hours at the cardboard cut-outs of President Reagan and of President Bush, as well as of President Gorbachev and of President Yeltsin, leaning against the White House iron fence. The Iranian was a nice guy and when Meredith asked him to take his photograph with all the presidents at the same time, he didn't think Meredith was strange. "Please do it for me as a favor," he said to Mahmoud, "I want my mother in Louisiana to know I have good friends in Washington *and* Moscow."

Mahmoud agreed to do it. He stood the four cardboard dolls in line on the sidewalk and told Meredith to stand next to them. But the experience was too much for Meredith. He put the snapshot away in his pocket and every time he looked at it chills would go up and down his spine. The figures were so life-like, the lens had captured the expression on their face so well, he began to believe they were real. To think that each of those four men standing next to him had enough power to destroy the world twenty times over was something that blew his mind. Meredith went mad. On a cold Sunday, when Mahmoud had put away his cardboard figures in one of the steel boxes vendors can rent on Pennsylvania Avenue, he ripped off the lock and built a bonfire with them. The event caused a commotion; police cars arrived immediately and whisked him away.

I also remember the guy who tried to get to the Mall ahead of us every morning, to collect the coins from the public fountains. When we approached him courteously and pointed out this was our territory, he excused himself and insisted he didn't want the money to eat, as was the case with most of us, but only to buy airmail stamps. He was a stamp collector, he said, and he carried dozens of envelopes full of stamps in his jacket. "I love to go to sleep at night knowing they're in my pocket," he used to say. "When I lay my head on a stone, or stretch out my legs on a park bench at night, it makes me feel I have wings. One day I'm going to take my stamps to a travel agency and I'll buy a plane ticket to China, where I'll go to find me a bride." This always made us laugh, because Mark, being gay, was going to have a hard time finding a woman who would marry him in China. One spring day it rained for hours and Mark got tired of waiting out the downpour in a blue plastic Portolet in the park behind the White House. He ran out into the rain and all the stamps in his pocket got glued to one another and he had to throw them away. He also went looney. Now he goes around saying he's no good because he's a stamp without wings.

Life in Washington D.C. can be entertaining; it's not a hick town like it used to be. But when winter comes things *can* get tough. The cold weather is always depressing, and one can't bathe or shave in the public fountains. Having to walk around with your body covered with scabs and dressed in rags is very disagreeable, and the stench makes people afraid of you. In winter everything is white outside and black inside. It's like living in the stomach of Jonah's whale until spring thaws everything out. One has to hibernate, live under bridges or in public restrooms. The soul grows lonely; one starts to talk to squirrels in the park, or to those few ducks and pigeons that brave the cold.

I still haven't told you what brought me to Washington D.C., how I joined the patrol that guards the capital against enemy attack. I was born in Springfield, Illinois, and during the Vietnam War I was a captain in the Fifth Infantry Division. I was stationed for three years near Saigon. I was never afraid of war; the army has always been my way of life. My favorite pastimes are going to Church and reading books on military strategy, masterpieces such as Clausewitz's *On War,* which lets you understand what martial art is all about. I guess that was the reason I never married. My sister Miriam lived on a farm next to where I lived in Illinois, all planted with golden corn, and we were very close. Miriam was the light of my life. When she married and had a son, Mickey was like my own child. Miriam divorced her husband after five years and I helped raise Mickey and sent him to the university, where he graduated at the head of his class with a degree in agronomy. While I was in Vietnam Mickey was recruited into the army, and he got sent to Southeast Asia without my knowing.

He had stopped writing to his mother at a time the army was moving people from place to place with lightning speed, so there was no way I could have learned where he was. One day I had to pick a platoon of soldiers to capture a palm-thatched bunker which we feared had been mined by the Viet Cong. I chose blindly from a list of names; it never occurred to me that Michael Johnson could be my twenty-one-year-old nephew, who had just turned fifteen when I left Springfield. I led the attack myself; I was there when the mine went off and saw the young private's head fly by like a football, spattering to the ground with blood as it rolled up to my feet. When I looked down I couldn't believe my eyes: Mickey was staring at me from the ground.

I couldn't sleep for months after that. They flew me out of Vietnam and committed me to Walter Reed Hospital, right here in Bethesda, where I received intensive psychiatric treatment for more than two years. When I recovered they made me a Colonel and I flew back to

Springfield, but my sister had died and there was no one to keep me company. So I put on my uniform, my helmet and my boots and flew back to Washington D.C., where I'd heard some of my colleagues had joined an outfit whose mission was to defend the city.

We meet randomly: for the POW and MIA demonstrations on the Mall, for example; or for the Veteran's Day march down Pennsylvania Avenue. There are a good many of us, a bit thick around the midriff and with less hair but still wearing our dog tags proudly around our necks, as well as the crosses or holy medals that saved our lives in Vietnam. In a few days we are going to hold an official conference which we expect all D.C. veterans to attend, because we have to discuss a matter that has been worrying us for some time.

It all started when the fuse of the Cold War went out, and suddenly the communists weren't our enemies any more. Thanks to our country's efforts global peace has been achieved. Today Russians, Lithuanians, Estonians, Poles and Czechs all stretch their hands to American citizens as if they had been friends all their lives. We've finally attained the right to freedom, the privilege to inhabit the world in peace. The Enemy, however, has not vanished; he is nearby, hovering somewhere above us. As Christ himself said when he withdrew to do penance in the desert, Satan may take many shapes to tempt us: that of pride or ambition, that of lust, that of betrayal.

Strange things are happening nowadays in our country. In the past anyone who wanted to could travel from Europe or Asia to Ellis Island, and he would be free for the rest of his life. Today immigration laws are becoming tougher, especially with immigrants from down South. I tell you, I can't understand what's happening in that part of the world. It's as if the United States were sitting on a giant anthill, and all of a sudden someone had poured a kettle of boiling water on it; the whole continent wants to burrow its way North. Mexicans are fished by the hundreds from the Río Grande. Haitians are pulled out by the thousands near the Florida coast. Dominicans prefer to swim over to Puerto Rico, where they try to survive. They don't all make it, though. Last year two thousand Dominicans drowned crossing Mona Channel, many of them in plywood boats which sank at the sight of waves three feet high.

I'm convinced Satan is to blame for everything. He's the one who inspires the Helicopters, a secret anti-patriotic sect which has lately begun to gain thousands of followers in our country. And I'm not the only one who thinks so. Our clandestine meeting last week in the basement of the Executive Building revealed that Helicopter's forces have multiplied inordinately during the past few months. You see them everywhere in Washington now, flying over this or that building like angry wasps, or pinning people down at night with their searchlights. We veterans have first-hand knowledge of what these creatures are like; of what really makes them fly. When we were children, we thought helicopters were wonderful toys; we all wanted Santa Claus to bring us one at Christmas. They were egg-beaters that whipped meringues out of every cloud; ponies we could ride over open country. During the Vietnam War, however, we discovered helicopters could do a great deal of harm. They could throw napalm and agent orange from their open hatches, for example; or persecute civilians through valleys and plains, hunting them in slow motion when there was no shelter in sight. That's when we began to believe there was a covert relationship between Helicopter and Satan; that maybe the Helicopters are Satan's secret host on earth.

Helicopters have been doing strange things in Washington D.C. lately. One day I saw one of them flying over the Mall during a Gay march, when it suddenly took a nosedive and scattered the terrified demonstrators in all directions. A giant quilt covered the Mall's grounds, in which the names of people who had died with AIDS were embroidered in red thread, and as the demonstrators ran they tripped on the quilt and screamed in panic. During the Gulf War there was also a large march, and several helicopters got out of hand and began nosediving into the crowd, killing several demonstrators, and not a word appeared in the *Washington Post* about it the next day.

Helicopters aren't always aggressive, however. Just a few months ago, when the Ku Klux Klan held a demonstration in Washington D.C. and about fifty hooded members marched down Pennsylvania Avenue, a squadron of helicopters flew at its head in perfect formation. When several hundred black Washingtonians countermarched in protest, armed with stones, bats, pipes and all sorts of homemade weapons hidden under their coats, the helicopters maintained their altitude and didn't mingle at all in the fray. They looked on impassively as D.C. police, most of them black officers, stood the brunt of the attack, and bricks and bottles were distributed wholesale.

This afternoon my men and I are finally putting into effect the plan we have been forging for a long time in the Executive Building's basement. That's why I'm here right now, by the way, boring you no end in the tourist line, in the middle of the White House Tour. You seem to be a nice man, you nod your head once in a while as if you agree with what I say. You've calmly kept on taking photos all the time of the East Room, with its portraits of our beloved Martha and George on each side of the large windows curtained in gold satin; of President Lincoln's bedroom, with its Victorian bed upholstered in burgundy velvet; of President Franklin's drawing room, with its Empire furniture upholstered in emerald-green brocade.

My men and I joined the tour at eight a.m., and we've been quietly admiring the rooms too, mingling with the rest of the visitors. We loved the French porcelain jars Jackie Kennedy donated to the White House, as well as Mamie Eisenhower's sewing chest and Lady Bird's collection of Lenox plates, decorated with iridescent American butterflies. If you stay by our side a while longer, until the tour reaches the esplanade of the South Lawn, you'll be one of the few visitors to witness the heroic and unequal battle between this humble servant and Satan's squadron, who will arrive shortly to kidnap our President. That's why my men and I have gathered here today, because we must save our President from Helicopter's coup d'etat and his plans to impose a military dictatorship on us.

Translated by Rosario Ferré and Lizeth Paravisini-Gebert

This Noise Was Different

❖

Olga Nolla

Although it was only around nine in the evening, she thought she heard a noise she couldn't identify coming from the garden. Anytime a branch or fruit fell, the dull thump could immediately conjure for her the tearing apart, the trajectory to the grass or to the galvanized steel of the garage roof. If it was a rat, she could follow its quick dash amidst the trees and underbrush. Iguanas, on the other hand, produced a barely perceptible whisper, the dry leaves alone could pinpoint their exact path. But this noise was different. Like the sound of a fist against a wall, she thought, and then perceived that her hands were trembling when she again dipped them in the soapy water to resume washing the dinner dishes.

I must calm down — she said out loud, and was surprised to hear her voice sounding so strong and tempered. After her teenage children had gone out, the house had been submerged in a hollow, glassy silence: the sounds from the garden, the wind, the insects, the vegetation encompassed the silence without canceling it. Her voice sounded like an echo, as if she had spoken in a cave. Yet it was not an old house, like those that look like mausoleums when you close doors and windows. It was modern and spacious, with two interior patios graced with beautiful plants and a fountain. She had never felt the silence in such a way. It was, perhaps, José Juan's silence which made her feel this way.

He had arrived at five, slamming doors and speaking loudly, and from the moment she heard his footsteps in the garden she had known he was drunk. That's how it had been for the last few years: first it was on weekends, later, more recently, almost every day. At the beginning, Mariana spent her hours of insomnia trying to pinpoint, amongst her memories, where she had gone wrong, what mistake she had committed to make the course of her life take such an unexpected turn. A drunkard for a husband was something that happened to other women. This was not something that could happen to Mariana Martínez, after all the precautions her father had taken to protect her from the evils of men. Besides, the culture of alcohol was something her family knew nothing about. They knew nothing of the custom of going out drinking with friends on Friday nights. Her father, if he went out in the evening at all, did so with her mother, to visit friends or relatives. To her father, drinking was not a manly thing, but something for nincompoops and charlatans.

So when José Juan started to drink and, later, to arrive home blabbing nonsense, like a spluttering idiot, Mariana didn't know how to react. It shocked her to see her husband, a distinguished architect, behaving in such a manner. What could have happened to make this transformation possible? To top it off, the oldest son, Pedro Juan, had begun arguing with his father, seconded, although timidly, by the youngest son. Now the father barely talked to his children. If Mariana attempted to have them all sit at the table for dinner, calling upon sacred traditions of family unity, and they gave way, the conversation was uncomfortable and slipped hopelessly into fruitless confrontations.

At the head of the table, José Juan insisted on the people's right to free determination. But alcohol made his exposition awkward and slow and the young men grew exasperated and attempted to give their opinions.

"Children and women speak when chickens pee!" — José Juan would say, red with fury.

Then the sons, ashamed, looked imploringly at their mother, and she excused them from the table so they could leave, please, she could endure José Juan's diatribes alone, it was her duty as his wife. Little by little, like one sinking into a cesspool, José Juan was alienating himself from his loved ones.

"I feel very alone," he told Mariana one day looking at her with a glint of the old tenderness that bound them.

"That's why I drink," he added, evading her eyes.

"The more you drink the lonelier you'll feel," she dared say as she swallowed her tears. But the cruelty of José Juan's words had wounded her. She felt the weight of guilt fall upon her shoulders. José Juan barely heard her feeble protest. He searched the bar for a bottle of whisky and sat in the library to drink himself into oblivion.

As long as Mariana, doing the dishes, kept turning the water faucet on and off, the strange unidentifiable sound had not worried her again. But when she finally turned the faucet off she once again heard the sharp flat thud. She shuddered. José Juan was sleeping off his drunken binge of the afternoon on the library couch. She went to him and tried to awaken him. It was hopeless. Then she heard two, three thuds one after the other.

She was stricken with terror. The house, big and empty, surrounded by the garden pierced with whispers, heightened her uneasiness. She once again tried to awaken José Juan. She shook him desperately, yelled in his ear, but he only sputtered nonsense and turned his back to her.

Maybe she should have called the police from the telephone in the library, but she grew so confused in her despair that she ran to her bedroom to lock herself in. She didn't have time to reach the door. The man grabbed her from behind, stuffing a towel into her mouth. She groaned and struggled, but later, when he threw her on the bed and tore up the sheet to tie her hands and gag her, she obeyed the instinct to remain very quiet, like an animal that wants to escape unnoticed. Hunched on the master bed, Mariana had a good look at her young assailant. He was about her sons' age, eighteen perhaps, tall and muscular, with a sallow complexion. His hair, which was very curly, grew into a bushy afro. He was wearing red sneakers laced to the ankles, and shorts. His sleeveless t-shirt advertised a brand of cigarettes.

He was opening drawers indiscriminately, nervously, searching among the clothing. When he reached Mariana's jewelry box he opened it avidly, but when he saw that it only contained a pearl necklace and gold earrings, he seemed annoyed. He took the gold and left the pearls. In José Juan's chest of drawers he tossed out the shirts and underpants with more fury, broke a crystal box, picked up the perfume bottles and tested the scents. As he perfumed his underarms he laughed like a child and looked at Mariana, who had begun to tremble; when he found the three hundred dollars in new bills that José Juan had hidden among the socks, he laughed louder still.

Then, smiling, he stood before Mariana and caressed her hair, softly, with the tips of his fingers. She whimpered and began to cry; tears rolled down her cheeks, soaking her gag, wetting her chest. He tore her blouse to expose her breasts and seemed disturbed by her animal whine. He slapped her brutally: twice. Mariana fainted.

When, after a minute, or perhaps it was seconds, she regained consciousness, the man had finished undressing her. He wanted her to look at him as he penetrated her. If she closed her eyes, he slapped her to make her open them again, or threatened to slash her face: he had a knife in his pocket that he would show her to force her to open her eyes.

"Look at me, sweet thing, look at me," he said to her again and again, gnashing his teeth. She looked and tried to see, through him, the beams on the ceiling, the cornice of the bedroom, the pink walls. Only for one instant did she feel that their gazes had crossed; then she fainted again.

When she awoke, she was laying on her back. She opened her eyes and was surprised at the bedclothes in disarray, the lights all turned on. Then she remembered and began to tremble again; she huddled in a corner of the bed. A dense and impenetrable silence surrounded her. She tried to listen; but not even the rustling of the leaves in the garden could pierce through.

"My God!," she exclaimed, overcome by terror.

The disorder of the drawers forced her to acknowledge that it had not been a nightmare, and only then did she realize that the young man, before leaving, had cut off her gag and the strips around her wrists, and that she was completely naked. She got up with an effort and put on the first dress she found, but suddenly she recalled more details and felt nauseous. She went to the bathroom and made herself vomit. Then she thought of bathing, the revulsion she felt was so strong, but she remembered José Juan and rushed, as if sleepwalking, to the library.

José Juan was laying on his stomach, motionless on the couch. She thought he was dead, but when she turned him over she realized that he was snoring. Then she began to strike him with contempt, with fury, and to scream, hysterically:

"You fucking bastard! You fucking bastard!"

When the police arrived, Mariana explained that the assailant, armed with a revolver, had tied and gagged José Juan. Then he had locked him in the library before finding his way to the bedroom where she slept, to steal her jewels and rape her. The officers listened to her respectfully, not daring to challenge her version of events. His eyes wide open with bewilderment, José Juan only said that it had all been like Mariana had told them. Before they left, the officers took fingerprints from the window the assailant had broken and jotted in their notepads the amount of the take.

Translated by Lizabeth Paravisini-Gebert

Requiem for a Wreathless Corpse

❖

Pedro Peix

The corpse was behind a glass pane "it's about time you died, you damned *gavillero*[1]; you were never good for nothing but breaking fences and branding other people's cattle; I hope the maggots devour you long before you're buried. It would be a pretty spectacle, a vengeance out in the open after spending so many sleepless nights waiting for you with a shotgun, rubbing my eyes and yawning until in my dreams I could hear you arrive, whistle to the beasts, damn you, soothe them with your cunning hands, and then it was too late, because by the time I'd wake you'd be long gone with the beasts, riding ahead into the night" *as people lined up to view it and some, craning their necks, began asking others how long it would be before they could see it, whether perhaps it was very swollen and that's why people stared at it for such a long time, whether it was true that he was dead or just pretending to sleep, whether it was really Alonso Bobadilla lying there and not some other carcass that looked like him* "you bastard, I wanted to see you like this, bloated by the bullets, purple, your eyes bulging out. Who are you going to trick now? Why don't you move, heh? You don't have the balls to get up and call your henchmen, answer me, why don't you speak out? Yes, yes, yes, you're quite dead and I can hardly believe it. How many times did I dream of grabbing you by the neck and slowly strangling you and then grabbing you by the neck

---

again and squeezing until there was nothing left between my fingers? But you would go, bastard, you would go and you went, leaving my house on fire, my wife and daughter raped and shattered, leaving neither trace nor track to follow. He went with the wind, that's what people said, because they were resigned and afraid, so afraid, you son of a bitch, that no matter how much money I offered no one ever dared go after you" *or whether it really was that women fainted at the sight or maybe threw up and the ones coming behind had to step aside and wait until water was splashed over the dusty ground before the line could advance. Others, aware that many hours would probably pass before they reached the body, had brought canteens to quench their thirst and pouches of tobacco to smoke while they waited their turn. There were those who brought reams of yellowed newspapers in order to amuse themselves with old accounts of the corpse's feats* "they ought to have shrouded him in the national flag and not exhibit him like a bloody pig. He was a real hero, bent on nothing but defending our sovereignty against those high and mighty gringos. He should be getting salvos, he should be decorated; the heroes' pantheon should be his resting place, Alonso, after risking your life to defend us from these freckled scoundrels. I don't know how people can be so mistaken as to think of you as a bandit, a highway robber, when all you did was restore honor to a people capable of nothing but closing their doors at the invader's approach. But of course, the gringos, always at their tricks, turned you into a villain in the eyes of the people because you were a patriot. Rest in peace, Alonso, some day your life will be more diaphanous than this dark vengeance" *reporting on which provinces and regions he had been through and describing the battles he had waged and the number of supplies he counted on as well as the strategies he had used not only to attack but also to slip away. Protected as much by their size as by their harmless presence, children sneaked up the line, slipping between adult legs, trying to edge closer to their goal, not imagining that they would find themselves tangled in a dark nest of skirts and petticoats forcing them, under a shower of reprimands and knocks on the head, to return to their place in the queue* "I never imagined he'd be so big; he looks a bit like a harpooned whale. How I would have liked to have seen his eyes. I don't know why they haven't shrouded him, even if it had been in an old rag. It's disrespectful to display him stark naked, he doesn't deserve this mockery, no matter how bad a bandit he'd been. I always wanted to be like this; what arms he has, and what a chest, no wonder everyone took off when they saw him coming. Now that I see him like this I can believe what they used to say about his shadow being broad enough to cover a dozen men and still leave room for his horse. How I'd love to stay a bit longer. It's such a shame I've run out of money."

More than six hours had gone by when fritter vendors started setting up their stalls on both sides of the line, lighting fires, heating up pots, quickly filling the air with the smell of crisp pork rind, tripe stew, fried fish and boiled plantains. It almost broke the ranks of those waiting in line, except that the people, uncertain, didn't dare leave the queue to get something to eat, fearing they would lose their spots, a problem happily solved by the corpse's relatives through the setting up of a delivery system, sending up and down the line a cadre of children armed with trays loaded with fritters and other victuals which were welcomed by the public with much enthusiasm since now they could eat without risking their places. A few squabbles broke out nonetheless when it occurred to two or three wiseguys to offer to hold people's places in line — for a sum — if they didn't want to digest their food standing up. An *al fresco* dining room had been improvised for this purpose, but when they went back after their meal, precisely at the moment of their rejoining the line, people would start bickering and the very guardian would claim that he didn't know what deal the other guy was talking about, that he had never seen him before in his life, the swindled one being left with no choice but to go to the end of the line *"oh, Alonso, how I would like to drive your death away with this rose I carry in my hands; I brought it for you, from that rose bush you took me to see when my woman's breasts were budding on my chest. We descended the hills hand in hand, and the dusk seemed to roll down with us, so quickly, so quickly, Alonso, that when we got down the night was already crossing our lips. I know that since then you've had other women; I know it, I sense it; they all seem to be here, or maybe far down the line, yes, behind my tears, hidden amongst the people's anxiety. Look at me now, Alonso, here's your son, bound to my waist; this son we made together under the shadow of a besieged almond tree, quickly, without exchanging a caress, while the dogs searched for you, barking, seeming to sniff our coiled bodies; this child I felt growing within me through the tremors of the war, and which I held in my womb just so I could hold on to something of your flesh and blood; this son who now bears your name and your silence; he too is looking at you; it's the first time he sees you, Alonso, and he sees you dead."* As evening came they surrounded the corpse with candles, but they burned too quickly, and so they decided to replace them with torches. They also lit with a lantern the box where people deposited a coin in exchange for the right to look at the corpse for a specified length of time, being able later — through the payment of an additional sum — to spend ten minutes with it in a tent and touch it. By dawn there were only a few stragglers left who had not seen the corpse. And those left were people who had refused to believe until the very last moment that the bullet-ridden corpse on display in the tent was really that of Alonso Bobadilla. Once they saw and touched the body, however, they had to capitulate before the clear evidence, acknowledging coldly what had been public knowledge for many hours. But, as a means of soothing their vanquished incredulity, instead of inserting their coins through the slot of the coin bank, they threw them at the relatives' feet, looking at them with as much derision as scorn. Afterwards, when no one else was left in line, a pack of stray dogs gathered around the tent. Wagging their tails, sniffing desperately, climbing one over the other, they lifted their front legs and glued their noses to the glass. It was then that the relatives decided to take down the tent and take the corpse to another town.

FORTUNATO BOBADILLA (this is the biggest score of my life I would have had to spend it sharpening knifes and blades not even a plate of rice and beans could I eat with this blue wool suit I look like a grand gentleman I'm going to get even for so many years with this moneymaking scheme it really looks good on me it's true I feel sorry for my nephew but he never thought of me and I having such a hard time out there on the streets ARE YOU RELATED TO ALONSO BOBADILLA? as if what he was doing up in the hills were my fault what did I care about the war he had to be crazy to fight the gringos that was no life almost alone and always hiding five years and they're still here at least they've stopped persecuting me I kept running into them everywhere that night they didn't lynch me out of pure luck I don't think we look so much alike I wish we did but I still had to go to jail at least ten times with no one to get me out and who among them would believe me YOU'RE ALONSO BOBADILLA'S UNCLE, YOU MUST KNOW SOMETHING and they pointed their rifles at my temple and pulled the trigger I was so afraid I lost my hair they finally decided I was too stupid to belong to the gang if they only knew they felt sorry for me but when they let me go it was probably because they already had him surrounded about eleven bullets went through the same wound that day the marines sweated and I saw how fifteen men had to drag him to the army post I heard the applause and how they embraced each other out of sheer happiness at having killed him and looked at me proudly thinking they had accomplished a great deed and that night they had a big party three lieutenants came to invite me now they've been promoted and they had me sit at the officers's table as if I were one of them and they got me drunk with a yellow rot the bwiski bottles or whatever they called it I forget the name were pretty and I wanted to take them with me and sell them as holy water it would have been a good business so I was left lying on the floor with piles of chairs on top of me they had left their caps and spats on the tables it would have been good business to sell them things like that are always occurring to me and I got up and they were waiting for me and they were very serious and a fat one with a mustache who seemed to be the chief HERE, TAKE AWAY THAT BANDIT'S BODY AND SHOW IT FROM TOWN TO TOWN SO THEY CAN SEE WHAT CAN HAPPEN TO THOSE WHO GO AGAINST US I was the first to see him and my blood ran cold but it seemed like a good business I should have done it by myself the other two are just a nuisance I'm going to have to leave that child behind in some village this so-called son of Alonso but this corpse is mine I'm going to strike it rich there won't be a town I won't take him to I'm going to buy more suits and ties and hats it's going to be wonderful living the grand life that awaits me), LINDA BOBADILLA (we used to play all the time he was always a man's man cutting twigs to make into swords he always liked weapons we waged war with stones and knocked down the plantain trees but his father never dared give him a whipping although he made a living out of those plantains he didn't care because Alonso could work morning, noon, and night one had to tell him to stop no one worked harder than him everyone felt so proud HE'S GOING TO BE A GREAT MAN and I believed it even after his mischief in the river he would swim under water cold and clear towards me but he would spread out my legs let the king through let the king through he would say as in the children's game and before I knew it he would lower my panties and me shivering and I liked it I don't know why I liked it and don't tell anyone let the king through you alone have seen it let the king through he pushed my head into the water so I could see it until I swallowed water and he at the bottom waiting for me to go up for air and dive down again with eyes open wide how nice it was to touch your dick and later we did it every day the two of us alone in the river how I liked it when he told me blow blow until it swells up and it was true that it would swell up I have never seen one like it nor better Papa liked us to go out together every one in the family liked to see us together they said that with him I ran no risk but Alonso's father was not so trusting although he never barred us from doing anything RESPECT YOUR COUSIN, ALONSO he suspected something though we were together until we were fifteen or maybe earlier but it wasn't longer than that I remember the day I went looking for him and no one wanted to give me an answer they were all silent but his mother had placed thick candles by his photograph and when I started crying she came to me so afraid they would hear what she had to tell me although she was in her own home she said it very quietly that Alonso had joined the war against the gringos his father arrived and looked at us and I suddenly ran out I remember that I knocked down a flower vase I don't know if there were orchids or any other flower all these years without seeing him so many years wanting him every hour in the river I have spent hours upon hours caressing myself and feeling the water washing my pleasure away, letting myself be drawn to the shore, walking out naked and crying they have all seen me what do I care now that I have lost him forever at least I have his corpse and every day I wash it and comb his hair he's still as beautiful as ever I would be alone with him if I could it hadn't occurred to me to bring him a different flower every day I will stay with him until he rots not one flower my hands will be his fragrance no matter where they take him they only want him for the money Uncle doesn't say so but you can see it in his eyes every time they deposit a coin in the box he rubs his hands he thinks of nothing but that and what is it to him since he never had what I had with him in the river I have wanted to take him away and sink with him forever how I would like that), VALERIO BOBADILLA (he could eat five fried eggs WHAT ARE YOU WAITING FOR TO PASS THE SALT it was Mamá's fault as if I had been her slave five bottles of milk like a good animal he could drink them as if they were water GIVE THAT WIMP SOME PLANTAINS laughing at my knobby knees and my long face always sick as I watched him play and I stood by the window he was so muscular I was afraid of him and didn't want to bathe with him I pretended to be sicker than I was COME ON, CHICKEN-SHIT, SOAP YOURSELF LIKE A MAN he would come into the room naked out of sheer mischief and stand at the window which really pleased the cook and I behind dying of envy that's why the cook always hung the clothes out to dry when Alonso took a bath so she could see him and then he wanted to go out and have rock throwing fights and he always came back victorious and sweaty to general accolades and I in a corner listening to descriptions of his feats, and then at night dreaming of doing the same things and feeling tall and strong like him DON'T TELL ME THAT THAT'S YOUR LITTLE BROTHER, ALONSO he would take me out for walks he walked so fast and I felt proud because everyone respected his strength women turned to look such idiots they said he was irresistible poor Linda is still going around thinking that I never forgave my mother who looked at him with eyes she never had for me everybody knew that Alonso was her favorite but if Mamá had not married again why did she do it I didn't come out looking like Alonso WHO DO YOU THINK YOU ARE? YOU'RE ONLY BROTHERS ON YOUR MOTHER'S SIDE I know she said it out of sheer meanness she liked to humiliate me and always started laughing when she looked at my fly butter wouldn't melt in her mouth when Mamá was around as if I hadn't seen her in the river the little whore she was the one always coming after Alonso he was never in love with her but it was convenient for him to go out with her without anyone suspecting anything as if their being cousins was a barrier to anything she never wanted to do anything with me good fine with me I never proposed anything I would masturbate under the bed and never looked at her but I watched from the corner of my eye when she came wearing her little blue dress she would lift her skirt so Alonso could see her saying that she was being eaten up by mosquitoes who was she trying to fool her legs so soft and with little hairs that's how they were how could I not remember later I discovered what she and Alonso did in the river and she would come to the house so cheeky as if nothing were going on WHY DON'T YOU PLAY WITH YOUR COUSIN VALERIO all manhandled how shameless she won't pay any attention to me not even now that he's dead and she looks after the corpse as if he were alive until the day I cut it into tiny pieces then she'll look at me she will indeed and love me, that's it, get rid of the corpse forever but before

that she has to like me I can do it so well she will love me if I have to
make you forget that carcass I'll tell her don't you doubt it that I want
it like in the river I would see you wet and naked and give you an
embrace that will be the longest caress all my skin for you) AND
ALONSO, CALLED THE YOUNGER (yes it was a very dark room it
wasn't a room or a cave maybe Mamá would remember it was dark
every day how could I forget her eyes when I could see through them
if they were wet there was bad news her lids rarely opened to laugh
oh Mamá all these years wandering around in darkness your fingers
stretching like bolts behind the door looking like walls I never slept
in the same bed two days in a row running from place to place without lifting my head staring at other people's legs only that and the
stones and dust and feeling her white hands sweating between mine
pulling me to flee don't look at anyone close your eyes I didn't dare
tell her that I was hungry I would see her with the same dress big
enough to wrap twice around her to escape through an alley she
would carry me she had learned to run like a goat we only went out
at night it was easier to flee in the night once she couldn't go on and
when the sun came out she was still asleep I couldn't move and
watched her breathe her heart bouncing against mine the gringos
were coming across the park that's the only way she could sleep
holding me tightly in her arms from a distance they pointed their
weapons at us and I didn't dare scream I saw one of them approaching and I started to cry I didn't want to wake her then there were
many of them and my tears ran down my face that's how she woke
up at the last moment DON'T GO OUT ON THE STREET, ALONSO,
DON'T GO NEAR THE WINDOW OR OPEN THE DOOR TO ANY-
ONE one day the war will be over only my father was fighting I wanted to meet him but she didn't know where he was luckily no one
knew they had trained dogs in the hills and we heard them bark and
they never captured him they were also pursuing us they asked in
every town and people were silent they supported my father they
came in and searched all the houses with bayonets piercing the
armoires and I was behind some heavy dresses which smelled bad
and the bayonets would slide by me I PITY YOU IF YOU HAVE
MIGUELINA AND HER SON HIDDEN they toppled tables and
opened doors and people stood against the wall they even ran their
bayonets under the beds COME, WE WON'T DO ANYTHING TO
HURT YOU IF YOU TELL US WHERE THE WIFE AND SON OF

THAT BANDIT ARE the clothes rolled to the floor and they opened the drawers out of pure mischief who was going to be hidden in them people loved father and we listening to their questions and Mamá hugging me in a basement where we spent a night once we spent a sleepless night in an outhouse HAVEN'T YOU SEEN A BOY AROUND TEN YEARS OLD Mamá would tell me that that wasn't me HAVEN'T YOU SEEN A THIN AND DIRTY WOMAN and I would watch her turn her face away to cry while they kept asking she didn't want me to see her tears the last time I saw her cry was when she took me to see Papá she scolded me I shouldn't have told her I sounded so stupid why did I tell her that and Papá naked behind a glass pane I am already a man and she was very quiet but I knew she was speaking to him how people behind us pushed we didn't eat that day so we could see Papá more than a day without eating and to have to pay to see him she had hidden her coins in her chest she was nervous afraid of someone recognizing us how she looked at him although maybe she wouldn't have cared if they recognized us HE'S YOUR FATHER, FOLLOW HIM WHEREVER HE GOES, HE BELONGS TO YOU MORE THAN TO ANYONE ELSE they didn't want to believe me at the beginning I told them very clearly I repeated it and that Linda looked at me in a strange way but I told them I was his son the half-brother's eyes almost killed me I can't think how he could be Papá's brother he looks like an idiot but when they saw me I know they were frightened I look just like him what does the Uncle think he's doing by giving me a coin the guy in his brilliance thinks that I'm some kid who wants to get something out of his death HIS LIFE AND DEATH BELONG TO YOU, MY SON exhibiting him from town to town as if he were a clown the bastards but don't worry Mamá they'll be sorry you can be sure of that). They reached the outskirts of Nueva Victoria, carrying the corpse in a wheelbarrow covered with a white sheet. But there was such a dust blizzard that every few minutes the sheet would blow away and the relatives had to go back for it. On one occasion, when they were all tired of retracing their steps, they decided to make do without the sheet and go on their way with the naked corpse. But Alonso, the one they called the younger, protested strongly and they agreed to give a money reward to the one who went back for it. "I do this out of love and respect for my father's remains," they heard him say suddenly, in a tone so severe and honest that they felt, for the moment, humiliated. At one point, when the duststorm had once again blown the sheet away, the three relatives all ran after it. But seeing that the relatives were taking longer than usual coming back, Alonso grabbed the wheelbarrow and went looking for them. He found them chatting by the side of the road, right as they were about to sell the sheet to a neighboring peasant claiming that it was the sheet with which the great Alonso Bobadilla had covered himself for the last time. Just as the peasant was about to hand over the agreed sum they grew ashamed in the presence of the boy and again covered the corpse with the sheet. After walking a long way, seeing how exhausted they all were, Linda proposed pushing the wheelbarrow herself. The relatives accepted with great relief. At the beginning Linda held the barrow with incredible vigor, but after a short while her strength began to wane, precisely at the moment when they reached a sinuous slope from which they could see the paths and roofs of a village. Without showing the slightest hint of fatigue she continued pushing her heavy load, but when they were beginning to descend corpse and wheelbarrow went careening down the hill while the others began running after it yelling curses and cries of alarm. Swift, zigzagging, skipping over rocks, crushing chickens, running over goats and calves, the wheelbarrow rolled down the slope and entered the town, startling the soldiers sitting by the door of the army post. Without stopping, it frightened the horses tied to their posts, knocked down the stalls loaded with pineapples and avocadoes erected on both sides of the street, smashed the milk pails carried by mules on their rumps, turned over the pots where they were frying lungs-and-blood sausage and destroyed all the vegetable gardens and corn rows that had been planted in front of the municipal building. Then, before the entranced eyes of the relatives and with the same uncontrollable and heartless speed, it stripped the bouganvilleas adorning the parish-house porch, disbanded a group of devotees hissing prayers before the church doors, threatened a couple of times to chase a bride just then emerging from church and broke the ranks of a funeral procession just coming around the corner, leaping over the coffin that the startled people had dropped to the ground. After traversing the village from one end to the other and forcing the residents to shut doors and windows, it went twice around the cemetery until it lost speed and came to a stop precisely in front of a freshly-dug grave into which it plunged, exhausted, tumbling into it head first with the corpse.

A short while later the inhabitants came out of their houses and began surrounding the relatives, fierce looks on their faces. And just when, angered, they were about to lynch them, the mayor and the priest interceded on their behalf, asking them how they planned to reimburse people for the damage caused. In a flash Fortunato Bobadilla explained the manner in which they were going to repair the devastation. "Get in line," he started to shout at the top of his lungs, "get in line and follow me to the cemetery." In a few minutes the multitude saw themselves at the cemetery gates, where, intimidated, they all stopped on their tracks. "The dead don't come out in broad daylight," declared Fortunato. The crowd, persuaded, entered the graveyard. And there, with pompous gestures, he pointed to the body of Alonso Bobadilla, narrated his life and death, described the privation they were suffering, and with improvised tears exhorted them to view the body, contributing whatever amount they could afford to restore, amongst them, the lost goods. The picture of bitterness and orphanhood he presented was such, and such the anguish and grief reflected on his face, that the inhabitants, moved to pity without even viewing the body, rushed to relinquish what little they had in their pockets; they went as far as to offer them shelter and food, a display of hospitality for which Fortunato thanked them but which the relatives declined, claiming that they were in a hurry to take the remains to the deceased's native village. Fortunato, however, seeing the number of outsiders coming in and out of town, insisted they accept the invitation. It was not until the mayor promised them a plot in the cemetery to bury the corpse that Fortunato gave the order to leave. Despite this the mayor — who wanted to join in with the feelings of the community — called a meeting of the Municipal Council which passed a resolution that stipulated the giving of a cart and a pair of white mules to the relatives so they could transport the corpse with more dignity. The bestowal of the donated goods was done with great solemnity, participating in it, not only the municipal band but also a committee of "friends of charity" ladies who, with deep emotion, presented to Linda a bouquet of roses and to the other relatives a beautiful silk shroud finished just a few hours before by the village women. During the ceremony the mayor, anticipating the approaching national electoral campaign, took advantage of the opportunity to remind all the relatives that the noble manner in which they had been treated was one of the current goals that the present government – presided over by the wise virtues of the Military Governor, Rear Admiral Thomas Snowden – had proposed with the goal of rekindling the ties of solidarity that should exist between all the peoples of the world. But when the mayor, pumped full of enthusiasm by the attention of the crowd gathered there, announced his intention of seeking reelection, a volley of stones and rotten tomatoes fell upon his fragile podium and the guards mingling in the crowd had to intervene quickly while the relatives loaded the corpse on the cart, and, lashing the mules, fled at breakneck speed.

Night fell as they traveled on (I thought we should stay on the highway) and there still wasn't a glimpse of a town (not me, Uncle; you know that this cart is too rough; we should go by train) although lights could be seen in the distance which could very well have been fireflies (Uncle is right, Linda; traveling by train would be too costly; there would be four of us plus the body; imagine how expensive that would be!) or the lights of some distant town still awake (that's true, Valerio, everything we have accumulated in the coin bank would be lost in train tickets) and which it was necessary to reach (but don't they realize that the body has fallen to the ground eleven times? What do they want, to show people his bones?) by crossing a fragile and swaying bridge (it's not that, Linda; the thing is that we're not going to inconvenience ourselves for the corpse's comfort. You know what a sacrifice it has been to take him from town to town only to waste it all now on useless expenses) which could barely withstand the weight of a cart and five passengers (and it's not only that, Linda, but that traveling by road we could show the corpse to many more people, because between village and village there are many settlements where the trains don't stop or even run through, isn't that so, Uncle?) unless they all got off the cart and crossed the bridge one by one (I agree, Valerio, who knows if Alonso fought on any of these fields; if that's so, then people would be willing to pay whatever it takes just to see him this restful, as they could never have pictured him) risking sending the cart across alone with the corpse (and you haven't thought of the fact that traveling by road it would be very easy to attack us and steal the corpse and everything else we're carrying on us; in the train we would at least travel under some protection) or maybe letting Alonso, the one they called the younger, since he was the lightest of them all, drive it across the bridge (but, Linda, who is going to steal a corpse; besides, how the hell will they know that this is precisely Alonso Bobadilla's corpse?) of course that was provided the river didn't rise because if it did then the waters would wash the bridge away (all right, I don't agree, but it's ok; but later, if something happens to us, don't go around complaining; remember I told you so) and the corpse would be lost forever and who knows if the people in the cart would also drown.

"Listen, little one, what's wrong? Why don't you speak? *He must hate us all I am sure but what do I care?*"

"You haven't said a word since we left that stupid town. Have you had enough? I had already told you this was no easy work. You came with us because you wanted to. It's not too late to go back home. *The only thing he's good for is to be a real nuisance why don't they all get fed up and leave this business to me alone looking at me as if it were somehow my fault he must blame us for Alonso's death me or all of us why not the others he must know what the gringos said to me but he's also involved in this.*"

"Leave him alone, can't you see he's only a child; maybe he's tired. *The more I look at him the more he looks like Alonso if only it were him my God he was like that when we bathed in the river the long arms he must be the same in everything but of course he won't listen to me he must feel that life is disgusting traveling with his father's body but it will be mine poor boy nobody else's but mine.*"

"Why have the beasts stopped, Valerio? *How frightful everything so dark and without a weapon one can't hear a thing what can that be damn it.*"

"It's a fine mess we've gotten into now. I had told you already the best thing for you to do is to climb off the cart to see what's going on. *I could seize that moment to turn the cart around but the boy is here where would I go alone maybe he would like to help me I would make him fall in love with me why not then I would be alone with the body I must do it now.*"

"You go ahead, Valerio, we can't leave the cart alone; I'll take care of Linda and the boy. *What the hell do I care I hope he doesn't come back I wouldn't leave the body for anything in the world I'm not going to take the risk of course not.*"

"Why don't you go, Uncle, everything is so dark. *What an asshole he's being just a bit too clever I'm not moving from here does he think I'm stupid I wouldn't walk straight into the lion's den who does he think he is, ha.*"

"Don't be such cowards and get off once and for all; don't you have any guts? *These chicken-shits won't make up their minds they're going to spoil my plan if only I could convince him but he doesn't trust me I know but who does or else I could squeeze his hand and look at him the way I do.* Well, we're not going to spend the night standing here, right? Do you want me to go alone, then?"

"If you go, Linda, I'll go with you. *I would have her all to myself I would undress her maybe she wants it for such a long time and she too because I haven't seen her do it I would hug her how nice from behind.*"

"Well, then let's go, Valerio. *If I let him I could convince him but it makes me sick I'm sure he would help me get rid of Uncle with a kiss I must hurry up and if he betrays me and rejects my kisses maybe later I would give him more he'll believe me.*"

The moon was far from dark (it would be a good time to get rid of him he's looking at me I know I don't want to turn around he's capable of anything it wouldn't be prudent) as the cart remained standing on the road (if he moves but he won't dare I could push him yes and leave with Papá or hit him on the head he seems so calm) and a regular and powerful murmur could be heard growing stronger each time.

"There's a river ahead," she returned, suffocated, smoothing down her disheveled hair with her hand, "a huge river, Uncle."

"Yes, and the bridge is swaying," behind, buttoning his shirt, "I don't think we can cross it riding on the cart."

The waters leapt over the bridge which swayed from side to side, disappearing every once in a while, drowning in the darkness. The relatives climbed off the cart and crossed the bridge one by one, turning their heads every instant to see if the one preceding them was still on the bridge. When, finally, their clothes dripping, they reached the opposite bank, they saw the flash of the white mules, furtively backing up, getting further and further from the bridge, becoming a distant point in the night. When they recrossed it they ran after the cart and had not advanced but a few yards when they found the corpse lying on the road. A little further ahead they saw the cart tilting to one side, as if it were missing a wheel or had gotten stuck in a rut. Later, above the distant roar of the river, they heard a deep and penetrating wail.

Dawn surprised them once again crossing the bridge. The waters had receded and ran dark and muddied, bearing tree trunks and shrubs under the thin shadow of the bridge. As they had abandoned the cart, the relatives had climbed on the mules, but seeing that the beasts refused to cross the bridge, they decided to leave them behind and carry the corpse on their backs. But the load seemed so heavy that every few minutes they had to stop to rest. It was then, when they saw the vultures circling over them, that they quickened their steps. They walked with their eyes glued to the sky, even the one whose turn it was to carry the corpse couldn't tear his eyes from the vultures, tripping and falling repeatedly on the dust without letting his eyes leave the sky. As they moved ahead, the vultures would sweep lower and lower, until they could see their heavy wings and bald heads. Some of them had alighted on the highest branches of the trees. However, when they saw that the relatives kept walking they flapped their wings and flew off. In a moment of desperation and in an attempt at distracting the vultures, Fortunato Bobadilla tried to rip off an arm from the corpse. But when he saw Alonso, the one they called the younger, marching towards him with an aggressive gesture, he gave up the idea. From then on they continued walking without further mishaps, although the menacing shadow of the vultures haunted them throughout their journey; not even when they had reached the railway station and even – to the surprise of the passengers awaiting the train on the platform – when they had placed the body under the bench on which they sat, did the birds abandon their stubborn persecution, which lasted six hours, alighting now on the rafters of the tracks, now on the station's roof. Inside, the passengers began looking at the relatives with mistrust, and when two vultures craned their necks towards the window, pecking on the glass, people got up from their seats determined on seizing the corpse to throw it to the vultures. But the faraway whistle of the train stopped them, leaving them, however, anxiously on their feet until the train wheels screeched right before the station. Only then, slowly and cautiously, did they open the door. Trampling each other, carrying bundles and suitcases, they stampeded to the train. Then, pushing and shoving, they climbed the steps in a frenzy, elbowing those behind, prodding those in front with their knees and screaming, before the first person was barely in, that there was no room left. Bringing up the rear with some perspicacity the relatives waited until all the passengers had climbed in, and when the train was beginning to move ahead, they hoisted the corpse up, ran cautiously over the dusty esplanade and climbed onto the last car, not aware that the passengers had been watching them, sticking not only their heads and half their bodies out the windows but also canes and umbrellas which they brandished in the air with as much hostility as indignation.

The gestures of hostility quickly became words of protest. The passengers gathered on the aisles and went to complain to the conductor. When he found out that there was a corpse in the train the conductor, preceded by the bustle of the passengers, marched to the relatives' car. Trying both to appease the passengers' wrath and elicit the conductor's sympathy, Fortunato Bobadilla, with sorrowful and reticent voice, explained that if the corpse was the reason for the discord they would all get off at the next station, but to please remember that the corpse was that of Alonso Bobadilla and it merited the respect usually given to great national heroes, to which the conductor replied that only corpses shrouded in the country's flag traveled in his train. Not letting himself be intimidated, and seeing that the passengers were approaching the corpse with evil intentions, Fortunato argued that the corpse under his care was more than illustrious, it was heroic, and that never in history has there been a flag sufficiently noble to serve as its tribute and its shroud. Emboldened by the impact of these words, Fortunato laid the corpse on the aisle, requested a hat, and exhorted the passengers to return immediately to settle themselves comfortably in their respective cars. Then he organized a collection: in return for a coin thrown into the hat they would have the right to come from their car anytime they wanted to view the corpse. However, figuring that the compartments were divided in diverse classes, he decided to take the corpse from car to car with the purpose of obtaining higher fees according to the category of passenger. As the people came and went up and down the aisles, the train almost derailed at a junction because the engineer, enthralled with the spectacle of the corpse, had refused to go back to his post. Rigid, with an idiotic expression on his face, he had to be dragged back to the engine. Right before they reached the next town, Alonso, the one they called the younger, observed through the window the yankee patrols riding their horses past the huts in the distance, and he saw too how some women had climbed on the soldiers' horses, and how some pot-bellied and barefoot children ran and ran trying to overtake the train.

COME, COME NEAR EVERYONE but Uncle, we're barely off the train COME AND YOU WON'T BE SORRY believe me, Linda, we must take advantage of all these people WHAT YOU WILL SEE WILL BE UNFORGETTABLE doesn't he ever get tired; let's go, Valerio, tell him to leave it for tomorrow, I don't understand what the hurry is HERE IT IS, LADIES AND GENTLEMEN, THE BODY OF THE GREAT ALONSO BOBADILLA they're listening to him, Linda; look how many people have gathered already; now we're really going to make some money SEE WITH YOUR OWN EYES THE TERRIBLE BANDIT ABOUT WHOM YOU ALL HEARD SO MUCH DURING HIS LIFETIME it's filthy because he's afraid of the gringos he said in the train that he was a hero it hurts to be your son, Papá, and not do something, it hurts DON'T CROWD AROUND, SIRS, FORM A LINE, DON'T PUSH I am truly sick of all this, Valerio, I'm sleepy and exhausted; I can't stand it a minute longer PATIENCE PATIENCE, GENTLEMEN, THERE'S PLENTY OF TIME calm down, Linda; before nightfall all this will be over; with the money we're going to make here we can rest for the rest of our lives CALL YOUR FRIENDS, YOUR ENTIRE FAMILY, TELL THEM THAT HERE IS THE BODY OF ALONSO BOBADILLA DEAD AS A DOORNAIL BY THE HAND OF THE LAW you're courageous everybody knows it the law is bad Mamá used to tell me if there were a law you'd be alive if there were yes DON'T BE AFRAID, COME NEAR, LADIES AND GENTLEMEN COME NEAR . . .

Despite the rain that was beginning to fall (what's going on, Valerio? Why did you wrap the body in the shroud?) and of the pools of mud forming on the street (the body is rotting, Uncle, can't you feel the stench?) people lined up sheltering under umbrellas and newspapers (good, better still, that way they'll be more impressed) while the yankee soldiers believing themselves to be a part of the spectacle (his bones are beginning to show my God!, Uncle, let's forget this) walked up and down the line with their rain cloaks (I told you to remove the shroud, can't you hear me, Linda?) pointing their fingers at the corpse and then pointing to themselves (but the stench is unbearable, Uncle, even we can't breathe; let's get him off the table and put him in the coffin) as if wanting to say that it was they who had killed Alonso Bobadilla.

When night fell the rain turned into a downpour and people — still covering their noses with handkerchiefs — left the line to return the next day. The pools of mud were so deep that the men had to roll up their pants and the women to gather their skirts to the ankles, and some to the knees, to be able to negotiate the mud covering the streets. Somewhat disappointed, the relatives saw how the yankee soldiers tried to take off their muddied spats while those riding on horseback got stuck in the mud. With nothing left to do, the relatives wrapped the decomposed corpse in its silk shroud and fording mudholes, went to spend the night at the nearest hotel. But, hours later, just at dawn, a small bonfire of blue flames lit the town. People, opening the windows, cried the alarm. When a night patrol finally reached the spot the fire had extinguished itself leaving behind a barely breathable air, an intense vapor like that of singed flesh.

The next morning the skies were gray and dry. People had started coming out of their houses very early. Lined-up and silent, they had been standing outside for more than two hours. Seeing that the relatives still hadn't arrived, the soldiers went to the hotel. No sooner had they turned on their heels that they heard, suddenly, the beckoning of a laconic and manly voice announcing in a dispassionate tone:

COME NEAR, LADIES AND GENTLEMEN those standing on line turned their heads around COME NEAR, PLEASE and they saw Alonso, the one they called the younger, with a small urn under his arm COME ALL TO HEAR and then they saw him with a long rope dragging by their feet THE STORY OF THE GREAT HERO ALONSO BOBADILLA three corpses over the hardened mud.

Translated by Lizabeth Paravisini-Gebert

[1]The gavilleros were guerilla-like bands in rural areas during the 1916-1924 U. S. occupation of the Dominican Republic.

Emilio's Visitations

Reinaldo Montero

I saw God peek into that window there last Monday, looking in, half-hidden, as if he didn't want to be caught at it. But I saw him. God in the flesh. I'm not telling tales, everyone around here knows me. I knew right away that that half-Chinese mulatto was him, he has one of those faces you can never forget. He has a God-like look that there's no mistaking. And he's mulatto and sort of Chinese-looking, yes, sir. Why does that surprise you? He wasn't going to be like that fair-headed, blue-eyed guy with his heart falling all out of his chest in a complete mess, no, that rock-n-roll singer type is nothing at all like him. It's clearer than water to me, God had to be mulatto, that way he'd be halfway between whites and blacks, and sort of Chinese-looking so he'd be halfway between indians and mongolians. Well, if you don't understand it it's because you don't want to. God is a guy on the know, he looks out for his public, and the son of a gun decided to give everyone his little bit, and, logically, to Him go the spoils. He hasn't appeared to any of those old pious ladies left around here not even as a joke, he confessed it to me himself. The poor little things, if they only knew, they'd fall headlong into the grave.

Like I was telling you. On Monday I saw him peeking in and the first thing that caught my attention was how old he has gotten. Listen here, this makes three times he's visited me.

The first time was in Cascajal, when I was a cane weigher and we were in the middle of that business of the sugar differential.[1] I was infinitely grateful for his making his way to my cane scale, because they had sent me to meet with Anisio, a turncoat who used to be a machinist, he must be dead by now, and the Party – because I don't know if you know, but though I have not been a card-carrying member of the Party I've been a communist all my life, and sometimes I've worked shoulder to shoulder with the communists – well, the Party commissioned me to control that fellow Anisio because he was rousing people up, when the most logical thing to do was to stay on your toes and build up the pressure if the matter of the differential didn't come through, but little by little, not to start running around in all directions like a chicken with its head cut off like Anisio wanted. And I told you that I've got to be grateful for his visit because the meeting was going to be tough, as in fact it turned out to be, and I wasn't clear how to go about it. It wasn't easy, there was already quite a group supporting the guy. One night, around ten o'clock, God made his appearance, suddenly, as he usually does. I remember that I was just finishing work, dead tired I was, but we talked about a million things. You can bet I took advantage of the opportunity, not knowing then that I'd have a second one, not to mention a third. You have to go about this thing one step at a time because Anisio is a real blowhard and if you come in pushing from the start he's going to start showing off, and what you or the Party don't need is to have to wind up giving the motherfucker a good whack even if he deserves it. That's what God told me and I'm still grateful for his advice.

The second time was when my son Ruco, the eldest, had joined Fidel's rebels. I hadn't heard from my boy in more than three months and the offensive, so touted by Batista, was at its height, or at least that's what they said, Otto Meruelos and the other one and the other one. You can't know anything about that because back then you were just a little brat, you would've been four or five, no? As I was telling you, I remember that in the last note I had gotten Ruco was around San Pablo de Yao, and that's where things seemed to be hottest, and on that at least Radio Rebelde and the dimwits on television could agree. Then I said to myself, if they kill my boy I'll grab my pistol and I'll go kill myself a trio of policemen, at least three, even if later, if I lived through it, the people in my cadre crushed me into dust and with good reason, because I wouldn't have solved anything by killing three of them. And that was when God appeared to me to tell me that tomorrow or the day after my other two sons would leave for the Sierra. Don't play dumb with me, you know that even the youngest has been messing around with pipe bombs for a while, they're just waiting for something to happen to join the rebels, and if Ruco has been killed, or if they do kill him, because I really don't know, then his brothers are going up there, which is like saying that Ruco is multiplied by two, and if for every one that these degenerates assassinate two go up, the dictatorship won't last.

I'm telling you that God is quite a guy. He doesn't come to you with fairy tales, he tells you I-don't-know with such a spiritual tranquility . . . that's why I liked him from the beginning and consider him a true man and a true friend.

As I started telling you, the son of a gun appeared again, old, tired, years don't go by in vain. And right away I felt a bit sorry. I was happy to see him, let me tell you, I like the guy, we've known each other for a long time. But I felt bad because I figured we had nothing to talk about, and that's the worst thing that can happen to two friends after they haven't seen each other for a long time. So, as if I hadn't noticed him, I turned around, and started heading towards the casting molds at the end of the factory floor, and no sooner did I turn my head than he is next to me, almost grazing my arm. The son of a bitch gave me quite a scare. Sure, I know he didn't do it to scare me. I think that as the years have gone by he's forgotten that he's different from people, even though he is a mulatto and sort of Chinese-looking, and he can always come up with something that to him is a piece of cake and to you is the strangest thing in the world. Ah, and the guy, and let this be clear, has never boasted of his power as far as I know. Wise, my friend, a man who knows. Shit, my man, you really scared me, I thought you were a ghost. It was the first thing I let out. He laughed. You wanted to slip away, he told me. And it was true. That's the way it is, you can't fool God.

And we had things to talk about after all. And we stayed up until the wee hours yakking away, not drinking or anything, because he doesn't even drink water, and if he wasn't going to keep me company I wasn't going to down a bottle on my own, not for nothing, but I don't go for that. And I was beginning to get hungry, but not he, I think he lives on air. And then I lit up. I mean, it was like he was massaging my brain. Because conversation with him is always intelligent.

And we hit on the problem. The economic technical plan was not the Economic Technical Plan, like production is not Production, do you know what I mean? We have so much bottlenecking and so many expenses and so many complications because we go around with our sights nailed to the goal, and nobody pays any attention to the equilibrium of the process, to the beauty of time, to the love that must be there from beginning to end, from the entrance of the raw material to the product that goes out. And it has to be this Chinese-looking guy the color of a paper bag who opens my eyes on purpose or not, he should know. I'm telling you that work should be like an Alicia Alonso ballet. Yes, my man, strong and elegant, and you'll see that in that way the Economic Technical Plan will be like a backdrop, and Production a pleasure to the hands, and you'll see that even fatigue disappears, and when people leave their shift it'll be like coming down from a temple, or from the bleachers of the Latinoamericano Stadium after a good game. One will always come out feeling like they want to come back, not just wanting to get out. And when you carry your children or grandchildren you will do so thinking of bringing them nearer to that which makes work such a big thing. And all this I have to be thankful to him for, or to his visits, which is not the same thing.

I tell you that I don't have any hope of ever seeing God again before he dies, because he looked bad, not frail, no, he has such dignity that his ailments aren't even noticeable, but on his face I saw the grim reaper's shadow, and I know for a fact that when he goes down to the river, when he becomes insensible, when he goes up in smoke, when his supreme hour arrives, I won't be there to close his eyes, or to see how they dress him, though according to what he told me I'm his best friend and it'll be sad not to assist him, and even sadder not to know he died and find out a year later, like with Ruco, my boy, who, even after having all the confirmation I could have of his death, and after the factory was named after him and all, I still waited for him, and although I'm over that fixation, every once in a while I forget, and when I come back to my senses, it's as if he died again, once again without warning.

Translated by Lizabeth Paravisini-Gebert

[1]An important moment in labor activism in Cuba.

Lillianne's Sunday

❖

Ana Lydia Vega

*Out of self-respect I will not interrupt the silence of the
dead. And I will keep my tale free of names in all refer-
ence to those who were responsible for the Ponce
Massacre, since most of them have already stepped
beyond life's frontiers and my very remembrance of their
deeds will bring sorrow enough to those few still alive,
awaiting their hour of departure, slipping away like
shadows in flight from their past.*

— Rafael Pérez-Marchand,
Ponce District Attorney
Historical Reminiscence on the Ponce Massacre[1]

*Each time the memory of that day rekindles in me, I relive the
immutable ritual that signalled the beginning and end of all the weeks
of my childhood.*

*Every Sunday we went to La Concordia, my grandfather's farm in the
Real Abajo barrio of Ponce. In the back seat of the square Packard my
three sisters, my brother, and I fought over the window seats. No sooner*

had we left Hostos Avenue behind and set out on our way across the city to the Juana Díaz detour, that we went through a thousand contortions before settling down, while Mother scolded us because of the racket and Father watched us, amused, in the rearview mirror.

I liked going around the Plaza de las Delicias, watching the young girls showing off their new dresses and the ladies entering and leaving the cathedral with their veils and fans. But I preferred crossing it on foot with Father on those afternoons when he allowed me to accompany him to the barbershop; on such occasions we always stopped at Eusebio's cart to buy the best vanilla ice cream I have tasted in my life.

That Sunday we left a bit later than usual. The night before, Father had taken us, against Mother's wishes, to La Perla Theater to see a zarzuela: Chaste Suzanna was, according to her, "too strong" for our tender ears. We had gone to bed well past ten, which in my house was considered, not only a threat to children's fragile health, but a real abuse of trust.

We had a light breakfast in anticipation of Mamina's arroz con pollo in the country. While Mother laid on my bed the pink pinafore with its little lace collar, I did my exercises with Father in the lean-to by the yard. At eleven we were on our way, begging in unison to stop at the Square for ice cones. People walked by with their holy palm branches in their hands, which made us redouble our entreaties and tripled our longing. But with the pretext of our delay there was to be no stopping and certainly no ice cones. Through the rearview mirror, Father gave me a consolation wink which didn't amuse me one bit.

As we drove past the Pila Clinic we saw a large number of policemen pacing the street and, naturally, we asked if there was to be a parade. "The Nationalists are coming," Mother said, quickly changing the topic. And that was the end of that.

Angel was coming from El Tuque. He had spent the entire morning at the beach gathering shells to make bracelets and necklaces for the girls. He had found many pretty ones, rimmed in pink and violet, and was carrying them in the basket on his bicycle, in a paper sack pressed between the coffee jug and the tin bowl.

He was eager to catch a glimpse of those Nationalists who had announced their meeting with such fanfare. He didn't much like that sort of thing, but, after all, there was nothing better to do to kill death-bound time on a Sunday afternoon in Ponce.

He tried to make his way into town up Marina Street. The police-

men, who had placed barricades on several intersections, would not
let him pass. He made an attempt at Aurora Street, but almost before
he reached the first corner they made him retrace his steps. Then he
hit on a master plan. He left the bicycle leaning against a tree in front
of the Ladies' Asylum, and securing the bag of seashells between his
chest and undershirt, limped across the street. He would ask the
guard with the long carbine pacing nervously up and down the
Alvarado Garage entrance to let him through so he could tend to his
twisted ankle at the Pila Clinic. The guard threw him a malicious
glance and, shrugging his shoulders, waved him on.

*The road was paved, a rare thing in the thirties, and the flamboyant
trees flanking it must have been scandalously red to have remained etched
in my memory for such a long time. That day, by dint of arguments and
shoves, I had earned one of the fiercely sought-after windows. As we
neared Coto Laurel I could comfortably watch the furious geese of
Hacienda La Constanza.*

*Father was singing old ballads and danzas with Mother providing the
chorus. Our faces contorted in incredible grimaces as we tried to repress
our laughter, which nonetheless would burst out without warning, the
more clamorous the more we tried to stifle it.*

From the balcony of the Amy residence, on a second story on
Aurora Street, the view was perfect: the ideal spot from which to take
sensational photos. In any case, it was pointless to search for another:
there was not a single balcony that was not crammed.

Carlos climbed the steps two by two. He had the pleasant surprise
of finding the door open. As he made his way to the balcony across a
living room crowded with the curious, he noticed with growing ill
temper that the best spots were already taken. If he had not had to
park the car so far away, if the walk had not been so long . . . But the
police had cordoned off the neighboring streets and not even his
press pass from *El Imparcial* had been enough to get him the necessary dispensation.

He took a cigarette out of his jacket pocket and lighted it with his
last match. Between puffs of smoke he began to study the faces
around him, hoping to recognize some acquaintance who would help
him achieve his goal. In the first row, the ladies had placed stools on
which to rest their buttocks, a noble and considerate gesture which

allowed those on the second row to enjoy the panorama. There, between two men discussing the merits and demerits of Governor Winship, he saw incontrovertible proof of the fact that, on that day, luck was definitely not with him.

We were still some distance from the curve by the pumpkin patch when I began to feel that vague anxiety that always seized me when I anticipated its approach. Mother had diagnosed carsickness, but the sensation was not the same. It resembled more the queasiness that gripped my stomach when, playing hide and seek, I was about to be found.

The curve of my dread finally appeared, with its wooden crosses, memorials to highway victims. Knowing my weakness, Father left "Happy Days" unfinished to intone, in a deliberately lugubrious voice, "Don't Bring Me Flowers." I surreptitiously reached for Lolín's hand, which I did not release until the irresistible attractions of the road claimed my attention again.

Climbing the fence that separated the hospital from the convent was not an easy task. The privet hedge bordering it presented an additional obstacle. The nuns, moreover, were looking out their windows. But they were, thank God, too absorbed in what was taking place on the other side. Angel concentrated, dug his fingers like hooks into the wall, and hoisting up his torso, mastered a jump that brought him down onto holy ground on all fours.

The removal of a neighbor by hammock to a place unknown, hospital or cemetery to be sure, forced my father to slow down while the cortege marched past. I remember that we could only glimpse, at one end of the hammock, a pair of skinny yellowish feet sticking out. As she hurriedly rolled up the windows to protect us from mysterious viruses floating in the air, Mother explained to us that water was probably the culprit and that that was precisely why it had to be boiled for ten minutes by the clock before one ever dared drink it.

The Inabón river now bordered the road. Lent had unveiled the intimacy of its rocky bed and dried its wide and foamy pools. Father stopped so I could toss out the window the garden pebbles I had brought in my pocket to measure the water's depth.

Crafty Conde, having arrived early, had sneaked between the ladies by dint of gallantries, and was already happily shooting with his camera over the crowd on the sidewalk awaiting the beginning of the parade. *El Mundo* had its front-page photo more than assured. Carlos bit his tongue with rage.

Just then a young girl, small and round, with lips as red as the hearts sprinkling the ruffles of her skirt, whispered very near to him, forcing him to lower his eyes:

"Are you a professional photographer or an amateur?

The question stunned Carlos, who had been, in the light of his present predicament, pondering that very same question. Fortunately, his masculine pride replied for him and the girl was suitably impressed.

We were not very far from the farm when the startling spectacle of what seemed to me like a house making its way by itself across the fields made me exclaim, in alarm, that the earth was shaking. Father's burst of laughter dislodged his spectacles, and Mother had to replace them on the bridge of his nose. It is not an earthquake, he said when he recovered his voice, it's simply a move.

Fascinated, we followed the house's progress, as it was pushed, riding on rollers, by more than twenty men. I wanted to know why, instead of moving the furniture, they had chosen to go through the trouble of moving the house. But I didn't dare ask, for fear of my sisters' eternal mocking laughter.

Once in the yard, Angel meant to go out quite nonchalantly by way of the alley that separated the convent of the Sisters of Mercy from that of the Sisters of Joseph and take a peek out the gate, armed with the genial excuse of being nothing less that the Bishop's messenger. But a nun who had been keeping an eye on him from the moment she saw him jumping the fence yelled out the window. Luckily, with the din coming from the street, he could pretend not to have heard.

The big iron gate with the hacienda's name emerged through the breadfruit trees. As we drove past the payment shack we saw the overseer's raised hand and noisily returned his greeting. The Packard found its habitual spot under the shadow of a carob tree.

Mamina and Papiño were anxiously waiting for us on the immense porch of the wood-frame house. Why were we so late? Had that thing in Ponce already started? Was there a lot of traffic? The questions alternated with kisses and embraces. In the kitchen, Ursula was putting the final touches on the gigantic plantain mofongo reigning supreme on a tray by the fire.

My brother left with my father to chat with the sharecroppers who had come out to greet us. Ursula and grandmother started to take the dishes and silverware to the table on the bohío, the palm-thatched hut in the middle of the grapefruit grove. Accustomed to Corsican gastronomic rites, Mother would have preferred to have her lunch comfortably inside the house. Of course, we would not accept any dining room other than the bohío. My sisters went to the swings. I lost myself amidst the coffee bushes, sniffing and exploring the aromatic mysteries of the berries. And I so truly lost myself that when it came time for lunch, Mamina had to come looking for me.

The conversation did not end there. The girl offered him a sip of her raspberry ice cone, red as the mark of her lips on the white cone from which she was sucking. Pleasantly surprised, Carlos accepted, and the ice cone bridged the space between the couple, whose hands lightly touched.

Suddenly, the irritating click of his rival's camera worked like an alarm clock waking him from his nirvana. Carlos remembered the sacred mission that had brought him with such difficulties from San Juan.

"Why don't we find another spot?" the girl then said, her face slightly flushed from the reflection of the ice cone. Carlos, who couldn't have hoped for anything better, bowed to her desire as if it had been an order, and joined the compact mass vainly craning their necks to catch a glimpse of the street. When he realized that she had not followed him, he looked behind him and saw her standing, arms akimbo like an impatient bride, at the end of the living room. Confused, Carlos thought she was signalling him to return. He attempted to justify himself, pointing a finger at the camera. But she shook her head insistently, and, torn between pleasure and duty, he stood still and undecided for a few seconds before retracing his steps, as fast as he could, towards the girl.

Without a word she guided him to the entrance, from which she pointed, with quite a mischievous smile, to another closed door. Making sure that only Carlos and no one else followed her, she took from her pocket a ring of keys and put the smallest one in the keyhole.

Atop a staircase, a slice of blue sky crowned his trust. Closing the door behind them, they ran triumphantly to the roof.

After lunch, no matter what and come what may, the grandparents always took a siesta. Father let himself down in the hammock on the veranda with a sigh of satisfaction. Mother laid down, with a novel she had had the wise precaution to bring, on the sofa in the living room.

Lolín took advantage of the adults' withdrawal to search at her ease in the small odds-and-ends room. From there she returned with an album full of old unglued photographs which unleashed a fury of sneezes that almost betrayed her. Carmen and Lina grabbed it and devoted themselves, to my great boredom, to its perusal.

The sky was so perfectly blue and the afternoon so dazzlingly white that I couldn't resist the animal's primitive call. I approached the chicken coop with the caution and bad intent of an egg thief. But the ruckus of the guinea hens immediately foiled my plans.

Then I slipped towards the pens where the rabbits grew and multiplied biblically. And I spent a lot of time pestering them, sticking them with a lemon-tree branch, hiding their food. I chased the goats, tried to milk the cows, and did not get to ride the horses because wise old Papiño had locked them in the stable. Emboldened, I carried my audacity to the barrel of landcrabs. Grabbing a long stick with a curved hook used to knock down loquats, I lifted them one by one to bring near my eyes the bluish threat of their claws and then dropped them, from that height, on the resigned carapaces of their companions.

When, from excessive repetition, I grew tired of doing mischief, a gluttony for fruit enticed me to climb trees. Soon, the ground was carpeted with the last oranges and grapefruits of the season. The mangoes, still green, climbed grudgingly off the branches. But the guavas accomplished their revenge. Not only were they all full of worms, but the thorns of a lemon-tree standing guard next to them left my fingers as if I had spent the morning grating plantains.

Angel had already reached the gate and was in the very act of sliding the latch to glide discreetly onto the sidewalk when he was surprised by a clarion call which made him stop dead on his tracks. Immediately the martial chords of La Borinqueña[2] imposed themselves by beat of cymbals and trumpets. Making sure no one was watching, Angel considered for a moment removing his hat as a sign of respect. A guard's frowning gaze, nailed on the musicians, forced him to reconsider. The Nationalist cadets clutched their black berets against their chests while their lips formed the words of the banned anthem.

The aroma of the coffee Ursula was brewing wafted over the farm announcing the approach of the mid-afternoon snack. Although the fruit had turned my intestines inside out, the image of the sweet buns, meekly lined up on the kitchen table, prompted me to return.

Amidst a melancholic ballad, my father's powerful tenor hovered in the still air:

> *There's no other heart like mine*
> *that suffers without a sigh*
> *a heart that suffers in silence*
> *a heart that suffers in silence*
> *is not easy to come by.*

It was his favorite song, the one he asked me to sing to him when he returned tired from the courthouse at seven o'clock in the evening and slumped onto the wicker rocker. I paused on the narrow space that separated the storeroom from the mill and, projecting as far as I could my weak girlish falsetto, I replied with the twin couplet.

> *I had a little white dove*
> *that was my pride and my glee:*
> *she fled from my little cage*
> *she fled from my little cage*
> *though my love for her was so sweet.*

Father applauded and yelled enthusiastic bravos from the veranda. At that moment, not knowing yet why, my eyes welled up with tears and my chest tightened up.

Carlos felt his ill humor dissolve, and a smile tickled the corners of his mouth. The girl had sat on the edge of the white wall, posing coquettishly, her legs crossed, inviting a photograph. With his usual skill, he pressed the shutter release to please his guardian angel and, with the pretext of seeking an angle, came closer to her.

La Borinqueña rose to the sky on the wings of the breeze. Shy or maybe just curious, who knows, the girl turned her head and evaded the kiss destined for her lips. She saw the Nationalists standing at attention with their wooden rifles; she saw, behind them, the women dressed in white and the line of Thompson machine guns, like a dark frontier between life and death, like a frozen river.

"Look at that, it's an ambush," she said, tracing a broad circle with her raised finger.

Carlos spread his legs, squared his body, and took a step forward to take his first photograph. A voice gave the order to march. Two sharp detonations were heard. A piteous chorus of cries and moans took possession of the air.

Before the buzz of a bullet forced them to throw themselves on the ground, Carlos was able to press the shutter and imprison in the astonished eye of his lens that scene of horror he would never be able to tear from his memory.

Wounded on the head, Angel barely had time to crawl towards the tall grass on the patio. His pierced cap covered his face. A long line of spilt seashells extended from his last hiding place to the convent gates.

Mamina was calling me. The sudden irruption of an iridescent butterfly had distracted me, delaying my return. It was then that the black car with an officer at the wheel and the police insignia on the rear bumper came through the gate, like a huge scarab of ill omen. The insistent croak of his claxon made my mother drop the steaming cup of coffee and run down the steps.

A veil of grey smoke was floating over Ponce when the black car stopped at the intersection of Marina and Aurora. It must have been six o'clock of a prematurely darkened afternoon. The few people on the streets walked hurriedly with heads bowed. The long carbines kept watch over the streets. Only the ambulances mocked with their shrill sirens the stillness of a city under siege.

The District Attorney had to lean against the door to remain standing as he faced the overwhelming smell of death that rose from the stained cobblestones. The muffled buzzing that filled his ears drowned the words of the Colonel, whose thin hands moved grace-

lessly accompanying his high-strung description of the "attempt."
When the District Attorney was finally able to formulate, with a wisp
of a voice, something as simple as what happened? or maybe a hopeless were there any deaths? and embark on a macabre tour through
the entrails of a bad dream, his bewildered eyes discovered, in the
bluish light of Ponce's twilight, the words painted in red on the white
pediment wall of the convent:

LONG LIVE THE REPUBLIC
DOWN WITH THE ASSASSINS

The District Attorney had the foreboding that those words, traced
with the waning strength of a dying hand soaked in blood, had the
power to overturn his life, a life that never again would run its course
as placidly as his day at the hacienda every Sunday.

Translated by Lizabeth Paravisini-Gebert

[1]The Ponce Massacre, a deadly confrontation between police and unarmed
pro-independence Nationalist Party supporters, took place in Ponce, Puerto
Rico, on March 21, 1937, a Palm Sunday.

[2]The Puerto Rican national anthem, whose original lyrics, based on a poem
by nineteenth-century writer Lola Rodríguez de Tió, were considered subver-
sive during the nineteen-thirties.

The Blind Buffalo

Mirta Yáñez

For Miguel Carralero and Iván García

For a long time I carried everywhere with me a coin that was a bit more than a good-luck charm. They say there are no secrets in a small town, but mine was very well kept. I feel compelled to make an initial confession: from a very young age I had been a butter-won't-melt-in-her-mouth kind of child, a designation I had truly and honestly earned, since the first notions that wouldn't fit into my brain were the discovery of that coin and the peculiar look of my town.

Around that time people used all sorts of expressions to refer to distant and little-known spots. Any number of remote dwelling places would always come up: in the boondocks, miles away from nowhere, in the back of beyond, to hell and gone, or even where the devil himself wouldn't tread. I'm not going to linger on the possible origins of these abodes, but speaking of the devil, you'd also hear people refer to remote locations as places where the devil hollered three times, or they'd compare them to far-off geographic zones like The-Ends-of-the-Earth or Timbuktu. But at the time I am writing about most people just said that my town, Esmeralda, was in the armpit of the world.

I agree it doesn't qualify as a pretty or poetic phrase, but it has the advantage of being a graphic way of expressing the exact sensation that crumbled over you as you traveled the kilometer upon kilometer flanked by sugar cane fields that separated Esmeralda from the district capital. Not to mention the chimerical road that linked my town to the resplendent Havana, barely glimpsed in dreams and newspaper clippings.

Esmeralda had the name of a green jewel, although during periods of drought it presented itself as a dusty, or better yet, as a hell-hole kind of a place. The only bright spot that opened like a skylight on our dark routine was the railway station. The red tiles of its roof neatly framed a platform that I was convinced of having seen in more than eighteen cowboys-and-indians movies. The platform even boasted the obligatory dry tumbleweeds dragged by the wind. To top this off, the station was called Woodin, a name that fitted perfectly the picture of the stagecoach, the saloon, the sign rusted by the prairie air which had been burrowed down to our bone marrow thanks to Metro Goldwyn Mayer. And despite the dearth of Hollywoodesque emotions at Woodin, it was nonetheless the magic landscape from which novelty arrived. My parents' house was barely fifty meters from the train station, separated from it by a grocery store of ostentatious doric, ionic, and corinthian columns – I need say no more. So that my favorite and not very original entertainment was that of watching the arrival and departure of the trains or of anything capable of moving on those tracks.

The neighborhood knew me well. I was the only daughter of the ne'er-do-well notary, a not very original one to boot. A common enough little girl, a bit given to awkwardness in movements and bows, noted for neither dazzling academic brilliance nor bad conduct reports. Because of my reputation as a pliant homebody, my secrecy about the coin didn't raise any concerns. But I must assure you – let me spell it out here in writing – that I believed myself to be a being from another world. Seriously.

When I say from another world, I mean not only exceptional or more intelligent than the rest, but in addition, quite literally, having come from another planet. No comments on the margins, thank you.

The blame for that conviction of mine had to be distributed evenly between the radio broadcasts to which my mother and I listened with anxious loyalty at noon or dusk, sitting on the porch as we awaited the mail or the newspaper from the aforementioned Woodin station, and the notions of grandeur I had acquired since my father began allowing me to roam his ill-assorted library at will. There I rummaged, morning, afternoon, and evening, without restrictions of any kind. In my incursions through bookshelves, glass cabinets, credenzas, corner cupboards, and armoires I was as enthralled by the novels arranged according to no logic, paired together by dust and humidity, as by those trashy tomes with worn-out spines and jack-of-all-trades contents which introduced themselves with the appellation of encyclopedia. Not to mention the enormous pile of full-color magazines in a strange language, full of illustrations of the entire planet Earth, the very same earth I felt the urge to get to know hither and yon. The ritual scene was completed by a globe, faded and bulging in inappropriate places, an inkwell with a faun's head, and a bronze figure of Don Quixote, trophies from my father's career at the university.

I think that the poor notary surnamed Balboa with the Christian name of Silvestre — witty joke or historical mania of my grandfather's which made my father's lot hard to bear — I repeat, I believe that my poor notary had no inkling of any danger lurking in the listless little girl I appeared to be. By then the imperative to keep my planetary condition a secret had been revealed to me with great clarity. If others had discovered my true personality I would probably have been lost. They would have carried me off without pity to heaven knows what jail cell, or worse, to the convent where they locked up those who dared break the regularity of life in Esmeralda. At least that's what had happened to a third cousin of mine after some love affair with a stranger, a Martian probably.

My intuition warned me that what is different is usually punished. And I was nothing less than an aboriginal from another world.

Another fact to take into account: my house was frequented by a great variety of characters. Be it for professional consultations, because of its vicinity to Woodin, or my mother's coffee, the rocking chairs on our front porch had their share of an heterogeneous parade of behinds. And you had to hear them talk. One of them, I no longer remember who, and it no longer matters, confided to me a certain fact. It concerned the existence of a five-cent coin, a nickel, with the figure of a buffalo of the common and ordinary variety. No one was to know this, but it was a matter of finding a surviving piece from a singular mint, with a buffalo on one side, your everyday nickel, but dated 1914. And then came the best part: it was valued at a million dollars.

My confidante's convincing and mysterious tone, coupled with the historical data related to the First World War, gave the story a persuasive veneer of verisimilitude. A million dollars! The mere mention of the amount made me dizzy. It was an astronomical amount equated in my fantasies with the light-years of distance between the stars, the same light-years that back then seemed to separate me from Havana. None of my dreams had dared encompass so much. I looked towards the station, the engine whistled, the wagons began to move slowly as I counted the railways' crossties, crosspieces, wooden rollers, girders, rafters to infinity. I calculated convulsively everything I would be able to do with a coin like that. And I had to stop, sit down, think of something else, let my mind wander, because it made me dizzy.

One day that seemed like many others, but of the sort that only later fix themselves in your memory, a bolt of lightning on a clear sky of identical days, mother sent me to the grocery store of doric, ionic, and corinthian columns to buy something as commonplace as twenty-five cents worth of capers. I paid with a dollar bill and, receiving my change, I spread it on my palms by force of habit, with little faith. But . . . Gentlemen! There was my coin! The buffalo minted in 1914 had fallen into my power. I don't have to describe to you how that breathtaking apparition amidst vulgar, ordinary quarters was interpreted by me as a revelation of the high place to which I was destined — ribbons, dirty nails, and scraped knees notwithstanding.

I was trembling by the time I got home, like a fragile squab with soaked feathers, and my mother mistook my frenzy for some malarial fevers that were going around. She sounded the infectious alarm and I was thrown under five blankets with a hot-water bottle by my feet. After drinking a disgusting tisane I fell asleep, the coin still in my hand, shiny with the lustre of time and the rubbing of countless fingers.

During the entire nervous semi-vigil of that night, I perceived my mother as a blurry silhouette which approached and receded from my bed, without succeeding in penetrating the ineffable haze that surrounded me. I had already gained possession of the first message from that other, superior world. To tell the truth her image blended with the versions of Havana I had heard repeated so often.

Under the morning light, in the absence of fever or other symptoms, my mother declared me cured. But as I nonetheless continued to behave strangely, she kept a close eye on me, watching me with a curiosity bordering on a spanking. In the course of that day I hesitated three or four times whether or not to share my secret with her. But I opted to leave my mother in her ignorance. How would she have received the sudden news that her daughter was the absolute owner of a million dollars?

When I finally managed to be alone, I again verified the date stamped on the edge of the coin. I confirmed with relief that nothing had changed and my buffalo was still there, with its olympic profile, a portent that fitted in any crack carved by a termite, and capable of getting lost for another forty years. The need to find a hiding place for it was forced upon me. Reader of detective stories that I was, I knew that what is most obvious is never seen. So instead of burying my coin in accordance with the traditions of piracy, or building a secret gothic drawer in an armoire, I wrapped it in pink Chinese paper and put it at the bottom of a box of powder. The buffalo well deserved all conceivable pampering since he was the keeper of my future – goodbye, Esmeralda!

Every night, before going to sleep, I dusted the coin, polished it, and sometimes placed it against my forehead, sometimes against my thumb. Through handling it so much I became convinced that the buffalo on my coin was not impervious to what was happening and addressed long orations to it, although its huge head never deigned turn around to look at me. Because of this I got set in the conviction that it must be blind. If that hadn't been the case, it had had more than time enough to acknowledge me, its owner. Its mistress.

My protector's blindness notwithstanding, a profound change had taken place in my soul. I stopped empathizing with my mother's financial struggles and my father's anxieties about my fate. I possessed the message. Besides, the blind buffalo would always be there to get me out of scrapes when required.

After that I completely neglected all radio programs and ceased to pay any attention to the up to then fascinating Woodin. Each time I had the opportunity, I locked myself in my room to whip together lists of the things I was going to do with the blind buffalo's help. I have no choice but to confess, with a pinch of shame, that my plans included no charity work: I wasn't going to donate my million to orphaned children or to found a ladies' association to combat polio; I wasn't even proposing to buy a marble bench for the Esmeralda park to give lustre to the Balboa name. Nothing of the sort. My ambitions were of bookish origin, adventurous, explorative. And they were closely connected to the pile of magazines, the thick mildewed novels, the encyclopedia, and the faded globe. My blind buffalo would take me to the Islam of *A Thousand and One Nights;* to Casablanca; to a medieval castle, especially to the one on Mont Saint Michel when the tide is out; with it I would roam the Winter Palace, Baker Street, and my grandparents' ancestral plot of land in Galicia; I would have my picture taken by the flag in the North Pole and next to a dog sled in Klondike; we would carouse in the Rio de Janeiro carnival; I would cross the Sahara on camelback and would arrive in Tahiti on a raft similar to the *Kon-Tiki;* we wouldn't miss the lion hunt in Africa and, of course, that of the white whale; I would feed the pigeons at the Piazza San Marco and would hear the roar of the Niagara Falls; I would follow Marco Polo's route, would sail the Amazon, and would find El Dorado; I would climb the pyramid of Teotihuacán and one or the other of the Seven Wonders of the World; I would visit, to say the least, Tom Sawyer's cave and Jean Christophe's Parisian attic. This may seem like an ambitious plan, but a million was a million. My blind buffalo could do anything.

You can imagine that the more time elapsed the less inclined I was to reveal to my relatives that they had a millionaire in their midst. I wasn't ready to provoke a scandal in Esmeralda nor to have them begin to treat me, at such a young age, with the deference I deserved. There would be time enough for that. I didn't want to embarrass my parents nor to disrupt the placid everydayness of Esmeralda.

In any case, around that time, something else took place to disrupt our small-town tranquility.

Across the street from my house there lived a flamboyant clan. As far as I could tell, the tribe was made up of old people, uncles, grandparents, in-laws, and two girls of marrying age. My two neighbors were nearing their late twenties and seemed to me another pair of has-beens, not only because the age of thirty seemed a long way off to a girl who was not yet ten, but because of the convent-like clothes, the immense eyes secured behind the tyrannical patriarchal iron gates, and the measured steps as they made their way to Mass every Sunday, the only stroll permitted the Misses Saínz. Their names were Silvina and María Isabel, although it was never very clear to me who was who.

On a day like any other, the two sisters were seized by the sudden fancy to take off for Havana. A rumor sizzled like gunpowder all through Esmeralda. The scandal exploded with a force commensurate with the neighborhood's dormant routine. Such a challenge to the rules that governed feminine behavior, unmarried girls raising cain, as people say, with no one to stop them. The tears of aunts and cousins-in-law, the parental indignation, the moral discombobulation of the brothers-in-law and grandparents, all were to no avail. Not even the "no dowry" hanging over their virginal heads. It was a disgrace, my parents commented in whispers at lunchtime. A horrible desecration of the most hallowed traditions. Those Misses Saínz were most definitely going too far!

The departure was announced, as was the "I-said-I-was-going-and-that's-the-end-of-it," the "if-you-leave-this-house-you'll-never-come-back," the "pack-up-and-go," and on the afternoon in question, a Holy Friday, they left dressed in their best, wearing the cutest little hats and carrying coffee-colored antediluvian suitcases, though a bit cowed under the condemnatory glares of the entire town of Esmeralda, which had gathered to sanction with their eyes the pair of reprobates. They walked the fifty meters that separated the patriarchal gates from the railway station where once a week the train that connected at Santa Clara with the longed-for convoy arriving from Havana, the mysterious and, as they called it, depraved Havana, stopped.

I too entrenched myself at our front window and watched them go by. My heart accompanied them in their daring walk, and amidst all the pleas for fortune crossing through my mind not the least of them was a demand to the blind buffalo to give them a bit of luck. How useful at least a fifth of my million would have been to them at that moment. The idea occurred to me as they climbed into the train car, leaving on the platform a mob of little kids and a few adults with sullen and pained expressions. The engine whistled — what could I do! I ran like a meteor with my coin in hand, reached the edge of the platform and there encountered María Isabel's (or was it Silvina's) yearning gaze escaping through the window, setting out for a faraway place. Then I heard a scream, a sort of sharp gurgling, as if something had broken into a thousand pieces. Two seconds later they were descending from the train, Silvina, or perhaps it was María Isabel, with head bowed over her chest, while her sister held those avid eyes fixed on a distant point.

Under the town's astonished eyes they retraced the short path to their house. When the gate closed behind Silvina and María Isabel I suffered, for the first time in my life, an unbearable feeling of frustration. Of course back then I didn't use such words, I barely managed to think that something very valuable had been taken from me, and I judged harshly, with the cruelty of childhood, those unfortunate girls who couldn't break away from all that I summarized in one word: Esmeralda.

That same evening, with my coin hidden between my chest and my pajamas, I reached a decision: I would leave for Havana even if I had to trample over the bones of Mazatín the bullfighter to do so. I would study archaeology and become famous. The blind buffalo was on my side.

The uproar surrounding Silvina and María Isabel did not die there. From that day on, the two sisters returned to the station every Friday of every week, with the two little hats becoming more and more frayed, and the set of coffee-colored suitcases more and more dilapidated from being carried back and forth. They would climb into the train car, settle on their seats — always the same seats — and wait there until the engine whistled before descending and reverting behind the paternal gates. Week after week, which later became month after month. At first people took it very seriously, later they found it amusing, until finally Silvina and María Isabel's weekly journey was observed with indifference, a voyage with its touch of the Sysiphean, a bit of Tantalus, and a lot of heaven-knows-what.

The years went by and nothing changed in my neighbors' lives, although there were a great many large and small historical changes. My hour of glory struck in the shape of a scholarship to an institute for know-it-all children. It was finally my turn to climb the train heading for Havana! By then I hardly ever thought of the blind buffalo or of the afternoon in which my eyes met María Isabel's (or was it Silvina's) hungry gaze bent on flight through the window of a train car waiting at Woodin Station. I had also for the most part forgotten my lunar origins.

As I said my farewells with an embrace to my parents I looked at my home's dark hallway without sadness, knowing that this was my last day in Esmeralda. But something occurred to cloud my happiness. As I was climbing onto the train I bumped into Silvina (or was it

María Isabel) with her bowed head and the dusty glare of a long drought. She barely mumbled a few words: "Never amount to anything." The phrase, not addressed to me, nor to anyone, jolted my heart, and I took it as if it had been a second message from that other world.

The story that follows has the triviality of the often repeated. I studied with great resolve, still under the remote influence of that being that believed me to be a saturnal elect. My grades were always excellent. I gathered prizes, honors, positions. I continued to be a butter-won't-melt-in-her-mouth kind of girl, but I must declare in my favor that I wasn't lacking in talent, effort, or an amiable air. I should add that the times were very generous to me and every so often I would think of the country bumpkin from Esmeralda, now a doctor of sciences, chief of a technical department, with a grand two-story house in Miramar and a bunch of other things that I need not mention here.

Every so often, when cleaning my desk or searching for something, I would run into my blind buffalo, relegated to the faraway realm of childish nonsense, despoiled forever of that limitless power once given to it by the girl I had been. Its appearance clashed with the straightforward, utilitarian objects on my desk, but for some reason I had qualms about throwing it away, and so it was moved from one side to the other of the odds-and-ends drawer.

Last week I attended a congress in the city of Camaguey. As I drove back I couldn't resist the impulse to take a detour and go through Esmeralda. A lot had changed in twenty years. The expected bustle of progress. My house no longer existed, but the invincible grocery story with its doric, ionic, and corinthian columns was still there. The wood and tile railway station, the sonorous Woodin, had given way to a cement building. Without allowing myself the time to change my mind, I strode to the Saínz sisters' gate.

It didn't surprise me very much when I glimpsed Silvina and María Isabel seated in their cedar rockers behind the gates, one of them with head bowed over her black muslin collar, the other with the all-encompassing gaze, two sisters captured for posterity as in a daguerreotype.

Displaying a confidence that I was very far from feeling, I pushed open the gate and sat down without asking leave on the Misses Saínz's portico step. I didn't mention the Balboa surname, nor the stories of the twenty years that had elapsed over the rest of the world, nor did I articulate many phrases in the conversation that for more than five hours I unraveled with María Isabel, or was it Silvina, while her sister followed the progress of the chat with her head broken over her chest, sadly marking the rhythm of the words with a slight, defeated, right-to-left movement.

For the first time in oh so many months I was oblivious to commitments and agendas. María Isabel's tempered voice (I suppose it was she) related in spirited tones the globetrotting exploits, feverish wanderings, and escapades of a traveler versed in all the routes, pathways and oceans of the earth's globe. From her chatter, which sounded so natural to my ears, flowed a whirlwind of tales told with an extravagance and passion that did not spring from any encyclopedia, not even from that pile of geographic magazines. Her yearning gaze seemed to be returning from the farthest corners of the earth, and an elemental happiness sprung from the pores of that traveler stranded in her charterhouse in Esmeralda.

During my drive back I asked myself if they still continued to take their places in the train car, week after week, and I realized immediately that it had ceased mattering.

When I got home I had time to think two other things. This is one of them: on the steps of a railway car, twenty years before, I had been incapable of apprehending the correct message. And this was the other: I had spent my time thrusting against life, without seeing it. I attended a scientific conference in Canada, but I didn't hear the Falls; when I visited Paris I forgot Jean Christophe's attic; in Leningrad, I had no time in my schedule to visit the Winter Palace; I preferred my car to rafts, sleighs, and camels; as far as the pigeons at the Piazza San Marco go, I must confess that I had to go to quite a bit of trouble to keep them from staining my new dress. I went to the odds-and-ends drawer and the poor blind buffalo was forced to listen to a few four-letter words I have no intention of repeating here and which were addressed, as you can surmise, to my own person. Then his huge head turned towards me and he opened his eyes wide. It must be the beginning of arteriosclerosis.

Translated by Lizabeth Paravisini-Gebert

Public Declaration of Love

Soledad Cruz

I love this man who I mount and ride without harness, saddle, bridle, or even a stirrup for the jump. He hesitates and defends himself with his usual fickleness. What a male! He's afraid that my gallop will speed up his stampede; he needs guarantees for his equilibrium. He's an ordinary man who guards the extraordinary, like his odors, in the most hidden places, where screams reside. I have given birth to him, once again, between my legs even though he's not legally mine. I am supported in this by our constitution which establishes no differences between legitimate and illegitimate children. And I have accepted this secrecy for our love despite the fact that the party, to which we both belong, has been in power for many years. I don't mean to say that our love is illegal. It's just that those who make the laws and statutes have avoided considering the case.

Before deciding to love him unconditionally, that is, forgetting the principles of commercial exchange according to which he would not suit me, lacking as he does a house, position, car and a good salary, I was haunted by the hatred of the wife of this man who comprises my penultimate failure. This shows that I'm a repeat offender, an explicable relapse, because I've never understood why wives are offended by the other and not by the one who had affirmed, with sign and signature, his exclusive worship of her person. In any case, as I was once a wife, I searched all the ways toward forgetfulness: I retraveled my gallery of ex-loves, took bourgeois vacations of escape, but I didn't have to consume three volumes of *Das Kapital* in order to find myself one day revealing in the most mawkish manner that I couldn't live without him.

I've already said that he is not an extraordinary man. He's afraid of his wife. All men are. It's the memory of the lumps his mother gave him and his gratitude because he owes her a lot. He owes her the secret of his stomach troubles and the discretion of his most hidden fears. Because this man I love is fearful, just like any other human being. And he lies like all the rest. He doesn't make vulgar promises but subtly stimulates the illusion of things that will never take place. It's a consolation he reserves for himself. He firmly believes that they are possible. Another consolation. He's in no hurry. The height of self-consolation! He's certain that he will live one hundred years. Perhaps he has flirted with the idea of dying beforehand, but that was probably in his first youth. I am speaking of a man in his fourth decade of a life that has confirmed his vocation for goodness.

He can be the best and most generous man on the planet, but he doesn't like it to be demanded of him. In general, he doesn't like demands at all. And yet, if he doesn't sense the pressure of a very small demand, he isn't satisfied. He's not even satisfied with himself. There is a very violent struggle between his audacity and his caution. Despite that, he has had achievements that have given him some satisfaction. Stripping himself of leftist tendencies, for example . . .

He isn't original or daring. Hardly anyone is anymore with respect to love. Every morning I look for a note in the flower pots of my window. A bouquet of rosemary. Or an african violet. He knows that I'm crazy about chocolates. But nothing occurs to him. My door remains a virgin at dawn without his hand to surprise or violate it. He prefers to announce his visits telephonically. It's a truly modern device that confirms the absence of witnesses. I think that my insistence frightens him. He used to think that I wanted to trap him. No man will tolerate that openly. Perhaps some of my eloquent messages reminded him of the danger. I'm a dangerous case. With precedents. Not penal, just painful. But trapping him was not my intention.

I don't want to be his lover or his wife. I'm uncomfortable with either of the two positions at our present historical juncture. I offered to be his accomplice, but he, machista after all, altered it to partisan. I didn't care. For a while now I have ridden him of the anguish that accompanies male infidelity. It's a type of prehistoric vice without immediate remedy. I believe in fidelity but in another sense, when the absurdities that justify it nowadays have been eliminated. One cannot be faithful to fetishes.

Although God has had a lot of responsibility in all of this. Think of that business of the rib, the female original sin . . . it's not the action and grace of the Holy Spirit that makes men lose control when confronted by our locally-produced abundant buttocks. Observe that with the ugly ones the male role doesn't come into play. I am certain that having not been favored by nature at the hour of prescribing female endowments, I quickly affiliated myself with Marx's idea (*Economic and Philosophical Manuscripts,* 1844) that all relations between men and the world, including those with women, should be human ones.

As you can appreciate, I have studied the problem deeply. The conclusion was to treat my different equals of the species, for whom sociohistoric evolution from the era of matriarchy to today had created the potential for animality, with much consideration. They are, in fact, as unfortunate as we women. Victims-victimizers of the process of alienation between two halves of the same being. Of course, they didn't pay it much attention and have relished it more, but it hasn't made them any happier. The evidence is their habit of unfaithfulness. Since they cannot satisfy one woman, they decide to unsatisfy two. I advocate attempting to humanize them.

My understanding of these phenomena conditions my search for a close encounter with this man that I love. On top of everything else, a poet. But first I want to rid myself of bio-historical-feminine conditionings, which also help to muddle the situation, in order to arrive at a love free of unrelated considerations. It's something I must attain in order to transcend my grandmother. I want to love without signing a contract, without the threat of joint property or the need to be thanked for the years of love I have given, without the threatening pleas—so feminine!—about what I have contributed to his personal fulfillment and how much the children are going to suffer.

It so happens that this man I love has the damned virtue of very much resembling the person I had anticipated for my experiment. I don't mean that he is exactly the same. It may turn out at the end that they don't resemble one another at all. Hope is a whore that can convert sundry scarecrows into knights-errant. If this should happen I'd never confess it to avoid altering his sense of self. I believe, however, in the risk of his grandeur and in his soul which, I suspect, has not yet been surrendered. These days no one has time for such contributions. We're too busy with social accomplishments. If I could conquer his soul, then he wouldn't be ashamed to have me see him during critical moments in the bathroom or stammer while reading me poems written for another, and he would come to see me even if he weren't in the mood or was too tired for a virile erection.

He's unaware that I love his noble fatigue, his vigilant pursuit of the general happiness of my country. I have said that this man guards the extraordinary, like his odors, in the most hidden places. Which doesn't exempt him from vanity. He's confident that he is masculinely enchanting, and there is so much puerility in this that I'm moved. He's so foolish that he gets angry if I suggest he is getting old. And so sensitive that tears fill his eyes relating how helpless the years have made his father. I never ask him questions. I abolished them all. Who has the right to question half a lifetime after having arrived on the last flight and on the waiting list? After all, I don't need a man to represent me or to leave me a pension when he dies. I can deal with all that, as well as with the discussions in defense of the legitimacy of socialism or the insensitivity of bureaucrats. When he arrived my vocation as a communist was already secure, but it's so comforting to have him understand and share my anxieties during the transition period . . .

As my girlfriends have concluded, he is egotistical in love, as are all of his sex, but contrary to the most recalcitrant of his gender, he is tender, timidly tender. So much so that by effort of hiding it, the tenderness has inundated the limits of his sadness, casting it into melancholy, a discovery that killed me one December night. From that moment on it provokes orgasms in my soul. Because one encounters with relative ease those that can provoke them in other places, but there, My God!, in that unreachable abyss of oneself, only he that dwells in the vacant half of the heavens. He possesses, moreover, the secret of rain. Just the sound of his voice is needed for the downpour to break loose. And he has restored astonishment in me. That chill that pierces your stomach like a knife, experienced in the roller coaster of my infancy and when a man's hand squeezed my own for the first time.

It's true that I have tried to undo the knot many times. I'm not inclined to participate voluntarily in a modern polygamy. In one of his visits to the war zone I declared him formally substituted. But he returned with a love poem. A man who returns from war with a love poem ought to be honored like a victorious field marshall. I surrendered once again and saluted the macho way he has of resisting the temptation of my demons. So Ochún has blessed me and now I wind up with you? He responded almost joyfully. I'm not so sure, however, that he can return my love with the same intensity. It's not for lack of wanting; I grieve for him and for the world.

If only he would love me as I love him, we would be powerful enough to avoid a nuclear war and guarantee world peace. That's why I don't want you to believe that I am justifying this clandestine love— not an impossible one, since its existence is as disproportional as the population of Havana, where I reside, favorable toward males, without childhood traumas and with the solitude I get along with so perfectly. Nor do I want you to think that I am asking for permission to be happy. It is my constitutional right. It's just that I've been told so many times since birth that a love like this, a pure love, is impossible, that feeling it makes me think that the whole planet should know about it, the same as if they should suddenly announce that Reagan died of a heart attack. Beside which it is a pleasure to inform the mediocre and the fearful, without consulting the honest people, of such end-of-century events.

I'm not to blame if the models provided by the adorable Engels in *The Origin of the Family, Private Property, and the State,* in the last century no less, have penetrated my consciousness. If, in love, I border on communism, the case should be considered, in the final analysis, as a stride, an expression of the development of socialism in Cuba. But not everyone evolves at the same rate in a society. I am prepared to avoid the suffering of third, fourth, and even fifth parties involved in the case. He is a much-loved being and I am only his partisan. I also love those who love him and those whom he loves; they are like relatives on love's side. Don't anyone fool themselves into thinking that I'm shamelessly confessing my vocation as a cuckold. Those who believe that haven't understood a word. It's just that I learned very early on that one cannot expend deeds to dreams.

I know that I'll be accused as an instigator, of not following the party line with respect to the care of the family. My male — and female — enemies will comment gleefully: "She always had anarchic tendencies," those more skilled in philosophy, that is. The others will simply say: "What a whore!" And there is always the one who will complain to my party cadre. But they're mistaken. I agree that the family is the basic nucleus of the society. Love has to be the basic nucleus of the family. But if the family that does not include this requirement is in crisis, it seems to me another indication of development is the fact that we are beginning to leave behind the hypocrisy of the bourgeois marriage. Which means to say the Revolution revolutionizes at home.

It's true that these are times of difficult changes. Hard times. My love is aware of this and transcends it without asking for sympathy, like anonymous heros who don't claim a medal in victory. If this love should die of lovelessness, I foretell great catastrophe for its corresponding half, but let no one dare speak of defeat. The victory of this love has been proven. It lies in its very existence. Its unselfishness. Its proven bravery which stands the warlike signals of the enemy, the prejudices of class allies, and the hesitations of my lover, who would be shocked at this public declaration of love with his pretensions as a sane, moderate, but determined man, although perhaps a bit overweight . . .

Translated by Margarite Fernández Olmos

Fritters and Moons

❖

Magali García Ramis

One evening, under a waning moon, an ill-omened moon, a moon not suited for beginnings, by the sonorous and dirty fountain of the town square, they became sweethearts. But from the very first moment Patricio Afanador looked into her eyes and heard her clear but distant "yes" he knew his days of love were numbered. That's why he rushed the courtship. That's why he took a second night job. By day he roasted under the sun in a used car lot; at night he struggled to stay awake teaching a class for mechanics at the vocational school. He knew that the days, months, and years of their shared love were precisely numbered. But the more he thought about it — on slow mornings, under the blazing noonday sun, and on humid nights — the more inner strength he bolstered to confront his fate just as those who witness a miracle draw energy from the vision.

He personally made all the arrangements for the wedding and she, lost in an ancestral reverie, accepted everything amiably, smiling and absent. He made sure he got the first-floor apartment at Don Sebas' house as their home, and he painted it all in yellow. He saved enough to rent a proper blue bridegroom's suit as she asked him. He saved to buy the lace and trims she would sew onto her mother's wedding dress, which she was borrowing for the ceremony. He tutored her for months so she could finally pass her high-school graduation exams.

He arranged with Father Gronninger to take the short pre-nuptial course; he ordered the wedding cake, the almonds and the nougats from the bakery owner; he ordered the wine and liquor, the flowers. All was arranged among men in a man's town. He decided and commanded, knocked on doors and opened hearts so as to get married and be happy in the brief time allotted to him.

He began courting her at sunset on a 25th of September, when the trial was behind them; she became his sweetheart, and he made her his wife in December of the following year. He loved her from the start, and felt that she too loved him. Once married he hurried to build a family. They had one, two, three children, one after the other. All boys. It's best, he thought, in case it can be inherited.

While they lived together he made a point of courting her everyday. He brought her flowers. He gave her candied fruit. He even bought her the wonderful modern sewing machine she had seen in a magazine and had admired with that distant note with which she dealt with just about everything in her life.

He devoted his weekends to her and the children. They would all climb into his jeep and take trips to the beach at the foot of the mountain range, or to the Capital to see the ancient walls and the old city, or to the mountains of the interior to see the brooks and waterfalls, trying to give her his all, to love her, to wrap her in the multiflowered cloak of his love. Because he had loved her from the very first evening he saw her with her father and brothers at the town's patron-saint festival. He loved her from the very instant their eyes met, he so sure of himself, she, so scared when her father embraced her after the shots were fired, and he, Patricio, standing behind them, looked at her father. It had been as if she were being entrusted to him, lovingly loaned to him to protect, cherish, and bide his time.

As long as the end remained in the distant future, Patricio was able to control the sadness that seeped through the weave of his feelings, so vulnerable, so tested. But when the fatal day was only a year away Patricio began to despair. He didn't want to lose her, he didn't want to feel her absence, he didn't want her to return to her origins, he dreamt up all sorts of mishaps that might spare him, remembering nonetheless that it was his fate to be a replacement, a surrogate. That's why his time for love came to an end with fate's unforgiving precision for repeating numbers and dates in the lives of its chosen ones. At sunset, on a 25th of September, José Antonio Grau came out of prison after serving six years for an illogical, spontaneous, and provincial crime which astounded members of the jury, reporters, and sophisticated city people, but not the immutable town folk who understood, naturally, what passion is all about.

She was, had been, and would always be the apple of his eye, his North Star, his equilibrium. Although José Antonio had had five other children with his wife and another three "outside," like his ancestors the now impoverished Grau planters, she, the youngest, was always *His* daughter. As an infant she crawled to greet him with the intense love that children feel at that age when they are bound with another, her small blue eyes transfixed in his, her tiny mouth smiling. At the age of three she clung screaming to his legs to force him to take her when he was off on his manly pursuits: cockfights on Sundays, the pool hall on Friday nights, talk of guns and hunting with the three policemen, his partners at target practice at the shabby little station, with his mother-of-pearl-trimmed pistol. And he, moved, had her dressed up in linen, a big bow in her straight hair, and took her with him.

At the age of seven she dedicated her first composition to him, and José Antonio reveled in the commendations of her teachers, who placed her "Song for Papá" on the school bulletin board as an example to the other students.

Her mother, her brothers and sisters, her grandparents and uncles, her aunts and neighbors, bemused beyond shock or surprise, understood from the moment she was born that she was his, and José Antonio thus accepted it. When people in town said "José Antonio's daughter" they meant her, not any of the others. He never meant to favor her over his other children, but she was his life. When he took the children for a walk she held his hand. Wherever she went, to the movies, the town square, the church, to eat fritters in the small neighborhood cafe-bars, it was always with him. She no sooner glanced at a dress in a shop window than he bought it for her. Any candy her eyes rested upon soon reached her mouth. In a feat of synchronized cause and effect, he fulfilled his fatherly role by making sure she never felt she lacked anything.

When she became an adolescent and began to attend small parties he would take her, dance with her for a while, leave, and return later to fetch her. His gaze alone was enough to make boys respect her, and when they had her in their arms, spinning her around the room, they never forgot for a second that they were dancing with José Antonio Grau's daughter, and not with just any girl.

At some point Father Gronninger talked privately with José Antonio's wife, asking her, with some concern, about the intense love between father and daughter. But the mother swore to the priest that José Antonio had never fondled the child, had never caressed or looked at her with anything other than fatherly affection. She assured him that he fulfilled his conjugal duty weekly and that what José Antonio and his daughter felt for each other was the outcome of fate, which had chosen them for these roles above all others open to humans in this valley of tears.

The girl, all this attention notwithstanding, never became spoiled. She was unpretentious, helpful, hard-working, and caring, all simultaneously and to all her siblings. She came into this world with one mission: to be above all else, his daughter. And his daughter, above all else, she had been.

Then came the time for the town's patron-saint's festival in her fifteenth year. As in previous years, José Antonio took all his children to the square to enjoy the festivities. They went together on the rides, to play games of chance, to savor cod fritters and *almojábanas,* to drink fresh fruit juices, and above all, to the Gold Club food stand to taste *alcapurrias,* the crab fritters made by San Antonio's best-known cooks, now growing old.

It was precisely there that the tragedy took place. José Antonio was walking arm-in-arm with his daughter, followed by his two eldest sons. They came to a stop amidst the noise, the music, the fireworks, the screams of the people on the ferris wheel, the heat, and the raillery of the Saint Ursula and the Eleven Thousand Virgins carnival band, which the town's faggots presented each year, scandalizing the pious and delighting the rest. In front of the old women's kiosk stood two children and a tall burly man in a sleeveless shirt open to reveal a red mole on his left shoulder. Inside the glass case, foggy from the heat, there were three large flat light bulbs, resembling phases of the moon, to warm the *alcapurrias.* There were meat turnovers, blood pudding, blood sausages, savory pies, and in a corner, a single, solitary, enormous crab *alcapurria* resting on a napkin soaked in yellow grease, lit and warmed by the third bulb, which resembled a waning moon.

"What would you like, honey?" José Antonio asked his daughter.

"Oh daddy, the crab . . ." but she didn't get to finish, because just as she was answering her father the tall man with the naked shoulders, unable to hear anything because of the din of the feast and the Saint Ursula revelers singing "Allá en el rancho grande," the old Mexican folk song, at the top of their lungs, reached his hand over the glass case, grabbed the last crab fritter, and brought it to his mouth.

José Antonio had only to glance into his daughter's eyes, watch her blink in astonishment, to feel that he had failed her for the first time, that she hadn't gotten something she wanted, for him to instantly draw the pearl-handled pistol, push his daughter aside with his left arm, and accost the stranger as he fired three shots which went unnoticed in the din. He embraced his daughter and as he released her, turning around, he saw a young man who didn't seem startled like all the other bystanders — now screaming, gesturing, restraining José Antonio, and trying to help the injured man — a young man who had appeared like José Antonio's ghostly double, and José Antonio seemed to beg something of him with his eyes. A few seconds later, in her despair, she too turned to look at the young man.

Arrested and jailed by his three policemen friends, José Antonio didn't utter a single word from that night to the day when the prosecutor called him to the witness stand during the trial held in the nearby capital shortly afterwards. Until then the newspapers and the radio and television newscasts had only spoken of a crime without motive, since no one but his daughter had known why José Antonio had shot the man, later identified as a traveling salesman named Juan del Valle. But when the prosecutor confronted him, José Antonio chose to speak out.

"Do you admit that you fired three shots at the deceased?"

"Yes."

"Why did you shoot him?"

"Because he ate my daughter's crab fritter," he answered point-blank. The tabloids had a field day with the headlines: "HIS DAUGHTER'S WAS EATEN; KILLS IN COLD BLOOD FOR DAUGHTER'S FRITTER; IT WAS THE FRITTER'S FAULT — all amazed, unable to understand, stunned at passions beyond people's grasp. In the town of San Antonio, however, José Antonio's family, his friends, the police at the shabby station, the barber, the cockfight fans, and even Father Gronninger, aware that each heart beats to its own rhythm, prayed for his quick return, and never considered him a criminal, either before or after the trial.

The day José Antonio began to serve his sentence his daughter was approached by Patricio Afanador on her way home. From that moment, in love and in pain, he knew that he was destined to be one with her for only a few years. Once she accepted him Patricio travelled to the state penitentiary to ask José Antonio's consent. José Antonio gave it to him. Then Patricio worked as hard as he could, saved as much as he could, married her, loved her, had children with her, took care of her, and dreamed of not having to return her.

That was until the 25th of September when José Antonio became a free man and was met at the penitentiary gates by his two elder sons who took him home. All his family was happily waiting for him. She was there. They looked into each other's eyes after such a long separation, embraced, and began to live again. Patricio too was there with their three children. When it grew late the children fell asleep. She helped Patricio take them to the jeep.

"Take them home," she said after kissing each of them. "I'll see you later, maybe I'll stay here tonight, we have so much to talk over with daddy." She spoke quite naturally, her eyes bright, once again entwined in her fate.

Vitally wounded, Patricio looked at her, climbed into the jeep and returned home. It may possibly have been another night of a waning moon.

Translated by Carmen C. Esteves

Corinne, Amiable Girl

❖

Mayra Montero

D o you know how many gourdes that can cost you?"

Apollinaire Sanglier lowered his eyes and discovered a small army of minute snails advancing on the earthen floor. They were fleeing the fields, the dizzying sun devastating the pasturelands, and the persecution of the birds. Papa Lhomond, also noticing the forward march, picked up a few at random and put them into his mouth.

"Many gourdes," he announced as he chewed the mass of blackened shells. "If you have dollars, so much the better. But you won't have them. This is more than you can pay."

The *houngan*[1] kept his gaze fixed on his cauldrons and on the rag warriors guarding the altars. He sucked the remnants of mollusks lodged between his teeth with his tongue and bent down to the floor to pick up more snails.

"There are few of us left, very few who know how to work the living dead. No one wants to get sucked into these dealings anymore. Least of all if we're dealing with a white woman."

"She's not white," Apollinaire lit up. "Corinne is mulatta."

"So much the worse," the *houngan* said. "Mulattas are tough to handle, tougher than black women, which is saying a lot."

Apollinaire shrunk like a humbled child and the other one rose to his feet.

"How much money do you have, finally?"

"I had saved a few dollars to leave for Santo Domingo. My mother's going to put up whatever else is needed."

"A hundred to begin with. When is she getting married?"

"At the end of the month. Next Sunday."

"The same day as the elections? There'll be plenty of shooting that day. Bad for you. Good for the work."

The *houngan* left the hut, and Apollinaire was inwardly grateful for the mark of trust implicit in his being allowed to remain alone in the temple. The air inside smelled of rancid fat and fermented tobacco, and he lied on his back, looking at the palm-thatched roof and listening to the dull sizzle of the insects getting scalded in the fields. Then his eyes dimmed and he tried to drive away all hurtful memories of Corinne. He no longer wanted to think of her, he wouldn't even try to see her until she returned from the blue well of the deceased, clean and submissive like God intended, with the pale gaze of those who never think, without that scowl of disgust she gave him every time he came near. Later they would go very far away, to the smoky coasts of La Cahouane and their children would be born there, broad in the beam and light-skinned like their mother.

"She will never raise her voice at you and will always give birth in silence."

His stepfather, Faustine Dondon, had said that on the very same day in which the family had gathered together to decide what to do with their misguided son, wallowing in the despair of his love like a victim of a blood spell. Apollinaire no longer ate, he spent night after night staggering through the bars in the harbor, and towards six in the morning, when his mother set out looking for him, he was to be found crouching on a pool of vomit, his arms bearing the scratches of his own fury, the face swollen with tears, and crying in a woeful moan, like that of a badly-wounded wild boar, which made the early vendors in the marketplace die laughing.

"Corinne's mother," his stepfather liked to stress, "sells fruit in the morning and squeezes it at night, at One-Arm-Tancréde's. She was always a whore, and her daughter will end up the same way."

Apollinaire had never felt such fury. His mother, meanwhile, looked at him as she used to look at hens sick with pip, a look between commiseration and stubbornness which heralded fast and pitiless cures. Finally, when his stepfather ran out of arguments, Eloïse Sanglier took in some air, stretched her bony hand, and grabbed his ear.

"Listen to me well, Apollinaire, my little son: you're spending the dollars for your voyage, your life's savings, in drinking bouts. That mulatta is getting married at the end of the month and I say to you, why don't you go to Papa Lhomond so he can bind her to you?"

"Papa Florvil already bound her," Apollinaire sighed. "They gave it to her to drink, but it didn't take."

"Remember she is the daughter of a priest," his stepfather muttered. "She has to be worked differently. Let them bring her down among the dead, and then you can take her away."

Following this, the old man bent over Apollinaire and whispered what he considered to be two great advantages of the business: once the girl returned from he-knew-where, she would never raise her voice, and were she to give birth twenty times, twenty times would she give birth in silence.

"And what is even better," he added with a slight smile, "only then can you be sure that she will not become such a whore as her mother."

Shortly after this conversation, and after a clandestine meeting between Eloïse Sanglier and Papa Lhomond, Apollinaire sailed to the Isle of Gonaïves, to meet for the first time with that ageless man with hardened face and teeth like a horse, whose skin was of such a gray color that it seemed kneaded in solid smoke. The *houngan* went straight to the point: if he agreed to do this work, it was because Eloïse, his favorite god-daughter, had asked for it. But he would have to move heaven and earth in L'Artibonite and that cost dough. Besides, he would have to place some people near the girl. He was ready to travel to Gonaïves on the eve of the wedding. But he expected Apollinaire to collaborate in everything necessary.

"You know that if we don't arrive in time she will die entirely?"

"My stepfather mentioned something about that."

"And you know that if she dies then I won't be able to return your money?"

"I know, " Apollinaire admitted.

"If the family realizes it, or if they get it into their heads to call a doctor, she could also die."

"Her mother doesn't have a cent."

"And the boyfriend, are you sure he won't call a doctor?"

It was a detail Apollinaire had not counted on. The truth was that he had never taken that emaciated guy who had gotten himself engaged to Corinne too seriously. He didn't feel jealousy or envy or any desire to beat Dessalines Corail to a pulp. He felt absolutely nothing. His thoughts were too occupied with the woman for him to concern himself with the man taking her away from him.

"Maybe the boyfriend will call the doctor," Papa Lhomond repeated.

"The boyfriend will be away all day," Apollinaire assured him. "He works for a politician and will come to get married in the afternoon, after people have voted."

"Well, by the afternoon she'll be quite stiff," Papa Lhomond stated sententiously, and immediately returned to devouring his snails.

Apollinaire, his gaze fixed on the sweltering surface that was the fields, now thought of what his life would have been like if Corinne had loved him like he loved her. There would have been no need for him to cross the Saint Marc channel to visit this remote *hounfort*[2] in order to force her into being an amiable girl. She would perhaps have given birth to his children screaming and swearing like all other women. But what did that matter. What did it matter that the mother spent her nights whoring at One-Arm-Tancréde's, since after all the daughter took after her father. Didn't Corinne have the same yellow eyes and the same disposition to communicate with the mute the Dutch priest had had? If she had loved him, he told himself as he watched another gray column of snails ascend the wall, he wouldn't have minded supporting them both. The mother too, so she wouldn't be rolling about in bed with just anyone for a couple of gourdes at the Salon Français. But Corinne had never loved him, and moreover, had chosen to marry one of the mutes that the priest had taught to speak by signs. That's how she communicated with Dessalines Corail, by means of a game of hands that made everyone who saw them walk by laugh. Maybe that's why he didn't worry about pushing the rival away, because he believed deep down that that man would never have the courage to snatch her away; because he knew that Dessalines would never be capable of whispering into Corinne's soft ear one single phrase to warm her soul, nor a torrid word that would make her willingly surrender.

The snails stopped, and he picked one of them to put into his mouth. He was sure he was not going to like it but he had to discover what strange pleasure Papa Lhomond derived from the chewing of those bugs, enough to eat them by the fistful, cutting his lips with the soil-encrusted edges of the shells. What he had forgotten to ask the *houngan,* he told himself as he was overcome by retching, was if it was true that the skin of women brought back grew hard with the years, like that of a brown pig. He didn't even want to think whether what old people whispered was true, that with time the living dead fell into the habit of devouring vermin they found on the fields. Faustine Dondon, his stepfather, had told him of the case of a French woman abducted by a slaughterer from Hinche who used to breakfast on a half-stunned *cul-rouge* spider her husband would bring before he awoke her.

Apollinaire Sanglier spat out a gray slime that tasted at once putrid and bitter. He had made up his mind, there was no other way. Papa Lhomond, by this time, would already be spurring on his contacts, unearthing bones, searching in solitude for the infallible substances used only for works such as these. Corinne, many miles away, could not imagine the stiff price she was going to pay for her disdain. And Dessalines Corail, absorbed as he was in politics, wouldn't be able to anticipate what was cooking either.

He dusted off his clothes and left the hut. The heat outside was so intense that he felt an impulse to return to the altars, to shelter in the shadow of the sawdust warriors guarding the virgins with the greedy look of those who would rather split their legs open once and for all. But he understood that it was time to set out on the long road home, await the emissary Papa Lhomond would send to pick up the dollars, and not go anywhere near the places where he could run into the woman or her boyfriend.

"Let no one see you prowling around her, let no one realize that you know she's going to get married."

To spare Apollinaire greater sorrows, it was decided that his stepfather, Faustine Dondon, would accompany the *houngan* in the difficult task of finishing off the work.

"If you accompany me," Papa Lhomond meditated, "you run the risk of being repelled by her later. You'll wait until we bring her to you. When you see her again, she will be clean and ready for you to take away."

Once back in Gonaïves, he asked himself uneasily what it was that had changed in the city. He had been away only a couple of nights, but when the packet-boat in which he made the return trip slowed down and started to enter the harbor, it seemed as if he had been away many years. The usual mild breezes that traversed the gulf of Gonaïves at that time of the year now dispersed into hot gusts that eddied when they reached the coast, choking the air moving inland. Maybe everything was the same as ever, he thought as he wiped away the dollops of sweat, maybe the strangeness was only inside his own brain. But later, when he set foot on shore and started to walk towards his house, the impression that something horrible had occurred or was about to occur assaulted him again. His mother, Eloïse Sanglier, received him coldly:

"On Sunday afternoon a man from Gros-Morne will come to take you both straight into Port-au-Prince. From there you will travel by boat to Jérémie. At Jérémie you yourself will have to find someone to take you down to La Cahouane."

Apollinaire remained silent. Then he snapped his tongue as if he had remembered something unpleasant.

"Papa Lhomond will send an old man from the isle for the money."

"The old man already came," his mother said. "I already gave it to him."

He looked at her in surprise and seemed about to ask her something, but Eloïse cut him short with a movement of her hand.

"That is not to be discussed with anyone. Do you understand me, my son?"

Apollinaire did not reply. He changed his clothes and set out as usual for his job at the Mariani Brothers' shop. He scrubbed the floors, emptied the garbage cans, and noon surprised him preparing the two-pound bags of black beans which would be sold at a reduced price all day Saturday. Antoine Mariani, his boss, alarmed his patrons every so often with hints that maybe he wouldn't be able to open the shop the following week.

"There'll be shooting on Sunday," he told them. "Who knows if we'll have to spend Monday under our beds."

The customers that had a few extra gourdes on them reacted by buying an additional tin of crackers and a few more pounds of rice. Those who had brought just enough looked at the shopkeeper, perplexed, and left without a word. Apollinaire trembled from head to toe when he thought that Corinne could appear at any moment and that with the same dusty hands with which he was separating the black beans he would have to sell her what he always sold her: ten of sugar and one of okra. Corinne, however, did not show up that day, and it was her boyfriend, Dessalines Corail, who came to the store for the provisions the girl had sent him for. Apollinaire, busy as he was slicing pumpkins in half, was unaware of his arrival until one of the Mariani brothers tapped him on the shoulder.

"Leave that and go cut a pair of herrings for the mute."

Apollinaire turned slowly. He knew that the mute could not be other than Corinne's boyfriend, and when his eyes met Dessalines' somber eyes, an incipient fury, a mixture of terror and pity, got stuck in his throat. The mute handed him a piece of stained paper where the order was written.

"I don't understand the handwriting," grunted Apollinaire.

"How could you understand it," they roared from the back room, "if you can barely read."

Apollinaire went on cutting the herring, and Antoine Mariani approached to read the list.

"Give him rice and beans. Five of each. And ten of corn meal."

Then he addressed the mute.

"You've been distributing leaflets, haven't you?

Dessalines denied it with his head.

"The nuns distribute leaflets," Apollinaire intervened in a biting tone.

"No one asked you," Antoine scolded him, and immediately insisted with Dessalines: "But you are working for that politician, Latortue, your mother-in-law told me."

The mute assented.

"Watch that you don't get your throat slashed before you get married. Mind you, there's more than one around with his eye on Corinne."

Apollinaire shuddered and dropped a whole scoopful of black beans on the floor. Dessalines remained very serious, grabbed his packages, and left the store with the same look of anguish with which he had arrived.

At dawn on Friday, two sharp knocks, like two stone blows, awakened Apollinaire Sanglier. Eloïse rushed to open the door, and from his cot he heard the whispers and the prattle of steps which stopped next to the little flowered curtain that led to his room.

"Apollinaire," his mother said, "get up and come look after Papa Lhomond."

He dressed in a hurry and when he came out he found Faustine Dondon, his stepfather, speaking with the *houngan* in a low voice.

"From this moment on," Papa Lhomond told him as soon as he saw him appear, "you don't know me, you don't greet me, you haven't seen me even if you're looking at me."

Eloïse served everyone coffee, and Apollinaire discovered on her face a vital and ardent look, an expression made iridescent by the light and which in any other person would probably have terrorized him. A bit later he left for work, leaving Papa Lhomond and his stepfather sitting around the table, exchanging small packages wrapped in newspaper and tied with shoelaces. That day Corinne didn't come to buy anything either, and when Apollinaire returned home in the evening his mother awaited him with the table set and a luxurious dinner: stewed meat and green plantains. Only then did he understand that this was farewell.

"You have been left without a cent," Eloïse Sanglier said. "And you owe me a great deal of money. As soon as you get to La Cahouane, you should set up as a charcoal-maker and try to save a bit."

Apollinaire moved his head with a vague gesture and remained staring at the curdled sauce of the stew reaching the chipped borders of his plate.

"To think that my grandchildren," he heard his mother say, "will also be the grandchildren of a priest."

"A priest of the kind that is allowed to marry," he replied, "not the other kind."

"So what?," jumped Eloïse. "What good did it do Corinne's mother to have him marry her, if when he left he didn't leave her a cent?"

"Corinne has yellow eyes thanks to him," Apollinaire dared add.

"Thanks to cat's claws, you mean. The mother always carried them on her so that her child wouldn't lack grip."

"She won't lack anything," Apollinaire promised and ate his banquet in silence.

When he got to the store the following day, he found a long line of early-risers awaiting the special sale on black beans.

"She died last night," he heard a woman who was speaking to all. "The doctor says that it was her heart, but she had had some fevers before. Her mother believes that the veins in her head burst."

He stood watching the woman, not daring to ask her anything. A doctor, he thought, and that very instant he heard Antoine Mariani call him to start serving the customers. If only he could have let Papa Lhomond know . . . But the *houngan* had warned him: "You don't know me. You have not seen me even if you're looking at me." People snatched the two-pound bags from his hands and he felt a cold sweat running down his face. They had called the doctor. Surely they had given her some potion to drink. Or in the worst of cases, they had opened her belly after death to see what had made her sick.

"She was going to get married tomorrow," he heard his boss say. "Poor mute, the girl had grown into such a beauty."

No one felt too sorry for Corinne. It's just that in Haiti no one feels pity for the dead, but rather for those who remain alive. Had the doctor killed her? The mute had had to call him, no wonder the mute had given Apollinaire an evil look. The mute suspected something.

At noon he left the store dragging his feet. He didn't feel like returning home, but he felt the need to tell his mother, since he couldn't tell Papa Lhomond, everything he had heard. They had called the doctor, the thought hammered in his head, a doctor that surely had felt Corinne's soft gut; one of these quacks who had perhaps ruined the work with his scalpels and potions. When he got home, his mother was waiting for him, still dressed in her mourning clothes: a gray shift with a high collar, laced black shoes, and brown stockings bunched at the ankles. Attached to her kinky hair, she wore an old-fashioned straw hat.

"I come from your future wife's wake," she announced in an edgy tone.

"The doctor went to see her," Apollinaire broke down.

"Papa Lhomond already told me," she said. "But don't worry, I don't think he did any harm."

Eloïse Sanglier went to the stove and returned a few minutes later with a steaming earthen bowl which she handed to her son. He started to sip the fish soup and she began to tell him what she had seen at the wake. No one in the neighborhood liked Corinne's mother very much. But in a critical moment like this, those trifles were overlooked. Not only had many neighbors stopped by to keep her company, but One-Arm-Tancréde, her boss in whoredom, appeared with two bottles of spirits to serve with the coffee.

"Your stepfather, Faustine Dondon, came by to express his sympathy. You should have seen how he embraced her . . . I'm sure that one good day he'll go around to the Salon Francais to finish comforting her."

Apollinaire smiled. He smiled for the first time in many days. It was true that Corinne's mother still had good solid flesh to paw. Warm and hard flesh made of the darkest molasses which drove the sailors from the islands mad. He knew because he had tasted it. At One-Arm-Tacréde's, for two miserly gourdes.

"In any case," Eloïse sighed fanning her bosom, "they'll bury her this afternoon, between five and six."

When he returned to work, Apollinaire found the Mariani brothers hammering a sheet of metal over the doors of the shop.

"There are many *macoutes*3 around. Things are going to get the color of stinging ants."

Apollinaire breathed a sigh of relief. He wouldn't have to listen to any more comments about Corinne's death. He helped his bosses seal all the doors and while he did so he saw a group of strangers armed with machetes go by.

"They are not strangers," Antoine Mariani whispered. "They're *macoutes*, crawling out of who knows where like cockroaches."

The people that normally roamed through Gonaïves on Saturday afternoons seemed to have vanished. Except for those men, the streets were emptying, and when Apollinaire started walking in the direction of the harbor, he felt again that tug of wind, as if the November breeze, held stagnant and putrid somewhere, had finally staggered down, freeing itself at last from the fiery gales that had confined it.

"You're not working today?"

It was the voice of his stepfather, Faustine Dondon, and at the very instant he turned to look at him, the distant sound of gunshots reached his ears.

"The Marianis closed up. It seems they're already shooting."

"Plenty of shooting," the old man told him. "People working at polling stations got beaten up."

"But the mute must have been spared," muttered Apollinaire, thinking that at that hour Dessalines Corail would not be distributing leaflets or pasting campaign posters. He would be with the deceased, bestowing his last kisses on her, attempting his last words in that damned hand language to which she would no longer reply.

"Have you seen Papa Lhomond?" he asked his stepfather.

"He'll be doing his job," the other replied drily.

They returned to the house together and Apollinaire, following his mother's advice, laid down to sleep.

"Remember that you will spend the night traveling. Even if you make good time, you will not reach La Cahouane until tomorrow afternoon."

He agreed it would be best. If he managed to sleep he wouldn't have to feel distressed later, between five and six, knowing that Corinne was being imprisoned under the first blows of that detested earth. Neither would he see his stepfather, Faustine Dondon, leave accompanied by the *houngan* from the isle of Gonaïves, together on their mission to conclude the most ferocious part of the work. When he woke up everything would be ready: his girl freshly bathed, domesticated and hidden in some spot in the forest, and the man from Gros-Morne waiting with his lights turned off and the engine running to take them to Port-au-Prince.

"You have to get up, Apollinaire. You have to come see."

He rubbed his eyes and felt his back being shaken again.

"Wake up, my son."

He calculated that he had slept but a short while, but he noticed, as he sat up, that it was night-time.

"Papa Lhomond and your godfather want to speak to you."

Eloïse Sanglier's disjointed face filled him with apprehension. He recalled immediately that he had dreamt of the coffin. The Mariani brothers were hammering a sheet of metal over the wooden lid while he begged them not to do it. At that very instant a group of crazed men appeared, naked except for the leather relic bags they carried, brandishing their rusty machetes in the air. Apollinaire recognized at once the rag warriors he had seen guarding the altars in the *hounfort* on the isle; warriors in love with their virgins; venomous warriors reddened with fury, like the assholes of certain spiders.

"Did they bring her already?"

"I told you to get up," Eloïse Sanglier insisted energetically.

His stepfather, Faustine Dondon, and the *houngan* were leaning listlessly on the stools. They were both sweating and panting as if they had just finished a long race. Apollinaire squared himself before Papa Lhomond.

"Was she dead?"

The *houngan* lifted his eyes as if surprised to see him. Then he lifted his hand to his chest.

"I don't know. We weren't able to reach the cemetery."

"We almost got killed," stammered Faustine Dondon, and he spat against the wall.

"Who wouldn't let you near?"

"There's plenty of shooting outside," Papa Lhomond said. "There are *macoutes* everywhere."

"But you're a *houngan*. Tell them you're going to the cemetery."

"They won't listen to anyone," Faustine Dondon cried out. "The streets are filled with corpses. I had never seen so many corpses together."

Apollinaire clenched his fists.

"Corinne can die."

The others did not reply and diverted their eyes. Faustine Dondon stared stubbornly at the floor and the *houngan* lifted one hand and called Eloïse.

"Why don't you warm a bit of coffee for us?"

Apollinaire recalled the noises in his dream, the hammering of the Marianis against the background of the panting noises of a thousand warriors. Then he let out a huge sigh and buttoned his shirt.

"I'm going to the cemetery."

"You won't get there," his stepfather said.

"And even if you get there," Papa Lhomond chimed in, "what will you do there alone?"

He seemed to hesitate.

"I will look for her. Come with me."

"Impossible," the *houngan* said. "There's too much shooting."

"Let him go out," Eloïse Sanglier intervened. "I want to see him go out."

Apollinaire couldn't quite understand whether his mother was challenging him. He went out onto the street and when the door closed behind him, he realized that the evening was cool and that the usual November breezes danced with their accustomed lightness amidst the trees. The streets of the city looked like the streets of a ghost town. No dogs could be seen, none of the beggars that usually sheltered under the eaves, none of the rats habitually zigzagging across from one sewer to the other. From time to time detonations and screams could be heard coming from a spot near the harbor, but he felt no fear. Instead he felt anguish. The anguish of having to traverse half the city knowing that at that hour no one could indicate to him where Corinne's grave was.

He stopped in front of the Mariani's shop and tried to get oriented from the smells in the air. Smoke from burning tires floated above the square, and counting on that being the shortest route to the cemetery, he decided to make his way across through the bonfires. Behind the church, next to the garbage cans of the cabinet-maker's shop, he sighted the first corpses. Their faces were covered with sawdust and the spilled shavings had stuck to their shoes. Apollinaire slowed down. He noticed the half-severed necks and arms and concluded they had been killed by machete blows. He started to run and felt that his mouth, his own mouth already tasted of blood; he spat without stopping and his spit stuck to his arm and trickled down leaving a trace of water, like the trail of Gonaïves-Isle snails. When he turned the corner, without having the time to avoid it, he found himself facing a mob that was suddenly upon him, dragging him along little by little. Some men where sobbing loudly, their faces covered with blood and their clothes torn, and in the midst of the exasperated torrent, he seemed to catch a glimpse of the face of Dessalines Corail. It was only for an instant and he lost him immediately in the roar of the stampede and the dense clouds of smoke.

"Dessalines! Dessalines Corail!"

A woman stopped next to him and without uttering a word pushed him towards a hiding place where three other men, squatting and numb, awaited them. It was evident that she had mistaken him for someone else, and when she was able to see Apollinaire's face all she could manage was to burst into tears and squat with the others, her hands on her temples, her gaze truncated.

"Dessalines! Dessalines Corail!"

He dove again into the crowd and traversed the street scrutinizing each face, avoiding the flying stones, flaying himself alive against the walls.

"Dessalines!"

The mute looked at him without seeing him.

"Dessalines, accompany me to the cemetery."

The other one tried to move on. He himself looked like one of those who had been brought back from the dead: very rigid arms, a fixed stare, the convulsive grin of the mouth, the bitter grin of all the creatures that like to eat vermin.

"You know where she is buried. You have to come with me."

He grabbed him by the arm, making an effort to drag him away, but the multitude didn't help. Then he noticed that his hands were drenched in a hot tar. He let go of Dessalines Corail; the mute was soaked in blood. The wound, an enormous slanting gash, seemed to run across his chest into his gut. Apollinaire remained paralyzed, watching that shadow wobble and finally disappear into the horrifying wave.

"Dessalines!"

He knew it was hopeless. The mute could not hear him and, contrary to Corinne, he would never be able to speak that lively language of the hands. He continued sneaking through like a shadow, he crossed the line of men firing and saw the others, the strangers armed with machetes butchering already exhausted bodies, remote and sweet like burst fruit. No one seemed aware of his presence, no one seemed to look at him, or maybe he really wasn't there. He wasn't in the city, he wasn't amidst the shooting and the fires. He, Apollinaire Sanglier, no longer existed, except in the tormented dreams of that woman who awaited him with bated breath and with her precious minutes counted.

"I am looking for a corpse."

The man dozing inside the wooden porter's lodge opened his eyelids slightly and looked at him indifferently.

"The body of Corinne, a girl they buried today. Do you know where her grave is?"

"Go away. This isn't the time."

Apollinaire made a gesture to keep going, but the man, behind him, called him with an energetic voice and showed him his gun.

"You're leaving right now."

Apollinaire looked at him with crazed eyes. Then he retraced his steps.

"There's a woman alive beneath the earth, under here."

"Such is life," the other one replied sarcastically. "See how many dead ones we have on the street and all of them have remained above ground."

He gestured with the weapon again, urging him to beat it.

"Go home, that is, if you don't get shot before you get there."

Apollinaire left, deranged, crying with his mouth open. He walked for a long time along the gray fence of the cemetery, smelling a putrid air that reminded him, suddenly, of the sad bitterness of the chewed-up snail shells. He returned to his house near dawn, avoiding the soldiers piling up bodies on tarpaulin-covered trucks. His mother was bustling around in the kitchen and Faustine Dondon, sitting at the table, was cleaning his nails with the tip of a knife.

"Where is Papa Lhomond?"

"Resting," Eloïse Sanglier replied calmly.

"They wouldn't let me enter the cemetery."

His mother didn't bat an eyelash. She placed the large jar of coffee on the table and wrenched the knife from Faustine Dondon's hand to cut a piece of cassava. She then looked at her son from head to toe.

"Papa Lhomond and your stepfather will return there tonight."

Only then did Apollinaire remember that his clothes were stained with blood and that the cuts and scratches were stinging his face brutally.

"You think that they will get there in time?"

Faustine Dondon and Eloïse Sanglier exchanged long sagacious glances. Finally, they smiled.

"Can you find a *cul-rouge* spider?" his stepfather asked.

"Of course I can," retorted Apollinaire.

"Then go find it. She'll come out hungry."

Translated by Lizabeth Paravisini-Gebert

[1]Priest in the cult of voudoùn in Haiti.

[2]Ritual altar and place of worship.

[3]Haitian para-military police force created by the Duvaliers.

Under the Weeping Willow

❖

Senel Paz

I wake up at dawn and I like it. I hear the bellowing of the cows in the barn and the voices of Grandfather and my uncles shouting at them. None is as stubborn as Caramelo, a red cow who knows she's the prettiest of the herd. In late afternoon, the moment I draw near the fence to look at them, she comes down the hill with the flowering pine-nut trees very slowly, so that I can watch her, and I do watch her, and I see how the early evening light is framed by the arch formed by her horns, and we talk. Grandfather gets up at three in the morning when the alarms go off. He wakes my uncles who have returned home late from seeing their girlfriends, and the three go off to tend the cows. I don't hear the clocks the first time, or the second time, at four thirty. Then it's Grandmother who gets up, makes coffee and sits down to wait for Grandfather to arrive with the first pail of milk, to boil it and send breakfast back to the barn. It's the bustling about that awakens me, the crackling of the burning wood on the stove, the clinking of a glass, the whispering between them. Or maybe it's the light from the oil lamp and the stove that reaches the dining room from the kitchen, makes a turn at my bedroom, and enters through the half-opened door. At that hour I'm alone in the room, and I like to look at that tiny red glare and listen to all there is to hear: the cows, the voices, the mice, now and then a horse, and I feel a little chill at my mother's being far, so very far away from this house. I'm carried away by my thoughts, and I'm as handsome as Uncle Armando on my horse, or I'm the boyfriend of Isabel, Uncle Alberto's girlfriend, or I come from the Canary Islands and meet Grandmother after having sold a tobacco plantation, wearing my new linen *guayabera* shirt, and we marry. Then I think of finding a lot of money and giving it to Mama, and I build her a house, and we all live there together. Because there are four of us: my other grandmother, Mama, my sister Gloria and I. My other grandmother works in Gavilanes picking coffee. I like it that she works there because she always brings us cheese and guava jelly and a new batch of stories, but she says they have crags and hills that can swallow up anyone who falls into them. I don't want her ever to get swallowed up, not just because of the little bags of caramels, sweet cakes, and sugar drops, but because when she visits me she sits in the dining room with the other grandmother and they start to talk about all the people they know. I look at both of them and try to decide which of the two is prettier or which one I love the best. If that grandmother has brought me plenty of sugar drops and sweet cakes then I think that she has won, but if I've been with this one lately to hunt for hen nests, or if she's taken me to the pond near the rose-apple trees to swim, then I believe she has won. Mama comes to see me less often than Grandmother does. She works in town and buys my clothes and shoes, and my sister lives with her godmother. Sometimes I go to the godmother's house and my sister stays here, or the two of us stay at Clotilde's, one of Mama's cousins, or at Don Gervasio's, who is some sort of relative to us. Sometimes they leave me with Mundito Gutiérrez, Grandfather's old friend, but not my sister because she's big already and so is Mundito's grandson, and he may have turned out fresh like his father was, may he rest in peace. Grandfather says that Gloria and I can't both be here at the same time, even though it's what we prefer, because we're too much trouble for Grandmother. We're sickly and two mouths to feed to boot, but first one and then the other is OK. Another thing he says is that Mama can come and go as she pleases, day or night, and when she arrives she's to be waited on and given the best there is because Mama wasn't the bad one, the bad one was my father, and my sister and I aren't to blame either. My three unmarried aunts are the ones who don't want Mama to come to the house, and they put brooms and salt behind the door, and hide in their rooms with puckered faces until she leaves, and what they dislike about us is that we wet the beds like little rascals, because how many times have they told us. The only place we can pee without getting scolded is at cousin Clotilde's, because over there we sleep together with the other little cousins all in one bed, and in the morning no one knows whose bladder took the leak. But it so happens that at cousin Clotilde's my sister and I are never the ones that pee, damned our little wee-wees. I don't know if Grandmother likes Mama to come, because she greets her in the living room and offers her coffee, and tells her how quiet and obedient we both are, you wouldn't even know there were children in the house, and if it weren't for the food we could both be here together. But in the end, all that's really needed for us to be here or for Mama to visit us is for Grandfather to say so, because no one would dare go against Grandfather's wishes. Not even Caramelo the cow.

But that's not what I was going to talk about, and it's not why I've been standing under this weeping willow since dawn, dressed in my best pants and shirt, with my hair still combed and my eyes still glued to the road. Early this morning I was talking with Grandmother in the kitchen, waiting for the fog to lift before going to the barn to watch them finish milking the cows, when Grandfather came in and asked me: "Do you know what day today is?" I didn't know and glanced at Grandmother for help. "Today is Christmas Eve and we are going to roast a pig," he said. "But the important thing is that today your father is coming to meet you. Have yourself combed and dressed early, and don't get dirty so he'll find you presentable." He stood there looking at me, and I looked at him, and then at Grandmother. "Let's go back to bed again for a while," she said when Grandfather had left, and carried me off to her room. But I didn't sleep. The first thing I decided was not to eat tangerines or guavas so that I'd be hungry and eat a lot in front of my father at the table. And as soon as my aunts heard that Papa was coming today they got very happy, and said they were going to clean and scrub the house, and polish the furniture, and then they combed and dressed me. I came out here to the patio with my hat to choose the spot where I'd wait for Papa. "Hey! Where is that one going so dolled up? He must think he's Mundito Gutiérrez!" the chickens said the moment they saw me, but I paid them no attention and told the ten o'clock carnations to open today at nine, and the night jasmine to release its bouquet by day, and the butterflies to keep watch and flutter around when Papa appeared, and each one of the cats to catch a mouse and greet him with it in their mouths so that he'd see what good hunters they are. I planted myself in the center of the rosebushes, thinking I'd stay there and act like I didn't notice Papa arriving, so that he'd ask: "And that man who's watching over the plants, who is he?" "He," Grandmother answers, "he is your son." But then it got too hot so I switched to the shade of the guasima tree in the patio and grabbed an axe to start cutting firewood so that then Papa would say: "And that gentleman who's working so hard, who is he?" "Ah," Grandmother says, "he is your son!" But then I decided I'd better not, because there's an awful termite colony in the trunk of that tree, so I came to this weeping willow and here I am, waiting, standing like a cowboy. "Who is that man, so serious and respectful standing over there?" Papa will ask. "That is your son!," Grandmother replies. "You don't say. So big and good-looking! Run over here, son, I want to say hello and give you your presents. How are your sister and your mother? Give them my greetings." And when I get nearer he'll say: "He's just like me. Now I'll raise him myself. I'll take him with me to Camaguey and put him in school." Papa will appear on the road mounted on his white horse with his saddlebags bulging with toys. As he's crossing the brook he'll stand on his stirrups and cry out: "Tell my son to come and meet me!," and I'll run as fast as I can, with my hat in my hand, and he'll lift me up to his saddle and the white horse will whinny so hard his coat will tremble the nice way horses do, moving his mane and his tail and opening his eyes wide with joy. My father is my father and I want to meet him. That's why I'm still underneath this weeping willow standing like a cowboy. He is the young man in the living room photograph, mounted on a horse, in his younger days. Grandmother says he's had more girlfriends than Uncles Armando and Alberto put together, and not just because he's the oldest, according to her, but because there wasn't a more handsome man in all the area, and no one who could improvise a better poem. My sister saw him once and told me that he's taller than Grandfather and stronger, but he has Grandfather's voice, Uncle Armando's laugh, Uncle Alberto's eyes and only got Grandmother's nose. Uncle Alberto is the one who is most like him in his walk, his eyebrows, and in his way of talking sort of out of one side of his mouth. They both like checkered shirts, black hats and standing like the cowboys that they are. I look like him too, everyone says so, they recognize me right away, and it's because we think alike, I have the same mole and the same way of walking, of sleeping, and all that without ever having seen him, only in that little picture in the living room, and it's because it's in my blood, the same blood as his. Grandmother says that when he was a boy he also was small and skinny something pitiful, but he wasn't so sickly and he worked harder than I do. At home I can't mention his name, and when Mama's relatives say that he's a scoundrel and that my mother's so good, and that when I grow up I must take good care of Mama, and if he needs me I must say no, that he should remember that he didn't concern himself with me when he should have, I say yes, that's what I'll do, but I feel sorry for my father with everyone speaking badly of him, when it was probably a potion that some woman gave him to drink. Sometimes I imagine that I'm my father, and I'm in the living room picture, on that same horse, and then I go into town and I bring Grandmother the groceries she likes so that she can save them in the old cupboard. Then I right away get married to Mama again. Other times I think that I'm sleeping with him and not with Uncle Alberto, and he covers me so that the mosquitos won't bite, and the best is when it's not Uncle Armando who's circling me around on the old mare but him, and we talk, and he asks about my sister, and I invite him to visit us.

But he's not here yet, and I went and ate a tangerine, and then another, without realizing it, and then a guava, without realizing it. I missed it when they stabbed the pig, and I didn't see how they jabbed it with the spit, or what a dead pig looks like inside. The aunts have got the house cleaned up and the last one is finishing her bath. Grandmother says yes, my father's coming, he'll be here any minute, and so I went to the palm groves and told the trees, who are my friends. Now they're also waiting for him to appear to greet him. The aunts cut fresh flowers for all the vases and Grandmother placed her white embroidered apron on a stool to put on as soon as he approaches. Every now and then she peeks out at the road and asks me if anything's happened yet. "That one will get here around twelve," she said. But twelve o'clock passed and I had to tell the ten o'clock carnations not to close at one, and the night jasmine to please continue releasing its perfume. Thank goodness there are some birds playing in the guasima tree. And I'm melting away because there's hardly any shade under this weeping willow. If my shirt gets dirty I don't have another. Mama will probably ask, "What did your father say, did he find you big, fat, cute, did he ask about us, about your sister, did he give you any money?" All I want is for him to finally get here.

"Joaquín is coming!," I hear my Aunt Rosa say suddenly from a corner of the porch. Letting go of the broom, she runs inside smoothing her dress.

"Joaquín is coming!," all the aunts repeat from the kitchen, and the uncles run off, leaving the roasting pig behind under the star-apple tree. Only Grandfather remains there, fixing his hat and his belt. The cats hunt their mice, Caramelo approaches the fence, the roof glistens, the butterflies stir about, the birds sing among the flowers, and all the chickens scurry to the front of the house as if corn were being scattered.

Joaquín is my father, and I spot him on his white horse, appearing and disappearing through the palm trees, over there on the main road. He'll reach the gate and take the narrow path. At that point we won't have to go out and meet him yet, until after the brook, when his horse gallops uphill to arrive slowly under the shadow of the leafy boughs. Then finally I'll see his face. Grandmother has come out of the kitchen with her white embroidered apron, wiping off the grease and soot from the stove. Then come the aunts, with flowers in their hair, everyone smiling, and later the uncles. I stay where I am under the weeping willow, with one foot on a rock and a hand on my waist as if I were my Uncle Alberto talking, and now everyone is coming through the garden. The ten o'clock carnations, the night jasmine, the gardenias, and the roses release their fragrances. Now my father is crossing the palm grove, he's almost as tall as the palm trees which have run to the border of the path to applaud him. The biajaca fish leap in the brook. The white horse is enormous and one can clearly see that Papa is smiling and my chest swells so the top button of my shirt pops off. Grandmother can't resist the temptation to run ahead. She reaches Papa in the center of the pasture. I hear their laughter, and he grabs out, pulling her up to the horse. Grandmother laughs and kisses him, and takes off his hat. I ought to go and cut firewood under the guasima tree but there's no time. The aunts await at the farmhouse door and my father's dog wanders around the patio, sniffing. Papa lowers Grandmother to the ground and with a jump dismounts and hugs his first sister, his second, without letting go of the first, the third, without letting go of the first, the second and Grandmother, and then it's the uncles' turn: hearty embraces and handclasps that I can hear way over here, and everyone is laughing and hugging. Will Papa like grapefruit preserves the way I do? They all approach the weeping willow. The second shirt button has popped off, and the little birds in the trees are chirping because they too want to see my father and his horse which is following the party, galloping proudly at being so white and pretty. They're here. I see my father who hasn't yet seen me. I see him from head to toe. From now on I'll always remember him like this, smiling, with such white teeth, spotless, standing under the weeping willow with the sun to his back. He's so tall! I'm afraid I'll be unable to say: "Your blessings, father, how are you? And your wife?" and I won't be able to answer now when he asks me about my sister and my family because . . . such a mustache, such a nice laugh, how everyone laughs so happily and I'm ashamed because I'm not laughing and they're coming. He's going to pass me by without seeing me. I'd better change positions but keep acting the cowboy like him. I know: I'll cough, say something. "Aunt Rosa, have you seen my jump rope?" Grandmother looks at me. It had to be her with all those flowers embroidered on her apron who would notice me. Now I know for sure, I love her more than the other grandmother. With her arm she brushes the tumultuous family to one side, opening a path than runs from Papa to me, and pointing me out says: "Look, Joaquín, this is your son." Why don't I have my good luck shell in my hand now? I start to run towards him, but his stare stops me, and I await the words he's about to say: "He's bug-eyed like his mother's family." He rejoins the circle of his family and they all follow to the house where Grandfather comes out with open arms. "I was beginning to think you'd never get here, Mister," he says. They embrace. They'll probably all go to see the roasted pig.

I'm going to eat some guava fruit and go hunting around for hen nests.

Translated by Margarite Fernández Olmos

Gnawing on a Rose

❖

Ángela Hernández

My eyes were still green. My mouth, instead of teeth, had little windows. People lamented when they saw me work. "So little, and stuck in the kitchen, one of these days she'll burn herself."

But I was happy in the complex alchemy of the cloves of garlic, the beans soaking in the pan, the fragrant blends of bitter orange and hot pepper, the transmutations that ensued from my play.

In my eyes, flayed by the smoke from the tender twigs burning on the fire, there was joy. The place had cracks and windows through which a fresh world, redolent of ripe pears and forests, filtered in. The present was contained in what my heart and gaze could encompass.

When I walked to the river, a tub of dirty laundry on my head, commiserating gazes traced my figure as it tottered along, framed by the fresh air in which it balanced itself cheerfully, as I felt my body capable of becoming the axis between heaven and earth, joining both through the guileless flow of my veins.

The day belonged to me. For hours I goaded lather, kindled the red-hot coals with the breath of my lungs, lived the intimacy of ashes and water. Washing clothes was a call to the water, to fire, to the nimbleness of the hands. Water, fire, hands . . . First the hands wrinkled and grew, then little strips would peel off and the nails would lose their borders.

If I was silent, everything around me dreamt. Hatching eggs, the

195

broken rhythm of well-muscled mares cradling in the sores of their rumps the unscrupulous eagerness of the insects. Animals in the prelude of heat. Dominion of birds and wetnesses. Things that fall or scatter themselves while others germinate in ceaseless movement.

From time to time, a sudden fright. An angel sliding down the rose-apple tree to my left. He is a deaf-mute, I know that, because he is oblivious to the leaps of my heart. He looks at the photograph in his hand and climbs back to the top of the tree.

I clap hands, splash in the water, whistle, but, as always, he ignores me. I have no fear left, I just want the angel to notice my presence.

I was the fourth sister and the eight child. I was, however, the oldest female still living at home, not counting my mother, that is. Girls leave first, I had learned. They don't need to join the army or find a job. They leave with a man, join a convent (nuns are always on the lookout for girls with a vocation for being locked up), or go to a relative's house to help with the housekeeping or to altogether take over the chores from the woman of the house. All we women need is a task before us to dispose of our energies.

Noraima, the eldest and best loved of the sisters, left with a man. My mother wailed, we ran from one end of the house to the other after she left, not understanding what there was of tragedy in this act of delirium; to leave in the early evening, with a glossy-haired youth, to an unknown place and an unfathomable fate, while the adult brothers scoured the hills, armed with machetes, supposedly ready to bloody their honor, since it was no longer possible to restore it.

Ah, Noraima, so beautiful, it was sheer bliss to look at her. In the mornings she would awaken with a small mirror in her hand and stand by the window, staring at her reflection without blinking. Then she would powder her face. Surprised still by the vehemence of her own eyes, she would go to the kitchen to stir the embers over which she would boil water for coffee. This she would make and then distribute around with chunks of bread or cassava. She disliked household chores, no wonder she left. She had to care for the younger siblings, counter the pressures put upon her by the older ones (who felt responsible for her protection, and not knowing how to fulfill this obligation, squeezed her like you do an orange, demanding cares and attentions to their clothes and food, all under the guise of teaching her how to be a woman) and then, to endure the difficulties posed by a beauty that sprouted too soon on her adolescent body.

The schoolteacher would never leave our house. On Sundays a fat and cheerful man would come from town bearing two boxes full of food which he handed to our mother, and sweet treats for us. He wanted to give Noraima a furnished house and couldn't understand why she refused the gift. Our mother could find no way to get him out of the house. She insisted that her daughter was not going to be a rich man's mistress, that a woman who sold her ass was worth less than a cat in heat.

Males swarmed around my sister. They pursued her with the fervor of lunatics; I am truly convinced that not one man in his right mind came near her. "They have screws loose in their noggins," my mother would say, deeply troubled by Noraima's hold on men seemingly searching in the deep and limpid peace of her eyes for the lucidity they lacked. The rich one, for example, laughed absurdly, even at wakes, or when he was eating or narrating some family misfortune. He spoke of his dead daughter with a nervous laugh. Of his business affairs with a stuttering laugh. Of his hopes relating Noraima with a lewd laugh. His raptures only made us somber in return.

No one would have wished the schoolteacher as a husband for a relative. More often than not the parents of his pupils, timid before his authority, felt obliged to protest against the bruises their children brought home on buttocks and extremities. Even I, Noraima's sister, once got a beating because I lost a pen he had lent me, precisely because I was Noraima's sister.

Noraima was the family's hope, and she left us just like that, with an enlisted man (if he at least had been an officer), jilting the suitor approved by all. Berto, his name was. His eyes were a beautiful blue, and dead. Dead eyes – looking at them was like looking on a blank page. My mother would place two chairs for them in the living room, making me sit nearby to keep an eye on them. Futile task. Berto wouldn't allow himself a suspicious glance, nor a slip of the hand, he didn't do one single thing I would have expected. Noraima didn't love him, and that's why she ran away with the cousin, the enlisted man.

Our mother sobbed. They hadn't even waited for the dead of night to elope. She hadn't even waited till she was fourteen. And poor Berto . . . (I could picture my sister running up the street – our one and only street – while I grieved because her lovers would no longer bring us treats.)

But something even better arrived from Noraima: a pair of white shoes for me and similar pairs for my other sisters. Three pairs of resplendent shoes, with straps and buckles at the ankles. I immediately wanted to throw away the faded slippers which had the gift of never wearing out (they were handed down from foot to foot, from sister to sister, their use a legacy that trickled down). But, oh terrible fate, the white shoes could not reconcile themselves to my feet, which were disproportionately large. I didn't succeed in making them fit, though I rubbed oil on my feet and coated my soles with soap lather. Stuffing the shoes tightly with rags for several days was to no avail. "They're good shoes, like we've never seen before, that's why they won't give," was sentenced to my dismay.

My mother sold them to the Marte family. And I saw my shoes in full display on the feet of a daughter my own age. They went very well with her dress of organza and the ribbons on her hair, they harmonized with her tidy garments. During Mass I would glance at her feet and it was like discovering something of mine which didn't suit me. I imagined that the butterfly that fluttered around my face as I washed the dishes would one good day feature on the girl's vaporous skirt.

Anything of value arriving in the neighborhood would eventually end up with the Marte family. Like a magnet that swipes away all surrounding metal, the clean poverty of the neighborhood clustered around the Martes' possessions. Even our lands were added to theirs when our father, gravely ill, undermined by the nearest doctor, who for two years mistook a stomach ulcer for a failure of the prostate, had to sell the farm at a low price to go to the capital to get well. The howling of the ambulance heralded his arrival a week later. He returned to the house in his death throes, with a long seam in his belly, his pockets empty, his soul worn-out by a pain that didn't prevent his acute consciousness of the orphanhood in which he was leaving us.

Taking advantage of a trip to town my mother bought me a pair of rubber moccasins, the profit from the sale of the shoes had not been sufficient for more. Black and ugly as they were, I fell in love with them. I paid no heed to words of admonition: "Try them on carefully. Make sure they're not too tight. If you get them dirty they won't exchange them at the store." I tried on the right shoe, and with the knowledge that if I rejected them I would have to wait until someone went to town again, something that could take considerable time, I exclaimed hurriedly: "They fit, they're very comfortable." My mother insisted: "That looks tight to me. You're going to have to wear them to school all year. It'd be better if they're a little big so you won't out-grow them right away." I insisted that they fitted perfectly. "Can't you see how well they fit?"

Then, horror-stricken, I realized the disparity in my feet. The left shoe bound my foot excruciatingly. But I couldn't go to my mother, who worked more hours than there were in the day to keep us alive, with tales of having one foot larger than the other. I bore my martyr-dom stoically.

My most vivid memory of my first communion was that of having to remain standing for hours. The exhausting narrowness in which my lower extremities were trapped destroyed my heels. Stiff bulges curdled in my groin. "Dry up," my mother commanded them, hum-ming incantations so they would not cripple me. I took this inflam-mation of the ganglions like a well-deserved penance for my multiple sins, mostly "bad thoughts" which, try as I may, I couldn't keep away. "Bad thought, don't come near me," I would command, and they would rush to me. Everything, like thinking of one's body, carried its risks. I made an effort never to look at my sex since the eyes would bring it to the mind: a sin. It was the same if I caught one of my brother's peeing. I would listen to the stream — bad thought — and then imagine the penis from which emanated the flow. How could one avoid bad thoughts? We all slept in the same room. How to van-ish from the thoughts certain parts of the body and what one does with them? The very effort to remove them from one's thoughts made one think of them. The thoughts were like an elastic band. You stretched them as far as they could go and when you let go they struck your hand. The unavoidability of sin: we are all sinners, we must confess before taking communion. A simple matter of being cleansed before one was stained again. In the midst of the infinitude of human beings only one had been free of sin, the Virgin Mary. I myself always committed the same sins: I had bad thoughts, I was disrespectful to my elders, I was arrogant. The well-known repertory of faults. But, like all mortals, I lived in fault, always on the verge of disobeying some ancestral code so remote that it was rendered unimaginable in its initial purity.

I surely felt more corrupt than Nero. The penance of the moccasins was a test of my desire for purity. Besides, it was a well-deserved penance, since even when making the greatest effort I couldn't keep myself awake during the Rosary. The monotony of the Holy Marys stupefied my eyes. My lips continued to respond long after I had fallen asleep.

Angels went around barefoot. I confirmed this with the deaf-mute angel at the river. But he paid me no mind, even when I stood right under the soles of his feet. To walk with liberated feet must be the reward for purity. They never touched the ground, that's why they could go around with naked feet. We, on the other hand, got chiggers, parasite larvae, red ringworm (so conspicuously alive it could devour your belly) encrusted in ours. Angels did not catch parasites. That's the reason they fascinated me.

If it was an easy thing to endure through mystic fervor the horrors of my imprisoned feet, it was not as easy in school. Very early in the morning I would soak the moccasins in warm soapy water. At two o'clock in the afternoon I would put them on and run as fast as I could to school. There I would take them off immediately, hiding them behind the wall on which the blackboard rested. To go barefoot during recess, to step on the cool floor of the classroom, were delicious circumstances which ended abruptly when school was out. My feet, expanded in their freedom, had to return to the shoes.

Armed with courage, after six months of dark mortification and with sores on the tips of my toes and the contours of my feet, I gravely requested from my mother that she cut their backs so as to turn them into slippers. I argued the growth of my feet and the heat, they would sweat so profusely that several times I was on the verge of fainting.

What decided me was a visit to the school by the Regional Education Director, during which I could not free myself from the shoes. The teacher, to make matters worse, ordered me to recite the poem to the fathers of the nation. My brother Paul had taught it to me, and I had modified it with the introduction of musical supplications.

My paleness and sweat must have made an impression on our guest. He asked the teacher to allow me to sit down, but the latter wanted to boast of his accomplishments and insisted: "This girl is very bright. You will see what a memory she has. Come, Cristina, recite the poem." I felt faint. I was most grateful for the gentleman's generosity in the face of my lividness. "Let her sit down. She will recite some other day. Maybe she hasn't eaten today." (If my mother had heard this she would have considered it an insult.)

Later I learned that not only the angels went around barefoot, but also the dead. Then I lost my fear of being buried one day. "This girl has a cold heart," they commented when they brought us the body of my oldest brother. The circumstances of my brother's death made people cry. It angered them that he had been precisely the only soldier killed by the guerrillas just before the soldiers killed all of the rebels. They sympathized with the dead, my brother as well as the guerrillas. Grown-up women had fits and fell to the floor. My mother was bathed in tears, recalling out loud details of her son's upbringing, from her pregnancy till he joined the army. From that moment on he had never failed to send ten pesos a month, thanks to which we had credit at the Martes' grocery store.

I had adored my brother. I remembered particularly the day he picked me up from the floor to explain to me why the image of Jesus Christ had its heart outside his chest. Nonetheless, I couldn't cry in sorrow like the others, because my brother had finally taken off his heavy boots and was barefoot like the angels. Some day I would see him go up and down the rose-apple tree, looking at my picture in the palm of his hand. He would pay me no heed, but he would be there just the same, and he would have to fight no more.

Translated by Lizabeth Paravisini-Gebert

Silvia

Verónica López Kónina

An empty bus halts a short distance from the bus-stop. Silvia looks around her, uneasily, at the people waiting. Fear ties a knot in her throat and then, like a shudder, the warning: *It's Bow-Legs!*

Slowly, the bus approaches. A pair of eyes scrutinizes the crowd. Behind the windshield, a hard face, there's no doubt about it, the same blond, bristly hair . . . *Where can I hide?* — she ponders in despair —. Can I run? but what if he catches me . . .

The man sees her. He stops the bus and summons her with a gesture.

"Listen, it's you I'm talking to . . ."

The girl doesn't respond. She leans against the wall. Her features freeze. *I'm not aware of his presence,* — she tells herself. She empties herself of fear. She dismisses a spot on her checked blouse, which she scrutinizes meticulously. She steadies her fingers. She clicks her heels instinctively and feels somewhat secure. *If only the bus were to come now . . .*— it is almost a plea. She scans the wet cardboard, the mud, the cigarette butts. *Calm down, calm down.*

The man watches her from behind the windshield, staring fixedly, insistently. *He thinks that after what happened I am going to give him the time of day!* Silvia reddens.

The queue grows restless: the man is blowing his horn, high-pitched, intense, breathless . . . The face is no longer a plea. The jaws grow tense.

Silvia again concentrates on the dirty cement of the pavement. She's afraid. *But here, in front of everyone, he wouldn't dare.*

The horn prolongs its alarming note. People watch Silvia, some with curiosity, others evidently annoyed. "What a place to come deal with her problems!"— some of the faces seem to say. *It has nothing to do with me,* Silvia thinks without lifting her eyes. *If only I could make myself invisible.*

The man suddenly revs the bus' engine. A couple of sharp turns and the bus, no sign to announce its route, disappears.

That evening she had gone out with people from Santa Fe. Since the group had split up she had been adrift, now with some, now with others, sometimes not having any parties to go to, sometimes as an impromptu partner to go to some club. That day the party had also been a bust, and "Fly," who had arranged to meet her, had not shown up. So that morning's rap ended up being a lot of bullshit, despite the kisses at the Casino, under the awnings, and the heavy-petting in the water. Nor did she want to be with Eddie, a dark-skinned cutie from El Vedado, a bit of a bourgeois, and boring.

That's why she decided to wait for the number 30 bus, maybe she would find a party at Buena Vista. *A disco-party for sure, or maybe a sweet-fifteen with salsa and Roberto Carlos, who is so mellow. Maybe I'll subject myself to a Saturday movie. There have been a few good ones lately, mysteries or ninja movies. As long as they have something new. I could stay at home. That is, if my brothers leave me alone and mummy doesn't show up with one of those guys who drop by with a bottle of rum and a slobbering smile.*

No doubt there'll be a guy. So better not try it. A party it is, then, that or finding someone so I don't have to return home until very late, when everyone is asleep.

The bus stop was deserted. A number 30 had shown Silvia its blackened rear, drowning her in exhaust fumes. The little houses nearby remained in silence. *It must be a bitch to live near a bus stop.*

I don't like being alone. Silvia looked behind her. *When I was in the group, everyone stood up for me. No one dared mess with me, or with Lis.*

Whatever became of the Russian? she remembered suddenly. *I haven't seen him again. One day I went by his house – quite a mystery.*

No one wanted to explain anything . . . Could he be in jail?

A bus stops. Silvia lifts her eyes: fingers on the steering wheel, blond hair, muscled torso, no shirt. *A strong guy, and quite young . . .*

The vehicle doesn't have a sign indicating its route. *A mechanic . . .* it occurs to Silvia. *The garage is around the corner. He's not old . . .*

The man signals to her. Silvia smiles, but lowers her eyes. The silence of the night stops at the dark aisle of the bus. *That man there, calling me. It is as if this had happened to me before.* She feigns nonchalance, watching the park nearby and the entrance to the so-called motel. The laughter rises, restlessly, she cannot contain it in time and bares her teeth. The man gains confidence.

"Come here, girl. Don't be afraid."

This guy could call attention to himself. Silvia tousles her hair and grazes her lips with her tongue. *Better ask him what he wants.*

"Where are you going?" It is the man who initiates the dialogue.

"To the Cosmos cinema."

"I'll take you."

Silvia glances at him for an instant, her hand resting on the front door and a foot on the bottom step.

"You don't have a shirt on . . ."

"It won't take long."

The girl hesitates. "It's late." She watches the man: wide pants, i.d. bracelet, rough leather gloves to grab the wheel, well-muscled chest, fine form. *He'll think I'm afraid,* it occurs to her. *What could happen to me? It won't be the first time I catch a lift . . .*

Silvia sighed with relief. She had left behind the vacuous Saturday festivities, the strident music, the bars full of drunks and recruits. In the middle of the night, putting up with flirtations and whispered propositions, and she not able to reply; alone as usual.

The empty bus stop, not a single soul in sight, a lightbulb caged within iron bars. *What damned luck to be always missing the bus,* she thought. A new uneasiness floods over her. *My God, Bow-Legs! If he catches me here, alone, he's capable of anything . . . Where can I hide?* Silvia scans the surroundings. *The important thing is to move away from the light.* She turns her steps towards the park nearby and sits on a bench, sheltered under the shadow of a tree.

A man approaches the bus stop. He traverses the darkness and stops. He is not very tall. A prominent belly and a satisfied expression. *Middle-aged,* Silvia decides. She returns to the bus stop and places herself against the wall, under the fat man's gaze. *Good idea,* she comforts herself, *to strike up a conversation.*

Can you spare a cigarette? – the usual pretext. The man looks in the pockets of his *guayabera.*

This is better, she thanks him with a gesture. *When he arrives, he won't dare . . .*

The fat man remarks on the evening's heat and recalls the delights of a moonlit bath. *Not a likely candidate for that.* Silvia lifts the corners of her mouth and nods affirmatively.

"Yes, of course."

From the corner of her eye she watches the street. A bus goes by, all its windows rattling. Silvia's smile freezes. A tremor makes her shrink inside: *He must be near . . .*

She sees it appear, around the corner, its headlights turned off. It doesn't have a sign indicating a route. A pair of eyes suck her away from the bus stop, but grow dim at the sight of the fat man's presence. The bus advances slowly, disappears into the park and returns from the opposite direction.

Silvia reddens. *Son of a bitch!* but she doesn't raise her eyes. With eyes lowered, she whispers to the fat guy:

"Look, that guy . . . he's been pestering me . . ."

The man listens to her, incredulously:

"And you don't know him?"

"No. I've never laid eyes on him . . . He must be crazy. It's not the first time he's followed me . . ."

A glint of fear appears in the fat guy's eyes; he shrinks and, his self-assured expression gone, begins to distance himself from Silvia.

Bow-Legs then gains confidence. He begins his monologue of gestures, more insistent by the minute, which give way to the horn and the hatred of his fingers on the wheel.

Silvia leans against the wall and crosses her legs.

How does he manage to find me every night?

The bus makes a strange detour, between small houses and flamboyant trees.

"Hey, this isn't the way . . ."

"This way we can't be seen from the bus stop . . ."

The dormitories of the Art School remain behind, and the narrow street, overhung by enormous branches, is a lampless refuge.

Several buildings, half-finished, surrounded by the illusory darkness, look like cardboard decorations yawning widely through the empty window.

"What are we waiting for?"

"Nothing."

The man abandons his seat and stands before Silvia. His legs are deformed, U-shaped. He comes near. The pants are tight, a noticeable detail. The muscles on his chest. He smells of cigarettes and his teeth are stained. He doesn't ask her name. The arms are hairy, the man lifts her and places her on his knees. Silvia feels his breathing, hot, near her ear. A hand. He has removed his gloves, pulls her by the shoulders. An unknown taste. The man searches her tongue. Hard teeth. Their salivas mingle.

The man lowers the straps of her blouse.

"You're pretty . . ."

His tongue is thin and scratchy, like a cat's. Silvia feels like crying.

"Come." Bow-Legs takes her by the hand and guides her to the rear of the bus. He sits her down and kneels at her feet. Holding each ankle, he unstraps her sandals and takes them off. He caresses her thighs through the thick cloth of her pants. Then he frees her shoulders and nibbles, softly, unhurriedly. He traces her nipples. His tongue is warm, so is his body. Silvia touches his hair, rough as bristles.

"Help me . . ."

The man gets tangled with the zipper of his jeans. He finally manages to open it and frees her from the remaining pieces of clothing, which he places on the seat in front. Once naked, he lays her down. Silvia feels cold. "What if someone sees us through the window?"

The man spreads her thighs.

"You're going to like it like this . . ."

It's a pity I can't think. I have to concentrate. The girls' head knocks against the glass. Her hands grab on to the blond hair.

"Move!" the man grabs her by the hips and pushes her. "Like that, mamma, that's good . . ."

A few more jolts and Bow-Legs arches up one last time and falls, completely crushing her under his weight. The beating inside the hard thorax slows down. The man gets up and closes his fly with a sporting gesture.

"Did you like it?"
Silvia grimaces with uncertainty.
"More or less."
The man stops at the button of his pants. His face darkens.
"You didn't like it?"
"Don't get like that . . . It's just that I'm with someone else . . ."
"So you didn't like it?"
Oh why did I tell him that?
"Yes, I liked it," she assures him. "I said that just to be a pain . . .
But take me home, ok?"
The bus takes her back to the stop, however. Silvia looks at the
man in surprise.
"Wait for me here." Bow-Legs opens the front door of the vehicle.
"I have to talk to my boss. I'll be right back."
The people at the stop watch Silvia with curiosity; she can't decide
whether she should go to the end of the line. She's displeased, with
herself and with the man.
The bus comes back after a short while, dark and empty, its driver
again without a shirt. *Isn't he planning to put it on?* Silvia senses some-
thing strange.
"Get in, quickly."
The girl stands by the front door and notices the route the bus has
taken.
"I told you I wanted to go home . . ."
"Calm down."
"I'm not kidding."
The dormitories of the School of Art, the same place under the
trees, the darkness. Dark holes in an opera buffa. Silvia bangs on the
door with both fists, trying to separate its two halves.
"Open it! I'm walking!"
The man rises from his seat. Silvia runs down the aisle, . . . *throw
myself out the window . . . there's no time . . .* towards the other door . . .
yes, it's open . . . but Bow-Legs grabs her by the hair and pulls her
roughly. He grabs her forcefully. He's as tall as she is.
"Be still! I'm not going to hurt you."
"I don't want to! Let go of me, damn it!"
His arms are like iron, they squeeze her and throw her down on
the floor.
"Asshole!"

Silvia hits his back, but only manages to enrage him. The man pulls her blouse down with one jerk and furiously bites the soft neck, the shoulders, the nipples, the lips that he sucks, trying to push his tongue through the clenched teeth. A strong hand grips both of the girl's arms, the other manages to open the zipper.

Silvia pulls in her legs and grazes his testicles with her knee.

"Oh, yeah?"

The man grabs her by the hair and slams her against the floor, her nape against the floor, the girl's head slackens.

"Will you be still . . . "

He scratches her hips as he pulls down her pants and panties together.

"Like that, very very still. You didn't want it the nice way . . ."

I can still feel him opening my legs. Son of a bitch! And there he is, I don't know what he's waiting for, waiting for me to be alone to do the same thing to me again . . .

The man looks at her through the windshield. Silvia feels the fixed stare on her. He's been there for so long that people are beginning to notice. Enough time has gone by for Silvia to think of her bad luck, of the number 30 bus, delayed on purpose, and of the advancing darkness which holds greater perils in store.

"Don't cry," he orders, "don't cry."

Silvia squirms in disgust.

"Let me go!"

The man forces her knees open. Tears of powerlessness spring from Silvia's eyes.

"I haven't done anything to you . . . Please . . . Let me go . . ."

She implores, begs, but the man, inevitably, bends over her and almost manages to penetrate her. The girl's tears wet his chest.

Silvia starts to scream, to shout with all her strength:

"Let go of me, damn it!" She tosses her head back and screams.

"Let go of me!"

The scream arches over the night, expanding throughout several blocks.

"Enough. Shut up already."

The man gets up.

"Don't shout anymore, idiot."

He speaks in a low voice. He's afraid. They could have heard her in the dormitories, or at the military station.

Silvia gets up. Her hands are shaking, her knees give way. She pulls her pants up and tries to arrange her blouse, but Bow-Legs pushes her toward the door.

"Go, go."

One last push makes her fall out of the bus which suddenly takes off. Silvia enters the ghostly building. She hugs the wall, whose cold surface calms her hiccoughs a bit. The tears mix with the snot which she spreads all over her face.

The noise of an engine forces her to squat. *Let it not be him coming back.* Not daring even to breathe, she flattens herself against the earthen floor.

Silvia climbs on the number 30 with relief. She looks for a coin in her pant pocket, her nerves tense . . . *no, it's not here* . . . she puts her fingers in the other pocket . . . *there* . . . she deposits it in the slot and notices a bus keeping up with hers, parallelling her eyes.

It's him. Bow-Legs' bus is right next to hers.

"Girl, it's you he wants . . ." the driver holds her back, and examines her face with concern.

"Are you all right?"

Silvia's pupil's darken. It's Bow-Legs. She lifts her eyes. Bow-Legs responds with an aggressive gesture. The girl holds on to the pole and closes her eyes.

She moves down the aisle, slowly, and feels the man, him, moving in reverse, moving in reverse, Silvia advancing down the aisle and Bow-Legs driving in reverse, the fixed stare and the i.d. bracelet, the tight pants and the strong torso.

The number 30 takes off and Silvia senses, through the rear window, a pair of hard eyes, the bristled hair and that bus, empty . . .

Translated by Lizabeth Paravisini-Gebert

How Do You Know, Vivian?

❖

Luis Manuel García

A kite has just plunged into the lenses of the Optyl sunglasses (made in Germany, US$23.50). A tinted kite has just crashed against the tinted waters of the Caribbean, splashing with tinted drops the surface of the tinted lenses. In their condition as objects, the sunglasses are incapable of apprehending that the kite's demise has been but the city's ploy to mask the death of unrepeatable memories now beginning to dissolve into that soft yielding substance which is forgetfulness. The sunglasses abandon the landscape and rest on the Snacks Nail Care file (US$1.50) polishing off with great care all irregularities, projections, protrusions, preparing the terrain for the Broadway Nail Hardener (US$2.50). The sky-blue Rocky panties (US$5.95 the set) stand up, revealing the distorted lettering of the printed "Thursday." The Cobra slippers (US$2.50) attempt a few half-hearted steps to the beat of the music issuing – bubbling like a Redstar Cola (US$0.30)– from the Unisef Stereo Walkman (US$32.00) whose earphones discharge their seventy milliwatts a few millimeters above the Black & Blue earrings (US$12.40). The Rocky set and the Cobra slippers head for the bathroom, abandoning the Snacks Nail file, the Optyl sunglasses, and the Unisef on the night-stand. In the shower, the stream washes off traces of Coppertone Suntan Lotion (US$4.95), vestiges of Nina Ricci's L'Air du Temps

(US\$10.40), and of Barbara Ward's Colored Lady Creme. New Rexona Natural Deodorant Soap coats the spots occupied a few minutes before by the Optyl sunglasses and the Rocky panties, as well as places where they hadn't been, but is quickly washed off by the water (no registered trademark). A few minutes later Old Spice Shaving Cream (US\$5.40) sows the lather to be harvested by the Gillette PerSona Track II (US\$3.00). A seraphic white halo of Valmy Shampoo (US\$2.50) quickly dissolves. Back in the room, Friday's Rocky replaces Thursday's. The rouge Lipstick (US\$1.90) draws two homogeneous traces that scrutinize their own perfection in the mirror but which, recalling their previous distraction, open to allow the penetration of the toothbrush loaded with Colgate MFP-2 mint-flavored fluoride toothpaste (US\$2.50). That omission rectified, the lipstick repairs the imperfections and achieves a state of bilateral grace and symmetry that is at the very least satisfactory. Everything is ready for the Guerlain Varnis à Ongles (US\$7.90) to cover the surface previously fortified by the Broadway nail hardener. All this is done with every precaution, with extreme patience, since total perfection is but a sum of minute ones; and the Lipstick, Varnis, Valmy Shampoo, and Madonna eyeshadows (deluxe case, US\$7.95) now occupying the place of the Optyl sunglasses, know it well. They also know that perfection can be a weapon, and that the effectiveness of a weapon is often undermined by trivial details, so that two sprays of Agua Brava deodorant (US\$3.00) and strategically placed dabs of Charlie, Revlon Inc. (US\$16.50) conjure away danger before a pair of Ladystar shoes (US\$35.00) replaces the Cobra slippers and a Pierre Cardin dress (US\$29.30) covers a space defined as somewhat above the Ladystar shoes and somewhat below the rouge Lipstick, whose two traces open now intermittently to allow in a few almond-stuffed La Española olives (US\$2.40) sprinkled with sips of Chivas Regal (US\$11.95). Then the Ladystar shoes walk out of the room and descend to the restaurant, where they are met by a pair of Adidas sneakers, St. Michel pants, and a Chemise Lacoste pullover. The orange juice slips down the Fantasy necklace (US\$34.20), a recent gift from the Pierre billfold now resting in the back pocket of the St. Michel pants. A few words escape through the two traces of Lipstick. The whisper-thin veneer of Colgate MFP-2 toothpaste begins to erode against the rough surface of the toast. The Madonna blush blushes (even further) at the warmth of certain innuendoes, contorts at the brink of certain jokes. The

Chemise Lacoste pullover and the Pierre Cardin dress cross the hotel's threshold and walk into the sea breeze which flutters the minute residual particles of the Valmy Shampoo — as in the full-color photos in *Burda.*

It is then, as she turns her head, that Sandra sees Vivian, hanging on a Mexican arm to which Sandra introduced her fifteen days before, when it was Sandra herself who, hanging onto that very same arm, had run into Vivian on her way home from school, in the neighborhood of La Mina. She had had no choice but to introduce him. I had no choice, damn it, but she had. It wasn't for this that I've been busting my ass for so long; you want a pair of jeans, here's a pair of jeans; you want a bathing suit, a walkman, a dress. Take them, but study, don't be an fool. And now. For me, ok. But her. It's not as if she had been raised by Aunt Aurora or had met Fermín, like I did, when she was eleven; I have never, not even today, been able to call him Father. But she, who didn't have to suffer Aunt Aurora's litanies: That happened to your mother because she's an ass, a martyr in training. The brightest thing going when she's out on the street but a zero at home. That father of yours wouldn't amount to anything even if he were wrapped in cellophane and stamped for export. What do I care. Let them send him to China. Or Angola. Angola. Home is where he should be. Not fluttering around chasing schoolgirls, with the slew of daughters he's got at home needing to be fed. But your mother had this coming. It's not as if his thing were made of gold. Every time one of his sluts kicks him out he reappears, and your mother's back washing his undershorts like an asshole. That's why I live alone. No one is going to make an ass of me. Learn that and look sharp because life's too tough to go around whining and sniveling. What does it matter if he's a man. If he hits you, grab a stick and smash it on his head. If you want respect he has to know you're not made of cookie dough. It's not as if Mama had made her wash diapers when she was seven, like she did me, or cook when she was nine while she went off to work and there was no other choice because Fermín would disappear for four or five months or a year at a time and she had to support us, even bringing home the milk for the little ones because so often we didn't even have the twenty-five cents to buy a half a gallon of milk; and then Mama would bring me home from Auntie's so she could go to work until the streak was over and Fermín came back, and then they would send me to Aunt Aurora's again, because there really

wasn't enough room in the big bed for me when he returned, or
when he announced he was returning, because he would give no
notice when he took off, but his returns were heralded louder than
those of the Savings Bank. But she, all she did was eat, cry, and wet
diapers. I understood. And that was the worst part. That and the constant switching from one school to another; ten years changing teachers and friends and the bastards, the ever-present bastards ready to
take advantage of you, but I was having none of that. I'm not crip-
pled. And I'm no one's patsy. My hide got so tough from washing-
ironingcookingscrubbing that I didn't even feel Fermín's whippings.
And it was better when he was gone than when he came back for
good after that really bad streak, when Mama finally showed up at his
job and told the people from the Party that he didn't even feed the
kids. And word got around. He lost his Party card for about three
months. And then he came back, but it was worse, because first he
went after Mama for going around telling tales; and when I got into it
he took off his belt and gave me such a whipping I still bear the
marks. And Mama going I'm sorry, I'm sorry, but I was having none
of that. Never, never. Especially not to him. I'd be damned if I told
him I was sorry. And it got worse and worse, and he kept whipping
me until I was lying on the floor. And the neighbors. Not one of them
dared show his face, because Fermín was always showing off his Party
card and his pistol. Mama sorrysorrysorry, it could break your heart.
But not me. Not that day nor any other. Not even when he said: no
movies, no beach, no parties. Not even the school in the country, after
they'd got a certificate and all. Someone had to stay with the little
ones. And I didn't shut up when he whipped me for coming home
late, for asking for money on the street — damn, if I hadn't I still
wouldn't know what an ice cream tastes like — for going to a party
without permission, for cutting school to go to that library, which is
why I stole his change; I didn't care if he hit me if I could have my
photo taken and get an i.d., and spend five or six hours reading novels in which people didn't have to washironcookscrub, and didn't
have a father, or if they did they left him out because there wasn't a
trace of him anywhere. Or when he whipped me for going to the
movies to see the same show three or four times until it seemed to me
that I was living in the movie; although later, when I had to come out
because my eyes hurt it was worse worse worse. And what hurt the
least was Fermín's belt. What hurt the most was a spot inside me that

Fermín couldn't reach. But you. You didn't shoplift, you weren't caught red-handed by the police, you didn't have to lie to them, I live in San Ignacio, no, in Aguacate, no, in. And go round and round in circles to see if they'd get tired and let me go, because if Fermín finds out. And at the end we found that high school, and I go to school here, and the principal, yes, leave her with me, I'll speak to her parents, and just like that she sat with me in the park and we talked and talked, although she didn't know me and I didn't go to school there, and she let me tell her everything, and she was very quiet and didn't scream at me or scold me or anything. And that made me feel like crying, but I held back, until she put her arm around me and her hand on my head; and then I did; I couldn't hold back any longer and I cried nonstop for an hour — if my aunt had seen me: wimpy, wimpy like your mother — but I couldn't care less, and the principal didn't give me a hard time or try to comfort me. She just let me cry. When I stopped I was so tired, so limp, so light, as if they had scrubbed me clean inside; as if they had lifted off a load I'd been carrying for a long time. I told her I would, but I never saw her again, I don't know why. Or I do, but. In any case, no matter how much I talked, I had to go back to the house. And it was worse. Speaking to her softened me up, and we had enough wimps with Mama. Sometimes I feel like going back and waiting for her in the park. But it's no use. She mustn't even remember me after such a long time. What for. After Fermín kicked me out of the house there was no turning back. If he only knew. Maybe he did. I was so afraid that day. I told Vico, but: Don't be silly girl. And since we didn't have anywhere else to go we went into the cubbyhole behind the stairs. And he kissed me and kissed me so I'd get over my fears, but no; although he was all hot and bothered already and took off my panties, and I, I'm so scared, and he, don't be silly, and I, I don't know how, and I think he didn't either, and we spent a few minutes like that, until he felt the warmth between my legs, and I squeezed him, and he moved a couple of times, and just then he splattered all over me, and right away Fermín showed up screaming and Vico took off running through the back, that asshole, and Fermín kicked me out (I don't want any whores around here). Of course, Sarita was old enough to washiron-cookscrub, and she was docile like Mama. And I even thought that was all there was to it, that's what it was like. People talk so much about it, and I didn't feel a thing. It didn't dawn on me until two months later, when I was already in that flower job (room and board and a hundred and five pesos), when I met Armandito, who really knew what he was doing. I found out I was still a virgin when I no longer was; two months later I learned that he had knocked me up, and that he wasn't going to lift a finger to do anything about it (you do whatever you want; who knows if that bun in your oven is mine), and as far as my family went, God forbid them finding out. Though, after all, it was the same to me if they found out or not and sooner or later Fermín did, later rather than sooner; not when I had to donate blood and had to arm myself with patience, a good eraser, and lots of care to change the name in the donor's card; and that was how Juan Pérez, or whatever the sappy name I gave him was, gave me the quarter of a liter for the abortion. But Fermín never finds out what can be of no advantage to him, and he didn't give signs of life until I left the hospital, when all I needed was a taxi, not Fermín or Armandito. But there they were waiting, both of them, Armandito looking like a calf on his way to the Luyanó slaughterhouse because Fermín had brought him at gunpoint, so that you can make an honest woman of my daughter. If you're man enough to knock her up, you have to be man enough to marry her. And he pushed us into a jeep and took us to the first hall of justice he could find, and got two witnesses from the corner bar, bought them a couple of rums, and married us unceremoniously, his hand on the pistol wedged between his belt and his belly. When we came out he took off in the jeep and left us standing in the middle of the street, the witnesses asking where the party was. I strode off towards Charles III Avenue to look for a taxi. I didn't even turn around to see what my husband was doing. I still haven't turned around, and I haven't seen hide nor hair of him since then. I had enough things on my mind to try to understand why Fermín, why? What was it to him if I got knocked up or not? Why why why? A period of time you'd rather forget rushes to your memory, a time I have no right to forget since forgetfulness is silence and silence a trap with bits and pieces of naivete as bait, lurking out to snare the unwary. It started the day you left Braulio — fortyish, divorced, a mid-level manager of a small firm. You had met him the year before, a year after he was released from a prison sentence for assaulting his parents. You changed jobs five or six times till he gave you a job as a cashier. Between the two of you falsified payroll signatures, taking advantage of the piecework payments to the tune of an additional four or five hundred pesos a month. A regular at the Venecia bar, he sometimes came home from his incursions with girlfriends with whom he incited you to have relations, something you preferred to attribute to the secondary effects of rum. You learned from him the voluptuousness of alcohol, black tobacco cigarettes, and marihuana, the product of some clandestine plantation in Baracoa. And those were the moments of greatest intimacy between you, when Braulio spoke to you of his stings, swindles, and other experiences, so that you wouldn't be expelled from the university of life. You started going to bed with others and got pregnant. Even though Braulio was sterile he insisted you keep it. I'll bring it up as my own, what does it matter; but you packed your belongings and moved in with the author of the baking bun. Two weeks after your second abortion you learned that the man was getting married in a month, and you can't stay here because as you can see we have to fix this place, replaster the ceiling, paint, and. Then came the worst: sometimes you ate at a friend's house, sometimes they lent you money for a meal. You took a bath where and when you could. You caught four or five hours of gritty sleep in funeral homes or long bus routes – the number seven, the number twenty, the sixty four. Five or six times you slept in motels with fly-by-night men, even with one who left without paying while you were asleep. At dawn, as you didn't have any money, you agreed to sleep with the innkeeper so he wouldn't call the police. It was during one of those nights, at the Infanta National Funeral Home, that you met Teté, who say what you want at least got me out of that hole, even inviting me over to her house that very same evening, and stay, it's ok, there's room to spare here; and she lent you clothes and paid you attention, something you had hardly ever received from anyone; and that's how your survival instinct started foundering, your protective walls, your fortifications collapsing, until you lowered your drawbridge on your seventeenth birthday, when she surprised you with a new dress, an invitation to dinner, leisurely conversation as you had drinks at the apartment afterwards, until you exhausted all topics of conversation and the bottle, and there was nothing left to do but go to bed together for the first time. And, in any case, if it hadn't been for her I wouldn't have met Maidoly, or the Guantánamo girl, or Adrián; although Teté never forgave you those friendships, since that's what I work for, so that you don't have to go around hustling in the park at Twenty-Third and G, or learn from Adrián – who had two whores working the docks – the tricks of the trade, the ins and outs of whoring, pick-ups at cabarets, the exchange of dollars, key phrases to attract clients in several languages, sophisticated agroturistic techniques for harvesting appetizing greenbacks: access to the government's tourist shops, duty-free shopping, alibis to avoid warning summons, the black market, and systems for blackmailing guards at hotels; although later she turned into a pain when it came to my comings and goings, assuming a motherly concern that I wouldn't take from my own mother, damn it, or even Aunt Aurora; until I had to give her two or three thrashings, followed by public scenes. Once I went too far and they locked me up for causing bodily harm but she wouldn't press charges and waited for me outside the station with her arm in a cast, and I felt sorry for her and I forgave her for ratting on me, although it's not something women do. But I made it quite clear that I had no master; not even Adrián who tried it himself, but soon thought better of it. Just partners and that's it, thank you. Until they locked him up I never had any bad dealings with him. He always settled our business punctually without any bullshit about I'll pay you tomorrow or look here it's three dollars to one peso now, not four or five or seven, like it's gotten lately. Tit for tat. Green for blue. All clear and above board. The one who kept being a pain was Teté, although now I had my own money and there were months when I could lay two or three hundred on the table. For the expenses, you know. But all she cared about was her jealousy and her slobbering, and that was no way to get on with it, with things getting tougher and tougher at the docks. We're not making enough even for pizza, Zaida Telegrama used to say, may she rest in peace, poor thing, she put up with plenty and kept telling me: this is no life, honey; look at that Tomasa there, she barely moves a finger and gets her slice out of us for her shitty rooms. Ten, fifteen, can you believe it? There's no putting up with this crap. And they say she hustled in her time. But ambition makes people forgetful and we're the ones wearing out our shoes prancing from Mosquito Park to Avenida de Paula and around the Amphitheater. I'm telling you, I, who have been at this for ten years, and got into it hoping to find someone who'd get me away from communism, because there's no freedom in this country, my friend, they're always butting into your life and busting your chops for no reason at all. And after searching and searching for someone to get me out of here all I have to show for it is the kids I had with that Greek. After three trips he was transferred to another ship line, or transferred himself. The fact is that he took a powder and go figure out where he is. And then there's that disease they gave you. Take it from me, Zaida Telegrama. Don't be an asshole. You have youth and class. Get yourself some nice clothes and go earn your bread in your own sweet time at the first-class hotels. And you delayed your decision for months until the day Zaida got stabbed by a drunken john because of an I-don't-want-to and let-me-go, when she was only twenty eight. You gathered together your savings and your bewilderment and took off for Cienfuegos for a week, not to rest but to think, and you reached a decision between the Prado and the Jagua Hotel; between the Palacio del Valle and Pasacaballos, at the edge of the bay. That's why when you came back you asked Adrián to lend you two hundred dollars to put together a trousseau to start with and take off in style from the Hotel Nacional to the Capri, from the Riviera to the Havana Libre, crashing at Caridad the Chinese's place every morning since the thing with Teté was over for good. And a bountiful era opened up: you woke up at four, went out at six, well dressed, scented, well-put-together, on your way to the good life, to places where you could start a casual conversation in the lobby with presumed foreigners, or a less casual one through certain hotel desk clerks and elevator operators in-the-know, and a lot of psychology, because young men are never good customers — tightfisted more often than not, whether because they don't have the wherewithal or because why pay for what you can get for free — neither are old men — irritable, prone to take certain deficits and softenings, certain natural deterioration of the equipment after many years of service, out on women — skeptical because the beauty of the thing is to make it appear to be other than what it is; a discreet offer, a piteous request — masked behind tales of half-paid debts, or vague complaints about how sad it is to have a red dress with no matching shoes — all very carefully masked behind love at first sight, uncontrollable desires unleashed by his masculine aura, how becoming that gray on your temples is, you're lying, why, you look fifteen years younger, all of which elevates machos of Latin origin to unpredictable flights of generosity — like that Spaniard who, moved by a tale worthy of the most tear-jerking soap opera, gave you two hundred dollars; or that Italian who climbed into the police van with you, accompanied you to the station, and got you out by claiming violations of your civil rights and lack of proof. Although no one has been able to free you from the persecution to which that guy (Danilo his name was? I think so) subjected you. It started one night when he called you over. Why are you in this business? There are all sorts of opportunities open to you, my girl. I have a daughter that looks like you. Why? I'm doing nothing. Tell that to someone else. Listen, why are you picking on me? I'm just picking on the kind of business you're in. But I don't . . . Look, I know that Candela, Tormenta, the Chinese girl and all those others are looking for someone to get them out of the country, but are you . . . Are you? No way. Then . . . damn it, can't you see what kind of image of your own country you're projecting? It reminds me of a saying: Ducks don't shit where they eat. And you're shitting on it. But look, officer, I . . . Don't say another word. Get out of this, because if I see you, wherever I see you, even if it's having an ice cream at Coppelia's, I'm going to throw you in jail and then you're going to have to listen. Either you get out of this business from conviction or you're getting out from sheer exhaustion. But the exhaustion and Danilo's memory (I think that was his name) bring to mind that Frenchman, do you remember? (I do) who kept taking jabs at socialism, and that's why this country, the Pearl of the Antilles, and you no, no, there are no beggars and no hunger, and education, free medical care, and he: Look who's talking: a whore and a communist. You don't sell yourself for pesos or rubles, you sell yourself for dollars. And you said no more and got dressed and tore the bills he had slipped into your purse into tiny pieces and ran out of the hotel and drank seven straight Carta de Oro doubles, but your memory can swim in oceans of rum, and forgetfulness is a long apprenticeship that you haven't mastered yet. And you, Vivian, who have been through none of this, not even. That. That pisses me off. You haven't ever had to swallow a fifty dollar bill so the fuzz wouldn't lock you up for seven years for illegal possession; nor have you been robbed three times with no recourse, which can be worse. And that's why I paid Anselmo the Nail forty dollars. A brilliant move. He almost killed Veitía. So that he learns not to play around with women nor to come to me with that ridiculous story about a friend of mine coming by and cleaning out my room while I was at Varadero. A friend my ass. Nor have they left you dead drunk in a gutter as if you were garbage. Nor did you meet Mercedes, who at the beginning was all yes, my friend, my good good friend; come by the house for dinner, and later began lend me that blouse, give it to me, and finally asked Mejías for a VCR in my name. When I found out I called her a thousand times on the telephone until her mother came on: Look here, young woman, don't call my daughter again. She's studying, do you know what that means? Her exams at the university start next week and . . . But. No buts. Do you want me to be more explicit? My daughter is a young revolutionary, integrated, well-adjusted, studious. And she neither has, nor wants to have, relationships with prostitutes. Click. (They were probably watching a movie on the VCR and I interrupted them.) Nor did you go to the Chinese girl's wake. A closed casket because she had doused herself with alcohol and lit herself up in her room in the Víbora district. She was already thirty, poor thing. Nor have you gotten up in the morning, Vivian, to count little wrinkles in the mirror, or sat down afterwards to cry and to try not to cry. And maybe that's why, because there's so much you don't know, because if you want jeans, a bathing suit, a walkman, a dress, there's your sister to get them for you; and you shut your eyes and ears and wear them, and now you come on his arm, damned the hour I introduced him to you; and who knows whether you're blind or just pretending; and Mama doesn't ask any questions either when her daughter shows up with an electric fan or a record player, a dream of hers with so many of Benny's records to listen to; and Fermín doesn't ask any questions if a nice pair of shoes just show up in his closet, or a t-shirt, or a digital watch. And it is not that I love him, god-forbid, never, dammit. And you would know why if Uncle Ernesto were to tell you more, but no, because she's not so innocent herself, that Elena, and I'm not going to add fuel to the flames, since in any case not one of them is worth the trouble, but him I wouldn't give the time of day to. Not even Elena. That man is worthless. He may be my brother and all that, but he's worthless. And he had the gall to tell me. Not four, not a hundred shots of rum would justify a man saying something like that and even less doing it. But he would tell the story like a joke. So that Sandra would get started, he used to say; if she was all set to be a whore then let her do it as a married woman. Let the husband deal with it and then they wouldn't come bugging him with her problems; and besides he took the burden of feeding her off his shoulder as well as the trouble two or three had in store for him for throwing a minor out of the house; those bastards will use anything, man, to avenge themselves, to smear one's reputation. But you don't know that, Sandra, and you know even less, Vivian. Nothing about anything. Not even that I gave him the shoes and the t-shirt out of hatred, so that later he can't say he didn't know. The fuck you didn't. Sure you know. Sure you keep silent, and cool yourself with the fan, and put on your new little t-shirt to visit that mulatta you have over in Santos Suárez. And you, Vivian, and you.

Right at that moment a screeching of brakes startles Sandra out of her fleeting reverie, and the taxi driver, with half his body out the window: Hey girl, go daydream on the Malecón, if I kill you I have to pay the same as for a new one. And a man practically carrying a pregnant woman seizes the chance and boards the taxi: To the Naval Hospital. Urgent. And Mejías grabs her by the arm: Are you daydreaming? Don't you ever again stand nailed to the spot like a statue not listening to what I say.

And the St. Michel pants, the Adidas sneakers, the Chemise Lacoste pullover, the Pierre billfold drag Sandra, who is no longer Sandra, or is, or not, who knows, to the Havanauto's Renault parked in front, a Sandra now overcome by an an after-the-fact terror which shakes a certain sector of her brain and a well-determined number of trademark neurons calculate the losses that the taxi could have caused if the driver's reflexes hadn't been on target, if there had been a flaw in the brakes, if it had stopped twenty centimeters ahead: US$23.50 for the Optyl sunglasses, US$0.85 for the Friday Rocky, US$12.40 for the Black and Blue, US$29.30 for the Pierre Cardin, US$35.00 for the Ladystar shoes, US$34.20 for the Fantasy, her most recent acquisition, and so forth, adding up to a hundred and thirty dollars and twenty-five cents. How tragic.

Translated by Lizabeth Paravisini-Gebert

Tosca

Abilio Estévez

For Arturo Arango

1.

A ccording to Ana, the first symptom showed itself during a lunch, she said, that was neither more nor less placid than all their other lunches in the past thirty years. As usual, she served the meal and sat before him, but the moment they were about to eat a bell chimed twelve times. Adolfo's gesture made her conscious of the clock's presence.

She recalled that, in the beginning of their marriage, the grandfather clock, an enormous resonant cedar box, distressed her with its strokes, mainly at night, when some worry would rob her of sleep; the incessant movement would force her to keep an exact count of the time she spent awake. That's how it had been at the beginning. Adolfo himself told her one day, "You'll get used to it," and he was right. Before the first year of marriage had expired, she discovered that from force of habit the chimes had slowly extinguished until they became inaudible. That's why she was surprised to see him interrupt something as sacred as lunch, walk toward the clock, remove it from the wall and remain staring at its yellowish dial with the Roman numerals that were no longer as shiny as before.

"Your food is getting cold."

Startled, he returned the clock to its place and finished his lunch.

Afterwards, as always, coffee on the porch chairs, the enjoyment of a splendid afternoon in late January, cool and brilliant, perfect for each one to pursue his or her pleasure: for him, reading a volume of Cesar Cantu's *Universal History* while petting Talleyrand's back; for her, the final touches on one of her useless mufflers.

The following day was Sunday. Ana adored Sundays because, after a week of housework, it was the day for enjoyable activities: bathing Talleyrand, gardening, visiting her mother with the gift of a flan or a pudding—the entire family would be there for a two- or three-hour lunch. As she herself would say, "Sundays have a different kind of routine."

She got up early, so contentedly — in her, joy manifested itself in a certain condescension toward others — and peered out the window. The streets were empty, the breeze that flowed made her happy. Strangely, Adolfo was not in bed, but she was conscious of her penchant for noticing trifles and thought: "He's probably in the patio preparing Talleyrand's bath, that Adolfo is so impatient . . ." Except that when she entered the dining room she saw him in his pajamas seated at a table covered with parts and screwdrivers and a collection of pliers purchased many years before but never used. She didn't have to glance at the dining room wall to know what he was doing: Adolfo had taken apart the grandfather clock.

He explained himself with phrases she couldn't understand, not knowing if it was because Adolfo was expressing himself unclearly or because the surprise — or perhaps her anger — had made her deaf and mute to the point of not even being able to say good morning. She entered the kitchen with trembling hands and burned herself several times with the coffee pot.

When she handed him his cup of coffee and noticed that he didn't even bother to look at her, trying to adjust two tiny parts, she was instantly assured of something she had already suspected: her Sunday was ruined. To spend the entire week working just to have some nuisance deprive her of a delicious Sunday was something perfectly miserable. Rebelliousness grew in her as she — all by herself — bathed Talleyrand who was more bothersome than ever. There and then she decided to go without Adolfo. The blessed grandfather clock and her husband's whims would not ruin the only enjoyment of her week.

"Aren't you going to mother's?" she asked in an attempt at reconciliation.

"I can't leave this like this," was his reply. He finished the sentence with a gesture toward all of the pieces scattered across the table.

Pretending to have regained her composure, Ana smiled and continued to perform her Sunday duties.

She returned late. The first thing she did was to enter the dining room. The grandfather clock was in its usual place, but Adolfo wasn't there; nor was he in the bedroom, the study or the patio. Talleyrand was also missing. Ana told herself that all was well, it was precisely the hour in which the dog should be taken for a stroll.

When Adolfo reappeared, it was well past the time when the clock had struck eleven. She thought she perceived a blink of surprise in his eyes at seeing her there, an impression she discarded at once as totally absurd: for thirty years she had occupied the same spot near the same porcelain lamp where she would knit and tally the day's expenses.

"I went to give Talleyrand a stroll," he said, anticipating the question she was not going to ask.

"It looks as if Talleyrand had a tremendous urge to walk," she replied, with an effort to avoid the impression of irony.

He seemed not to be affected by the reply, not even looking at her. Nor did he grab his bedside book, the well-worn *History* by Cantu, opening instead a bound package he had brought back from his walk. He removed a book on whose leather cover she managed to read *Puccini Operas,* and left the room.

Ana arose and saw him reading, lying on the sofa – the sofa for which she had sewn a laborious damask cover and on which she preferred that no one, not even guests, be seated – and her indignation had no bounds: he was smoking a cigar and throwing the ashes on the floor.

She approached and tapped him on the shoulder, telling him in a low but firm voice to get up from the sofa immediately and put out the cigar, that he was soiling the floor which she, with her hard work, had managed to keep as shiny as a mirror. Adolfo, however, never even took his eyes from the book and, as if to show that he did as he pleased, tapped the cigar against the sofa, flicking away the rest of its ashes.

Ana could not recall in her entire life being as irritated as she was that night, with a fury so powerful it left her sleepless, listening to the chimes of the clock.

Upon awakening, she recalled that the last chimes she was conscious of were five; she had slept less than an hour.

Adolfo was no longer in the house. Very strange: they always — absolutely always — had breakfast together and he never had a class before ten. She didn't mind, on the contrary, she experienced the joy of being sole mistress of the house. She worked frantically despite the fact that her fatigue reminded her of an earlier one, many years before, after a twenty-four hour journey by train. The house was her passion. She enjoyed declaring that since the first day of her marriage she had dedicated herself to the household duties with energy and devotion. The mufflers were only her pastime: her obsessions were the shiny floors, the clean and pressed curtains, the dust-free furniture, the meals on time. It sickened her to see an object out of place. "Anyone can see I was educated by nuns," she used to say. Adolfo would praise her: "You are the perfect woman." Out of self-respect, she would change the subject, knowing inwardly that he was right, that in the entire town no other house was as clean or as orderly.

And Adolfo, who had lived his youth "in a somewhat disorderly fashion," — she would explain — "you know, Havana, the University, in short, the bohemian life," had adapted himself magnificently to the life that she, with enormous skill, had indicated for him. Ana was of the belief that the woman makes the man. Gently, unobtrusively, she brought him over to her perception of domestic discipline. "What is a home without habits, without good manners? Unruly family, unruly nation." Ana explained her ideas unharshly but with the solemnity and lack of passion with which she always expressed herself.

She worked so much that she didn't realize, until it was too late, that Adolfo hadn't returned for lunch. She called his school and was told that his classes had ended at twelve and that he had already left. Then she called his sister under the pretense of borrowing a skein of blue yarn, so that Beatriz would say: "What a coincidence, your husband is here;" instead, she said: "Tell my brother he's a phony. I haven't seen him in two weeks."

Adolfo arrived at three in the afternoon. He searched agitatedly among his papers. At three thirty he had a class in ancient history. He explained his absence from lunch in passing saying that he had had to go to the Municipal Library to consult Plutarch. He didn't know what had become of his copy of *Parallel Lives*. He kissed her on the forehead and left as he had arrived, unbathed, unchanged and without a morsel of food.

Ana, who habitually dusted the books daily, went into the study and, on the desk on which he prepared his classes, for all to see, discovered the Espasa Calpe edition of *Parallel Lives,* stained with the perspiration of her husband's hands.

2.

The following days would have been perfect had it not been for the clocks.

Adolfo prepared his classes, walked Talleyrand, read, conversed with her and the only thing unusual was that he returned home each day with a new clock. The first was a bronze girl, the second, a horse on hind legs, the third, the London Parliament tower, the fourth, a simple Westclox . . . Some fifteen clocks had accumulated on the dining room table.

With her practical common sense, Ana asked: "Why so many clocks if one is enough?"

He responded smilingly:

"I share Proust's passion."

She didn't understand his reply, just as she didn't understand Adolfo's new passion, even madder than the maddening tic-toc of so many clocks. That passion displaced Cantu's book and manifested itself one afternoon. At first, it was something simple, too simple: Adolfo lifted the cover of the RCA record player, an enormous console that was practically just a decoration as it was never used – she hated music – and placed inside one of the dusty disks that had piled up in the study, relics he had saved from his bohemian years and that she had not thrown out in one of her general housecleanings because it was the only thing he had forbidden her to do. At once a saccharine and unbearable music filled the house and a soprano's voice intoned an incomprehensible song.

"What kind of pain is that woman in?" she asked, knowing that her vulgarity would annoy him.

But Adolfo didn't respond. He had knelt down to adjust the volume and the needle on the record, and remained in that position for a long while; then he began to double over, fists clenched as if the one in pain were he, and when she approached he uplifted a transformed face.

According to Ana, it was the first time she had seen Adolfo cry.

From that day on, perhaps the least important fact was that he hardly touched his food and spent his time not in reading or conversing but rather listening on end to that soprano who "shrieked" in the console. She began to concern herself. He avoided answering questions. One afternoon he may have said something about shattering for two or three glorious days "the crystal of routine" — was that the phrase he used? — "to transform himself into another ephemeral stranger that would illuminate with greater clarity the joys of everyday life."

Ana discussed three reasons to be opposed to this criteria. First, they were not "two or three glorious days," but rather several intolerable weeks. Second, she disagreed with that affirmation of shattering the crystal of routine: for her, there was no happiness outside the bounds of routine, categorizing as madness all deviation from tradition. Third, she knew Adolfo much too well: "seven years of courtship and thirty years of marriage made for a complete life," she stressed.

She never mentioned the number of years without emphasizing that her marriage was perfect — or almost perfect: it lacked children who, for most people, are the vulgar measurement of marital perfection. They, on the other hand, took pleasure in God-given solitude. "Children at times are only good for getting in the way," Adolfo would say and she, who was unable to bear them, was grateful for his understanding and tactfulness. Thirty-seven years, one beside the other, had formed solid, inviolable habits, blissful days that passed spotlessly, perfectly, adorably, "the epitome of happiness."

And that good fortune had never been disrupted by Adolfo's late arrivals or much less by his being dirty and unfed, like a motherless bachelor. Now it turned out he was arriving later and later, at unsuitable hours, and when he opened the door he didn't even deign to greet her — a woman as selfless as she, the exemplary wife — nor did he explain his conduct. He simply threw himself on the sofa with filthy, disgusting clothes, the same suit he wore to teach his classes and which, despite her insistence, he hadn't changed in days.

One night he delayed so long that Ana lost patience and began to search for him in town. She thought she heard a church bell but couldn't be certain for the simple reason that she couldn't be certain of anything that night, except that she walked and walked through empty, dark streets – everyone knows that those street lights only darken the roads rather than illuminate them. The houses, secured under lock and key, and she wandering without knowing where to turn or whom to ask. She arrived at the square in the park. No one was there. Not even a drunkard sleeping on a bench as one would imagine there to be in every park. She circled the small walk that ridiculously imitated Prado Street in Havana several times. She went to the high school which was silent and in darkness. She paused in front of Beatriz's door but decided not to knock and cause alarm, perhaps unnecessarily. Finally, when she had decided to turn back, disappointed and more anxious than before, she heard Talleyrand's unmistakable bark. At first, Ana refused to believe what she should have: those barks were emerging from the ruins of the Teatro Principal. Still uncertain, she crossed the dilapidated entrance flanked by several columns. Now it wasn't barking she heard but something even more incredible that had to be credible (for Ana, reality is never mocking, lesser yet deceiving). She *had* to give credit to what she was hearing: Adolfo was singing. With his appalling voice, his worn-out voice, he managed to intone the unbearable aria that Ana was condemned to hear fifteen or twenty times a day. She was seized with fright. The walls of the theater were still faithful to sound, and his voice resounded and reverberated with a tone far removed from sarcasm or joy, because he sang as if he had no other alternative, as if some terrible grief compelled him to express himself in that way. Ana entered the old theater that no longer had a roof, barely illuminated by the February night. As she passed, several cats ran by her. The smells of humidity and putrefaction in the enclosure made her nauseous, the garbage horrified her.

And there in the detritus, amid the decay and the dust, the rubble and the debris, Adolfo sang out, embracing the time-worn boards of the stage floor.

3.

The clocks began to make their presence felt. Adolfo

acquired the habit of cleaning them daily. He neglected his classes and everything else that prevented him from dismantling those artifacts and oiling them with care.

Ana soon learned that the clock-cleaning ritual was only the preparation for a much more complex ceremony. She discovered it during the early hours of one morning when her husband's laughter awoke her. She recalls getting up and moving silently, gropingly through the darkened house and the long hallway that separates the living and dining rooms, which seemed longer than usual. She paused before approaching the dining room and saw, first, the reflection of a light on the wall and Adolfo's shadow, a gigantic copy of him with arms raised and head pulled back. She advanced until reaching the threshold of the door. He was bent over the open clocks. The table was full of dials, jars with an amber liquid, pieces of cotton, pendulums, coils, springs, clock-hands, cranks, chimes. Agitated, in semi-darkness, wrapped up warmly despite the asphyxiating atmosphere of the closed room, he examined the clocks' movements and analyzed each part, constantly adjusting his jeweler's eye loupe. Motionless, with a perplexed expression and open mouth, he then removed the loupe and babbled incomprehensively. Later, after he had calmed down, he breathed a sigh of relief and started to laugh again.

They remained that way until sunrise: he adjusting the clocks, she, suspecting that no good would be coming of this. At daybreak, Ana opened the windows "to allow God's blessings to filter in," she said, and in a falsely indifferent tone asked him the time.

He raised himself triumphantly — the question meant a lot to him — and responded:

"My love, it is two o'clock in the morning."

She repressed a smile.

"How can it be two a.m., Adolfo, if dawn has already broken?"

Stretching himself, he yawned and shrugged his shoulders:

"It is no more than two a.m. Time for bed."

He went to the bedroom and fell asleep.

Ana searched through the clocks in wonder and discovered that, in effect, they all pointed to two o'clock. At first she thought he had put them back, but had he done so they would have continued to advance anyway, that is, although on a different hour, clock time ensued with a before and an after following the natural succession of hours, that constant and repeated order according to which life transpires. But the opposite took place: the clocks marched backwards, going from the after to the before, as if, instead of serving to observe the present on its way to the future, they pointed the way to the past: after two o' clock they indicated one, then twelve, then eleven, and Ana watched as the implacable precision of the machines dissolved the day and her actions, her everyday actions, her cherished habits, transforming them into monstrous aberrations.

As a result, the clocks isolated the household from the rest of the world. The house seemed to avoid time and place itself in limbo, a non-existent zone. Ana would awake at dawn and notice the clocks pointing to the most unexpected hours. At twelve, for example, when the sun blazed down on the rooftops, the alarms went off announcing the start of the morning of the prior day; when the grandfather clock chimed a midday long past, the sun had already begun its decline and the streets, the actual streets, the real streets, were descending into that languor that dims the shine on asphalt. The town's evenings were a five o'clock of an earlier afternoon.

To live governed by an illusory time conferred on each of her actions such a marked sense of unreality that she no longer felt like herself, but rather as if her life had been converted into a movie that, despite everything, she was unable to view from afar. And to complete the madness, the background to the day was an indefatigable soprano.

4.

Ana related the above without the slightest emotion, without abandoning her hieratical affability. I had gone to visit them more as Adolfo's friend than as the Principal of the school, concerned with his absences from the history class. I recall that when I arrived Ana exacted my silence with a gesture and informed me that my friend was asleep. She explained that, despite the sunlight, for him it was evening.

"Let's go to the back," she said in a tone deplete of irony. She, who had never had a sense of humor, was even more somber than usual.

After listening to her story in silence, I asked her for her opinion.

She didn't respond, but raised her finger to her temple to avoid pronouncing that terrible word she preferred remain silent.

"The doctor must be called in," I recommended with unavoidable banality.

"Never!" she exclaimed impassively. "He never would have permitted it. He is so intelligent . . .! I'll shut myself in and fulfill my obligation."

This declaration of principles put an end to my visit, the first of several throughout the following days.

During that time I only saw Adolfo twice. On one of those visits, I arrived at eleven a.m. and he, although friendly, greeted me with sarcasm:

"Do you believe that this is an appropriate time for a visit?"

"What time is it?"

"One a.m. yesterday," he responded.

I smiled despite myself.

"And you, why aren't you asleep?"

"Tosca kept me awake."

I was speechless. Ana, who had entered at that moment, stopped breathing for a moment, as one who awaits a revealed truth.

"I was thinking of poor Victorien Sardou," Adolfo continued, "how sad it must be over there in eternity to realize that *La Tosca* is more famous for Puccini's opera than for his mediocre melodrama."

Ana and I gave each other a glance of relief. In that sense, his conversation was as always.

"Do you know the play?"

He was astonished at my ignorance.

"No one. No one knows it, I suppose. Perhaps two or three unemployed scholars."

And he began to relate the story of *La Tosca,* about how Puccini had become interested in Sardou's libretto and the circumstances surrounding the opera's debut in 1900. I could perceive no incoherence; on the contrary, he demonstrated that excellent way of narrating the most prosaic story as if it were a fairy tale which had earned him his reputation as a good teacher. Perhaps the only suspicious thing was that, upon completing his account, when my watch displayed midday and the dining room clocks pointed to eleven-thirty, he explained that it was eleven-thirty p.m. of the twentieth of February.

"Today is March twenty-fourth," I replied foolishly.

"It cannot be denied that you're just a sorrowful anatomy teacher, " he said, only partly in jest.

The second time I saw him he invited me for "a stroll." I suspected, when I saw that he made me turn near Martí Street to arrive at the park in front of which one could see the eclectic facade with the name and the two undamaged familiar masks, that he was taking me to the ruins of the Teatro Principal.

I haven't yet mentioned that in other times the theater had been our most prestigious structure, the pride of our people. A fire destroyed it and one fine day it was converted into a warehouse, and later a mechanic's workshop before becoming the dismal relic it is today. Despite the transformations it suffered after the fire, it retained several balconies and the proscenium which had been an attempt to imitate the Garnier style. Deteriorated, falling to pieces, the Teatro Principal was now a shelter for ferrets and stray cats. The neighborhood used it as a garbage dump.

When we stood before it, Adolfo observed the facade and mentioned the architect's name, some Serrano fellow who had studied in France and was overwhelmed by the monumentally vulgar Paris Opera. Adolfo grinned, perhaps because of Serrano's naivete or perhaps due to his ability to relate with such ease the theater's history, something he did — and I must stress this — in a most singular manner: from its recent history, supported by an erudition of which he alone was capable, he slid back to the very day in 1908 upon which the mayor set the first stone on land won in a claim against poor Spanish herders. Before my eyes, and thanks to Adolfo's narrative gifts, the building shed its present decay, recovered the artisan's woodworkings, erected its statues intact and its velvet curtain, and radiated an enormous floodlight. He took me by the arm and made me approach the ruins.

"Although he affected French style, Serrano did not lack talent. This theater had perfect acoustics."

We entered. Adolfo advanced through the debris rapidly, as if he were at home. He stopped in the center of the vast hall that had at one time been the orchestra section and was now a breeding place for mosquitos, and raised his arms in an ambiguous gesture that was meant to show me either the space the theater had occupied or the extent of his own ambition, of his dream, and at the same time of his disenchantment, because he lowered them again, clearly dejected.

"Perché, signore, perché . . ." he cried and left the ruins vibrating with the sound; he left without noticing me, totally forgetting that I was there.

5.

The following day Ana came to see me at school. Her solemn resignation, her gentle gravity had given way to a barely-controlled indignation. I believe I asked her for the reason and, ignoring me, she sat down and abruptly flung an envelope on my desk. I questioned her with my eyes.

"You'll soon see," she said softly, so much so that I'm not quite sure she actually did. I do recall clearly that, as I was about to remove the papers from the envelope, she prevented me from doing so with a brusque gesture.

"When I've left."

Her tone was imperious: she had the air of a wronged woman. I said yes, of course, that's fine, I'd read them later, that evening perhaps if the children didn't take up all my time.

She rose with the mien of a deposed sovereign and left the way I suppose one does in these situations: slamming the door.

The moment she was gone I opened the envelope. Inside was a portfolio, obviously very old, tied with blue strings. When I untied them the folder came apart. Dozens of yellowing papers and theater programs fell upon the desk as well as a sepia-colored photograph. I glanced first at a program dated 1918 which, in meticulous Bodoni typeset, heralded the great German singer Clarissa Men and her company in the production of Giacomo Puccini's *Tosca* in the Teatro Principal. It was followed by clippings from *La Clarinada,* our local newspaper at the time, with articles on the performance. They were signed by a certain fellow called Gaspard de la Nuit who had been unable to conceal his enthusiasm for Men and spent almost the entire article describing in detail the moment, magical for him, in which Floria Tosca calls to Cavaradossi. "Her voice is not human," he wrote. Another article referred to Clarissa Men's appearance on stage. If listening to her voice moved Gaspard de la Nuit, watching her made him "experience the bitter taste of tears." The last of the columns, the one dedicated entirely to studying the soprano's interpretation of "Vissi d' arte," caused him to proclaim: "Music of the heavens." The word "sublime" was used profusely. I couldn't help being touched, however, by the final sentence: "It was an evening that will always remain in my memory," because I should note that those passionate words, despite the platitudes, were far from the usual style of such articles. Gaspard de la Nuit was genuine. Behind the false name was the reality of a fiery nature, a sensitive man with no little musical understanding. I also found a sheet of notebook paper on which was written the following sentence: "Clarissa Men arrived early. Her hair is like wheat. She is dressed in black." And it was Adolfo's writing. Although more carefully written, I recognized his singular, unmistakable penmanship.

Other reviews, published in the Havana papers, revealed that the subject in question was a highly-esteemed singer, a diva who had been applauded in the world's most important opera houses and who, in one of those decisions tactlessly referred to as eccentric, had decided to remain in Cuba where she founded her own opera company.

From other critiques and program notes I learned that the name Clarissa Men was the pseudonym of Marlene Innitzer, an Austrian born in Salzberg in 1876. In Vienna, she was Ulrica Ben-Heim's favorite pupil and had performed *Tosca* in Brussels for Puccini himself who was enchanted with the purity of her voice and the emotion she conferred on "Vissi d' arte."

She established herself in Cuba after the outbreak of the First World War, choosing a mansion in Cerro where she was accompanied by two greyhounds and a voice tutor, a German from Munich, as robust as one of Wilhelm II's officers — the comparison is Adolfo's. Popular imagination attributed every manner of salacious nuance to the singer-tutor relationship that I prefer not to mention. I learned of these details because my friend described them without the slightest indignation on paper with the letterhead of the Telegrafo Hotel which had been the most elegant hotel in town.

On another sheet from the same hotel I discovered, in reddish ink, Clarissa Men's autograph: a phrase in German — which I was unable to decipher — and another in imperfect Spanish: "something more to grateful," ending with the simple, unadorned signature of the singer.

I cannot deny that I was impressed by Men's photograph. "Profoundly Prussian," Adolfo had written, among admiring comments in a corner of one of the programs, and he was right. Despite the deterioration of the photo, she appeared to be blond, with a perfect oval face, pronounced cheekbones and "a smile envisioned by Leonardo," another of Adolfo's phrases. In her eyes I believe I discerned a peace that was in no way human, considering as I do that human life is uncertainty, a permanent struggle between ignorance and the audacity of wanting to know. In the photograph, Clarissa Men seemed to be a woman removed from of all anxiety, including that of her character. Looking at her one could not help but agree with the statement Adolfo had left on another page: "She isn't a woman but an idea. She doesn't belong to this world."

Clarissa Men, however, did belong to this world. A long article, written in the scandalous tone so typical of that type of news item, appearing in a 1934 issue of the magazine *Bohemia,* described the mysterious circumstances surrounding her suicide. Just like the heroine she embodied best, she hurled herself from the small tower of her private Sant'Angelo. Adolfo's sole comment was written on the borders of the article: *Vissi d'arte, vissi d' amore, non feci mai male ad anima viva . . .!*

I saved Clarissa Men's photograph and the autographed sheet from Hotel Telegrafo in my desk drawer. The rest was returned to the portfolio and tied with the blue strings.

6.

Impatient to see Adolfo and tell him who knows what, anything to cause a response, elicit a clue that, in reality, I wasn't sure what I'd do with, I went to his house. I discovered it as it had never been before: with doors and windows wide open, and so illuminated that it seemed to be aflame. I didn't knock. I entered the living room and called out. She responded telling me "come in" with her usual serenity. I passed through the long hallway and arrived at the dining room.

Ana was seated at the table with the jeweler's loupe in her right eye, attempting to dismantle a clock. The rest of the clocks, including the grandfather clock, were open on the table.

"I never imagined that the workings of a clock were so complicated," she said by way of a greeting.

I asked her anxiously what she was doing.

With total calm she laid the screwdriver and clock on the table, removed the loupe and sighed. She cast a glance at the mess of pieces that were piled up around her.

"They're more work than a muffler!"

When I inquired about Adolfo she shrugged her shoulders.

"I don't know," and she rose and went to the kitchen. She waved me to follow.

"Did you bring the papers?"

I handed her the portfolio. Unopened, she placed it on the flames of the range. It seemed to me that she was smiling as she watched the pages burn, that the shine in her eyes was not a reflection of those flames but of the inner ones that consumed her. She turned toward me and I can swear that it was the first time I had seen her jubilant, with a joy so visible she could hardly articulate.

"Just because she is dead," she said, "she is not going to be more powerful." And she returned to the disassembled clocks.

I left, knowing already where I had to go. One didn't have to be overly suspicious to figure it out. I ran across the park and reached the ruins of the Teatro Principal. Talleyrand met me at the door with barks of joy or perhaps of hostility. Upon entering, I saw my friend in the middle of the debris. I called him. Not answering, he simply turned around and began to look forward toward what had been the stage and advanced slowly, although somewhat easily, through the rubble. I followed as best I could and stopped at his side. The night had closed in and the silence was so perfect that everything, even the town itself, seemed like an extension of the ruined theater. He raised his eyes and I followed. At first I thought he was staring at the sky and I was about to admire it, to tell him that it was really lovely with so many stars, that there hadn't been a night like that one in a long while. But I stopped myself, because I saw him raise a hand, just one hand, to his chest with his palm facing outward and smile, I saw him smile and close his eyes, and then open and close them again. The extended hand began to move rhythmically, as if to the beat of a nonexistent music.

At that moment I felt defeated. Don't think that my defeat arose from my inability to speak with him and extract something about Clarissa Men. The cause was a petty one and I'm ashamed to confess it. In an instant I knew that Adolfo had not looked at the sky but at a roof decorated with nymphs and fauns, where a Viennese chandelier was beginning to dim. I knew that for him the three hundred seats of the orchestra section were filled to capacity, and a man in black, from his pit, conducted the music that to my friend was unequaled; and the curtain rose with the scenery and a wooden cross that revealed a Roman church in the year 1800. I felt defeated because he *saw* and I didn't, because he *heard* and I couldn't, because despite the fact that we were in the same place, we *were* in different places and as much as I tried to penetrate, to tear apart the veil that separated us, my eyes only managed to perceive the remnants of a stage, whereas his had reencountered a soprano who sang just for him.

Translated by Margarite Fernández Olmos

BIOGRAPHICAL NOTES

❖ EDITORS ❖

MARGARITE FERNÁNDEZ OLMOS is professor of Spanish at Brooklyn College of the City University of New York. A recipient of a Ford Foundation Fellowship and a Post-doctoral Fellow of the National Research Council, she has lived and studied in Europe and Latin America. Professor Fernández Olmos has lectured extensively on contemporary Latin American literature and written for such journals as *Studies in Afro-Hispanic Literature, Revista/Review Interamericana, Hispania, Revista Iberoamericana, The Lion and the Unicorn, La Revista Canadiense de Estudios Hispánicos, Revista de Crítica Literaria Hispanoamericana, Heresies,* and *Third Woman,* as well as for several anthologies on Latin American and Puerto Rican literature. She is the author of a book on the Dominican writer Juan Bosch, *La cuentística de Juan Bosch: un análisis crítico-cultural* (1982) and co-editor with Doris Meyer of *Contemporary Women Authors of Latin America: New Translations and Introductory Essays* (1983). In 1989 she published a collection of essays on contemporary Puerto Rican literature, *Sobre la literatura puertorriqueña de aquí y allá: aproximaciones feministas.* Her most recent book is *Pleasure in the Word: Erotic Writings by Latin American Women* (1993), co-edited with Lizabeth Paravisini-Gebert.

LIZABETH PARAVISINI-GEBERT is associate professor of Caribbean and Latin American literature in the Department of Hispanic Studies at Vassar College. She received a B.A. (magna cum laude) from the University of Puerto Rico, and an M.A., M.Phil, and Ph.D. in Comparative Literature from New York University (1982). Professor Paravisini has written on contemporary Caribbean, American, and Latin American fiction, and on popular culture, for such journals as *Obsidian, Plural, Clues, Callaloo, Sargasso, Cimarrón, Anales del Caribe, Nuevo Texto Crítico, Contemporary Literary Criticism,* and *The Journal of West Indian Literature,* among others. She has contributed chapters to several anthologies, including *Comic Crime, Spanish American Women Writers: A Bio-Bibliographic Sourcebook,* and *History of the Literatures of the Caribbean.* She co-authored *Caribbean Women Novelists: An Annotated Bibliography* with Olga Torres Seda, and is the author of *Phyllis Shand Allfrey: A Caribbean Life,* forthcoming from

Rutgers University Press. She has edited Ana Roqué's 1903 novel *Luz y sombra, Green Cane and Juicy Flotsam: Short Stories by Caribbean Women* (with Carmen Esteves), *El placer de la palabra: literatura erótica femenina de América Latina* (with Margarite Fernández Olmos) and its English version, *Pleasure in the Word: Erotic Writings by Latin American Women,* and the forthcoming *The Collected Poems of Phyllis Shand Allfrey.* Her translations have appeared in *Cimarrón, Her True True Name: An Anthology of Writings by Caribbean Women, Callaloo,* and other reviews and anthologies.

❖ AUTHORS ❖

HUMBERTO ARENAL was born in Havana in 1923, the son of one of the first women to graduate from a Cuban university. An indifferent student but avid reader, he left school early to pursue a series of odd jobs as messenger, telephone-book delivery man, office clerk, translator, and secretary. He studied English with a series of private teachers and in 1948 left for New York with a scholarship for further studies in English. In New York he worked as a newspaper reporter and joined a revolutionary cadre. Arenal returned to Cuba after the 1959 Revolution and became a full-time writer. He has published three collections of short stories, *La vuelta en redondo* (1963), *El tiempo ha descendido* (1964), and *El agua mansa* (1986); two novels, *El sol a plomo* (1959) and *Los animales sagrados* (1967), and various plays and poems. He is currently working on a biography of Cuban poet and dramatist Joaquín Lorenzo Luaces.

LUIS RAFAEL SÁNCHEZ, Puerto Rico's foremost contemporary novelist, was born in the island in 1936. An accomplished dramatist, Sánchez's 1966 groundbreaking collection of short stories *En cuerpo de camisa* changed the course of Puerto Rican short fiction for the following decades. Sánchez's first novel, *La guaracha del Macho Camacho,* published in 1976, won the author international recognition. In 1988 he published his second novel, *La importancia de llamarse Daniel Santos.*

RENÉ DEL RISCO BERMÚDEZ was born in San Pedro de Macorís, Dominican Republic, in 1937. He studied law at the Universidad Autónoma de Santo Domingo and was politically active in the cause against the Trujillo dictatorship. Before his premature death in an auto accident in 1967, he published two collections of short stories, *Viento frío* (1967) and *Del júbilo a la sangre* (1967). At the time of his death René del Risco Bermúdez was considered one of the Dominican Republic's most promising young authors. His stories and poems were collected posthumously in 1974 in *En el barrio no hay banderas*.

HILMA CONTRERAS was born in San Francisco de Macorís, Dominican Republic, and educated in Paris. She started writing short stories while still in Paris in the 1930s and is said to be the first Dominican woman to write short stories. Her first collection, *Cuatro cuentos,* appeared in 1962. Her only novel, *La tierra está bramando,* was published in 1986. Her work covers a wide spectrum of themes and styles, ranging from the political novel to the fantastic tale.

AÍDA CARTAGENA PORTALATÍN was born in Moca, Dominican Republic, in 1918 and pursued advanced studies in music and theory at the School of Plastic Arts in Paris. She was a valiant supporter of intellectual freedom during the harsh period of the Trujillo dictatorship and founded a press, Brigadas Dominicanas, to publish the work of local authors whose work was unacceptable to officially-sanctioned publishing houses. She is the author of two novels, including *Escalera para Electra* (1978), several collections of poetry and numerous short stories, and is the editor of an anthology of Dominican short stories, *Narradores dominicanos* (1969). Cartagena Portalatín died in 1994.

MARCIO VELOZ MAGGIOLO, born in Santo Domingo in 1936, is an anthropologist, literary critic, university professor, journalist, and diplomat, as well as possibly the best-known writer of fiction in the Dominican Republic after Juan Bosch. He is the author of numerous works, including several novels, among them the Dominican classic *De abril en adelante* (1975), poetry, drama, and cultural essays on a wide variety of Latin American themes, and several collections of short stories, including *Cuentos, recuentos y casicuentos* (1986).

NORBERTO FUENTES was born in Havana in 1943. He showed an early talent for drawing and was enrolled in the San Alejandro Art School, but his real vocation was that of a news reporter and after a stint as a cartoonist got his first reporting assignment chronicling the early days of the Cuban Revolution. He has worked for a number of newspapers and magazines in Cuba. Fuentes earned the 1968 Casa de las Américas Prize for his first collection of short stories, *Condenados de Condado*. In 1970 he published a second collection, *Cazabandidos*. Since them he has been working on a massive novel about the Revolution and on an equally massive book on Ernest Hemingway's life in Cuba. He now lives in Mexico.

MIGUEL ALFONSECA was born in Santo Domingo in 1942. He shared with other Dominican writers of the 1960s a passion for literature and social justice. Poet, short story writer, and professor of literature, Alfonseca was imprisoned for his political activities during the Trujillo regime. A collection of his stories, *El enemigo*, appeared in 1970 and other works are included in several anthologies both in Spanish and in translation. Alfonseca died in 1994.

TOMÁS LÓPEZ RAMÍREZ was born in San Juan, Puerto Rico, in 1946. He studied literature and social sciences at the University of Puerto Rico and the University of Madrid. After having published several of his poems, López Ramírez began publishing short stories and in 1970 won a national short story award in Alicante, Spain. He is presently a professor of literature in Puerto Rico. His works include two collections of short stories, *Cordial magia enemiga* (1971), *Tristes aunque breves ceremonias* (1992), and a novel, *Juego de las revelaciones* (1976).

EDGARDO SANABRIA SANTALIZ, born in Puerto Rico in 1951, received a Ph.D. in literature from Brown University. He is the author of several highly-regarded collections of short stories, among them *Delfia cada tarde* (1978), *El día que el hombre pisó la luna* (1984), and *Cierta inevitable muerte* (1988). His work has been praised for its delicately-nuanced satire of the Puerto Rican middle class.

JOSÉ ALCÁNTARA ALMÁNZAR was born in Santo Domingo, Dominican Republic, in 1946, and is considered the foremost short story writer of his generation. Known for his insightful explorations of his country's political situation, Alcántara Almánzar is also a respected scholar and literary critic. He has published five collections of short stories dating from the early 1970s, many of which are gathered in a recent anthology, *El sabor de lo prohibido* (1993).

ROSARIO FERRÉ was born in Puerto Rico in 1938 to a prominent upper-class family. In the 1970s she and her cousin and fellow author Olga Nolla founded *Zona de carga y descarga,* an important literary magazine devoted to innovative Puerto Rican literature. Her first book, *Papeles de Pandora* (1976), a collection of stories and poems, earned her recognition throughout Latin America. She has published four collections of stories for children, a collection of feminist essays, *Sitio a Eros* (1980), two collections of poetry, a novella, *Maldito amor* (1986), and several collections of literary essays, including *El coloquio de las perras* (1990). She is at work on her first novel written in English.

OLGA NOLLA was born in Puerto Rico in 1938. She began her literary career in *Zona de carga y descarga,* an influential literary magazine co-founded with Rosario Ferré. She was later editor of *Palabras de mujer,* the journal of the Federation of Puerto Rican women, and of *Cupe,y* the journal of Puerto Rico's Metropolitan University. Known primarily as a poet, Nolla is also the author of a novella, *La segunda hija* (1992), and of a collection of short stories, *Porque nos queremos tanto* (1989).

PEDRO PEIX was born in the Dominican Republic in 1952, where he was trained as a lawyer. He works as a reporter for *Listín Diario* and produces radio and television programs. Peix has published one collection of short stories, *Los fantasmas de la calle El Conde,* and a number of short stories in Dominican journals and literary magazines. He is also the editor of a collection of Dominican short stories, *La narrativa yugulada (1989).*

REINALDO MONTERO was born in Ciego Montero, Cuba, in 1952. He has published a play, *Con tus palabras* (1984), poetry, and several collections of short stories from a series, *Septeto habanero: Donjuanes* (1986), winner of the Casa de las Américas Prize for short story, and

Fabriles (1988).

ANA LYDIA VEGA was born in Santurce, Puerto Rico, in 1946, and obtained a Ph.D. in Comparative Literature at the University of Provence. She has published four collections of short stories, *Vírgenes y mártires* (1981), *Encancaranublado y otros cuentos de naufragio,* winner of the Casa de las Américas Award in 1982, *Pasión de historia y otras historias de pasión* (1987), and *Falsas crónicas del sur* (1991). Vega's fiction has received international recognition for its innovative and liberating use of language. Vega teaches French at the University of Puerto Rico.

MIRTA YÁÑEZ was born in Havana in 1947 and received a degree in literature from the University of Havana, where she once taught. The author of several collections of poems, children's tales, and short stories, most notably *Todos los negros tomamos café* (1976), she has also published a novel, *La hora de los mameyes* (1983). Her work draws on her experiences as a member of the agricultural youth brigades and gives testimony to her deep interest in cultural history and the Cuban peasantry.

SOLEDAD CRUZ was born in Camaguey, Cuba, in 1952 and has worked as a reporter for *Juventud Rebelde* and other newspapers. Well known in Cuba for her feminism and other controversial ideologies, she has published two collections of short stories, *Jinete en la memoria* (1989) and *Fábulas por el amor* (1990), a novel, *Adioses y bienvenidas* (1990), and a daring collection of poems, *Documentos de la otra (archivo incompleto)* (1988).

MAGALI GARCÍA RAMIS was born in Santurce, Puerto Rico, in 1946, and started her professional life as a journalist. Her first collection of short stories, *La familia de todos nosotros,* appeared in 1976. Her novel *Felices días, Tío Sergio* (1986) established her as one of Puerto Rico's best contemporary writers. She received a Guggenheim Fellowship in 1989 to work on her second novel, *Las horas del sur,* which is nearing publication. She recently published a collection of essays. A new collection of short stories, which includes "Fritters and Moons," the story translated here, is scheduled for publication in 1994.

MAYRA MONTERO was born in Havana in 1952 but has lived in Puerto Rico throughout most of her life. She began her career as a newspaper correspondent in Central America and the Caribbean and later wrote editorials for *El Mundo,* a San Juan newspaper. In 1981 she published her first collection of short stories, *23 y una tortuga.* She has gained considerable acclaim for her novels, which include *La trenza de la hermosa luna* (1987), *La última noche que pasé contigo* (1991), which has been translated into several languages, and *Del rojo de su sombra* (1993). Montero's fascination with Afro-Caribbean culture permeates her narrative.

SENEL PAZ was born in Fomentos, Cuba, a remote town in the center of the island, in 1950, and spent most of his youth in the Cuban countryside. Paz won the David Prize in 1979 for his first collection of short stories, *El niño aquel,* the Premio de la Crítica for *Un rey en el jardín* in 1984 and has also written several film scripts. He is best known for his daring treatment of the theme of homosexuality in his short story, "The Woods, the Wolf, and the New Man," which was awarded the prestigious Juan Rulfo award in Paris in 1990. Paz is considered by most critics to be one of the foremost writers of his generation.

ÁNGELA HERNÁNDEZ was born in Jarabacoa, Dominican Republic, in 1954. Although trained in chemical engineering, Hernández has worked primarily as a researcher and feminist activist. A poet and essayist, Hernández published her first collection of short stories, *Alótropos,* in 1989 to immediate and enthusiastic acclaim. "Gnawing on a Rose," the short story included here, belongs to her second collection, *Mastica una rosa* (1994). She is at work on her first novel.

VERÓNICA LÓPEZ KÓNINA was born in Moscow in 1968 of Russian-Cuban parentage. She has studied journalism at the University of Havana where she also worked as a translator. Her first collection of short stories, *Adolesciendo,* received the Premio David in Cuba in 1988.

LUIS MANUEL GARCÍA was born in Havana in 1954 and is a journalist, short story writer, and novelist. He has published several collections of stories, among them *Los amados de los dioses* (1987), *Sin perder la ternura* (1987), and *Los forasteros* (1988), and a novel *Aventuras eslavas de don Antolín de Corojo y crónicas del nuevo mundo según Iván el Terrible* (1989). His recent collection, *Habanecer* (1992) won the 1990 Casa de las Américas Prize for short story.

ABILIO ESTEVES was born in Havana in 1954. Poet, dramatist, and short story writer, Esteves has also dedicated his efforts to the study of nineteenth-century Cuban letters. His play, *La verdadera culpa de Juan Clemente Zenea* won an award from the National Union of Cuban Writers and Artists, and his stories are collected in *Juego con Gloria*.

❖ TRANSLATORS ❖

BETH BAUGH STHAPIT received her B.A. in Spanish from Middlebury College. Her translations have appeared in the *New England Review/Breadloaf Quarterly*. She is currently working toward a Masters degree in Special Education and a credential in bilingual education. She lives and works in San Franciso.

CARMEN ESTEVES teaches Spanish and Latin American literature at Lehman College of the City University of New York. She has translated into English works by Latin American women such as Magali García Ramis and Elena Poniatowska. She is co-editor (with Lizabeth Paravisini-Gebert) of *Green Cane and Juicy Flotsam: Short Stories by Caribbean Women* (1991).

PAULA SHARP is the author of the critically-acclaimed novels *Lost in Jersey City* (Harper Collins, 1993) and *The Woman Who Was Not All There* (Harper & Row, 1988), and of the prize-winning short story collection, *The Imposter* (Harper Collins, 1991). She is the translator of the Chilean writer Antonio Skarmeta's novel *The Insurrection*, and of numerous pieces of Latin American short fiction. She wishes to thank Clara Nilda Comesanas for her assistance in translating Cubanisms in Arenal's story.

BETH WELLINGTON holds an M.A. in advanced international studies from the Bologna Center of Johns Hopkins University and a doctorate in Hispanic languages and literature from Boston University. She teaches Spanish and Italian at Simmons Collge, Massachusetts. She has translated works by her husband, Dominican author Norberto James, as well as works by René del Risco.

❖ ARTIST ❖

MARIA DE MATER O'NEILL was born in 1960 and raised in San Juan, Puerto Rico. She graduated from The Cooper Union School of Arts and Sciences, New York, in 1984. Prizes she has won include the *III Bienal Internacional de Pintura*, Cuenca, Ecuador (1991), and the first prize in graphic design given by *Publish* magazine, San Francisco, (1993). She has participated in the traveling exhihition *Cien años de creatividad: Latin American Women Artists,* organized by the Milwaukee Art Museum (1995) in the United States and in Europe in *Otro País: escalas africanas* organized by Simon Njami, editor of the *Revue Noire* (1994).

Other Titles in the Dispatches Series

Other Latin American Titles

The Secret Weavers Series

Series Editor: Marjorie Agosín

Dedicated to bringing the rich and varied writing by Latin American women to the English-speaking audience.

Volume 8
HAPPY DAYS, UNCLE SERGIO
A Novel by Magali García Ramis
Translated by Carmen C. Esteves
ISBN 1-877727-52-0   160 pages $12.00 paper

Volume 7
THESE ARE NOT SWEET GIRLS
Poetry by Latin American Women
Edited by Marjorie Agosín
ISBN 1-877727-38-5   368 pages $17.00 paper

Volume 6
PLEASURE IN THE WORD
Erotic Fiction by Latin American Women
Edited by Margarite Fernández Olmos & Lizabeth Paravisini-Gebert
ISBN 1-877727-31-8   240 pages $19.95 cloth

Volume 5
A GABRIELA MISTRAL READER
Translated by Maria Giacchetti
ISBN 1-877727-18-0   277 pages $13.00 paper

Volume 3
LANDSCAPES OF A NEW LAND
Short Fiction by Latin American Women
Edited by Marjorie Agosín
ISBN 0-934834-96-2   194 pages $12.00 paper

Volume 1
ALFONSINA STORNI: SELECTED POEMS
Edited by Marion Freeman
ISBN 0-934834-16-4   72 pages $8.00 paper

White Pine Press is a non-profit publishing house dedicated to enriching literary heritage; promoting cultural awareness, understanding, and respect; and, through literature, addressing social and human rights issues. This mission is accomplished by discovering, producing, and marketing to a diverse circle of readers exceptional works of poetry, fiction, non-fiction, and literature in translation from around the world. Through White Pine Press, authors' voices reach out across cultural, ethnic, and gender boundaries to educate and to entertain.

To insure that these voices are heard as widely as possible, White Pine Press arranges author reading tours and speaking engagements at various colleges, universities, organizations, and bookstores throughout the country. White Pine Press works with colleges and public schools to enrich curricula and promotes discussion in the media. Through these efforts, literature extends beyond the books to make a difference in a rapidly changing world.

As a non-profit organization, White Pine Press depends on support from individuals, foundations, and government agencies to bring you this literature that matters — work that might not be published by profit-driven publishing houses. Our grateful thanks to all the individuals who support this effort and to the following foundations and government agencies: Amter Foundation, Ford Foundation, Korean Culture and Arts Foundation, Lannan Foundation, Lila Wallace-Reader's Digest Fund, Margaret L. Wendt Foundation, Mellon Foundation, National Endowment for the Arts, New York State Council on the Arts, Trubar Foundation, Witter Bynner Foundation, and the Slovenian Ministry of Culture.

Please support White Pine Press' efforts to present voices that promote cultural awareness and increase understanding and respect among diverse populations of the world. Tax-deductible donations can be made to:

White Pine Press
10 Village Square · Fredonia, NY 14063